Leaving Independence

Leaving Independence

LEANNE W. SMITH

Waterfall
PRESS

Published by Waterfall Press, Grand Haven, MI

www.brilliancepublishing.com

Amazon, the Amazon logo, and Waterfall Press are trademarks of Amazon.com, Inc., or its affiliates.

ISBN-13: 9781503934788
ISBN-10: 1503934780

Cover design by Shasti O'Leary Soudant

Interior map by Mapping Specialists, Ltd.

To Stan, who waters my flowers.
Thank you for traveling the road with me.

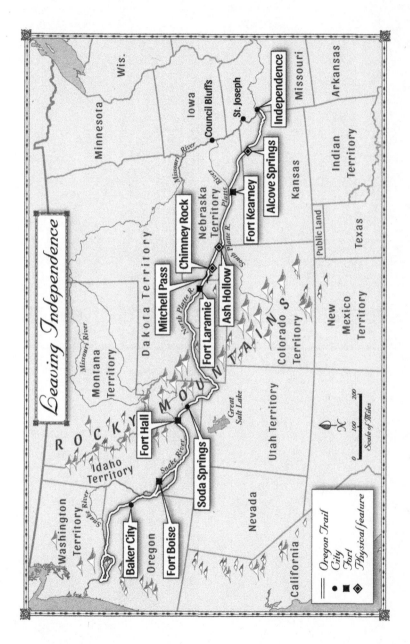

AUTHOR'S NOTE:

Marston County

Marston is a fictional county in Tennessee.

Several years ago I had the idea to create a fictional county to which all my stories connected. My only explanation for why this appeals to me is that when I was a girl, still small enough to lay my body across the narrow shelf behind the backseat of a car, I listened, as we traveled Highway 13 off I-40 west, while my parents told stories of the families they knew.

I grew up in Nashville, but my parents were from Perry County. When we visited relatives, they talked and I listened. The stories they told didn't all happen in a single time period—they were stories that wove in and out of decades and lingered in the mind.

Later, I married and moved to Hickman County, which neighbors Perry, also west of Nashville. An old statue stands in the middle of a field there, visited only by cows, birds, sunshine, and rain. If the statue could talk, what stories might it tell of the interesting people it had observed over time?

Marston allows me a common spring from which to dip for all my stories.

Leanne W. Smith

Western Migration and the American Dream

Leaving Independence is a fictional story about a woman who joined the westward migration movement with her children after the Civil War. She wanted to know why her husband had never come home. She wanted to secure her own and her children's futures now that Reconstruction had begun. In short, she was pursuing the American Dream.

This quest for the American Dream that drove all settlers—white, black, Asian, Hispanic, and otherwise—ever westward into lands already occupied by native peoples is a controversial one. The settlement of America by non-natives had a dark side, as does the settlement and history of many nations in the world.

I have not sought to glorify or justify westward expansion. History accounts and diaries written by both men and women on the wagon trains paint differing views: natives who seemed lazy, dirty, and beggarly and natives who seemed ingenious, majestic, and proud.

Depictions of the pioneers themselves are also mixed. They senselessly shot bison and prairie dogs for sport, carelessly raped and pillaged the land along the routes, and gave little thought to the native people they were impacting or the ecological effects of herding thousands of cattle, horses, oxen, and a migrant people through lands that had been home to tribes and beasts. They've also been depicted as hardy, hardworking, determined, and deeply religious.

There is likely some truth in all of these depictions. People were—and still are—multidimensional and varied in both their characteristics and perceptions of one another.

I've characterized most of my travelers in this story as hardy, hardworking, determined, and religious because those are the kind of people I admire and wanted to write about.

CHAPTER 1

Early-morning sunbeams

An early-morning sunbeam reached through the glass of the post office window and laid a warm hand on Abigail's shoulder as if it knew she would need some anchoring.

She unfolded the letter.

Dear Mrs. Baldwyn, It is my duty to inform you that your husband, Captain Robert Baldwyn, is not deceased as previously reported . . .

Abigail's eyes kept sliding over the ink, but few of the other words would come into focus. Feeling the gaze of the postal clerk on her, and wanting to protect both her family and her heart from any more Marston gossip, she refolded the letter.

The sender's name sat with a commanding finality at the bottom of the page: *Major Frank Talbot.*

She eased the letter back into its stiff governmental envelope and pressed the flap down, then smiled up at the clerk and reached for the door.

How could Robert be alive after all this time? And why was she hearing it from someone other than Robert himself? Surely this was a mistake. The cold wind whipped past her face and her heels click-click-clicked on the brick sidewalk as she walked home, helping her heart find its rhythm again.

The brick turned to gravel, then dirt.

When the sole of her boot swiveled and she turned up the sidewalk, Abigail peeled off a glove and reached out to fan the brown limbs of the willow tree—the tree she had planted the year she pledged herself to Robert. She caught a branch and brought it close to her eyes—eyes still seared with the imprint of Major Talbot's words.

The bark scratched against her fingers. It felt good. The rest of her was numb. Her fingers traced the bumps along the draping stems. The buds would soon sprout. God and the seasons could always be counted on . . . If only men were so reliable.

Sudden movement from the corner of the Baldwyn home drew her eyes. Her feet followed. Behind the house, a man poked his cane at the light snow that still covered plants at the base of the springhouse. Her breath caught as he turned.

"Mr. Palmer!" The banker. Relief washed over Abigail. "For a moment I thought . . . I thought . . ." Abigail stopped herself. Of course it wasn't Robert; this man was too short. "What brings you by the house, Mr. Palmer?"

Mr. Palmer rushed to remove his hat. "No one answered my knock. I shouldn't have taken the liberty, but was curious about your gardens. They have rather a reputation here in Marston."

With his Northern clip, Abigail was surprised anyone in Marston would tell him anything. But there was no denying it: the Baldwyn gardens *were* lovely, even in winter.

Her heart sank nearer to the frozen Tennessee ground as Abigail realized why Mr. Palmer was poking around her springhouse. "This is not really the best time to see them. Perhaps you could come back . . . later in the year."

"Ah . . . yes. About that." Mr. Palmer took a sudden interest in his cane.

A strong wind swirled around Abigail's neck, caressing it with icy fingers. She closed her eyes and wished that when she opened them the banker would be gone.

He wasn't.

Abigail took a deep breath. "Would you like to come inside, Mr. Palmer?"

As she walked up the front steps and pushed open the wide oak door, Abigail's hand trailed over the railing . . . the copper knob . . . the etched glass in the center. She turned and saw Mr. Palmer's eyes cataloguing the walls and the furniture.

"When could I bring my wife to see the house?"

Major Talbot's letter had ripped open an old wound, and now the banker was laying a fresh knife in the tear.

"She's welcome anytime."

Mr. Palmer stepped down the hallway, craning his neck toward the bedrooms. Abigail's upbringing demanded she be polite, but she refused to invite the banker to nose through every room so he could decide if all would be to his wife's liking.

As he turned back to the parlor, he noticed marks on a door frame and pointed with his cane. "What is this?"

Abigail loosened the folds of her wrap and sat down on the mahogany sofa. "That's where my husband marked the children's heights. Don't worry, we've not marked them on all our door frames."

"Oh. Yes. Novel idea." He took the upholstered chair across from her. "He must have marked those before he left. I understand he supported the Union."

Abigail wondered what else Mr. Palmer had heard about her and Robert. He seemed unable to look her in the eye, but she was used to that. Few men would hold a steady gaze with her. Instead, his eyes traveled around the room, taking in the butter-yellow walls, the deep-purple curtains, the pale blues of the furniture and the green plants in porcelain pots that gave even the inside of the Baldwyn home a garden-like quality.

He glanced back to the door frame. "You have four children?"

"Yes. Lina—the youngest—isn't on there. She was born after Robert left."

"Oh? How long after?"

"About nine months."

The banker's face reddened. "I see. I understand you have a woman slave?"

"A helper. Slavery was recently outlawed."

"Of course." He twisted his hat in his hands. "And what does she do?"

"She cooks."

"I see. Did she make all these fancy window coverings?"

He was stalling and Abigail resented it. Why not just say what he'd come for?

"I do the sewing."

"I heard you worked in the gardens."

"I do work in the gardens."

"So what else does she do?"

"She cooks."

"I see."

Patience abandoned her and Abigail stood, wishing the conventions of the day would allow her to toss the little banker out the door. "Just say it, Mr. Palmer. Why are you here?"

He stood to face her, clutching his hat with both hands as if to use it as a shield. "As you know, Mrs. Baldwyn, the bank, like every other business in Marston, has over the past few years suffered losses that are . . . no one's fault."

"I was hoping to have the money by now."

"We are a business, Mrs. Baldwyn."

"I understand that, Mr. Palmer."

"You borrowed against this house. If you can't pay the loan, you'll have to forfeit it."

"There's been a delay."

"What sort of delay?"

Abigail reached into her pocket and ran her fingers around the sharp edges of the major's letter. Why did her and the children's fates always rest in other people's hands? "My husband might be alive."

Mr. Palmer slapped his hat against his thigh. "Mrs. Baldwyn! You led us to believe he had been killed."

"That's what I was told, Mr. Palmer. Robert was a committed husband and father, he . . ."

How could Robert be alive? Had she driven such a wedge in their marriage when he left that he didn't want her—or the children—anymore?

If Robert was alive and had deserted them, she had no way to pay back the money she'd borrowed to keep them fed and clothed. She pushed down a surge of panic and lifted her chin.

"I asked the army for confirmation of his death so we could draw his benefits, and now they say he isn't dead." Abigail held out Major Talbot's letter to show the Washington postmark.

Mr. Palmer reached for the letter, but Abigail pulled it back. She wasn't even sure what most of it said; she'd only caught a few words after the first sentence.

"Then where is he?" Mr. Palmer demanded.

Abigail's confidence dropped. "He might be at a fort in Idaho Territory."

"Might be? Idaho Territory? In the *West?*"

"I question the validity of such a claim myself."

Mr. Palmer pursed his lips and jerked his head side to side. "Regardless, Mrs. Baldwyn, your payment on the loan is past due."

"Will you give me an extension so I can investigate? If he is alive, he'll surely return and resume his law practice."

"Will he?" The banker's eyes narrowed. "Why hasn't he done so already?"

Abigail felt a hot rush of blood to her face. "I can't answer that."

Mr. Palmer looked out the back window at the springhouse, then circled the room again with his eyes. "Even if Mr. Baldwyn—"

"Captain Baldwyn."

"Even if Captain Baldwyn returns and resumes his law practice, it could take months—perhaps years—for you to pay your loan, Mrs. Baldwyn."

"If the major is wrong, we're still due his death benefits."

Mr. Palmer's eyes narrowed. "How do I know this is not some trickery you and Mr.—Captain Baldwyn have contrived?"

"I don't know what you mean."

"It would not be the first time I've been lied to."

The nerve of the banker, to suggest she'd intentionally deceive him!

Abigail held the letter up again, working hard to keep her voice steady. "This same Major Talbot wrote to me in 1862, only months after Robert left, to say he had been killed. But I kept receiving letters from Robert through 1864, so the major was wrong. The government tried to send his death benefits then, but I sent them back, because contrary to what you may think, Mr. Palmer, I am not dishonest. But Robert's letters stopped coming two years ago. I kept thinking we would hear something. I wrote to the government once, before I came to the bank for the loan, but was told it was taking time to process things. Finally, last fall, I wrote again asking for information and to collect his death benefits if something had, indeed, happened to Robert, and now they say he is alive."

Mr. Palmer took his hat and cane and stepped toward the door. "This sounds like it could take a while to sort out, Mrs. Baldwyn. The bank has been generous to wait this long. So unless you have other ready resources, you'll have to vacate."

⁓

Independence lingered thick in Hoke's mind—thick as the early-morning sunbeams on the Texas trail he now traveled. Twenty years he'd avoided the Missouri town, and then she showed up in his dreams three times in a fortnight.

If the stallion hadn't alerted him to danger, thoughts of Independence might have been his last. But when the shoulders of the black horse tensed, he felt the sudden rise of his own neck hairs.

Hoke didn't wear spurs—he didn't like the way they dug into a horse's flesh—but his swift kick and jerk on the reins were enough to send the stallion off the trail and crashing into the brush.

He heard James, several yards behind him, pull up his horse and cock the hammer of the Colt Walker that was never far from his hand.

Hoke just caught the shape of the mountain lion over his shoulder as it sprang. He hadn't been aware of reaching for his own gun but felt it kick as he twisted in the saddle and squeezed off two quick shots.

Four bullets in all ripped through the formerly peaceful woods, then through the head, heart, and soft underbelly of the mountain lion, the shots' echoes followed by the hard thud of the animal's carcass landing on the ground.

Hoke relaxed the squeeze of his legs on the stallion's middle and waited a minute for the horse's pulse to slow before stepping him over to look at the cat. The stallion didn't like it, but the sure stroke of Hoke's hand on his neck was convincing.

James couldn't get his horse to go near it—it danced nervously a safe distance away. "Good thing you moved over. How'd you know that cat was up there?"

"I didn't."

"What do you mean you didn't? You spurred left, didn't you?"

"I knew it was somethin' but I didn't know it was a cat."

"You didn't see it move?" James looked up at the ledge. "Another cat could be up there now and a body couldn't see it. How do you do that?"

"I felt it."

"You *felt it.*" James looked up at the ledge again. "You don't feel any more up there, do you?"

Hoke shook his head.

James looked back down at the cat and shivered. "I don't know how you know things, but I ain't complainin' about it."

As they traveled on, Hoke was careful not to let his mind wander again. A man couldn't afford to daydream in the wilds of northern Texas. But that cold February night when he and James made camp, he pondered the isolation of his existence. Had he been killed by a mountain lion that morning, who besides James would have felt it enough of a loss to mourn for him?

⌒〇

The man's uniform jacket lay at the top of a neatly folded stack of clothes, caught in an early-morning sunbeam. He had been the one to fold them, not the woman who reached across him now, her black hair sweeping the top of his chest.

She ran her hand across the stitching on the pocket. "This is your name?"

The woman's raspy voice never failed to irritate him.

"What's it to you?" He slapped her hand away. "Don't mess my clothes up."

She lay half-covered by a horse blanket on the dirt floor of the shed they were in. It couldn't really be called a cabin. Only one strong wind would be needed to knock it down, but strong winds didn't often reach down in the base of this holler where he was keeping her.

"I never learned to spell, but I know that's a *B*." She reached over and traced the circles of it with her finger, then down the rest of the name: "aldwyn."

"I like this 'un that goes down." She meant the *Y*. "But the *B* is my favorite. *B* like in 'Bonnie.' My pa's Irish and called my maw a bonnie lass. That's how come she named me Bonnie."

"A half-breed Piute living in Idaho named Bonnie." He laughed and ran a hand over his neatly trimmed beard. "You are quite the enigma."

"What's that mean? I don't have no negra blood in me."

He shook his head. "That's not what it means."

When he got up to stir the fire, she opened the pocket flap on the jacket. A worn picture was inside.

"Who's this?" Bonnie frowned. "She's awful pretty."

He snatched the picture from her hand. "Leave it alone, will ya? That's my wife."

"Your wife? I thought you said you wasn't married no more."

He looked at the picture, drinking in the neat outline of Abigail's blond hair and the dark-rimmed eyes he knew to be deep blue. She was a beautiful woman and God knew he'd rather have her than Bonnie reaching across him under a horsehair blanket. But he wasn't going back to Tennessee. He preferred the freedom of the life he had now.

He put the picture in his pocket.

"It's complicated."

CHAPTER 2

Trains leaving Independence

As they stood in the kitchen, Mimi pointed the rolling pin at Abigail.

"I know you don't want to go ask Mr. Walstone for them ready resources, but I'd say it's time." She stretched over the table and rolled out the biscuit dough.

Abigail looked out the window. Her mind was sore from trying to think of alternatives to asking her father for help.

"I was mighty proud when you married Mr. Robert."

Abigail turned back to the table and watched Mimi pat the flattened dough with loving hands. When they were kids, Abigail and Mimi would lay their hands together and marvel at how, on the inside, their hand color was the same—pink and pale.

"He was the only one of all them suitors who would've done for you."

"I did not have a lot of suitors, Mimi."

"Why you always actin' like you don't know how fine you are? When you goin' to realize people admire you?"

"Boys came to the house because of—"

"Your brothers." Mimi sniffed and reached for the biscuit cutter. "No, they did not. They may've acted like that was why, but they did not. And they was almighty disappointed when Mr. Robert showed up and caught your eye, especially that Hadley Wiles. I *know* you know how love-struck he was."

"Let's not talk about him." Thoughts of an embittered father and a husband who had left her desperate were bad enough. She didn't want to think about the former suitor who made her skin crawl, too.

"Robert Baldwyn was just as foolish over you."

"You sure about that?"

The fissures in Abigail's heart cracked deeper every time she thought of Major Talbot's letter, the contents of which she'd finally had a chance to absorb. *Captain Baldwyn requested and was granted three weeks' leave prior to his departure. It surprises me he did not report news of the transfer to you himself.*

Surprised her, too. She'd thought the letters she and Robert had exchanged after his volatile departure had mended their relationship.

"Don't you doubt it," cautioned Mimi, waving the biscuit cutter. "I can't understand him not coming home, though . . . that ain't like Mr. Robert." She slapped the flour off her hands as she reached for the pan. "But that don't mean he didn't love you."

The word *didn't* rolled back and forth in Abigail's head as she stepped closer to the window and looked out at the spot where the banker had poked at the icy base of the springhouse wall. Her eyes fixated just beyond that spot, on a small headstone.

Several yellow jonquils had cracked open, front-runners after a few winter crocuses, hinting at the symphony of colors to come. She needed to clear the winter brush from around the springhouse and that headstone so the daffodils could breathe. Robert had built the springhouse with stones from Mill Creek—the coldest creek in Tennessee—which ran off Treetop Ridge, looping around its base like a lasso. Abigail felt like her own neck rested in the crook of a lasso. All it needed was a little more tightening to become a hangman's noose.

～

When the sentry walked the letter into his office and laid it on the desk, the man immediately recognized the handwriting and swore.

How had she found him? The memory of Bonnie pulling out her photograph floated back to him.

Prophetic.

He carried the letter to his private quarters before opening it. Then he held it to the lamplight with his right hand—a hand missing two of its fingers.

> *Dear Robert,*
> *Words fail me in knowing how to pen this letter. If Major Talbot's words are true and you are alive and serving in Idaho Territory, why have you not written to tell us this news yourself? Our resources are quite low. The banker, a Yankee, threatens to take the house if we cannot soon find payment. Tell me . . . do you have any intention of returning home to us, or are we left to face this new dilemma on our own?*

She was out of money. He felt marginally guilty. But wasn't her father one of the wealthiest men in Tennessee? Didn't that old man have some of the finest horses in the South on that large plantation of his? And he would have bet a large sum that not all the slaves had skipped out on old Mr. Walstone, either. He knew that Mimi's sister, Annie B, and her husband, Arlon, were particularly devoted to the old belligerent.

If Abigail lost the house, so be it. He wasn't going to feel sorry for her. All he had to do was remember their last conversation to stop feeling sorry for her.

It took him several days and drafts to settle on the proper tone in his reply. Repentant? Evasive? Authoritative? Or nonchalant? He finally decided to strike a balance between them all—all but repentant.

Repentant was struck from the list.

౿

Abigail tightened the string of her hat. "You're sure you don't want to come with me? Ride out and see Arlon and Annie B?"

Mimi wrapped two blackberry pies in flour-sack cloths and sniffed. "I'll just send the pies."

Every clop of the horse's hooves on the familiar, hard-packed path to Franklin brought back a memory for Abigail. The late-February wind chilled her cheeks, but her heart, under woolen wrappings, was fever-hot.

First she stopped at the cabin overlooking the Harpeth River. Three small children ran out, all smiles and gangly arms. Abigail hugged Annie B over the bobbing heads and handed her one of the pies.

"What brings you all the way out here deliverin' pies without your brood?"

"Came to talk to Daddy. What kind of mood is he in?"

"Ornery as ever, accordin' to Arlon. He's up there now breakin' the north pasture."

"It's too early."

"And another freeze is comin'. I can feel it in my bones. But your father wanted it broke."

Abigail shook her head and kissed each of the children, then hoisted herself back on the horse and turned toward the big house.

Her throat tightened as her eyes swept over the horse trails she once rode with her brothers, trees she'd climbed with Mimi, and the spot on the hill where Robert first kissed her. She veered off the path and stopped briefly at a small cemetery, dismounting so she could brush leaves off the headstones.

Half of her thirty-four years had been spent at Walstone Plantation . . . happy years, mostly. But her childhood home had also been scene to some of Abigail's bitterest heartaches.

Abigail understood why Mimi hadn't wanted to come with her. Mr. Walstone, whose outlook had always leaned toward overcast, had become increasingly caustic since Mrs. Walstone's death. A heavy cloud had settled over the Walstone house and fields. But Abigail rode through it. She was out of options.

Her father stood leaning on a rail of his expansive white porch and watched her approach. "That's a sorry horse you've borrowed," he mumbled as she came into earshot.

Leo Walstone had never been one to soften sentiments, not even for Abigail, his only daughter.

"What brings you out here?" he wanted to know as she dismounted and tied her horse to the porch rail.

She walked up the steps and kissed his cheek before answering. "Mimi baked you a pie."

"Blackberry?" He accepted her kiss but didn't offer one in return.

She nodded and went inside, setting the pie on the kitchen table, then returned to the parlor, the room he most often inhabited. "The banker came to the house yesterday."

"I knew it! I knew it as soon as I saw you coming from Arlon and Annie B's without your family. He wants his money back?"

Abigail looked at him—this man she had once loved above all others. He had not wanted her to marry Robert Baldwyn and had shown his displeasure by withdrawing his love for the past seventeen years.

"Yes. I'll have to sell the house if I can't find another way to pay him back."

"If you're here to ask me for money, I can't help you. If damned idealists like Robert Baldwyn had left well enough alone and stayed the hell off my land and away from my horses, I wouldn't be left with nothing but worthless bonds!"

Abigail crossed her arms and tried to avoid looking at her brother's bloodstains on the floor. Seth had bled out here after being wounded at the Battle of Franklin. That had been the beginning of the end for the Confederacy and had sealed her father's hatred for all things Federal.

"You can have all the Confederate bonds you can carry," he said. "I got a trunkful—but the only thing I have that the bank would see as collateral is my land, and I'll be damned if I give those Northerners a single acre!"

Abigail shook her head. "Why can't you let go of your hatred, Daddy?"

He scowled and pointed at the parlor floor. "How can I, Abby? I have to look at that every day, thanks to men like your husband. For all we know, he's the one that shot your brother."

Abigail had reached in her pocket for Major Talbot's letter, intending to tell her father about it, but now she stuffed it back down. What good would it do? She had long ago grown tired of hearing her father criticize Robert, and before that, of hearing Robert criticize him. So without mentioning that Robert might still be alive, she reached for her wrap. If Robert ever did come home, she wasn't sure he and her father could ever mend their broken bonds. She ought not to have come. Every time she came her father managed to stamp out another remnant of her love. Soon, there'd be nothing left.

"Give my best to Thad and Nathan," she said, trying to quell the tide of emotions that had stirred her heart since her decision to ride out and ask her father for help.

She was outside, mounted, and had pointed the horse toward Marston when Mr. Walstone called from the porch, "Wait! I have something for the children." He walked back to her minutes later from his barn, a black puppy in his arms.

"Name's Rascal." He lifted the dog up. "In memory of Robert."

Abigail leaned over to kiss the bald of her father's head as she took the puppy from him, heartsick at the events that had changed him into the acidic stranger who stood before her now. "I guess I should be glad you didn't name him Damned Idealist."

"I'll give you land, Abby—tried to give your husband land but he never would take it. You can come back here and your brothers will build you a nice house."

Abigail's throat tightened. She wanted to protect the good memories she had of him and her upbringing, and she didn't want his venom infecting her children. "We have a nice house now, Daddy. I'm sorry you've never accepted my invitations to see it."

She held her tears to the end of the lane. Then Rascal's tongue licked them as they dropped, as the sorry horse she'd borrowed walked the long road back to Marston in the cold.

༄

When a letter from Captain Robert Charles Baldwyn arrived a week later from Idaho Territory, Abigail stood once again under the gaze of the postal clerk. But this time she did not slide the letter back into its envelope and press the flap down. She did not smile, she did not nod, and when she reached for the door, her legs were strong and ramrod straight.

The warming wind whipped past her face and her temperature rose with every click-click-click on the sidewalk as she stepped toward home. When the sole of her boot swiveled and she turned up the walk she peeled off both gloves, her shawl, even her hat, so great was her risk of overheating.

Mimi was in the kitchen when Abigail burst through the door and handed her the letter.

"What's this scrawl?" Mimi peered more closely at the letter. "That ain't Mr. Robert's handwritin'."

"His hand. Remember?"

"Oh, that's right."

His hand had been injured in a battle—two fingers shot off in a skirmish. The words were legible, just not written in Robert's formerly neat penmanship.

Mimi read the words aloud. "'Abigail, it looks like you tracked me down.'"

Her eyebrows shot together in a V.

"'You always were a resourceful woman, so I am sure you will figure something out on the house. Here is my suggestion, if you care to know. Sell the house. Drop those children at your father's or leave them with the colored woman.'"

"*The colored woman!* What, he forgot my name? And *those* children?"

"Keep reading."

"'Come join me in Idaho Territory. I like it here and do not intend to return to Tennessee.'"

Mimi stared at the letter a minute as if trying to process its contents. "Well, Lord have mercy. What has got into that man? The Lord ain't whispered nothin' about this in my ear. I had no idea, Miz Abigail. How could any decent man have that to say after so long with no word?"

"Keep reading."

Mimi eyed the paper suspiciously before finishing.

"'You are a beautiful woman. Lord knows, I wouldn't mind having you here.'"

Mimi's jaw dropped. She read over the letter again and shook her head. "I don't know what to make of it."

"I told you he was altered. It's the first time in years he's even mentioned the children."

"What do you mean? He loves his children."

"He did when he left. I thought he loved us all."

Abigail paced the kitchen. Rascal, who had followed her in, stood in a safe corner and watched.

How could Robert do this to her? She put a hand to her chest, as if that could soothe her heart. It hadn't ached this badly in years. She looked at the letter that now lay like an unwelcome cockroach on the table. "Why couldn't he have just died, like we thought?"

"You don't mean that, Miz Abigail!"

"That would have been more kind than choosing not to come home to us!"

❦

That night when Charlie slapped his hand on the dinner table and said, "We should go out there," Abigail waved the suggestion off.

"No, I mean it."

Charlie, oldest of the blue-eyed Baldwyn children, was also the most serious. It wasn't like him to be impulsive, so it surprised Abigail when he looked to Corrine, Jacob, and Lina for support. "We should go. Join him! I bet he loves it out there." He turned back to Abigail, his eyes bright with hope. "We could make a new start. You said the banker—"

Abigail stopped him by raising her hand. "No."

She knew Charlie and Corrine felt Robert's absence the most. They had been the oldest, eleven and ten, when their father left five years ago. Charlie had wanted to follow in his father's footsteps . . . attend law school in the East. But he'd stopped talking about it, knowing they no longer had the money. Going west was the other direction. No . . . she would think of something.

"Trains leaving Independence go right by Fort Hall," said Charlie. "I've studied the maps!"

"What trains are you talking about?" asked Corrine, her blond brow twisted. "Track hasn't been laid that far west yet."

"Wagon trains!"

"Live in a wagon? With strangers?" Corrine sized up her older brother. "Are you out of your mind, Charlie?"

"We would have our own wagon, Corrine. With a cover over it." Charlie grew more excited, which got Jacob excited.

"We'd see buffalo!" Jacob's nine-year-old eyes grew as large as Mimi's biscuits. "Me and Charlie could shoot some."

Corrine huffed and looked at Abigail. "I hope you're not listening to him."

"People do it all the time," insisted Charlie. "Thousands of people."

"And how many get scalped by Indians? Bleed to death on the side of the trail?"

"That's enough, Corrine." Abigail watched Lina's face wrinkle in worry.

Corrine had talked earliest, walked earliest, and asserted her independence earliest of all the Baldwyn children. Two schoolmasters at the Marston schoolhouse had declared her the brightest student ever to grace the building. But the quickness of her mind sometimes caused her to be impatient with others. Lina, on the other hand, was all gentleness and sensitivity.

Abigail looked across the table at Mimi, who was watching Charlie with her brows pulled together.

Jacob was the rash one, not Charlie. What made Charlie think of such a thing . . . going out west to be with Robert? No. There had to be another solution.

"We are not going to Independence and joining a wagon train so we can chase your father out west," said Abigail, signaling an end to the discussion.

But she was wrong.

⌒⊙

Hoke's eyes locked on a white filly. He and James sat on their mounts and stared at a herd of wild horses in the Texan basin below.

"Yes, sir." James grinned. "Just settin' there waitin' for us. My luck, the day I met you. There's something about not seeing you get clawed by a two-hundred-pound cat, then coming out on this rise looking at our next year's income, that makes me sentimental."

Hoke took off his once-black hat and smoothed back his dark hair. He needed a haircut . . . and a shave . . . and a bath. Afternoon sunlight sparkled off a creek winding through the picturesque basin below. "You think that creek's deep enough for a full-body bath?" It would make for another cold one, but that was the kind he was used to.

"I make a profession of gratitude and you want to know if the creek's deep enough to wash in? That really hurts, Hoke."

"You rattle on more than I got ears to tolerate."

"But I was sayin' nice things. It looks like you could tolerate listenin' to nice things."

As their horses picked a careful footing down the slope of the hillside, James asked, "Take 'em to St. Jo or Council Bluff?"

"Independence."

"I thought you didn't like Independence."

"Why'd you think that?"

"You never want to go there when I suggest it."

"Well . . . suggest it now."

James shot him a look. "Is the trail dust itchin' you?"

Hoke didn't answer. He was watching the white Appaloosa, who was now watching him. He and James were nearly to the bottom of the hill. Several horses in the wild herd had raised their heads to eye them. That Appaloosa had been the first.

"Always said I wouldn't keep a white horse," Hoke said. A white horse was easy to spot. It made a man a target. "But she's a beauty."

"I think that cat done spooked you. That's what I think. And now you're drawn to the angelic. Say, aren't you from Independence?"

"It's where my folks are buried." The cat hadn't spooked Hoke, but his dreams of Independence had. Why was he suddenly filled with longing to see those grave markers again . . . to walk those dusty streets? Independence was calling him back after a twenty-year absence. He'd fought with Federal troops in other parts of Missouri during the war but had been thankful to avoid the town that held his childhood nightmares. Hoke's gut usually served him well. It was trying to tell him something . . . but he didn't know what.

Dreams of Independence had spooked him good.

James thought for a minute. "I'm trying to remember if I know any women in Independence."

Hoke cut him a sideways glance. James was younger than Hoke by nine years, taller, leaner, with a thick, full beard, and a talker. Hoke wouldn't have had the tolerance for most talkers, but James knew when *not* to talk, and he was capable. Hoke held a capable man in high regard.

"Women love me, Hoke. And I can't say I blame 'em. Don't be jealous just 'cause you ain't had any luck with women. There's always new women in a jumpin'-off town. That'll make things interestin'."

They had reached the valley where they would spend the next few weeks hovering around the wild herd, roping and calming, letting the horses get used to the smell and sound of civilized men—if he and James could be called that. Capable men . . . reliable men . . . but men with hearts as wild and free as the western horses running loose in the basin into which they'd descended.

"I wouldn't mind tackin' on to a wagon train one of these days," mused James. "Be kind of nice to see the upper half of the Rockies, wouldn't it?"

Hoke cast him a sideways glance. "I wouldn't mind seeing 'em, but I'd hate to be shackled to a train full of people while I was doing it."

❧

Abigail sat brooding in her rocker, a cherry box filled with letters open at her feet. Rascal lay next to it, his eyes grown heavy from the rhythmic sound of the rocker hitting the slats of the wood floor. The children were at school. Mimi would be back from the butcher's soon.

When the screen door banged in its frame, Rascal's head popped up. Abigail was already in the hallway, itching to get the newly formed decision out of her mind and over her lips before she lost her courage. She could hear the dog's toenails skidding across the floor as he scrambled to get his balance and follow her to the kitchen.

"I'm selling the house, Mimi, and going out there. I can't sit here passively, expecting some miracle to fall into my lap."

Mimi covered her mouth.

"Don't try to talk me out of it. My mind is made. If I sit here one day more than necessary without trying to reclaim my husband and put my family back together, I'll go mad. Suddenly this house—"

Mimi put her hands on Abigail's arms and peered into her eyes like she did with the kids when they ran a fever. "You love this house, Miz Abigail! You stitched every curtain."

Abigail wiggled out of Mimi's hold. "This house is choking me. Every room holds reminders of Robert and how our life was before the war came and tore us apart." She could hardly believe she was speaking these words herself but knew deep in her gut they rang true.

"Charlie's right. We need a new start. If we move to a smaller house in town I'll be sad every day it's not this one. If we move back to

Daddy's, he and my brothers' families will resent us for our neediness. And I don't want the children to finish growing up under that burden. If we leave Marston we can start fresh. Why shouldn't that be where Robert is? If we get out there and he doesn't want us, then at least we'll know where we stand."

❧

Rascal peed on the floor.

Corrine thumped her younger brother on the head. "You were supposed to take him out an hour ago, Jacob."

From where he sat hunched over a newspaper with Charlie, Jacob rubbed his head and called, "Mimi! Come clean this up."

Abigail, who was folding clothes into a trunk nearby, turned, grabbed Jacob's arm, sailed him back to her bedroom, grabbed his father's old belt, and held it under his nose. "If you ever speak to Mimi that way again, I will have your hide, do you understand me? That woman loves you as much as I do. She was present for your birth and has fed you and cared for you every day of your life. You will respect her for it!"

For the first time in his nine years, Jacob went mute.

Abigail released him and took a deep breath. She resisted the urge to smooth his hair. Jacob's hair was darkest of the Baldwyns and stayed as unruly as his spirit. But he wasn't mean-tempered, and Abigail knew it.

When Mimi came into the room he threw his arms around her legs. "Don't clean it up, Mimi. I will. I'm sorry."

"You're all right, Jacob. Corrine done took care of it." When he left, Mimi turned to Abigail. "What was that all about?"

Surprised as anyone by her reaction, Abigail sat on the bed and stared at the belt in her hands. "He shouldn't have said that to you."

"I appreciate you sticking up for me, but what's really bothering you?"

There were too many threads of fear to name just one, and she had let them grow fatter than she realized. "I guess I'm feeling the weight of what lies in front of me."

Mimi sat down beside her. "Which part scares you the most?"

Abigail shook her head. "That he won't want us. That I smothered every ounce of love he had for us when he left . . . when we fought."

"That letter didn't sound to me like his admiration for you was smothered. Didn't he say come join him?"

"Why would he not want me to bring the children, Mimi? Did I do something to make him stop loving them?"

"No!" Mimi shooed the thought away. "Maybe he's ashamed, Miz Abigail, and knows he'll have trouble looking them in the eye. But if there is any woman who can help a man find hisself again, it's you. Devil's going to make you doubt this decision. That's his job."

"He's good at it."

"He's had lots of practice."

"How do you not hate us, Mimi? How do you not hate me?"

Mimi turned Abigail's hand over and opened hers beside it . . . pink and pale on the inside. "I could never hate you, Abigail Baldwyn. You didn't set up the way of things."

Abigail clasped Mimi's hand in both of hers. "You don't have to come with us. You're free to make your own choices."

"I know. You told me every year on my birthday since you and Mr. Robert married."

"I wish you'd take your freedom papers. I know you don't need them anymore, but Robert wanted you to have them. He wanted you to know that no one owned you."

"That ain't true. Lord owns me just like He owns you."

Abigail looked deep into Mimi's eyes. "I need to know you're not coming out of obligation. This is a chance for you to—"

"You got mighty big burdens on your shoulders, Miz Abigail. Don't let me be one of them."

Tears pooled in Abigail's eyes. "Corrine thinks I'm making a mistake. If it doesn't turn out well, I'll have her blame."

"You'll have her blame no matter what. She's fifteen years old. Don't you worry about Miss Corrine . . . me and Lina can handle her. She'll come around."

But Mimi didn't handle Corrine like she promised.

⌒

The day before departure, Arlon showed up at the house. Annie B had fallen ill. Arlon was desperate for Mimi to come to them.

Blood proved thicker than love.

"I have to go to her, Miz Abigail. Everybody else is up north, and you know Arlon's never asked me for a thing before."

Abigail couldn't begrudge Arlon his request. Hadn't he walked through soldier-infested hillsides to till her garden the past four springs? Hadn't Abigail herself encouraged Mimi not to forfeit her own independence just because she thought the Baldwyns needed her? Still, Abigail couldn't fathom a future without Mimi's brown eyes and good sense. Impending doom seeped into her veins and swam straight to her heart. Suddenly sure she was making a horrible mistake, Abigail felt powerless now to stop the chain of events that had been set into motion.

As Abigail hugged Mimi one last time before she climbed onto the buckboard to leave with Arlon, Abigail whispered in Mimi's ear, "Am I doing the right thing?"

"Yes, ma'am, you doin' the right thing. I know it in my bones, Miz Abigail. The Lord, He whisper it to me. I couldn't let you go otherwise."

It gave Abigail hope because Mimi wasn't one to stretch or alter what the Lord said.

"I'm only sorry I won't see with my own eyes how much these children are goin' to grow up out there. 'Specially this little miracle baby." Mimi folded herself over and smothered Lina to her.

Laying herself across Mimi's bent back, Abigail breathed deep, trying to memorize every inch of her. "You smell like cinnamon," she whispered. Then frowning suddenly, she said, "You should have made me learn to cook."

"You know, I'm sorry about that." Mimi straightened up. "Maybe you can trade off sewing with some of them other ladies for cooking. Or get Corrine there working the stove." Corrine rolled her eyes at the mention of her name. "That's right. I know you heard me. And I know how much you been helpin' me in the kitchen, too. You know what to do. And you better be helpin' your mama. If I hear otherwise, I'll be chasin' down that wagon comin' after you. You hear me?"

Lina smiled up at her. Mimi had never laid an angry hand on the children.

"You got mighty fine"—Mimi had to shake her head twice to get the words out—"mighty fine children. I can say that since I helped raise 'em. And I love 'em like they was my own. My very own." Mimi didn't look down at Lina again, fat tears welling in her eyes.

Charlie, Corrine, and Jacob each hugged her tightly, then stood awkwardly by, the boys trying not to cry, Corrine shaking her head, still unhappy with Abigail's decision.

CHAPTER 3

The sudden click of heels

Come join me in Idaho Territory. I like it here . . .

He had chuckled when he wrote it, and chuckled again when he retold it to Bonnie as he buttoned his jacket, getting dressed to leave the cabin.

She had a small cracked mirror and had held it up so he could see if his waist sash was even, but now she lowered it, alarmed. "What if she comes out here?"

"Some chance. Abigail is too fine to travel out here. And she'd never leave her children. Hold that straight, Bonnie."

She complied. That was why he put up with her and the squalor of this cabin—she complied.

"*Her* children? Ain't you Robert Baldwyn? Don't that make 'em both y'all's children?"

He frowned as he polished his sword handle with his sleeve. "I suppose it does."

"How many are there?"

He leaned in to check his beard. "How many what?"

"Children!"

He straightened and looked out the window. "I forget exactly. Three or four."

⌒

They arrived by boat in Independence, Abigail's nerves pinging like the sounds of Reconstruction. The air was ripped with the sounds of sawing, men hawing horse teams, and the clangs of metal hitting iron. Not one face that passed by on the riverbank was familiar. After they'd disembarked, Abigail stood on the boat dock and clutched Lina's hand, wondering what to do.

She was just before putting them back on the boat to Tennessee when the riverboat captain's wife put her hand on Abigail's shoulder and shouted, "Percy!" to a man in a wagon. "Get over here!" Then to Abigail, "Percy can haul you over to Mrs. Helton's. She's particular about who stays with her, but she'll take you."

Charlie and Jacob helped the man load the heavy trunks, then lifted Rascal and their sisters into the wagon bed. Abigail didn't flinch when Percy offered a grime-caked hand as she climbed onto the wagon seat, but her heart did lurch with a sickening thud. What was she doing? Loading her children and all their earthly possessions in the back of an unsavory man's wagon?

"That there is Cannon Hill," he said loudly as they jostled under the branches of oaks and maples past homes and storefronts. The symphony of Reconstruction grew louder as they neared the heart of town. "That's where the Northers loaded up their cannons couple years back when the second battle swept through." He nodded his head. "That boardin' house there took some bullets, see 'em?" He pointed to a nearby house with chipped bricks, and Jacob's eyes grew big. "But lucky fer her, Mrs. Dandy's place is over yonder."

"I thought her name was Mrs. Helton," said Corrine.

Abigail turned to give Corrine a look of warning, being well familiar with her oldest daughter's sharp tongue.

"Yeah, I reckon it is. But she's uppity. You'uns ain't uppity, air ya?" He laughed and raked his eyes over Abigail, who fought the urge to scoot farther away from him on the wagon seat.

When they arrived at the boardinghouse, Mrs. Helton, an elegant woman with a neat gray bun, was busy cooking dinner. "Room five at the top of the stairs is the biggest one I have right now." She flipped a key off a hook. "The boys'll have to sleep on the floor." Her eyes paused on Charlie. "How old are you, son?"

"Sixteen." He stood straighter. "Almost seventeen."

"Is that right?" She looked down at Rascal. "He'll have to stay out back. Here's the key to your room. I run a tight house and do my best to keep out the rabble." She looked out a window at Percy as he drove away. "But you'll want your door locked. You never know about folks around here."

Abigail insisted the children change from their travel clothes for dinner. A family of Irish children—whose mother had not made them change from their travel clothes—eyed them as they came to the table. Charlie and Corrine exchanged glances.

A large, dusty man asked Jacob, "What are you all duded up for, son? Y'all just bury your pa? Look like you been to a funeral."

"No, sir. We're here to join a wagon train. We're going to Fort Hall to find our pa."

Abigail put her hand on Jacob's shoulder. "I'm sure the gentleman doesn't care to know our plans."

Mrs. Helton watched them, her gaze often resting on Charlie. She, too, had changed for dinner and sat as hostess at the head of the table. When the other guests dispersed after dinner and the children went to check on Rascal, Mrs. Helton invited Abigail to the parlor for tea.

"You've got mighty nice children," she said, eyeing Abigail over her porcelain cup and saucer. "Are you sure you want to take them west of here?"

Abigail wondered what had brought Mrs. Helton to Independence. She was more refined than most of the town Abigail had seen so far. "I can't remember the last time I felt sure of anything."

"I've seen a lot of folks heading down the trail, Mrs. Baldwyn. You and your family don't fit the normal mold. I'm curious . . . why are you here?"

Luckily the children came in just then and Abigail had an excuse to avoid answering. But the woman's question lingered. *Why are you here?* Abigail wished she knew the answer. She wished she felt more confident in her decision to come to Independence.

Later, as she lay with Lina nestled in the crook of her arm, Mrs. Helton's words continued to pick the scabs off her fears. Everything around them felt so raw. All that was familiar, like the eastern shore of the Mississippi, had slipped away.

A soft knock brought her tiptoeing to the door. When she opened it, Mrs. Helton handed her Rascal.

"Here. He won't stop whining. Don't let him pee on the floor."

❦

Hoke's soul hadn't quieted. Two weeks he'd been back in Independence and while he leaned casually enough against a post outside Granberry's Café listening to Colonel George Dotson and Gerald Jenkins talk about their plans to travel the Oregon Trail, his dark eyes combed the sidewalks as if the answer to his restlessness were still somewhere moving along the planks.

"It's God's providence you happen to be in Independence, Hoke," said Dotson. "We could use a man like you. There are quite a few eastern folks on this trip."

Hoke knew both men by reputation. Jenkins had owned a hotel in the East and Dotson, a native Missourian, had been a Union officer. Men who served under Colonel Dotson swore by his leadership and his character. Hoke looked Dotson in the eye. "I don't have plans to settle that far west."

"Who says you have to settle?"

"Settling's not required," added Jenkins with a grin. "You can head down to California or come right back along the trail. Oregon leads to anywhere."

These were good men. Hoke would hate to hear about them having trouble. "Heard there were some problems on the Bozeman."

"That's north of Laramie," said Dotson. "Things have been quiet on the Oregon. The Indians mostly just pester the soldiers at the forts. It's more likely white men could give us trouble. You'd be a welcome addition."

"What brings you to Independence, Hoke?" Gerald Jenkins was married to Colonel Dotson's wife's sister. He was short like her—not as bubbly, but he wore a constant grin.

What brings you to Independence, Hoke? Jenkins's question echoed and clanged in his head.

"James Parker and I rounded up a herd in Texas. Broke 'em and brought 'em up. I already sold some stock to your group—to an old man from Boston and a young doctor."

Dotson grinned. "Careful now, that old man is my age."

"We've got some good folks going on this trip." Jenkins leaned in. "Several single women."

Hoke's eyes swept the sidewalks again. "James and I have our eye on another herd in southern Kansas." They had seen it while coming up from Texas. Add the sales of that one to the horses they'd already sold and Hoke would have more than enough to set up his own ranch . . . if ranching was the answer to what was making him restless.

He didn't like the feel of restlessness. Jenkins's question gnawed at him . . . *What brings you to Independence, Hoke?*

Hoke wished to God he knew.

He turned back to Dotson. "Be a long time to be tied up. Take you what, five months?" That herd in Kansas wasn't going to sit and wait on him.

Dotson nodded. "We pull out Tuesday."

That was early. Most trains wouldn't leave for another three or four weeks. Hoke was flattered Dotson had approached him.

"I'm determined to get down the trail first," continued Dotson. "We've got a good stock of supplies—got a blacksmith going—several families planning to open businesses. A few of these folks will split after the divide and go down the California to pan for gold, but most of them want to settle a town, complete with a newspaper and a preacher for the church."

Hoke raised his eyebrows. "You got a preacher on this trip?"

"That's right." Jenkins's eyes were jolly. "And several single ladies, like I said before. If you see someone you like, you don't even have to depend on the colonel here to marry you."

The sudden click of heels on the wooden slats of the sidewalk caused all three men to turn and look toward the south end of the street. An attractive woman wearing a stylish tweed suit and brown hat approached. She was taller than most women, graceful and fair.

Jenkins jabbed Hoke with his elbow. "There's a pretty lady now."

Hoke shot him a sideways smirk. The paternal nature of these men appealed to him.

"Is one of you Colonel George Dotson?" asked the woman.

Dotson put out his hand. "I am."

"My name is Abigail Baldwyn." She took his hand and smiled. "I'm interested in joining your wagon train. I understand you're leaving next week?"

"Yes, ma'am. And we're still taking good folks. Trying to talk Hoke here into going." He indicated Hoke with a nod.

She smiled over at Hoke, then turned back to Dotson.

Something was troubling her. Hoke felt it and wondered what it was. She was a nice-looking woman—a woman wearing an expensive outfit and well-made boots, from what he could see of them poking out from under that long tweed skirt. A man could tell a lot about another man's station in life by his footwear. Or a woman's.

"I'd like to ask you some questions before I make a final decision," said Abigail to Dotson. "But if everything I hear about you is true, we want to sign on—me and my children—as far as Fort Hall."

Hoke's eyes rested on her face. She sounded Southern, but not country Southern—refined, educated, well-bred Southern.

He didn't see a lot of refined women in the western towns where he'd spent the better part of his life. He didn't see a lot of women with blond hair and blue eyes, either. Like most trail-riding men, he'd developed a heightened sense of smell. Lavender . . . she smelled like lavender. He'd smelled it in a shop once, and once was all it ever took for Hoke.

It suited her.

"Would you like to step into the eatery here and discuss the details?" Dotson motioned Abigail toward the café. "Mrs. Granberry makes the best rolls you ever tasted. Hoke, will you join us?"

"Thank you, no. Better get back to the stables." Hoke pushed himself off the post and smoothed his dark hair back before placing the hat on his head. "Good luck, ma'am." He nodded. "If you're in the market for horses, come see me."

"I'll take twelve. Your twelve best."

Hoke stopped. "That's a lot of horses." And his best wouldn't come cheap. She looked like she could afford it with her fancy clothes and well-made boots, but . . . what would a stylish woman with money be traveling out west for?

"I plan to get two wagons, four horses for each, and a fresh team to rotate as needed or to double up on steep inclines. I intend to treat my horses well."

"You'll need at least six on a team. Some folks like oxen better. They're cheaper to feed, strong, hardly ever run off, and Indians don't try to steal 'em."

Her brow twisted. It was a unique gesture. One eyebrow arched up and the other angled down, causing a pleasing little curve in her forehead. "I thought you had horses. Why are you trying to talk me into oxen?"

"I'm not. I just thought you should know that a lot of folks use oxen to pull the teams." Damn woman! What was she being hardheaded about?

She smiled. "I can't ride oxen."

Hoke didn't know what to make of it. She was confounding him, and he didn't like to be confounded. Where was her husband anyway? Abigail Baldwyn had mentioned children but no husband. He suddenly wanted to know but wasn't about to ask.

"I'll pick you out twelve of my best." He again turned to leave but felt her hand on his arm.

"I'd like to pick them. Horses are one of the few things I feel like I know, Mr. . . ."

"Hoke. Just Hoke. No *Mr.* required." Hoke looked down at her slender fingers on his arm, hot to his skin through the fabric, then down to her boots and back up her travel outfit. "Western horses aren't like show horses from the South."

By the look on her face he was sure he'd nicked a nerve, and he wasn't sorry about it, either.

She lifted her chin. "The characteristics of a good horse have nothing to do with the location of its birth, Mr. Hoke. I appreciate your willingness to sell me twelve good horses if you have them—maybe more if I really need six on each team. I would simply like to approve the selection."

Hoke stared at her. Well, of course she could approve the selection! Didn't a buyer always? But he didn't like anybody insinuating he might sell 'em low quality. Why were women always making him feel like a fool? He needed to get away from her, and fast.

"Fair enough." He tipped his hat again and walked away.

Even with his back turned, Hoke could feel her frown.

He heard Dotson say, "Don't worry about Hoke. He'll get you the finest horses to be found in Independence. Come in here to Granberry's and tell us what's calling you west."

Hoke stewed all the way back to the livery stable, cursing under his breath for the luck of running into Dotson. After all, he hadn't planned on a trip up the Oregon. And now, in the space of thirty minutes, it had overtaken his mind—that and the smell of lavender.

Damn.

CHAPTER 4

Hot and darting

When Abigail stepped out of Granberry's she turned her head briefly in the direction Hoke had gone. Colonel Dotson said that was the way to the livery stable where Hoke had his horses.

"Man who owns that livery knew him when Hoke was a kid. Thinks a lot of him." That was all the information the colonel had offered.

Fighting the temptation to lift her chin again, Abigail turned the opposite direction and started walking. The letter . . . the banker . . . Mimi . . . and that last image of her father putting Rascal in her arms all crossed her mind before she realized a man standing on the boardwalk across the street was staring at her.

She recognized him.

A shiver ran up her spine as she remembered Mrs. Helton's warning: ". . . you'll want your door locked. You never know about folks around here."

The question Mrs. Helton had asked her after dinner the first night—*Why are you here?*—hadn't stopped running through Abigail's mind. She wondered again at the answer to that question as she continued to put one foot in front of the other down the boardwalk.

A store clerk ran past her with an empty bucket, bringing Abigail back to the moment. She saw him dip it in a water trough down the street, and then she spied the flames that had sent him running for it.

Stepping briskly through the open door, she picked up a blanket that had been on display at the end of the counter. By the time the clerk ran back in with the dripping bucket, she had already beaten the fire out.

After running her hand over the wool to check for damage, she handed it back to him. "Good as new. See for yourself."

The surprised man just blinked at her. "Thanks," he mumbled as she walked out.

Why had she introduced herself as Abigail Baldwyn to the three men when she approached them? She should have said Mrs. Robert Baldwyn. It must have been Hoke's eyes—his eyes had nearly burned her skin. They were as hot and darting as the fire she'd just stamped out. They licked up every detail.

Abigail had no reason to lift her chin at him, but he had stepped on her pride. It was surprising she had any left after the last two months . . . and the five years that preceded them.

She turned down a side street and didn't notice the man who'd been watching her earlier until he stepped from behind an empty rig and blocked her path.

He swept off his hat and bowed. "Howdy-do, ma'am. Haven't seen you since I hauled your pretty little family over to Mrs. Dandy's. What brings you out today . . . ?" He craned his neck to look behind her, then grinned. "Alone."

Dread gripped Abigail's heart at the luck of running into Percy again.

Alone.

~๑~

"I owe you a debt, Mr. Branson," Hoke said to the livery owner. They were mixing feed to give to the rest of Hoke and James's horses.

"You don't owe me a thing, son. All I did was put you to work when I found you sleeping in my stalls."

Hoke pointed to the mixture of apples, oats, honey, and hay. "You fed me." Fed him more than food, too. Mr. Branson had seen to it that Hoke got an education—on horses and on life. Hoke turned and pulled a worn copy of *Oliver Twist* from one of his saddlebags hanging on a post nearby. "I traded for this in Denver. It's about an orphan." He handed it to Branson. "He had it rougher than me."

Branson smiled. "He must have had it rough, then." He pointed the book at the nearest corral. "That white filly sure is a beauty. Will you sell her?"

Hoke took his time in answering.

What brings you to Independence, Hoke? Jenkins had asked. The question wouldn't leave his mind.

Independence had gotten him in a choke hold from that first dream, two months ago. He had never expected to see Branson again, but here he was, standing with the man who had been so good to him when Hoke had needed it most.

"I'm thinkin' I'll keep the filly."

"Surprises me, if you stay on the move."

"I'm thinkin' about startin' a horse—"

A woman's scream pierced the air.

As Hoke rounded the corner he saw a young woman throw a change purse to the ground. "You mean to tell me that's all we have left?" An older gentleman he recognized as the man from Boston winced as if the woman had struck him.

"Irene. Lower your voice."

A younger version of the irate woman stood off to the side. Both females were dark-haired and pretty . . . if an angry-looking woman could be called pretty.

"Don't tell me what to do," spat Irene. "You're the one who's gotten us into this mess."

The younger woman nudged her. "Irene, people think we're being attacked, for God's sake." She turned to Hoke, who was holstering his gun. "We're fine. Just got some bad news, is all."

Irene noticed Hoke for the first time. "Were you coming to my rescue?"

Hoke nodded toward the man. "McConnelly, isn't it? Everything all right here?"

"Yes. I'm sorry, remind me of your—"

"Hoke."

"Of course, Hoke. Let me introduce my daughters, Irene and Diana McConnelly."

Hoke introduced Branson. When Diana took Irene to the side to scold her for making a scene, McConnelly winked at Hoke and Branson. "Irene is a little high-strung."

Hoke tipped his hat and bid the McConnellys good day.

When they were nearly back to the livery Branson said, "I'd be willing to let you run my livery, Hoke. Could even make you a partner."

Hoke's throat tightened at the offer. "That's mighty generous."

"You're the closest thing we ever had to a son. It hurt me and Ruby when you left."

Hoke's throat squeezed tighter still. "I hope you got my letter. I tried to explain things in it."

"We got it. And we read it. But nobody ever faulted you for what happened. That woman went on to prove what kind she was. It was just a bad stroke of luck you were caught up in it. I blame myself for you being alone on the road that night."

Hoke turned to look him in the eye—this man who'd been a surrogate father to him. Twenty years he'd avoided this conversation. He'd missed his chance to say these things to Mrs. Ruby. He would say them to Branson, man to man, like Branson deserved.

"Don't ever blame yourself for not doing enough for me. I'd have turned out rotten as that man I killed if it hadn't been for you." He lowered his eyes. "I'm sorry I hurt Mrs. Ruby. I just didn't want to bring shame on you, not after you'd been so good to me."

Branson laid his hand on Hoke's shoulder. "Ruby died nothing but proud of you, Hoke. She just missed you, is all. We both did." He smiled. "It's good to have you here now. Think about my offer."

~

The sound of boots on gravel floated to Abigail from the adjoining street. She looked at Percy. "I'm not alone." Craning her eyes past a clapboard building, she called, "Sweetheart!"

A man with a small boy on his hip came into view. She waved him over.

"Sweetheart, come meet Percy. He's the gentleman who brought us to Mrs. Helton's the other day." The man looked confused, but came toward her. "I didn't mean to run off and leave you." She turned back to Percy. "May I introduce my cousin, Mr. Percy?"

The gentleman, who Abigail had recognized could easily pass as a family member with his sandy hair and blue eyes, handed her the boy and extended his hand to Percy. "Marc Isaacs."

Frowning, Percy shook hands with him. "Pleasure." He tipped his hat to Abigail and boarded his rig. "Afternoon, ma'am." Then he yawed his team and drove away.

Abigail let out her breath and was so relieved she kissed the little boy on the cheek.

The man grinned. "You're a kissing cousin."

Abigail laughed and handed the boy back to him. "Thank you for coming to my rescue. He was making me nervous."

"May I walk you to your destination?" Mirth danced in Marc Isaacs's eyes. "In case there are any more men who make you nervous between here and there?"

"I'm only going to that boardinghouse." She pointed in the direction of Mrs. Helton's, then extended her hand. "Thank you, Marc Isaacs."

"Pleasure." He mimicked Percy, holding on to her hand. "Miss? Or Mrs.?"

"Mrs." He let her hand go. "Baldwyn."

"Ah."

Abigail smiled as she walked on, thinking how much Marc Isaacs reminded her of her brother Seth.

An April sunbeam snaked through the branches of an oak tree in Mrs. Helton's front yard as Abigail approached it. She stretched out her hand to catch its light.

It was the first good omen she'd had in months.

CHAPTER 5

The twelve best horses

April 6, 1866

Dearest Mimi,
We arrived safely in Independence three days ago and already have much to tell.

First, it's clear I should have married a riverboat captain. The wife of ours was a lovely creature who sent us to Mrs. Helton's boardinghouse. Mrs. Helton, in turn, sent me to George Dotson, a retired Union colonel she claims is the finest man traveling the Oregon "this season or any other."

I shudder to think how I would have floundered— both here and all my life—without the wisdom and generosity of other women, you foremost among them.

Daddy will have gotten my letter by now. Look after him for me, as much as you can tolerate.

Now that Abigail had settled on Colonel Dotson's train, there was no time to waste as they finished preparations. The children were full of questions—all but Corrine. "I wish I'd stayed with Thad and Sue Anne."

"Oh, you don't mean that, Corrine." Charlie was wrestling Rascal on the floor. "You would have ended up playing nursemaid."

Abigail's older brother and his wife had a new baby, born after the war.

Abigail folded her letter to Mimi. "Corrine, you'll have a much better trip if you decide now to embrace this experience."

"The colonel served the Union?" asked Charlie.

"Yes."

"So did he—"

"No. He didn't know your father." It was the first question Abigail had asked Dotson when they went inside Granberry's.

"Corrine." Lina took her older sister by the hand. "Aren't you excited about living in a covered wagon and seeing the mountains? What if we see a moose?" She giggled. "I bet they are this big." Climbing on a chair, Lina reached her hands as high as they would go.

"And buffalo!" said Jacob. "They're the biggest of all and I'm going to shoot me one with Pa's rifle."

"No shooting while we're gone." Abigail put on her hat. "Lina, step down, sweetheart."

Charlie hopped up and swung Lina off the chair.

"Charlie and I are going to the post office, then to buy the wagons and horses." Abigail handed Corrine a list. "You're in charge, Corrine. Check over this supply list and see if I've left anything out. Jacob, take Rascal out every hour, on the hour." She handed him her watch chain.

"Yes, ma'am."

"I mean it, Jacob. Don't forget."

Jacob looked at his brother and sisters defensively. "I won't forget."

"You'll clean it up this time, if you do," mumbled Corrine.

Charlie and Abigail went to the wagon maker's first.

"You don't want Conestogas," he said. "They're too bulky and hard to turn. And they'll kill your animals before you get there 'cause the load's too heavy for 'em all that distance."

This threw off Abigail's careful planning. She'd been counting on more space. But on the wagon maker's suggestion, she bought two lighter spring wagons instead—schooners, he called them—with smaller wheels in front for better turning.

"I'd advise you to get oxen or mules, too. Colonel Dotson said you were thinking about horses, but horses don't do well for the long haul."

"So everybody tells me." She was going to look like a fool when she went to see Hoke saying she had changed her mind about the horses.

As Abigail hoisted herself up and looked inside what was to be their home for the next several months, a shiver ran up her spine.

Someone was watching them.

She peered up and down the street but didn't see anyone. Was she just feeling paranoid after that run-in with Percy yesterday?

"This isn't a lot of room," said Charlie, scrunching in beside her. The schooners were only half as long as Conestogas and only four feet wide. She and Charlie couldn't even stand up straight inside. "Two of these wagons put together is less space than we have in Mrs. Helton's room."

With their trunks, that room was overflowing. They exchanged looks. The Baldwyns would need to prune through their belongings again.

Abigail snapped her fingers as they left the wagon maker's. "We can use burlap sacks and attach them to the inside walls. Corrine and I can make cloth sacks for our clothes, too. Let's run over to the mercantile and see if they'll buy our heavy trunks."

The owner agreed to give her several bolts of fabric and trim in exchange for the trunks. As they were leaving the mercantile, Abigail once again would have sworn someone was watching her.

From the doorway she looked up and down the street but again saw no one.

As she turned to say good-bye to the owner she spotted a high-backed rocking chair with a torn seat sitting in the corner of the store.

"That's not new; it was actually my mother's," explained the owner.

"I'll take it if you'll sell it." Lina still liked to be rocked.

The owner said he could whitewash it, so Abigail arranged to pick it up on Monday, making a mental note to get enough twine when she came back to repair the seat.

Next she bought two feather beds, and bedrolls for the boys to sleep in under the wagon. Jacob had proclaimed, "Me and Charlie can't sleep in the wagon, Ma. Men sleep on the ground." She'd resisted the temptation to remind him that he was nine.

Instead of buying a table and chairs, she had a carpenter fashion sawhorses—tall ones for a table and shorter ones for benches. Then she went back to the wagon maker to have him add iron rings under both wagons to which she could tie ropes and slide long wood planks through. She would use them for tabletops.

When they passed Granberry's Café Abigail noticed a small garden in the back. On a whim, she went in and asked Mrs. Granberry about her vegetables. Then she hurried back to the wagon maker a third time to see if he could build side boxes on her wagons.

"What for?" he asked.

"An experiment."

"I need to know what they're goin' to hold so I know how strong to anchor 'em."

"Strong enough to hold about ten inches of dirt." People sometimes used wooden boxes for growing things. Even Thomas Jefferson had used container boxes in his massive gardens in Virginia. Why not a floating vegetable garden for her?

When Abigail and Charlie left the wagon maker's this time, they turned west toward the livery stables.

Hoke was talking to two burly, bearded men when he saw Abigail and a boy approach. His gaze fastened on her from under the brim of his once-black hat, but he made no move to greet her.

When a dog ran out from the stable growling at the boy, Hoke instinctively started toward them but before he could take two steps the woman deflected it with the side of her foot, redirecting the cur like a rolling tumbleweed.

The dog ran on several yards before stopping to look back, as if he couldn't remember his original purpose.

Hoke smiled down at his boots as Abigail pointed the boy toward the nearby corral. When the men left, he joined them at the fence. He chewed on the soft end of a hickory stick, liking the taste of it in his mouth. "You picked out the best twelve yet?"

"Mr. Hoke, this is my son Charlie."

"Pleased to meet you, Charlie. And you can drop the *Mr.* Just call me Hoke."

"*Mr.* Hoke," said Abigail to Charlie. "I'm raising a gentleman, Mr. Hoke. It's his habit to address superiors this way."

This woman had a way of saying things to which Hoke could not think of a tart response. He wasn't glib like James, but neither was he usually tongue-tied. Feeling far from Charlie's superior, he extended his hand. The boy took it heartily.

Charlie was tall and stately like his mother but with darker blond curls. Same blue eyes . . . different nose and chin.

"Sir," said Charlie, "you've got some fine-looking horses there." He pointed at the corral. "How many you got altogether?"

"Why, you lookin' to buy the whole bunch?"

Charlie laughed. "Oh, no, sir. I was just curious."

Hoke liked him. Seemed like a good-natured kid. Couldn't really help who his mother was. He turned his back on Abigail and concentrated on Charlie.

"Which twelve would you pick?"

Charlie pointed out a sorrel, two chestnuts, a quarter horse, and a large black mare. "I like that spotted one, too, but I'm not as familiar with that kind of horse."

"Those are mustangs—better for speed than pulling. Wild herds in the West attract all kinds. Some of these, like that quarter horse, were once tame and had been ridden, then got loose and joined this group. Others were born in the wild. I think the sorrel wandered up from Mexico. It had a piece of bridle on it with some fancy jangles like Mexicans use. A few of these had war brands. When soldiers and Indian war parties clash, horses without their mounts run off. Sometimes wagon trains are attacked and horses cut loose."

Charlie looked at his mother. "Now that's a happy thought."

"The ones with brands are more compliant," continued Hoke, turning so he could see Abigail again. "The wild ones are temperamental at first, but they calm down. If you're putting together a team, you want to consider gender. Geldings and mares work best together. Stallions cause problems. Personally, I prefer to ride a stallion, but he's willful. He'd fight with any other stallion if he were on a team with it and that's a waste of precious energy when you're looking at a two-thousand-mile trek."

Abigail looked uncomfortable. Hoke wondered if he'd nicked another nerve by turning his back on her.

⁓

Abigail's collar grew warm as she listened to Hoke talk to Charlie about the horses. Her comment the previous day about wanting to approve the selection seemed silly now. Hoke's intuition had been right—her father raised mostly fine breeds, along with a few plow horses, nearly all of which had been confiscated first by the Confederacy, then the Union. These were western horses and Abigail knew nothing about them.

Hoke looked at Charlie. "Your six are fine selections from what I have here, but I've already put the best ones in a separate corral for you. Cleared the brands, rubbed 'em down, even worked 'em together in teams."

He was looking squarely at Abigail now. "Like I said yesterday, you really need six on each wagon if you're going to drive the twelve-foots, and I understand that's what you bought."

She had only purchased those wagons a few hours ago! "How did you know that?" Was Hoke the one who'd been watching them earlier? No . . . she was certain she would have noticed if it had been him.

"There are few secrets out here, Mrs. Baldwyn."

His voice was as deep as a rumbling waterfall. He needed a shave . . . a whole bath, really. He smelled like horse sweat—horse sweat with a hint of pine needles and chipped cedar.

Yesterday she had thought his eyes were dark, but today she could see that a gold rim circled each iris. And what eyes! They were unsettling. Not unsettling in the way Percy had made her feel yesterday. This man didn't make her skin crawl, but his eyes did make her feel sensitive . . . alert . . . because he was so alert.

His eyes ate everything.

What did he mean by "few secrets"? Had he talked with Colonel Dotson? Did he know why she was making this journey?

Abigail forced herself to meet Hoke's eyes. It wasn't easy to hold a steady gaze with him. "Do you think I'm making a mistake with horses?"

"Yes."

"Why?"

"'Cause horses sweat. They'll dehydrate before you get to Nebraska."

Abigail looked away. She'd just been thinking he smelled like horse sweat. Had he yanked that thought from her head?

Horses were loyal. That was what she loved about them. Abigail had thought they would be the better investment for the long term.

"What do you recommend instead?"

"For you, mules."

"Why for me?"

"They're the most like horses, but stubborn. I've got a feeling you can handle stubborn."

She opened her mouth to reply, then shut it.

Hoke turned to Charlie. "You ever work mules?"

"Yes, sir. A couple times at my granddad's plantation."

Hoke looked back at Abigail with his eyebrows raised. "Plantation?"

"I grew up on a plantation," explained Abigail, feeling defeated because of his "show horse" comment the day before, "and our help used mules to plant corn and tobacco."

"Your 'help'?"

"Our slaves. My mother always called them our help. Listen, are you going to be upset with me if I change my mind and decide to use mules instead?"

"No."

"You're sure? Because I told you I'd buy twelve horses. If I get mules from someone else, I'll only be able to afford a couple of your horses. I hate to have misled you on a sale if you were counting on it."

"I've got mules for you."

"You do?"

"Um-hum. I had a feeling you'd come around, so I went ahead and traded for some mules. Heard you changed your mind on the wagons—and even had some smart ideas on how to prepare your wagons—so I was betting on you wising up to this."

"But you said you put the twelve best horses in a separate corral for us!"

Hoke grinned and took the hickory stick out of his mouth. "I never said they were horses."

CHAPTER 6

Twenty-dollar gold pieces

Hoke led Abigail and Charlie around the side of a barn to another corral. Two harnessed teams of mules stood at one end and two horses at the other. All of them were big, strong beauties. Neither Abigail nor Charlie was going to argue about the selection.

Reaching for the muzzle of a large gray dun, Abigail ran her hand over it, then looked at his teeth. He was young and healthy.

Stooping down, she eased herself through the fence railing so she could feel his back flank and lift his foot. His hooves were filed and clean, his coat brushed and gleaming. These animals showed every sign of being cared for—excellently cared for. She reached into her jacket pocket and pulled out a sugar cube, holding it out for the dun.

Hoke leaned on the railing. "I see you came prepared to make friends with my horses."

"Just the ones that are soon to be *my* horses." Abigail smiled broadly, then scowled. "But now I wonder if I can afford them."

"How much were you expectin' to pay?"

Abigail leaned her back to the railing so she could look at what she was buying. These mules put Arlon's Bess to shame. Their long ears flicked at gnats and the sound of Hoke's voice—a voice they apparently found comforting, given the way they kept watching him and gravitating toward him. Her brother Seth used to have that effect on animals . . . Seth used to smell like horse sweat, too.

"During the war, the price of a good horse rose to over a hundred dollars. But they're only about half that now, right? I know oxen are cheaper and less expensive to feed, but I don't know anything about oxen." Craning her head back, she asked, "What about mules? Is their cost comparable with horses?"

"The price of anything, mules and horses included, is what the buyer and seller agree on," he said softly. "Tell me what you were expectin' to pay, and I'll tell you if I can live with it."

Abigail swung her head over to Charlie. She had expected Hoke to name his price. Was it foolish to tell him how much she had to spend? Would he take advantage of her because she was a woman and he wouldn't expect her to have any sense?

On Charlie's nod she looked back to Hoke. "I was hoping to get twelve good horses for six hundred. This is twelve mules plus two horses, and honestly, their quality is better than I had anticipated. I'm sure you can get a lot more than six hundred dollars for what's standing in this corral."

"I can." Hoke nodded. "But what's standin' in this corral hasn't cost me six hundred, so I'd come out ahead."

Hoke wondered if Abigail Baldwyn knew how lovely she was, and whether she was in the habit of batting those heavy-lashed eyes at men in the hope they would work something out for her. That McConnelly woman's voice yesterday had been laced with mockery. *Were you coming to my rescue?*

There was no question that Irene McConnelly used her looks for gain. Was this Baldwyn woman doing the same? And if she had a husband, why wasn't he making this horse deal?

Hoke couldn't really lose. He had traded horses for the mules, and the horses had been waiting for him in a little valley northwest of Washita, but . . . damn if he could think straight.

"I wouldn't feel right giving you less than seven," said Abigail. "And I'd still feel beholden to you."

Hoke looked down at the ground. "Charlie, does your mother have a surplus of money she's tryin' to get rid of?"

Charlie laughed. "No, sir. But you know she's right about the value of these mules and horses. You're still selling low to us at seven."

Hoke looked back up at Abigail. "Would you feel better payin' eight?"

She grinned. "I can live with seven if you can."

He moved to open the gate for her, but she slipped back through the fence railing before he could get to it. Hoke prided himself on his ability to get in the heads of most creatures, but women . . . women were a mystery. It had been a long time since he'd felt anything like peace around one.

"I'll bring 'em to you Monday at the jumping-off spot."

She laid a blue crocheted bag, heavy with twenty-dollar gold pieces, in his hand. He followed her eyes as they etched the outlines of his fingers.

They walked past the open door of the barn. Abigail stopped and pointed. "Whose horses are those?"

"Those aren't for sale. They're mine."

"Do you mind if I look?" She walked toward the black stallion in one stall, then the white filly in the other. "She's beautiful," crooned Abigail, stroking the filly's nose.

Hoke would have been irritated had he not liked watching her. Charlie showed respect for his mother, which told Hoke the husband had respected her, too.

"Are you sure you won't sell me *her*, Mr. Hoke, instead of the gray?"

"I'm sure. But I'll let you ride her sometime."

"I'd love to, but I leave on Tuesday."

"It's a two-thousand-mile trip. I expect there'll be a few chances between now and September."

Her eyes got big. "You're going?"

"I am."

"Oh."

She turned back to the filly but not before he caught the upturn of her lips. Was she hiding her smile from him or the boy? Charlie was several feet away now, admiring the stallion.

"What do you call him?" Charlie asked Hoke.

Hoke stuck the hickory stick back in his lips and took a final measured look at Abigail Baldwyn.

"My horse."

∞

"George Dotson's been after me to join his wagon train," Hoke told James later that day. "I believe I'll do it."

"How come?"

Hoke shook his head. "I don't know. Branson offered me a job here."

"I'm surprised at you joining Dotson's train then."

"Me, too."

Hoke and James had talked about a lot of things in their years of evenings around a campfire but had never once discussed long-range plans. They'd just kept riding together, tackling one job at a time, one town at a time.

When Independence first lured him back, Hoke had thought it must be time to settle. Branson's offer should have felt like a sign of affirmation. But ever since he'd heard the sound of her boots clicking toward him on the boardwalk and looked up, all he could think of was the way sunlight glinted off Abigail Baldwyn's hair.

James looked at him a long minute before slapping his hands together. "We better go, then. When you start making decisions you can't explain, things always get interesting."

Relief washed through Hoke to know James was open to the idea. There was his affirmation. Men he wanted to keep riding with didn't often come along. "You think you can be around people that long?"

"I can—but I don't know if *you* can. How long will it be?"

"'Bout five months."

James clapped Hoke on the shoulder. "You can probably tolerate people for five months."

Later, when Hoke told Dotson that he and James were going, Dotson asked, "What made you change your mind?"

"I don't know. Just feel like I'm supposed to go." Even at the risk of disappointing Mr. Branson again, the pull to go was flaming strong in his chest.

Colonel Dotson nodded. "The Baldwyn woman signed on, too . . . her and her four children, as far as Fort Hall. Her husband's supposed to be a captain out there. But somethin' . . . somethin' don't seem right about it to me. Nobody I've asked knows anything about him. I guess we'll find out."

"I guess so," agreed Hoke, not liking to hear she had a husband. But his decision was made—his gut told him to follow the scent of lavender.

⚬

April 9, 1866

Dearest Mimi,
Today we leave Mrs. Helton's boardinghouse. Her home lies within sight of the house of a famous artist, George Bingham, from whose porch one can watch the workings of the town.

In our short time here, I have grown fond of Independence—it's been both bustling and bittersweet. The folks are less genteel than what we are used to . . . more straightforward and hardworking. I like them very much.

We spend tonight in our wagons and roll out in the morning.

Independence buzzed.

Families moved out of hotels and boardinghouses and loaded supplies on farm wagons to take to the jumping-off spot near the Bingham place. Farmers lined both sides of Main, selling produce.

Even Corrine had trouble containing her excitement as the children helped Abigail buy sacks of potatoes, apples, beans and peas, seeds, and a slip of sweet potatoes for her wagon garden. Mrs. Granberry gave her a dozen strawberry plants and some dahlia bulbs. To Abigail's joy, she also gave her a small cherry tree that had sprung up the season prior.

Mrs. Helton took a final stroll with the Baldwyns, her arm linked through Charlie's, which made Jacob smirk. She pointed at the train depot. "The train loops down from Chicago now, but soon it will replace the boats for bringing folks out here. I expect they will build the railroad on out your way before too many years, although if men don't quit robbing trains, decent folks will be too scared to ride them."

At the top of a hill they came to a cemetery.

"I came up the Missouri, just like you, fifteen years ago. Was planning to join one of the trains, just like you. But Edward took sick the week we got here." She pointed to a headstone. "He died a month later. We were staying at the boardinghouse and I just kept staying there. The man who owned the house got shot one night in a saloon fight. He's around here someplace." She looked out across the sprawling cemetery.

Abigail noticed fresh flowers on a grave nearby and stepped over to read the name: *Ruby Branson.*

"I get letters back all the time filled with stories about people's travels and the homes they make . . . who gets married and who has children . . . who loses children." Mrs. Helton touched Charlie's cheek. "I lost a baby boy, Charlie. He would have been sixteen. Almost seventeen. And then Edward died before I could have any more."

Corrine swatted Jacob for his earlier smirk, and Charlie looked sympathetically at his mother. Abigail saw the small headstone for the first time: *Benjamin Helton.*

Mrs. Helton, her eyes full, turned to Abigail. "If you get to Idaho Territory and it's not what you're expecting, you bring these children back here and run this boardinghouse with me."

Lina tugged on Abigail's skirt and pointed. "Look, Ma." Across the cemetery, a man stood up from where he had just laid flowers on a grave. He turned toward the Baldwyns, smoothing back his hair before putting his hat on.

It was too far away to see him clearly—he was a black silhouette against the waning afternoon, one that turned and quickly faded to a small dot going down the hill.

"Can we go see?" asked Lina.

They walked to the grave and Lina smiled to see the flowers.

"We had jonquils at our home in Tennessee," explained Abigail to Mrs. Helton before turning back to Lina. "Did you see the flowers on the other grave near Mr. Helton's? They were jonquils, too."

Lina shook her head. "Can I have one?" she whispered.

"Let's not disturb them, Lina. They're a gift meant to honor someone else."

Rachel Mathews, Beloved Wife and Mother. Reading it made the children smile. When Mrs. Helton raised a brow in question, Abigail explained, "Rachel was my mother's name."

As they turned to leave, Mrs. Helton took Charlie's arm, and even though she leaned in and spoke low, Abigail still heard her. "If anything happens to your mother, Charlie, you and the rest of the children come back here to me."

⌒᳾

Abigail came around the wagon holding a rope. She handed it to Jacob, whose eyes grew large as they followed the cord to its other end.

"What is *that*?"

"A cow. Don't act like you've never seen one before. Your job is to milk her every morning."

"Wa—wait a minute! Where did it come from?"

"I traded for it." When the Baldwyns moved their things to the wagons, Abigail realized her folly in thinking she could jostle all the way to Idaho Territory with a porcelain washbowl and pitcher. So she'd gone back to the store where she put the fire out to see if the merchant there would trade her for a tin set. He was so grateful to her for saving his store that he threw in a Jersey cow.

"When?" asked Jacob.

"Just now."

"I never milked a cow before."

"You'll get the hang of it. Tie it over there, out of the way."

Charlie had been sent for a stock of firewood, and Corrine and Lina were repacking the food. Corrine didn't like the way it had been stacked the first time.

"I'm going to the mercantile one last time, Corrine, to get a churn." Abigail noticed mud clumps covering the foot of the wagon. "And a broom."

Corrine poked her head out of the wagon. "Why do we need a churn?"

"We have a cow," said Jacob, holding the rope high.

Before going to the mercantile, Abigail paid a final visit to the post office. She handed the first letter to the postal clerk. *I have taken your advice and am coming to Fort Hall.* Robert would surely be surprised— this was the boldest thing she'd ever done.

Then she reached into her pocket for Mimi's freedom papers and slid them into the second letter. Robert had drawn them up years before the fighting began. Mimi couldn't refuse them now and Abigail wanted her to have them—to remind them both that Mimi had never been hers to own.

She smiled to see the clerk postmark each letter *Independence.*

"I feel like I'm forgetting something important," she later confessed to an attractive brunette woman behind her in line at the mercantile.

The woman smiled. "You prob'ly are. But maybe I'll have it, and you can borry it."

"You're with Dotson's train?"

"That's right. Melinda Austelle." The woman extended her hand. Abigail could see she wasn't shy. "Mr. Austelle and I have two boys and a girl. We're from Georgia."

Melinda Austelle seemed to know everyone and everything. Abigail quickly learned that Mr. Austelle was the blacksmith traveling in Colonel Dotson's wagon train.

"Mr. Austelle has been workin' in that big lot across from the courthouse helpin' make shoes for all these stock and iron wheels for the local wagon sellers. Would you believe they's over twenty smithies down there? If the wheels ain't prepared right, the wood shrinks and the irons fall off. Some people soak the wheels in creek beds at night, but Mr. Austelle says you shouldn't have to, if they're prepared right."

Melinda was better prepared for this trip than Abigail. She had a husband to help educate her on things like wheel irons. Abigail wondered again what she was forgetting.

With the stoneware churn on her hip and the broom in the crook of her arm, Abigail wove through the growing maze of wagons. As she neared her own, she heard a deep, now-familiar voice and saw Hoke talking to Lina and Corrine.

"When you start the team you give a little flip on the reins, like this. Mules are stubborn, but if you show them you're boss and get them into a routine, they'll do fine."

Abigail stopped, curious to see what Lina and Corrine thought of him. Hoke's back was to her . . . same dusty black boots, same once-black hat, different buckskin shirt.

"What if they see a snake?" asked Lina.

"If it's a big rattlesnake, it'll scare 'em."

"What do you do then?" Lina's eyes were large.

"Better hold tight. If they take off running it'll be hell to pay."

"Mr. Hoke!" Abigail stepped forward.

"Just Hoke."

He didn't turn. Had he known she was standing behind him?

"Please don't say *hell* in front of my children."

He turned to her. "They don't know about hell?"

"Hoke brought our mules and horses, Ma!" Lina ran to tug her skirt, whispering up to Abigail, "I like his growly voice."

"*Mr.* Hoke," corrected Abigail.

"Is Charlie around?" Hoke asked. "I'll show him how to harness the teams and hobble them at night so they can't wander off." He stooped to rub Rascal's ears. Within seconds the dog's eyes rolled back in his head.

"I know where the boys are." Corrine reached for her sister's small hand. "Come with me, Lina."

Rascal loped after them, turning several times to look back at Hoke.

Abigail grinned. "You certainly made an impression on the dog."

Hoke stood and came toward her. "Could you stop correcting me in front of people?" He was clean shaven and no longer smelled like horse sweat, but the scent of pine and cedar lingered.

Hugging the churn, she took a step back. "When have I corrected you?"

"I told Charlie the other day to just call me Hoke and you said, no, call him *Mr.* Hoke. You just did it again, plus you scolded me for saying there'd be hell to pay. Here, give me that, it looks heavy." He took the churn from her arms and set it in the back of her nearest wagon.

"I'm sorry. But I've worked hard to teach my children a strict moral code. If you can refrain from cursing in front of them and promise not to offer them liquor or teach them to gamble, then I won't have to correct you in front of them."

"Do you think I'm a scoundrel?" He reached for the broom.

She couldn't read him well enough to know if that smoldering look in his eyes was hurt or anger. Why should it hurt him for her to think he might be a scoundrel?

"No," she answered hesitantly, letting go of the broom, which he set by the churn. "But you do have a piercing . . . hard way about you."

He turned back toward her and burned her with his eyes. "Does that make me a bad person?"

Abigail looked from the churn to the broom, and back to Hoke. "I guess not."

Charlie came bounding around the wagon. "Mr. Hoke! Good to see you again." They shook hands. "This is my brother, Jacob."

"Good to meet you, Jacob."

Hoke took Jacob's hand in his like he was shaking hands with a man. Jacob stood straighter.

"You boys probably already know this," said Hoke, "but let me show you how to hitch and hobble these mules and horses."

The boys looked at each other with raised eyebrows and followed him. Abigail didn't know if she was glad or upset to have Hoke on the trip.

She looked at the churn and broom again, wondering how he'd managed to take them from her hands in such a way that she had barely noticed, then stepped to the back of the other wagon to put her reticule in the cherry box.

Immediately she knew: someone had been in here . . . one of the children, maybe. Things she had left sitting on the top of the chest were strewn to the side of it. When she raised the lid and looked inside, it was obvious someone had rifled through her letters. Panicked, she checked the drawstring purse that had held the last of their twenty-dollar gold pieces.

It was empty!

CHAPTER 7

Mere suggestion of money

Fear nearly stopped her heart.

Abigail dug under the letters for the small box that held her jewelry. When the lid flipped up, she felt her heart beat again. The cameo brooch and pearl pendant were still there. The cameo had been her mother's. As a girl, Abigail had thought the silhouette in the carved ivory was her mother's profile.

Robert had given her the pearl pendant as a wedding gift.

Abigail tucked the jewelry box under her arm and searched for Colonel Dotson, but found his wife, Christine, instead.

"Mrs. Dotson!"

"Hello, Mrs. Baldwyn. Is everything all right?"

"Money is missing from my wagon . . . over a hundred dollars in gold coin. Nearly all we had left." Fear and doubt squeezed her heart in equal measure. How could they possibly survive this trip on the few remaining coins in her reticule? Was she a fool for bringing her family out here?

Christine left to get Colonel Dotson while Abigail went to find her children. None of them had seen anyone near the wagon.

Hoke arrived with the colonel, and Abigail showed them the cherry box. "This is where I keep important letters. The money was in here, along with a small jewelry box."

"They didn't take the jewelry?" asked the colonel.

She shook her head.

The colonel looked out darkly over the camp. "I won't tolerate thievery."

"Be hard to know if it was someone in our group. People have been coming and going all day," said Hoke.

"Mrs. Baldwyn, we could go wagon to wagon," said the colonel, "but Hoke's right. It could have been somebody from town. We could have everybody in our own group turn their pockets out, but how would we know your coins from theirs?"

Abigail thought of the bag of coins she'd laid in Hoke's hand only days ago. She wasn't sure she would recognize those same coins again if Hoke handed them back to her, so how would she know her missing coins if she saw *them*?

She bit her fingernail. "I don't know if we can still afford to go. Unless . . . how much time do I have before the group meeting, Colonel?"

"Two hours."

"Charlie, Corrine, watch Jacob and Lina. I'll be back in an hour."

⁓

Mrs. Helton looked surprised to see Abigail standing in the door of her kitchen. "Did you decide to stay?"

"No. I'm hoping you'll help me go."

Abigail told Mrs. Helton what had happened and showed her the jewelry. "Do you know anyone who might buy a pearl pendant?"

Mrs. Helton wiped her hands on a cloth and inspected the jewelry. "Not the cameo?"

Abigail shook her head. "I can part with the pendant more easily."

The older woman looked at her a minute. "I'll buy it."

She was so humbled she could hardly speak. "I'm not asking you to buy it; I was just hoping you could refer me to a jeweler."

"I have money. And I like it. If your circumstances change I'll sell it back to you."

Abigail's eyes burned as Mrs. Helton laid twice the amount Abigail had paid her for their lodging back in her shaking hands. She clutched the older woman's fingers and whispered, "What if I'm making a mistake, Mrs. Helton? What if I lose more than my money?"

The older woman studied her face before answering.

"Come here, I want to show you something." She led Abigail to a cabinet in the parlor and opened a drawer filled with letters.

"These are postmarked from every territory west and south and north of here. And they don't all have a happy ending. Sometimes people lose more than their money. But I am amazed at what they find.

"I know it took courage for you to come here, and it's going to take courage for every hardship you encounter on the way. I admire you for it. If I knew Edward was out there somewhere . . ." She looked out the window, in the direction of the cemetery. When she looked back at Abigail, her eyes brimmed with tears. "Or my boy? I'd walk two thousand miles to get to him."

Mrs. Helton brushed away the tears and smiled. "I don't know what you'll end up with, but don't ever fault yourself for trying. And don't let something like stolen coins stop you when you've still got the means to replace them."

⤵

At the five o'clock meeting Hoke spotted Abigail on the opposite side of the circle of travelers, sitting quietly on a hay bale with her children.

So she hadn't pulled out . . . not yet, anyway. *Good for her . . . good for her.*

Since delivering the last of his horses that afternoon, Hoke had been wondering what he'd gotten himself into. He and James had made good from the sales off the herd. There was land aplenty right here in Missouri, and the offer of a job from a man who was like a father to him. So why go on this trip?

His only answer was the memory of that regal yet exasperating woman rubbing the muzzle of his white filly. That was the moment he had decided to go, surprising himself.

Or maybe it was when she leaned her head back at the corral.

The thought that he might not have control of his own independent mind was infuriating. She was already a worry to him . . . her money stolen before she even left! It made sense she'd be a target, with her fancy clothes.

He intended to give her back the five gold pieces she'd overpaid him—they were jangling in his pocket now—he just wasn't sure of the best way to go about it. He didn't want to embarrass her in front of anyone. The way she squared her shoulders and lifted her chin showed she had pride.

He had no business worrying over a married woman, just like he had no business keeping the filly. No western man rode a white horse. It was too dangerous. But that filly had captured his heart somehow. She had fire and spirit! And he didn't know when he'd seen a prettier horse. Keeping her was a foolish vanity and he knew it. He just hoped it didn't prove to be his downfall.

Hoke's gaze fanned out over the gathering circle again. Who from this group would get buried along the road? It was said that for every hundred people that started down the Oregon Trail, five wouldn't live to see the end of it.

There were all kinds of folks here: educated and uneducated, wealthy and poor . . . and perhaps one who was a thief.

Abigail Baldwyn and her children stood out in this crowd. The mere suggestion of money and pedigree didn't just make people a target for stealing, it made them a target for mean talk, too.

Irene McConnelly waved to him from across the circle. He tipped his hat and looked away.

◯

Abigail looked around the circle of travelers, her eyes stopping on Hoke. He stood tall and brooding beside several other men. His arms were crossed and he was chewing on a stick again, talking to no one.

Even at this distance Abigail could tell that his eyes—his whole body—simmered. His gaze seemed locked on her, but then it darted away, seemingly catching every movement at the gathering. A tall, bearded man in suspenders and calf-length boots stood next to him, beside a low, flat-bed wagon someone had pulled to the middle of the ring.

Colonel Dotson hopped on the wagon and cleared his throat. "Welcome, everyone! We've got twenty-seven families, forty-six wagons, and seventy-eight souls on this train."

"And two thousand miles to get to know each other," yelled a man from the back of the crowd. Several people whooped and clapped.

"That's right." Dotson laughed.

Abigail realized with a sinking feeling that she should have brought simpler dresses. Several curious stares, some hostile, kept aiming in her direction. She wondered if word had gotten out about her money being stolen. What if folks didn't believe her? Few would feel sorry for the Baldwyns' present circumstances when it would appear they'd had plenty in the past. Abigail leaned toward each of the children and told them not to mention their stolen money to anyone.

The blackest stares in the group were coming from a petite, dark-haired woman who sat several feet away. When Melinda Austelle came toward her, Abigail nodded at the woman. "Who is that?"

"Irene McConnelly. And to answer your question, yes. She always looks like she's been suckin' a pickle. Her and that other woman over there, Sue Vandergelden."

"I was worried she thought I was overdressed."

"She *is* probably jealous of your looks and your nice clothes. I really like your shirt, by the way. It's got the prettiest sleeves."

"Thank you." Melinda's kindness felt extra warm after the cold stares she'd received from Irene McConnelly. "I can show you how to make them."

Abigail liked the loose fit of Garibaldi sleeves and usually paired a white shirt with a black Swiss waist or a striped vest with pockets to hold her thimbles. She wore a blue-and-green-striped vest now, and her deep-purple skirts billowed over high-quality boots. Abigail had thought her everyday clothes were dated, but compared to most of the other women here—including Melinda, who wore simple muslin dresses and bonnets with little trimming—she was the very picture of fashion itself.

She noticed that a small pink rose was embroidered in each corner of Melinda's bonnet brim, though.

"That's good stitching," said Abigail. She disliked wearing bonnets herself—they blocked her view on the sides. She wore hats instead, with a string tied under her chin. She didn't like parasols, either. A woman needed her hands free to work in the garden.

"Nothin' like this, though." Melinda inspected the collar of Lina's cotton dress. "Aren't you smart? Look at this embroidery, Emma! Is that not pretty? So detailed."

"Your boys are handsome, too, in those vests and boots," said Emma, Melinda's daughter who was Corrine's age.

Charlie looked at Emma, his face reddening.

Melinda introduced Emma to Corrine and told Charlie and Jacob, "You need to meet my boys, Clyde and Cooper."

Dotson was speaking again. "We've divided into four companies. Company A will be led by Gerald Jenkins." Jenkins stepped up on the wagon so everyone could see him.

He read the names of everyone in Company A, including three single men—brothers fresh from Scotland—who didn't have rigs of their own but would drive supply wagons for Dotson. A family named Peters planned to open a general store. Two older spinster sisters wanted to open a library. Dotson was also part of Company A. Not leading a team himself kept him free to handle larger issues that might arise.

"Anyone in Company A with an issue should report it first to Gerald Jenkins, who'll bring it to me as needed," said Dotson. "If we have to put something to a vote, having a train leader and four company leaders gives us an uneven number."

"What difference does that make?" Jacob whispered to Charlie.

"Think about it, Jake."

"Oh. I get it."

Company B's leader was Rudolf Schroeder. Abigail recognized him as one of the burly men she had seen talking to Hoke at the horse corral. "The Schroeder family is the largest family we have on the trip," explained Dotson. "They're from Pennsylvania. How many of you in all, Rudy?"

"Twenty-one, including my mother, Inez, who just turned seventy." Rudy Schroeder's scratchy voice didn't quite match his exterior. There was more cheering. Inez Schroeder, who wore small round glasses on the end of her nose, stood up and waved.

Several barefoot children ran by and Melinda leaned toward Abigail. "Those are the Schroeder children."

"They won't go barefoot on the trip, will they?"

"I won't be surprised if they do. They're wild as bucks."

Abigail thought the children weren't the only folks at the gathering who looked wild as bucks—in fact, several looked like the type to have taken her money. Some had simple farm wagons with homespun cloth coverings on top. Abigail had bought the best linseed-oiled coverings for her wagons that she could find. That was what Robert and her father would have done. She had spent nearly everything on supplies for this trip. She had even insisted on paying Hoke more than he had agreed to for his mules and horses.

Abigail saw now how naïve she had been, and how naïve not to have hidden her money better. The possibility of theft had never occurred to her. She felt deeply aware of her dependence. She was dependent on Mrs. Helton, dependent on God's grace . . . and ever more dependent on the husband she was traveling toward . . . the husband who had abandoned them.

"Company C will be led by Hoke Mathews. Hoke is a former scout for the cavalry and served as a US Marshal in Colorado Territory, along with James Parker, also in Company C."

Hoke raised his arm but didn't hop up on the wagon as the others had. James Parker was the tall, bearded gentleman standing next to Hoke, judging from the reaction of the other men, who suddenly sized the two up with visible appreciation.

Mathews . . . where had she heard that name before?

Jacob slapped Charlie's arm. "I told you he looked like a sheriff!"

"He wasn't a sheriff, Jake. He was a US Marshal."

"That's even tougher."

Corrine elbowed Jacob. "Shush!"

Abigail frowned and the children quieted but continued to trade threatening stares. Lina crawled into Abigail's lap.

"Other families in Company C are the Baldwyns, Austelles, Dr. Isaacs, Mrs. Atwood, the Becketts, and Tam Woodford."

So . . . they were in Hoke's company. Abigail was glad. Now she understood why Dotson and Jenkins had been so eager to have him join the trip. She, too, would sleep a little easier knowing his wagon was to be close to hers. Had her inclusion in his company been mere chance?

Melinda hugged her. "In the same company! And with a lawman for a leader. I've got to go find Mr. Austelle and see what he knows about those other families. By the way, that gentleman over there's been smiling at you."

Abigail turned in the direction of Melinda's nod as the gentleman stepped forward. "Mr. Isaacs!"

"Mrs. Baldwyn, it's a pleasure to see you again." He grinned. "Most people call me Doc."

"You're the physician the colonel just mentioned?" Abigail set Lina down and stepped back from the ring of travelers to speak to him.

He nodded.

"And part of Dotson's wagon train?"

"I am. And it sounds like we're in the same company."

Abigail was thrilled. Melinda Austelle was starting to feel like a friend, and now here was another familiar face . . . so unexpected. "Where's your son?"

"He's my nephew." Doc Isaacs smiled warmly at her. "I'm not married. Will's over there." He pointed to a woman standing several feet away with the boy on her hip. "My sister, Caroline, is recently widowed." Abigail could see the family resemblance. Doc Isaacs and his sister were both fair-headed and attractive. And Will, with his snowy white hair, was as angelic as Lina, Abigail's youngest.

Irene McConnelly and another dark-haired woman with her both turned to stare at Abigail and Doc Isaacs from under pinched brows.

Doc winked at Abigail. "I think we're being scolded."

Colonel Dotson finished talking about Company D, whose leader was a large, affable man named John Sutler.

"We'll rotate the lead group each week," said the colonel. "If a wagon falls out of formation, let your company leader know. Fall back in as soon as you can. If there's any sign of danger, get word to your leader. He'll have someone mounted each day that can run up and down the train with word. If there's trouble, we'll circle up just like we do at night, in a double ring, putting the women and children inside."

Dotson called Harry Sims, the preacher, to the front and asked him to say a few words. Harry Sims was barrel-chested and softer spoken than any preacher Abigail had ever heard.

Doc Isaacs excused himself to go back to his sister.

"What was his name?" whispered a woman standing behind Abigail.

"Marc Isaacs," said Abigail. "He's a physician."

"No, the preacher."

"Oh. Sims, I think."

The woman was attractive, but—Abigail felt guilty for thinking it—masculine. Her dress sleeves were rolled up past her elbows, revealing the strongest forearms Abigail had ever seen on a woman.

"Huh." The woman looked hard at Harry Sims as he read Psalm 23. "He don't sound like no preacher I ever heard." She thrust her hand at Abigail as soon as Sims finished. "Tam Woodford."

"Abigail Baldwyn."

"These all your kids?"

"Yes."

"They're a good-lookin' bunch. No husband?"

"He's in Idaho Territory, fighting the Indians," said Jacob. "We're going to meet him."

"I reckon he'll be glad to see you'uns. I don't have a husband. Never had one."

"You're traveling by yourself?" asked Corrine.

"Yes, ma'am. Mr. Woodford could be waitin' out there for me. Thought I better go find out, 'cause he ain't back there in Independence." She jerked her thumb toward town.

Lina smiled shyly at her as they said good night.

That night, Abigail had a tough time settling the children and doubted she'd sleep herself.

CHAPTER 8

Sleeping in a covered wagon

April 10, 1866

We begin, Mimi.
    Charlie read that over 300,000 settlers have left from Independence, St. Joseph, and Council Bluffs. How many of them will be in Oregon? California? Salt Lake City? Montana? Or Idaho?

Abigail's eyes opened. Where was she? On a strange bed with Lina nuzzled close. Corrine lay on the other side of Lina. Both were sleeping soundly.

> *Remember when our mothers let us sleep on the porch at night? How the dew seeped through the screen and we woke up under damp quilts with the taste of Tennessee dust in our noses? Sleeping in a covered wagon feels like sleeping on the screened porch again.*

The quilts were heavy with damp and Abigail's mouth tasted like new-wagon sawdust. Their bed, which lay on top of the burlap sacks that held their clothes, was so high she could reach out and touch the coarse canvas that flapped in the wind all night. It was surprising she had slept at all. Horses and cattle moved in the grass nearby, their earthy scent seeping through the cracks of the wagon's planks.

She shivered. It was cold, but not freezing.

Abigail eased Lina's arm off her stomach and scooted to the end of the bed. In the predawn light she couldn't tell the time but thought she heard people moving around camp. Wagons were spread over several acres in no real order. Last night there had been introductions and laughter, dogs barking excitedly, children running, parents scolding, and continued packing in the wagons. Now all was silent but for a few soft stirrings.

This was it. Tuesday. They would set out at sunup.

The colonel and Christine had come to check on her last night after the meeting. No one else had reported missing money. They assured her that the money she had after the sale of her pendant should be enough to pay for incidentals along the way.

"We're all in this together," said Colonel Dotson. But Abigail was determined that her family not be a burden.

As she dressed and smoothed her hair, she wished for more light.

I've nailed a round mirror at a downward angle at the top of the wooden slats, securing it with string to keep it from moving as we jostle. Beneath that sits an upturned wooden crate with a blue tin washbowl and pitcher. It is a poor substitute for the sideboard dresser with its beveled mirror and porcelain wash set I had in Marston, but I am resolved not to feel sorry for myself.

Raising the back flap, Abigail eased out into the moist predawn air. Her long skirts made it hard to see where to step. She envied Lina and

Corrine their shorter dresses but didn't know how they were going to fare climbing in and out either, especially short-legged Lina, who would have a far hop to the ground.

A couple of fires burned in the distance, but she could see little else. Feeling her way to the nearest wagon, she climbed up to check on the boys. Rascal's head popped up. Charlie and Jacob had lifted him in during the night to quiet his whining.

Charlie whispered, "That you, Ma? Time to get up?"

She had asked the boys to sleep in the wagon this first night just to ease her mind. The feeling of having been watched in town, then having her money stolen, had made her uneasy. Hopefully the feeling would go away once they got on the trail.

"It's still dark," she whispered. "Get a little more sleep if you can. I'm going to start breakfast."

As she stepped off in the dark, Abigail slapped into something hard—a body!

"You all right, ma'am?" She recognized the deep voice as an iron-strong arm reached out to steady her.

"Yes. Sorry. I can't see a thing."

"Why don't we fix that?"

He moved off before she could thank him. She heard twigs breaking and the striking of a match. Soon a small fire crackled, the light dancing patterns on his face and hands. Abigail liked the hot smell of the wood burning—it helped cover the stench of manure that hung over the camp, trapped in the mist of the coming morning.

She felt for the dish crate she had prepared the night before and pulled it from the boys' wagon, nearly dropping it.

"Need help with that?" Hoke was at her elbow.

"No, I've got it. Thank you." She didn't want him burdened by her lack of a husband. Was that why they put her in his company? "You don't have to look out for us, Mr. Hoke. We'll get the hang of things."

"Just Hoke. You're going to have a sore back if you pull that off there every morning. Here." He took the crate from her hands and set it by the fire. "Mind if I put a pot of coffee on and share this fire with you?" He smelled like the dawn—like sod and the horses—like the wooden sticks now popping in the flames.

"That would be fine."

Surely he wasn't going to stand there and watch her! She couldn't make herself stop rattling the dishes until he walked off into the distance.

Mrs. Helton told me how to make skillet biscuits, saying that would be easiest, but she went through the directions fast, assuming I had some basic knowledge of cooking. I was too embarrassed to admit otherwise.

Soon Charlie and Jacob were at the fire. Abigail handed Jacob the milk bucket.

"How much?" he asked.

"As much as you can get." Abigail smoothed his unruly hair.

Jacob retousled it and set off swinging the milk bucket.

"I'll feed and water the teams," said Charlie. She was pleased to see that Charlie had combed his hair.

Jacob soon ran back, sloshing the milk. "I'm helping Charlie with the mules!"

"Slow down, Jacob," she hissed, but he was already out of earshot.

Abigail tried to ease the milk into the flour and lard like Mimi always did, but the dough stuck to her hands. Wiping them off as best she could, she pulled out a wire rack to place over the fire for the skillet to set on. How was she going to manage this without burning herself every morning?

Smoke blew in her eyes. Hoke was back with a small table for her to work on.

"Are those biscuits?" he asked.

"I hope so." Abigail wanted to show appreciation for his help but hesitated to offer him any, fearing her biscuits wouldn't turn out. "Should I make extra for you and Mr. Parker?"

"That would be nice. I'll send James with some bacon."

The sky lightened and roosters, so close Abigail jumped at the sound of them, began to crow. Someone came toward the fire chuckling. "Those roosters belong to the Schroeder clan yonder," the person said, pointing. "They've fastened chicken wire to the sides of their wagons and made floatin' henhouses."

It was the tall, bearded man she'd seen with Hoke last night.

"My God, you're pretty. I don't believe we've met. James Parker." He stuck out his hand, then drew it back when he saw hers were tacky with the dough. "Hoke has sent me over with bacon and coffee." He held up a small black pot and a grinder.

Abigail looked up. "Nice to meet you, Mr. Parker."

She went back to her work, expecting him to leave. But he didn't. When she looked back up, he was grinning.

"Why don't I grind the coffee and slice this up?" he offered. "You know, if we fry the bacon in that pan first, those biscuits might not stick as bad. Pan looks new. Fryin' a pan full of bacon grease will help it cure."

She looked down at the pan. "Oh, yes. Good idea. Thank you, Mr. Parker."

Abigail picked her sticky biscuits back out of the pan and handed it to him. "I don't have much experience cooking."

"Well, I got lots. What do you say we do it together?"

She offered him a grateful smile.

"You know, I been tryin' not to smile at the dough on your cheek."

"Oh!" Abigail reached up and felt one of her cheeks.

James Parker was grinning down at her over his thick beard again. Then his voice dropped and his eyes got serious. "If you won't think I'm pryin', who did your cookin' before now?"

Abigail appreciated the man's ability to put others at ease, but she didn't know him well enough to trust him with much information. She also didn't trust herself to talk about Mimi without setting her heart to aching. "I had a woman who helped me. She went back to her sister, who was sick."

⁓

Hoke was rubbing down the legs of the stallion, getting him ready to saddle, when James walked up.

"You'll be glad to know I've got the bacon frying, the coffee ground, and the water boiling."

Hoke didn't answer.

"You keep rubbing that horse's legs, you'll wear the hide off."

"Hast thou given thy horse strength, James? Hast thou clothed his neck with thunder?"

"I know that comes from the Bible you tote around in your saddlebags with all that 'thou' language in it. Now that I've met me a proper preacher, I mean to ask Harry Sims if he knows where that horse bit comes from. But I ain't as dumb as a rock. I been over to deliver coffee, and now that I've seen that woman up close, I think I got an idee why you were suddenly so keen to go on this trip."

Hoke didn't bother looking at him. He kept working on the stallion.

"I ain't as smart as you, but I ain't as dumb as a rock," James repeated.

Hoke still didn't comment.

When James finally started to walk off, Hoke called after him, "We got enough extra wood to make the Baldwyns some steps on the back of their wagons? It's going to be hard for those girls to climb in and out with dresses on."

"Yeah, we got enough."

"Good. Plan to help me with that when we stop this afternoon. And I'm studyin' on how to make a grub box for those dishes so Mrs. Baldwyn doesn't have to reach up for that crate every day."

James shook his head. "You can think of more jobs than any man I ever met."

⁓

Abigail's back ached.

Driving a team isn't hard, Mimi, not with how slow everyone is to get in formation, but four hours of sitting makes a wagon seat feel like a slab of moving rock.

James Parker was driving his and Hoke's wagon. All morning Hoke had been on his horse, then off his horse, as he worked his way down the line of Company C helping people get adjusted to moving in a wagon train.

"You're doing fine. Let 'em know you're the boss. They'll get the hang of things. Fall in behind that one, there," Abigail heard him say to Charlie, then to her, then the Austelles, Doc Isaacs, Tam Woodford, and so forth.

Marc Isaacs waved to her from three wagons back.

"Who is that man?" asked Lina, standing in the wagon bed behind her.

"Dr. Isaacs. He has a nephew close to your age."

Abigail's back ached from spending a restless first night on a lumpy makeshift mattress, sitting on the hard wooden bench, turning so often to check on Lina and Corrine, and feeling so keyed up about the journey. Or maybe Hoke had been right about her getting a sore back from pulling the heavy dish crate down at breakfast.

When Colonel Dotson stopped the train at midday, she eased off the seat and reached up for Lina, feeling soreness down to every bone. As she unwrapped lunches she'd prepared for the children, Hoke came by with a bucket of water and swabbed the mules' mouths and noses.

"Aren't you going to stop and eat?" she asked.

"I will directly."

Charlie ran to help him.

All too soon, it seemed to Abigail, Colonel Dotson was back on his big red horse motioning for each company to roll out again.

♍

When the train stopped to make camp that evening, Hoke and James nailed steps to the Baldwyns' wagons. Corrine walked by and asked, "Why are you doing that? We don't need those."

"Sure you do," said Hoke. "It'll help you get in and out easier."

"I can get in and out just fine."

"What about your little sister?"

"She's got plenty of people to help her in and out."

"You got something against people making your life easier, Corrine?" asked Hoke.

When the girl twisted her brow she looked just like her mother.

"No, sir."

"Then quit acting like you don't want to be helped." He stuck a nail between his lips and held another step in place.

Corrine raised her chin and walked off.

James watched her go. "You don't see many girls that pretty with such a healthy dose of sass. Now me, I favor a sassy woman, where some men take it as a contradiction to their pride."

"She's just hurt is all," mumbled Hoke.

"Hurt from what?"

"Hurt about bein' left, I 'spect."

"Who left her?"

"Her father."

James looked from Hoke to Corrine's retreating back. "What do you know about it?"

"I just know the signs."

Later, when Hoke took the tools back to his wagon, he noticed Abigail Baldwyn sitting on a sawhorse. Her boots were peeled off and she was squeezing a rag she'd pulled from a bucket, rivulets of water spilling out as she bathed her feet. He put the tools away slowly, stealing glances to see how long she'd sit there.

She hadn't complained all day.

He could tell her back hurt when she got off her wagon at midday, but she never said a word about it. And she'd raised those kids well. Charlie had helped swab the mules' noses without being asked, and he'd been quick to unhitch the teams at the end of the day and rub their coats with a handful of hay, same as Hoke did.

Hoke wondered what she was thinking and whether she would come to regret her decision to make this trip. It wouldn't be easy . . . but maybe she was up to it.

After washing her feet, Abigail climbed up on the sawhorse with the bucket still in her hand, her toes curling around the wood, and poured what was left of the water into her box garden.

Hoke shook his head. She didn't need to be standing on the sawhorse that way; she could turn her ankle.

Damn woman.

CHAPTER 9

Covered in dirt stains

April 14, 1866

Each morning fires flare up in clusters, Mimi. As the smells of coffee, bacon, and pan biscuits fill the early dawn, roosters from the Schroeders' henhouses crow before the first rays of light. Everyone scrambles from sleep. We splash water on faces, eat a quick breakfast, water the livestock, hitch the teams—the mules often kicking—tie up bedrolls, wrap extra biscuits to make the lunch stop quicker, wash out pans, snuff out the fires, and jump in our seats for the roll out.

Abigail's skirts caught fire.

If Hoke hadn't walked up with fresh firewood at that moment, dumped it on the ground, and taken his hat off to swat the fire out, she might have gone up in flames.

Her face flushed with embarrassment for appearing so inept.

"Thank you."

Irene McConnelly had just been over to speak to her. "Why, Mrs. Baldwyn, how many fancy clothes did you bring on this trip?" Abigail had been bent down, laying a pan of bacon on the fire, and when she looked up, Irene smiled and added lightly, "I just came over to see if your wagon was stuffed full of them."

Abigail straightened then and held out her hand. "I haven't formally met you yet, Miss McConnelly. Abigail Baldwyn."

Irene waved Abigail's hand away. "Oh, please, attend to your food and don't mind me. I just came over to stir the pot."

Abigail looked at her a minute before stooping down to turn the bacon. A moment later, Hoke walked up, dumped the firewood, and swatted out the fire in her skirts. When Abigail looked toward Irene, now several wagons over, the woman's shoulders appeared to be shaking in laughter.

Had Irene raked Abigail's skirts in the fire? Or was she just taking pleasure in Abigail's own blunder?

Feeling the sear of Hoke's eyes on her, Abigail looked up.

"You might ought to rake those back when you're working by the fire." He pointed at her smoking hemline. "You got the sweepingest skirts I ever saw."

Abigail scowled and inspected the hem. "I thought I was. Maybe I'll take my skirts up. Most of my hems are getting covered in dirt stains anyway."

Her heart was covered in dirt stains, too. Could Hoke see those? He missed little else.

She expected him to leave—after all, the man was never still—but he lingered.

"Who was that man at the creek last night?" he asked.

Abigail's eyes shot up. "What man?"

"There was a man talking to you. When you went to get water. You seem a little distracted this morning. Did he upset you?"

Abigail shook her head. Yes, the man had upset her. But she didn't want Hoke to know it. She looked down, not trusting her eyes to hold up under his constant inspection. "He was looking for somebody. It wasn't one of our group."

"Who was he looking for?"

"Somebody that killed his brother. From Arkansas."

Hoke's voice dropped low. "What details did he give?"

"None, really, except that he felt his brother had been killed unfairly. He left before I could ask him much about it."

Abigail reached for the pan that held the biscuits. When she turned back around Hoke was gone. Surprise . . . then relief swept over her. She needed time alone to think. Irene's snide behavior was the least of her worries now.

Yesterday afternoon Abigail had wanted water for her plants. Charlie and Jacob were busy watching Hoke and James reshoe one of their oxen, so Abigail grabbed the bucket herself and walked to the nearby creek.

Just as the hairs on the back of her neck prickled and she got the feeling of being watched again, a man had stepped from the trees.

"How-do, ma'am."

They were only four days' travel from Independence. People who weren't part of their group had come by the train continually, peddling wares, asking questions, and offering reports of what to expect along the route. Abigail hadn't seen this man before, but he looked harmless enough with his homespun clothes stretched tight over a soft belly, and boots that both had holes in the toes.

She assumed he was selling something. So it surprised her when he asked, "Are you Robert Baldwyn's wife?"

How did he know who she was?

"I am."

The man removed his tattered hat and looked down at his feet. "I heard in town you were travelin' to meet him. I thought you should know I'm lookin' for him, too."

Before she could ask why, the man added, "And I aim to kill him when I find him."

A trickle of fear slid down Abigail's throat. She tried to swallow but her mouth had gone dry.

The wagons were pulled into the double circle Dotson had them form each evening for protection. Abigail looked back to the camp to see if anyone else had noticed her talking to the man—and to judge the distance in case she needed to gather her skirts and run.

The man held his arms up. "I don't aim to harm you, ma'am. I ain't a bad man. But your husband killed my brother and I can't let that go."

It didn't match up. The man's words were threatening, but nothing about his physical appearance frightened her. He seemed timid. And he wasn't even carrying a weapon that she could see.

"Who are you?" she asked.

He could hardly look her in the eye. "Cecil Ryman. You ask anybody . . . they'll tell you. I ain't a bad man. My brother's name was Dan—Dan Ryman, from Arkansas." He pulled a piece of paper from his pocket. "This is the article the paper wrote. They don't name your husband as his killer, but I know a man says he was the one who cut him—cut him with a fancy-handled sword and he bled out."

Abigail shook her head, wondering if Cecil Ryman was of sound mind. "Mr. Ryman, this has to be a misunderstanding. I know my husband, and he has a strong sense of justice. He would never do the sort of thing you've described."

"He may not be the man you think he is."

Cecil Ryman's words tumbled out so fast he was in danger of tripping over them. "Look, I'm not trying to upset you, ma'am, and I know this must seem strange, me coming out here to tell you this, but I saw you back in town and you seem like a nice lady with a nice passel o' young'uns. I just thought you should know before you get too far down the trail. I'm sorry if it puts you in a bad spot, but I aim to kill him when I find him for what he done. I wouldn't have rode out here to tell you if I was a bad man."

He refolded the paper in his hands and turned to go.

"Wait!" Abigail tried to stop him. She looked back to the camp to see if anyone was watching. Should she call for someone to come help her talk sense into this man? But no one had noticed them as far as she could tell. "Please don't do this, Mr. Ryman. Bring it before a court of law if you think he's committed a crime."

He put his tattered hat back on. "I'm sure courts and laws are coming west, ma'am, but they ain't there yet. I swore on my brother's grave I'd make it right, and I aim to keep my word. Don't worry, I won't lay for him dishonest. Maybe I was wrong to come out here and tell you this. I don't like killin' no one—I hate it. And I hate it for you. Just remember . . . I ain't a bad man."

Cecil Ryman apparently had said all he'd intended. He stepped back through the woods, leaving Abigail with an empty water bucket and a racing heart.

That had been yesterday at sundown. She'd hardly slept all night.

If Robert had really killed this man's brother, she didn't want the children—or the Dotsons and Melinda and Marc Isaacs and the rest of the group—to learn about it. What would people think of them? Could Cecil Ryman be right about her husband?

Abigail had been so angry with Robert for not coming home to them. She'd thought it was her fault—for the way she'd sent him off. But what if Dan Ryman was the reason he hadn't returned? She had expected obstacles, and she wasn't so naïve as to think Robert might not be greatly altered, but he wasn't supposed to be a murderer.

No . . . Abigail shook her head. She refused to believe a stranger. It just didn't sound like the Robert Baldwyn she knew.

Should she get word to Robert? Write a letter or send a telegram to warn him? Yes. That was what she would do. Couriers came by the train nearly every day collecting mail.

She wouldn't say anything about it to the children or anyone in Dotson's train. She would tell Robert. He'd know how to handle the news. He'd know how to make it right. And her warning him would show him that she was his partner and his ally, not the opponent he'd seen her as on the day he left.

It was only four days ago that she had sent the letter from Independence to say they were coming. And in that letter she still hadn't told him everything . . . she hadn't told him she was bringing the children.

She would need to be honest with him about that, too.

∽

April 17, 1866

Each day the colonel's goal is to cover seven or eight miles after breakfast. Tim Peters, who is planning to open a general store, has a device on his wagon wheel that will log the miles. Each time the spokes turn, it counts the rotation. So many rotations make a mile.

Colonel Dotson says he doesn't need a mile counter; he can just tell by the sun and the distance. There is a constant discussion among the men about how much we have actually traveled each day and whether Tim Peters's mile counter has an accurate reading.

At midday we stop for lunch—just long enough to rub down and water the animals, stretch our legs, and feed ourselves. Then it's the goal of another seven or eight miles before supper and making camp for the evening.

"Why don't you let Corrine and Jacob handle the teams?" Melinda Austelle asked Abigail a week into the journey.

"You think they're old enough?"

"Of course. Don't you see all my young'uns drivin' our teams?"

Cooper was only a year older than Jacob. Since Corrine and Jacob were eager to take the reins, Abigail let them. Now they had four drivers to rotate between, which left her free most days to walk or ride the gray dun.

Charlie had claimed the brown horse.

"I'm calling him Molasses," Abigail heard him tell Jacob as he brushed the horse one evening. "But don't tell Mr. Hoke."

"Why?" asked Jacob.

"'Cause Mr. Hoke doesn't name his horses."

Tim Peters, in Company A, is the only one who has been over this route before. He has three grown sons—Timmy (married to Nelda), Orin, and Bart.

Company B is made entirely of Schroeders. Mrs. Inez is the matriarch.

Rudy and Faramond (which all his family pronounces "Fairman") are the oldest brothers. They remind me of the sons of Zebedee . . . the sons of thunder.

Faramond's oldest two, Ingrid and Jocelyn, are in charge of all their thunder-sired cousins, and Melinda Austelle says that only they, being Schroeders themselves, are really up to the task. Rudy's youngest daughter, Prissy, is especially unruly. She does not fit her name any better than Faramond fits his.

Duncan Schroeder is married to Katrina. They have twin girls who ride on the hips of their older cousins. Katrina says they'll never learn to walk because they'll never have to.

Bridgette Schroeder is not married.

Hoke looked up from repairing a harness and saw Prissy Schroeder stroll by the spot where Corrine was working on supper.

For three days Abigail Baldwyn had had something heavy on her mind, and not knowing what it was weighed heavy on Hoke's. It was her habit, he'd noticed, to write letters of an evening. For the last three, she really took her time about it. It must have done her good because earlier that day her smile had come back.

"What are you cookin'?" Prissy asked Corrine.

Prissy Schroeder had to be close to Corrine's age, but she acted more like she was six. She was never required to help with evening chores, so she nosed around other people's wagons.

Corrine, by contrast, acted older than her years. She and Charlie were both more mature than others their age in the group.

"I'm cooking food," said Corrine.

"What kind of food, exactly?"

"Potatoes, corn, and apples, if you must know."

"Don't you got no meat? We're havin' pork. My paw's got three ham hocks salted."

Jacob, who was sitting nearby, said, "Does it take three to feed your whole bunch?"

"Naw. That's just for us—rest of 'em have their own ham hocks. We raise pigs."

"We noticed," said Corrine.

Hoke smiled down at the harness in his hands. One of the Schroeders' pigs had gotten stuck in a bramble earlier that day when the Douglas brothers' sheep got after it.

"Not very brave ones either," said Corrine, "to let sheep run 'em up in a bramble."

James was right; Corrine did have sass. He liked hearing her sling it toward Prissy Schroeder—every one of those Schroeder children swarmed the camp like unwelcome horseflies, but none was more worrisome than Prissy.

"Where's your other brother?" Prissy asked Corrine.

"Charlie went to get water."

"Where's your little sister?"

"She's with Mother."

"Where's your maw?"

"She's off looking for flowers."

"How come?"

Corrine rose to her full height, nearly as tall as her mother, and put both hands on her hips, apparently about done with Prissy Schroeder. "Because she likes them and wants to make the table pretty."

Prissy scrunched her nose. "Yeah, well, I'm tellin' my maw y'all don't got no meat."

"Are we in trouble?" asked Corrine.

After Prissy shrugged and took off, James rode up holding a turkey by the neck.

"Howdy-do, little lady!" He slid off and handed Jacob his reins. "You mind tying my horse, Jacob, so I can pluck this for your sister? Or did you want to pluck it?"

Jacob shook his head and took the horse. He waved to Hoke as he walked past.

"I don't think we've properly met," said James to Corrine. "I'm James Parker."

With level eyes that signaled mild interest at best, she looked at him a few seconds, then turned back to her work. "Well, now we have. I'm Corrine."

Hoke tried not to laugh when James looked at him.

CHAPTER 10

The art of biscuit making

April 18, 1866

*Ours is Company C, led by Mr. Hoke and James Parker.
They are a contrast. James Parker is much more lively.
All the women on the train, including the spinster sisters
from Company A, are in love with him.*

*In spite of Mr. Parker helping me cure the pan, my
biscuits have burned on the bottom every day. Sewing
skills are of no use whatsoever when what everyone wants
is food. Corrine is the only one who has complained about
it, though.*

"They aren't rising like they should, Mother. They're hard as rocks."
Corrine whipped up a batch one night at supper to prove she knew how
to make them rise.

"I swear! You keep cookin' like this, Corrine, I'll have to marry
you," said James, enjoying his fifth or sixth biscuit.

"And just how old are you, Mr. Parker?" snapped Corrine. "Forty?"

"Whoa now, I'm not even thirty! Is my beard makin' me look old? Hoke, is my beard makin' me look old, or are your crusty ways rubbin' off on me?"

Hoke glanced at him sideways but said nothing.

"That is downright hurtful, Corrine, you thinkin' I'm that old," sulked James.

Abigail looked at her daughter. "Show me how you made these or you'll have to cook breakfast from now on." Currently it was Corrine's job to get Lina ready in the mornings.

James rubbed his beard. "I'm partial to good biscuits. These are just like my grandmaw cooked 'em."

Corrine ignored James and turned to Abigail. "You've got to get the salt portions right."

"I used the same amount of salt as Melinda."

Mr. Parker and Mr. Hoke take their meals with us regularly, which is adding to my desperation as I seek to master the art of biscuit making. Even with Melinda Austelle building her fire close and watching over my shoulder, I can still ruin the biscuits. Corrine, on the other hand, is a wonderful cook as you predicted.

"Melinda!" Abigail called. "Didn't I make mine exactly like yours?"

Melinda came over to inspect. "I thought you did, but somethin' ain't goin' right. Maybe you knead 'em with a heavy hand."

"My grandmaw had a big wooden biscuit bowl to make her biscuits in," said James. "Hoke, did I ever tell you my grandmaw raised me?"

Hoke never looked up from his plate. "Yes."

"How do you know when you've kneaded them long enough?" Abigail asked Melinda.

"I don't know, you just know. You want to keep your dough ball nice and pli'ble."

James turned to Melinda. "Does my beard make me look old, Mrs. Austelle? Do you think the ladies would like me better without it?"

"I like Mr. Austelle better when he shaves."

Tam Woodford, four wagons over, called, "I got me a sharp razor if you need one, James! And some soapy water!" Tam and James, cut from similar cloth, had struck up a fast pick-at-one-another friendship.

Ignoring Tam, James scratched his jaw again, looking darkly at Corrine.

Abigail's brow twisted. "The dough should be soft? Well, no wonder. Is that with all bread dough?"

"It depends on the kind you're makin'," said Melinda. "Elastic dough makes a chewy bread."

"I don't care if you like my beard or not," James said to Corrine.

Corrine looked him level in the eye. "I don't care that you don't care."

Hoke started laughing so hard he nearly choked on his bacon.

Abigail, forgetting about the biscuits, turned to look at him. They all did. It took a lot to even make Hoke smile.

By the time Hoke got his food swallowed, tears were rolling from the sides of his fierce, weathered eyes. "James, I believe that's the first female you've met that don't care for your prattle. Good thing it doesn't contradict your pride."

Abigail looked from James to her daughter. "I didn't hear what you said, Corrine. Were you disrespectful?"

"She wasn't disrespectful . . . just honest." James stood up and shook the grinds of his coffee out in front of Hoke, who was still laughing. "Don't you have some work that needs doin'?"

Hoke stood. "Always." He smiled at Abigail as he left.

It lit a warm fire in her chest, and for the rest of that day the sound of Hoke's laughter filled her head.

Colonel George Dotson and his wife, Christine, lead us. The colonel is tall and commanding. Gerald Jenkins, his right-hand man, is short and smiles even when irritated. They are married to sisters. Mr. Jenkins's wife, Josephine, is the merriest woman I've ever met. Children adore her, Lina especially. Josephine rounds them up to sing in the evenings and makes every chore a game. Christine is more reserved, but like a sage mother to us all.

One afternoon Christine Dotson hooked her arm through Abigail's as they walked beside the wagons. The grasses of eastern Kansas were just deepening into green as spring reached its full height. Christine bent down and measured the stalks with her hand.

"Folks back in Independence will be hot on our trail, now. That'll worry George until one of them catches up with us. He wants to be the first group to Oregon this year." She patted Abigail's hand. "George says you're going to meet your husband."

"Yes, ma'am."

They walked in silence a few minutes, and then Abigail asked, "If you had two pieces of jewelry and needed to sell one, which could you part with easiest? The one from your mother, or the one from your husband?"

"I'd sell the one from George, because I still have him with me."

Yes . . . of course that was why she had chosen to sell Mrs. Helton the pearl pendant. She'd soon be with Robert again, but to have lost her mother's cameo would have felt like losing her mother all over again.

When Christine looked up at her questioningly, Abigail felt that she should explain herself. "When Robert left, we fought. He was an attorney and was against slavery."

"And you were for it?"

"No, but my family owned slaves. I grew up with them. It was a point of contention between Robert and my father. When Robert decided to join the Union I knew my father would never forgive him. I begged him not to go. I felt there were other ways he could have served his interests without fighting directly opposite my family."

"So you had family that fought for the Confederacy?"

"All three of my brothers. Seth—the one I was closest to—was killed. Thad and Nathan got him home after the Battle of Franklin, but he died in my father's parlor."

Christine sighed. "George had soldiers in his units who sometimes had family standing in the field across from them. Can you imagine taking aim on a sea of gray and knowing your son or brother was taking aim on your sea of blue?" She shook her head. "Have you forgiven him?"

How did Christine Dotson know Abigail had struggled to forgive her husband for his choice to leave?

"I thought I had, but . . . I also thought he had been killed. I didn't hear from him for nearly two years. When I learned a couple of months ago that he was still alive and just never came home . . . I was plenty mad all over again." This was the second time Robert had put her in a difficult spot.

Christine didn't say anything, just tightened her hold on Abigail's arm.

Abigail found it deeply comforting, so she plunged on with her confessions. "But I've gone from being mad to afraid."

Christine stopped walking and turned to her. "Afraid of what, sweetheart?"

"At first I was afraid he wouldn't want us anymore . . . that he wouldn't want me."

"I can't imagine that! Can't you see the men in this group admiring you?"

What men? Admiring her how?

"No." Abigail shook the thought from her head. "But anyway, now I'm worried something could happen to Robert before we get there."

"Something could happen to any one of us any day, I suppose." Christine squeezed Abigail's hand. "We'll just pray he's waiting for you with open arms and an open heart."

⌒⊙

Robert,
I have taken your advice and am coming to Fort Hall.

It took reading the letter three times for the words to finally sink in. "Well, I'll be damned."

He looked at the date again and the postmark . . . Independence. That gave him three, maybe four months.

He pulled an old wooden box from under his bunk and blew the dust off the top. Inside were dozens of letters, all written in Abigail's neat penmanship. He added her latest letter to the pile, then sorted them by date and started to read, starting at the beginning.

There were four children, not counting the one buried by the springhouse. Of course he knew that, though he'd never seen Lina, the youngest. He wondered what they looked like now. Corrine had always been pretty, like her mother.

Hours later he looked up when Sergeant Smith tapped on his door frame.

"Yes?" He hadn't realized it had grown so late.

"Just wanted to remind you we have new recruits coming in tomorrow, sir."

"Thank you, Smith. I'll be ready." When Smith hesitated in the doorway he added, "You can go now."

He pretended not to notice Smith's dark look as the man walked away. When he realized the light from his room must be shining in Smith's eyes, he got up and closed the door.

∽

As children in the train warmed up to each other, they ran from wagon to wagon in the mornings asking, "Who's driving for you today? Can I sit with you? Want to come ride with us?"

April 24, 1866

Once we are rolling, the children have strict instructions not to jump off or run up to other wagons. The Kensington sisters in Company A cautioned all the mothers to be careful. They had heard of babies falling off and getting crushed by the wheels. Deep ruts in the trail and the strain of the animals as they pull attest to the massive weight of the wagons.

One morning as dawn broke, sounds of squawking, barking, and then yelling came from the direction of Company B. Abigail looked around. "Charlie? Where's Rascal?"

A moment later, Hoke came walking toward the fire with Rascal in his arms.

"What happened?" asked Charlie, alarmed.

"One of the Schroeders' chickens got out."

"Oh, no!" said Abigail.

"Oh, yes." Hoke set down the dog and rubbed his head.

"Did he—"

"He did."

Abigail groaned. "I made two bonnets that I exchanged for Schroeder eggs just yesterday. They may be the last eggs we ever get."

Sure enough, the whole German clan cast Rascal dirty looks the rest of that day, as if he were the devil. That didn't sit well with the Baldwyn children. Abigail offered to pay for the chicken, but the Schroeders said, "We can't put a price on the lost eggs," and refused to take her money.

When Prissy came around that evening to let Abigail know that her mother said the chicken had been one of their best layers, Hoke said, "He was just being a dog!"

"Yeah. Eat the chicken and enjoy it," added James. "It'll be a nice break from all that pork."

> *A doctor named Marc Isaacs, his widowed sister, Caroline, and her baby boy are in our company. I had the good fortune to meet Doc Isaacs before we left Independence.*
>
> *Some in our group apparently fault him for being bookish and handsome, like a woman named Sue Vandergelden, who refused to let him near her wagon to tend to her boy when he came down with mountain fever. But I find it a comfort to have a doctor on the train.*
>
> *Doc Isaacs's nephew, Will, has developed a fondness for Corrine. It's nice to see her soft side as she cares for the toddler.*

"Is the sky bluer out here, Ma?" Lina asked one day. She was perched on the saddle of the gray dun with Abigail.

"Certainly seems like it. *The heavens declare the glory of God; and the firmament sheweth his handiwork.*"

Lina's face twisted up toward her. "Did you read that somewhere?"

"Grandpa used to say that . . . a long time ago. It comes from the Bible. Remind me tonight and we'll find the verse." Abigail kissed the top of her head.

It sounded like David. When Abigail pictured David sitting on the hillside watching over his sheep, she pictured hillsides like these. The land sloped softly. A tree line ran along their left, gently rolling waves of earth stretched for miles in front of them, and a well-worn path reached out like an endless blanket beneath the wagon wheels.

For the past three mornings Abigail had found ice crusting the top of the wash tin. But the days were getting warmer, and the sun was staying out longer in the evenings. Abigail had an internal debate going in her head—was sunrise or sunset her favorite? Funny how she'd paid so little attention to either event in Marston. But out here, where they were living like Israelites wandering the wilderness, the sunrise and sunset wrapped a person inside them. You were part of the experience—standing in the center of it—feeling your hope rise in the mornings, and your peace float back down at the end of the day.

Never had she witnessed anything to equal it—never had she spent so much time looking heavenward. But now, every day—from her midmorning rides, like the one she was taking now with Lina, to her afternoon walks looking for wildflowers with Melinda, and into the deepening blues of evening, which arrived as they finished eating—she found her gaze rising upward to see what kind of masterpiece God had painted that day. The sky was always changing. It was always beautiful.

Mimi would have loved these skies. If Corrine could capture a good likeness with her paints, they would have to send one home to show her. Corrine was a gifted artist, but there was no way anyone could brushstroke the bigness of the sky, or depict the thrill it shot through the back of one's spine, on a single sheet of parchment.

Was Robert seeing these same skies where he was?

In some ways, Mimi, this journey has proven harder than I expected. We have bugs in the sugar sack, my feet are covered in blisters, I can't seem to master cooking, and we've managed to alienate the largest family in camp thanks to Rascal. A woman named Irene McConnelly dislikes me, too, but I don't know what I've done to her.

In other ways the journey has proven easier than expected. Not one of the children has complained. Corrine has fussed about my biscuits, but that isn't really complaining. In fact, they are all thriving under the influence of the open air, the morning and afternoon chores, the evenings spent playing games or singing songs with fellow travelers. How can I complain about blisters or bugs when we are surrounded by such good, hardworking people?

And this land . . . these skies . . . the stars scattered so thick against the black back of evening. If Robert hadn't come west, we never would have known it was here waiting for us.

❧

Hoke watched as James hoisted Lina onto his saddle one day. Little peals of laughter floated back toward the wagons.

The next day, when Hoke hoisted her up, she went to sleep.

When he brought Lina back to Abigail, with Lina's head lolling on his arm, Abigail looked up at him accusingly.

"What did you do to her?"

"Nothin'. Rode out and showed her a den of baby foxes in that stand of trees yonder. She fell asleep on the way back."

Abigail reached for her.

Hoke nudged the stallion away. "Mind if I keep her till we stop?"

He was afraid she was going to say no.

"That's fine. Are you sure you don't mind? I can take her on the dun with me."

He looked down at Lina's soft curls. She was the nearest thing to an angel child he had ever seen. "I don't mind."

He had already turned the stallion when she said, "The dun's saddled and I was about to ride. Mind if I join you?"

"I don't mind," he said again.

Abigail ran to unhitch the dun from the back of the boys' wagon. "Lina still takes a nap every afternoon," she explained when she rode back to meet him. "But it's usually not until after we stop."

"Will it hurt anything if she keeps sleepin'?" Hoke had never been around children much.

"Not at all." Abigail smiled. "I try to feed them when they're hungry and let them sleep when they're tired."

Hoke smiled back. He had noted what a good mother she was. Not like that Vandergelden woman who nagged her boy to pieces, or the Schroeders who let their children run wild. Abigail was relaxed but watchful. He figured that must work because she had good kids.

"Why are those so rare?" asked Abigail.

"What?"

"Your smiles. You bestow them rather sparingly." Then she added, "Your laughter is even more rare. I've only ever heard it one time."

"I guess I haven't had a whole lot to smile or laugh about."

Bridgette Schroeder, in the wagon column nearest to them, stirred the air with her stout arms as she rode by. "Nice day, ain't it?" she called to them.

Abigail nodded and waved.

Hoke angled his horse away from the wagons. "She's got a voice that travels," he muttered, gingerly moving Lina's head to his other arm. Her hair was slick against his forearm where the tan buckskin of his sleeve was rolled up.

"Did she pull her bonnet off again?"

"It's in the back saddlebag."

"She doesn't like it. Her head gets hot." Abigail laughed. "One of the sweetest smells on earth to me is the top of Lina's sweaty head. That probably sounds strange to you. When she gets too old to sit in my lap, I'll miss it."

Hoke leaned down to smell Lina's head and tried not to make a face. Maybe you had to be a mother to appreciate it.

"I used to wonder why people came out here," said Abigail, "pulling up stakes and carting all their belongings with them to start over in the West. Some of the men were talking last night about Mormons who walk this whole trail on foot with nothing but a handcart." Abigail shook her head. "I don't wonder anymore."

Lina moaned and Hoke tried to reposition her again. "Say," he said, "should she be this hot?"

Abigail dismounted and came to feel her daughter's forehead. Her face fell and she snatched Lina from his arms. "She's burning up with fever. Get Doc Isaacs!"

∽

For four days Abigail rode in the back of the wagon, sponging off Lina's hot body. She rode in there all day and never left Lina's side, not even when they made camp in the evenings. Hoke felt as helpless as when he'd been a kid and watched his mother die.

One day he took the reins of his and James's wagon, so he'd only be one wagon over and could get to Abigail quick, in case anything happened . . . in case she needed him. But he couldn't stand the confinement of it, so the next day he put Jacob in the seat. It helped to keep the other Baldwyns occupied, anyway. The children said little, but worry creased their foreheads and their eyes all shot a dozen times an hour to the wagon that carried Lina's feverish body in it.

Corrine, who was a quiet thinker by nature, grew quieter still. She slept in the boys' wagon at night. Emma Austelle stayed with her so she wouldn't be alone while the boys slept below it on the ground, the dog between them. Corrine prepared breakfast and supper each day, with James lending a hand and taking a break from his usual teasing.

Meals were eaten in hushed tones.

On day two, Hoke rode back through the wagons of Company C, stopping to ask Charlie, "How is she?" Charlie looked back into the wagon at his mother, who was bending over Lina's body, and Hoke's stomach tightened at the boy's subtle wince.

"No change."

"And your mother? She still won't eat?"

"No, sir."

Long after the camp had gone quiet that night, after Corrine and Emma's voices had silenced and Hoke could hear steady breathing coming from underneath the boys' wagon, he stood next to Abigail's box garden and listened. He could hear the sound of water being squeezed through a rag and what he guessed were whispered prayers.

Doc Isaacs slipped in and out of the wagon every morning and afternoon. He was the only one Abigail would let in.

"Don't come in here!" Hoke heard her scold Charlie on the third day when the train stopped for the midday rest. Charlie had opened the canvas to set a fresh water bucket inside. "We don't need anyone else getting sick."

"What about you, Ma?" Charlie asked her. "We don't need you getting sick."

"I won't get sick."

"You're not eating. You're not sleeping."

"I won't get sick. Now go away. Don't come in here."

Charlie turned to go.

"Charlie!" she called. The boy turned back toward the wagon. "I'm sorry." Her voice cracked and the sound ripped a slice through Hoke's midsection.

"For what?" asked Charlie.

"For losing the house. For bringing us out here. For running your father off in the first place. For not . . . for not being able to fix everything."

"Ma." Charlie started to climb the steps.

"No! Don't come in here, Charlie. I couldn't bear it if any of the rest of you were to get sick. Thank you for the water. Now go."

That night as he stood outside her wagon, Hoke heard her curse Robert Baldwyn, call out for someone named Mimi, and plead to God not to take her miracle baby.

∽

At first, Abigail tried to keep count of all the offers for help she heard whispered through the canvas. People were being so kind to them; she must remember to thank them. And yet something in her pushed against that kindness. She didn't want people feeling sorry for them— she felt sorry enough for herself without anyone else tiptoeing around her, reminding her of her losses.

She was vaguely aware of Charlie, Corrine, and Jacob—she heard Hoke ask Jacob to drive his team. She almost poked her head through the canvas to protest—Jacob had never handled a team of oxen!—but she didn't. Hoke wouldn't put Jacob on a task and then not hover close by to see if he could really handle it. She'd been around him long enough now to know that.

Besides, she didn't want to talk to Hoke. Abigail was angry with him, even though she could hear him watering her box gardens every afternoon and could see it was his strong hands handing in most of the fresh buckets of water. He hadn't caused Lina's fever, but if the forearms he'd wrapped around her daughter hadn't been so strong . . . so inviting . . . Abigail might have noticed how flushed Lina's cheeks were and taken action sooner.

She had been almost jealous of Lina as she'd been held by him.

What kind of woman was she to let herself think such thoughts? And while her daughter was burning with fever in his arms! Of course, she hadn't known that then, but it still shamed her to think about it.

Each time her fears about the trip started to lessen, something else happened. She should have known things were going too well. Why hadn't she listened to the fears . . . to the warnings?

"When Arlon came to the house to get Mimi—after she'd made plans to come with us—I should have taken it as a sign that none of us were supposed to come," she moaned to Doc Isaacs on the third afternoon of Lina's illness.

"Who is Arlon?"

"It's not important. What's important is that I plowed stubbornly ahead. And I had another chance to back out in Independence when our money was stolen."

"Your money was stolen? I didn't know that."

"And I still came!" Abigail hung her head. "That's how foolish I am."

"Abigail, you are not foolish."

When Abigail closed her eyes she could still see Mimi riding off in Arlon's wagon. Mimi . . . if only Mimi were here!

"Tell me she's going to make it," begged Abigail, not caring to hide the desperation in her voice. She kept picturing Mrs. Helton at the graveyard back in Independence. *Who gets married and who has children . . . who loses children.* And she kept picturing those fresh yellow flowers on the graves—the same flowers she had planted around the headstone by the springhouse. Surely the flowers at the cemetery had been a sign, and she had been too blind to see it.

Doc laid his hand on her shoulder. "Ned Vandergelden pulled through just fine and I never even tended to him."

Abigail lifted her head and searched the doc's eyes. "Is that supposed to make me feel better?"

"It should. Lina's getting better care. But I'm not God, Abigail. I can't make promises about life or death."

"I lost one baby." Abigail was surprised to find herself telling him this. But there was something about Doc Isaacs. Hoke had Seth's way with horses, but Marc Isaacs had her brother's mischievous inner spirit and calm outward demeanor. "During pregnancy. Before Lina. I had gone to my father's. They had new horses and Seth wanted me to ride with him. Two days later I lost the baby. Robert never came right out and said it was my fault, but . . . that's when things started to fall apart."

Doc Isaacs took her hand. "I'm sorry," he whispered.

"I didn't mean to burden you with that, it's just that . . ." She hung her head again. "I can't lose another one. I can't put another child in the ground, then leave her. Not Lina. She has been the presence of the Lord to me every day of her life. I couldn't bear to live without her."

"Why don't you let me give you something?" Doc Isaacs said. "Are you sleeping at all?"

Abigail shook her head. How could she sleep when constant prayer was needed? Others in the group claimed to be praying for Lina, but no one else was going to say the things she would. No one loved Lina more than she did. No one else would be so shattered to lose her.

No one else had brought Lina on this trip. Abigail had. Abigail was responsible.

Melinda's voice, calling her children to supper, drifted through the canvas.

"Let me go get you a plate of food," said Doc.

Abigail shook her head again. "I don't have any appetite." The very mention of food made her ill. "What is that you're giving her? Are you sure it's the proper dose? It doesn't seem to be helping her fever come down."

He smiled at her patiently. Abigail wondered if this was something he'd learned in medical college. But his patience was making her anxious.

"You don't have to stay." She brushed his hand away from hers. "I know you have other folks to see to." Abigail knew that Nora Jasper, a young married woman from east Tennessee, had also fallen ill, as had one of the Schroeders.

By the fourth afternoon Abigail was exhausted. Her whole life had become a chain of constant motion: combing Lina's silken hair back on the pillow, brushing her red cheeks with a cloth, dipping the rag—hot from Lina's fever—into the bucket to cool it down, twisting it out, sponging it back over her arms and legs, laying her head over Lina's chest in order to hear the beating of her heart and feel the breath coming out of her mouth, then forcing some liquids down Lina's throat, and finally combing her silken hair back again.

Feeling dazed, she raised her head off the bed. The wagon had stopped. She must have fallen asleep. Sounds of evening camp trickled through the canvas. She groggily stroked Lina's forehead.

It was cold.

"No!" she wailed, fully awake now, her heart leaping.

She heard the sound of feet running. The wagon flap was torn back and Hoke looked inside as she hugged Lina to her breast.

Abigail smiled at him through her tears. "I was wrong," she whispered. "Her fever broke."

Then Doc was there, climbing into the wagon with his stethoscope. Lina watched everyone with large eyes.

"Why are you crying, Mama?" she asked.

Abigail laughed. "Because I get to keep you, sweetheart."

CHAPTER 11

Burrowing her toes into the grass

One evening the men congregated on one side of the camp to talk about how far the wagon train had come and plan rotations for guard duty. Josephine Jenkins had the children singing on the opposite side. Lina, now recovered, sat in Christine Dotson's lap.

The children's sweet voices sang *Oh, say can you see . . .* and a deep voice floated in to join them on the words *. . . by the dawn's early light.*

It was James. The men had finished their meeting and were coming over.

April 30, 1866

Each evening as the supper dishes are cleared, Josephine Jenkins calls out, "Who's going to sing with me? Hannah Sutler? Cooper Austelle? I bet you kids know this one!" Fast-paced spiritual hymns are her favorites. They fit her personality.

*The men start bringing extra benches over and the
women lay out quilts as children circle around her. "Here
We Are but Straying Pilgrims" has become a regular. Mrs.
Jo says it perfectly captures the essence of our journey.*

Hoke spied Abigail working on the seat of her rocker off to one
side of the circle, away from the others, weaving colored fabrics into
the twine as she worked. It looked like she was nearly done. A small
group of children who weren't singing with Josephine were watching
her, fascinated.

"How did you know to do that?" Prissy Schroeder asked Abigail, her
green eyes squinting under brown hair that always looked uncombed.

"I just had the idea and thought it would be pretty." Abigail smiled
at her.

"Ma's always making things pretty," said Jacob.

"Who knew you could sing?" called Tam to James.

"He can play, too," offered Hoke.

"Play what?" Tam demanded.

"Oh, I have a guitar," said James demurely.

Josephine heard him say it and hopped up. "You have a guitar and
you haven't said anything about it! Why, Mr. Parker!" she scolded. "Go
get it!"

Hoke saw Tam watching Nora Jasper, who looked at her husband,
Nichodemus. The Jaspers were one of the poorest families on the train.

"Anybody else sittin' on an instrument they ain't told about?" Tam
looked hard at Nora.

"Nichodemus has a hog fiddle," Nora admitted.

"What's a hog fiddle?" asked Prissy. No one answered her.

"What's a hog fiddle?" she asked again, louder. It was impossible to
ignore Prissy Schroeder for long, although several in the group had tried.

"It's a dulcimer," said Abigail.

"What's a dulcimer?"

"An instrument they make in the mountains, where the Jaspers are from," said Doc Isaacs, who was sitting nearby.

Hoke scowled. Doc Isaacs hovered near Abigail Baldwyn more than he liked. They seemed all the closer since Lina had fallen sick.

Harry Sims, the preacher, produced a harmonica and Alec Douglas, who seemed to have little else to his name besides sheep and Scottish brothers, a violin.

"Where have you been hidin' that fiddle, Alec?" asked Colonel Dotson. "I'll be . . . I thought I knew everything."

Hoke understood what he meant. A man in charge had to know everything. The Peterses' wagons rode low, for example, and it wasn't just because of merchandise they'd brought for their general store. Hoke figured they had enough gold to start a bank.

Sam Beckett had a lousy gun, but it didn't matter. He didn't know how to shoot it anyway. He was a writer and always had his head in the clouds.

Old man McConnelly and Ty Vandergelden were no good in a fight, either. Irene McConnelly word-whipped her father as bad as Sue Vandergelden word-whipped her son and husband.

But Michael Chessor, a young adventurer in Company D, was a keeper. So was Harry Sims, the preacher. The verdict was still out on the Schroeder men. They liked their hogs, he knew that much.

Hoke, like the colonel, had been assessing what benefit each traveler brought to the whole ever since leaving Independence. The colonel had just missed this one. Hoke couldn't blame him. Nobody would have guessed those simple Douglas boys possessed anything of value, or any musical talent.

Josephine scolded the group. "I can't believe we had this kind of bounty right under our noses and no one has said a word about it! If James Parker hadn't started singing, we might have gone all the way to Oregon without discovering it." She demanded that those who hadn't produced their instruments already go get them at once.

James made it back first and said, "Sing with me, Hoke."

"Hoke sings?" teased Doc Isaacs, who was bouncing his nephew on his knee.

"No," said Hoke, shaking his head, glaring over at the doc. Doc Isaacs spent most evenings bouncing someone's child on his knee or doling out advice to mothers who had questions about fever, diet, or sickness.

"Sings like a bird." James winked. "Like a deep-throated songbird. Makes weak-kneed women swoon."

"I'd like to hear that," said Irene McConnelly, who had perched herself nearby, staring hard at Hoke.

Hoke threw James a dark look.

James muttered, "You started this."

"A rare mistake. I won't let it happen again."

"Come on, Hoke. Sing with me."

"I don't sing in public."

"Hoke, don't be selfish."

"I'm not bein' selfish, James.

"Yes, you are. You're hurtin' Mrs. Josephine's feelin's, too. Ain't that right, Mrs. Jo? Tell him he has to sing."

"Aw, you two quit arguin' and give us a song!" bellowed Tam Woodford.

Hoke bowed his head and James elbowed him. "That's a sport." He strummed a couple of chords and winked at Hoke. Together they sang.

> *I had a true love,*
> *Who was sent from above,*
> *But she broke my heart in two.*
>
> *She got cold feet in the spring,*
> *And slipped off the ring,*
> *That I had given her to.*

She will never be mine,
She will never be mine,
But I have decided that's fine.

Because I found another,
I went back to my mother,
For she still loves me true.

Everyone laughed. Irene McConnelly fanned her face and pretended to swoon.

"Did you make that up?" asked Prissy. "I never heard it before."

"James doesn't have a wide selection," said Hoke.

"Now that's not true, Hoke. Mrs. Josephine, I even know some spirituals."

"Let's hear them!"

Doc Isaacs picked up his nephew and carried him toward the wagons, and Irene stood up and headed in Hoke's direction, so he slipped from the circle and went to sit by Abigail.

"You're about to finish that seat. What are you goin' to do with it when you're done?"

"Rock!"

Abigail's eyes sparkled. Hers were quite a contrast to Irene's, which had grown dark, as she'd just located him again. Hoke shut Irene out and concentrated on the woman beside him.

"Lina loves to be rocked." Abigail smiled at Jacob, who was still sitting nearby. The other kids had gravitated to the music, closer to the fire. "All my babies loved to be rocked."

"Ma," groaned Jacob.

"What did I say?"

"I'm going to look for Charlie," he muttered.

Abigail was sure that only moments ago Jacob had been proud of her. Now she had embarrassed him in front of Hoke.

Rascal looked longingly at Hoke before he followed Jacob. Rascal often ran at the heels of Hoke's black stallion during the day and followed him around camp in the evenings.

"To a stranger, it would look like Rascal is your dog, not ours," said Abigail.

Hoke ignored her comment. "How do you like the trip so far?"

"Other than thinking I might lose my daughter, it's been fine. I mean, the mattress is lumpy, the cow's being stingy with her milk, there's a layer of dust on everything from morning till night, and my feet have never been so sore . . ."

She laughed. At least her back had finally quit hurting . . . in part because of the side box he'd built for the dish crate. "But I like it. I like being part of a close-knit community. I like the hope that hangs in the air when everyone talks about their plans and their dreams. And I love seeing my children so happy."

"You have good children," he said.

Those had been Mimi's last words to her.

His buckskin shirt lay open at the neck and his hat was off. Hoke's black hair—or was it dark brown?—fell in waves down to his collar. Abigail looked at his boots next to her once-slender feet that were so swollen she'd left her shoes off since supper. The cool grass felt good on them, but now she dug her toes deeper into the stalks, suddenly shy about their bareness.

Trail dust covered his black, worn boots, which seemed intensely masculine, as did his hands. She had first noticed his hands at the corral in Independence, the way he had stroked the horses. His hands were always working, it seemed . . . always busy.

Her own hands were coarse all the time now, and she often had dirt under her nails from working in her gardens. She tried scrubbing them, but stubborn traces of soil hid in the corners, only to show up in the light and embarrass her later.

Hoke needed a shave again. And those eyes . . . his gaze was so full of heat it nearly burned her skin.

Abigail looked back down at the rocker seat. Why was it so hard to meet this man's eyes? Why did he make her feel so self-conscious? Few men had ever done so.

"Thank you. Your approval means a great deal to them, especially Charlie and Jacob. I hope you didn't think I was mad at you over Lina. Her fever scared me. But I know you didn't cause it. I appreciate all the kindnesses you've rendered us."

∽

Hoke loved to hear Abigail Baldwyn talk. She was perhaps the most refined and educated woman he'd ever met. He had a strong desire to ask about her husband but couldn't bring himself to do it.

"Scared me, too," he said instead.

"I've been meaning to talk to you about that."

"About what?" He looked up at her.

She kept her eyes on the rocker seat. "The kindnesses you've been rendering us. I don't want to be a burden to you, Mr. Hoke."

"Just Hoke."

"You're doing little things for us that you shouldn't have to do."

"I don't know what you mean."

"I'm afraid Colonel Dotson wasn't fair to you, putting us in your company." She laid a hand on his shoulder.

He looked down at it, trying to remember when he'd last been touched so casually. By her . . . when she laid her hand on his arm the day he met her. "I don't see it that way."

"We can pull our own weight." She removed her hand.

He nodded, missing the warmth of her touch already. "I'm sure you can. You do."

"We're not as experienced as some, but we're fast learners."

"I can see that."

"Like watering my plants, for example."

He tried to think of something to say that would make her lay her hand on his shoulder again. "Water's heavy and those boxes are high."

"I know, but that's my problem, not yours."

"Well, you're in my company."

"I know. That's my point. I'm sorry Colonel Dotson put us in your company."

He jerked his head up. "You don't want to be in my company?" he asked, hotly.

"That's not what I meant."

"What did you mean?"

A fire lit in her eyes. "If you would stop cutting me off after every sentence, I would tell you!"

She sounded testy, but Hoke didn't care. He was just glad to be near her. His own hungry eyes couldn't drink in enough of her.

Her yellow hair was pulled into a knot at the back of her head, but little strands were sneaking out like always. He loved the way they curled around her face in the heat of the day. She refused to wear a bonnet like the other women, so he didn't know why it surprised her that Lina wouldn't keep hers on, either. There was the brown hat she'd been wearing the day he met her, and another wide-brimmed straw hat she wore more often.

Both suited her nicely.

She looked the way he imagined all Southern ladies looked—genteel women in cotton frocks, with wide-brimmed straw hats, gathering flowers from a field.

Each afternoon she wore the straw hat as she and Mrs. Austelle gathered flowers for the porcelain pitcher on Abigail's makeshift supper table. Girls from all over the camp would come by asking if they could have the flowers to make necklaces or bracelets, which they'd wear until they wilted.

He loved having her wagon so near his own. It allowed him to steal glances at her as she pulled her hat off in the afternoons.

He had expected her to be spoiled and take his offers of help readily, but she hadn't. In fact, she never complained or asked for anything. So far as he could tell, she only allowed herself one luxury—a small basin of water that she used to wash the back of her neck and her feet before she got supper ready. So he'd started bringing her water when they made camp in the afternoons.

He'd reach up and water her plants, leaving enough in the bucket for her feet, then set the bucket down at the back of her wagon without saying a word. This had been happening for several days.

Abigail yanked at the fabric of the rocking chair seat she was working on. "I feel guilty that you are working harder than you would have to if you didn't have a woman with four children and no husband in your company." She seemed flustered.

It pleased him. "I was told you did have a husband."

"You know what I mean. He's not here."

"That is a curiosity to me."

She turned to look him in the eye then. "And to me, Mr. Hoke."

"Just Hoke."

"What kind of name is that anyway?"

"It's my name!"

She lifted her chin. "Is it your Christian name or your surname? Because Colonel Dotson called you Hoke Mathews. Is Hoke really your Christian name?"

He gave her a sideways smirk. "Why do you care?"

"I want to know how to address you properly."

"I keep tellin' you and you keep ignorin' me."

"Just Hoke."

"That's right."

She shook her head. "I'm trying to set an example for my children. They are to call you *Mr.* Hoke, unless they should be calling you Mr. Mathews."

"Are you avoidin' my question?" he said, avoiding her question.

"What question was that?"

"About your husband."

"You didn't ask me about my husband, you only said it was a curiosity to you that he wasn't here. To which I replied—"

"The question was implied."

"And the question is?"

"Are you always this difficult to have a conversation with?" he bellowed.

She tied a final knot in the rocker seat, jerking it harder than he suspected she had to, and turned to face him. He could feel his eyes blazing and knew all of his emotions lay on the surface, but he couldn't seem to tamp them down.

"No. I don't consider myself difficult at all. And I don't know how I manage to make you angry. You aren't short-tempered with anyone else. Why are you short-tempered with me? It must be because I'm a burden to you. I've not asked for your help. If you resent giving it, then don't!"

Hoke *was* angry, but not with her . . . with himself. Now that she had said the words out loud, he could see how she might interpret his irritation that way. He needed to keep a better handle on his emotions.

Frankly, he didn't know why she affected him the way she did. It made no sense. She was a married woman with four children! But he had trouble imagining the husband—had trouble believing he really existed. It would not be the first time a woman had purported to have a husband when she didn't, just to keep other men at bay. Why had she cursed Robert Baldwyn when Lina was ill? And what did she mean by saying to Charlie that she had driven him off?

If this woman really did have a husband, Hoke had no business looking at her feet and the cute way she kept burrowing her toes into the grass.

"Mrs. Baldwyn, I'm sorry you feel that way. I assure you, you are not a burden to me or to anyone else in this group. Tell you what . . . tomorrow I'll try to turn over a new leaf. How about I let you ride that white filly as a peace offering?" He stood and offered his hand.

"All right," she said hesitantly, standing up to shake hands with him.

Instead, he raised her hand to his lips and kissed it. Then he picked up the rocker and took it to her wagon without asking if she needed or wanted his help with it.

He could feel her puzzled expression through the back of his shirt.

CHAPTER 12

Where the world dripped with hope

Cecil Ryman never made it to Idaho Territory. He never even made it to Fort Kearney, north of Kansas.

After he spoke to Abigail Baldwyn, Cecil Ryman traveled due west, thinking to shave some time off his journey before turning north to get on the Oregon. But a lone man gets lonely weaving through unfamiliar land, so when Cecil Ryman spied a faint light at dusk one evening, he turned his horse to meet it.

Because he wasn't a bad man, he called out as he neared. "How-do, there!"

There was no reply, but Cecil Ryman didn't let that stop him. He nosed his horse on in, drawn to it by the hope of food and company. He got all the way to the camp—to the fire—and saw no one about.

Thinking the builder of the fire couldn't be far, Cecil sat on a rock and warmed his hands while waiting for the stranger to return.

And the stranger presently did.

A trapper, deciding that Cecil was harmless, emerged from the trees. One minute Cecil Ryman was sitting alone on his rock, and the next minute a trapper was squatting at the fire across from him.

Cecil jumped like he'd been shot.

"Lord, have mercy!" A nervous laugh escaped him. "If you'd a been a snake, I'd been bit 'fore I knew you was there!"

The trapper only looked at him.

"You travelin' alone?" asked Cecil.

"Are *you* travelin' alone?" asked the trapper.

Cecil was quick to nod. "You sound Irish. My name's Cecil Ryman. I'm headed to a fort in Idaho Territory. Man up there killed my brother and I got to make it right." Cecil reached in his pocket for the folded paper, even though the fire was small and didn't offer enough light to read by.

"This story gives the details but it don't name his killer. A man travelin' through Arkansas about a year ago, though, he seen it. Said it was a man named Baldwyn. Carries him a fancy sword and run it through my brother Dan's heart. The man didn't know why—said they apparently was friends and had served in the war together—but Baldwyn cut him, then stood and watched him bleed out. Baldwyn didn't think he was seen, but he was, by this man."

"Interestin'," said the trapper. "And you're not afraid to face him?"

"Well, truth be told, I hate to do it. I come across Baldwyn's wife back in Independence and I made apologies. But like I told her, I swore on Dan's grave I'd make it right and I mean to keep my word. I never killed no one before, but I've never had to. Not even in the war. I's a cook."

The trapper reached down and pulled a knife from its scabbard in his boot. He selected a long blade of grass from the ground and set it over the knife's edge. It sliced cleanly.

"Baldwyn has a wife, you say?"

Cecil frowned. "Yeah . . . pretty yellow-haired lady. I feel bad this is going to put her in a spot—her travelin' out to meet him and all. They got nice-lookin' children, too. I never had no children myself. Dan left two boys. That's why I got to go ahead and make it right. If I don't, those boys'll feel the need to when they get older."

Moments later Cecil Ryman lay dying by the fire. He bled out, just like his brother, Dan, wondering what he'd said to the trapper to set him off and make him want to slit his throat like that.

∽

May 2, 1866

. . . I realize in reading back over my letter, Mimi, that I failed to finish telling you about Mr. Hoke, the gentleman who leads Company C. He is alternatingly wonderful and disagreeable. He bosses the children, and sometimes bosses me. Then he'll go and do a thing so thoughtful it will leave me speechless.

The next morning, true to his word, Hoke brought his white horse, saddled and ready to ride, to the back of Abigail's wagon.

"I hope I haven't kept you waiting," she said, coming around the corner. "I got behind, but everyone should be settled now."

He grinned with that sideways smirk he had. "I heard Rascal cornered Paddy Douglas's coon."

"We don't need anybody else mad at us because of Rascal."

"He's just being a dog."

"Since he's partly your dog, could you try keeping him in line? And of all the animals in camp—Paddy Douglas's coon! Paddy would be crushed if anything happened to him."

Paddy Douglas's sweet simple-minded nature has won the heart of everyone in camp. When Michael Chessor

*found a baby coon the first week of travel, Paddy's brother,
Baird, said, "Give that coon to Paddy. He's a great one
with critters." And sure enough, Paddy had it tamed in
no time. His stature with every child in camp increased
after that. They seek him out now every evening to pet the
coon he keeps inside his shirt on a sling that his brothers,
Alec and Baird, have rigged for him.*

"What'll Mrs. Austelle do without you today?" asked Hoke, coming around the horse toward her.

"She's helping Caroline Atwood with baby Will. Oh!"

Instead of making a cup for her foot like her brothers always did, Hoke had put his hands on either side of her waist and said, "Jump." She barely had time to comply before he lifted her up like she weighed no more than a horse saddle. Surprised, she swung a leg over.

"I wasn't ready for that." Color crept into her cheeks. Abigail pulled at her sleeves, hoping he wouldn't notice that the lace of her blouse was starting to fray. Her dark-green skirt was about twelve inches shorter than she normally wore her skirts and split, then sewn up the middle like wide-legged pants. Brown riding boots covered her calves.

"I thought Southern ladies rode sidesaddle." He grinned again, adjusting her stirrups, then patting at the filly's stomach with the back of his hand to make her exhale before he cinched the belt tight.

Abigail stroked the horse's velvet neck, relishing the feel of Hoke's shoulder brushing against her leg. "Some do, but I grew up with brothers. They made fun of me if I rode sidesaddle. So my mother made me split riding skirts. That way I could keep up with them."

The filly danced and pranced, causing Abigail to smile as she worked the reins to get the feel of her.

Hoke mounted the stallion. "Looks like she wants to run."

"Should I let her?"

"Why not?"

Abigail let the white have her head, racing her out far ahead of the first wagons. Dotson and Jenkins, who were riding in the lead, waved as they passed.

It had been a long time since she'd ridden like this back in Tennessee. But out here, where the world dripped with hope, the urge to fly over the land was irresistible.

"Now you've done it!" she shouted as he came along beside her on the stallion. "I was liking my gray horse."

This white Appaloosa was something special, though. Abigail suddenly felt younger than she'd felt in years. Her hat flew back, caught by the string at her neck, and her hair started falling out of its tight bun, but she didn't care.

How long had it been since she'd *really* ridden a horse?

Not since she lost the baby.

She remembered how she had loved riding as a child. But then thoughts of racing Seth over her father's land, Mimi wiping blood from between her legs, and Robert angrily shoveling dirt behind the springhouse all ran through her mind.

Tears sprang to her eyes as the filly slowed. She ached to be young again and free of the memories that weighed on her.

Hoke's stallion slowed in front of her and she swiped at her eyes, embarrassed. He pulled up beside her and they slowed to a trot.

They rode in silence for what seemed a long time. It might have been awkward with anyone else, but Hoke was the sort of person with whom you could ride in silence. If he'd started talking and acting moody like he'd done the night before, her tears would probably have dried quickly. But his more jovial spirit this morning and now his thoughtful silence only made them worse. She couldn't seem to stop. There was no question now that he had noticed, but he had the decency not to comment.

Hoke wanted so much to know what was troubling her and whether he could fix it. Fixing things was what he did. He could repair or build most anything that needed to be repaired or built. But unlocking the mysteries of a woman's heart . . . he had never learned to do that.

"See that track?" he said finally, pointing to marks that crossed the trail in front of them. They were far ahead of the train.

She nodded.

The land was growing flat. Out here a person could see for miles on a low rise like the one they were on now. Each tree and bush they passed was budding with its own shade of green. Wild yellow flowers dotted the landscape in random clumps.

"Elk." Hoke nodded down at the tracks. "Herd of elk came through here. About four days ago."

Abigail swiped at her nose. "How can you tell it was four days ago?"

"The debris left in the tracks, and the dullness of the edges. You learn to tell if you study them long enough. An elk has a cloven hoof just like a deer, only bigger, thicker. A deer's are a little more spread out and sharper at the top." There were even fine differences in the track of a buck versus a doe—a doe's toes were more pointed. Hoke didn't like to track a doe this time of year when she might be pregnant with a fawn.

Abigail pointed to the nearest clump of flowers. "Did you know that jonquils are part of the narcissus family?"

Hoke grinned. "No, I didn't know that." He thought for a minute. "Is that the guy that became so enamored with himself that he drowned in a pool?"

"According to Greek mythology, yes. He was purportedly very handsome." She swiped at her nose again and grinned, and then her smile faded. "Yellow jonquils lined my front walk at home."

She squeezed her eyes closed, but one more tear slid from between her lids. He wished he knew what was making her sad.

She brushed it away and turned to face him.

"Have you always lived in the West?" she asked.

"No. I was born in Kentucky."

The horses had fallen into a nice rhythm, stepping slow and steady, their strong shoulders rolling Hoke and Abigail in a side-by-side motion.

She'd bravely fought whatever had made her sad, so he decided he'd bravely share, too. "My folks came to Missouri when I was eight. They both died before I was ten. A lot of folks got cholera in those days from diseased people coming off the boats."

"That's terrible! Who raised you?"

"Raised myself. Ed Branson and his wife, Ruby, were awfully good to me."

Abigail's breath caught. "Ruby Branson . . . and Rachel Mathews. You were the man we saw at the cemetery that day!"

He'd seen her there, had known it was her from the way she walked. "It's where my folks are buried. Anyway, I traveled to Texas when I was fifteen; been somewhere between Texas and Missouri ever since."

Hoke didn't look to see her reaction but felt her eyes travel the length of him.

"I can't bear to think of Jacob having to raise himself, or Charlie going all the way to Texas alone. Did you not go to school?"

"Not formally. Mrs. Ruby made sure I knew how to read and write. I never saw a woman who loved to read more." Abigail read to her children every night. Hoke could hear them through the canvas.

Her eyes were studying him again. He liked the feel of her eyes on him. "You've no other family?"

Hoke looked at her then, relieved to see she'd stopped crying. That had been his goal. Her eyes were bluer when wet. And the tip of her nose had turned pink.

He wasn't used to talking about himself. Even James knew little of his past. But for some reason he wanted to tell her. He wanted her to know—not so she could feel sorry for him, but so she could know him. Understand him. Forgive him for faults he knew he had, like clamming up and holding his cards too close to his chest.

"No family that I'm aware of. I'm sure I've got relatives somewhere, but as a ten-year-old I didn't pay close attention. I faintly remember some talk of it, but they weren't folks I recalled well enough to seek out when I found myself alone."

Hoke had been alone for years but for the occasional riding partner, like James. He was tired of being alone. Freedom was important to a man. At least, he had told himself it was important. He never thought he could travel with a group like this and not go mad from being tied to the responsibility of it. But it wasn't bad.

Some of these folks were annoying and downright funny in their choice of things. It was all he could do not to belly-laugh at those Schroeders for getting bent out of shape over a chicken. And those mindless sheep! Who in his right mind had the patience for putting up with sheep? But the Douglas brothers were good at it. Alec and Baird were as patient with the sheep as they were with simple-minded Paddy. Hoke would have lost patience long ago if John Sutler or Tim Peters had been in charge of this train, but they weren't. Dotson was. And Dotson was a man he could follow. Dotson had sense.

Hoke studied Abigail's face again, eager to know what she thought of him, but he couldn't tell.

"What made you leave Independence?" she asked.

It was the question he had dreaded, the one he had known she would ask. And he had thought he might tell her, but now he couldn't. "Just restless."

"So you traveled from Texas to Missouri, but you've not traveled this route?"

"No. I've seen the lower half of the Rockies but not the upper half."

It didn't seem either one of them could look on the other and lock the gaze. Each time he looked at her, she looked away as if not entirely willing to be known. And he did the same.

"Is the lower half where you marshaled? In Colorado?"

"Yes. I didn't do it for long—only a year."

"It must have been dangerous."

"I been through some scrapes. You learn to do what it takes, or you die. It's that simple. The will to live is a great teacher. Only real skill it takes is knowing how to track people."

"And how to bring them in," she corrected. "Staying alive when you find them."

He winced. Then he caught her gaze and held it. "I didn't like tracking men, then having to kill 'em when they started shooting back at me."

There . . . he'd told her that much: that he'd killed men. Would she think less of him now for knowing it? He hadn't forgotten the look she had in her eyes when she'd told him about her conversation with that man at the creek bank in Missouri, how troubled she'd seemed at the thought of one man killing another.

But she held his gaze, and he read no judgment in her eyes. Warm relief washed through him. He felt safe to continue.

"I always loved working with horses. My dad had a half-decent horse when he died. After I found myself alone I slept in a barn with that horse for a long time. That's how I got to know Mr. Branson. He gave me my first job. It was always my favorite job. So I went back to working with horses after I met James."

"And then you decided to come out here. To see new country."

He watched her as she looked out over the land ahead of them. "Yeah." He couldn't tell her that he'd come because of her. He didn't know how she felt about him and it was making him irritable, that and wondering if she really had a husband. All the evidence said she had one, so where was that nagging doubt in the back of his mind coming from? What would Hoke do *if* and *when* the husband showed up?

Do what he'd always done, he reckoned. Get up. Make coffee. Ride off. Survive.

What had Dotson said? The Oregon Trail was a road to anywhere.

He'd figure it out. It was just that for the first time in his life, he didn't want to live only for himself. He wanted to make a difference for someone else. He felt like she and those kids could use a guy like him—or at least he could make their lives easier. They could sure make his life more meaningful . . . they already had in a short time, whether they realized it or not.

Something unexpected had happened to him. It had stolen in slow and subtle when he showed those boys how to hobble the mules, figured out why Corrine was so sassy, and held that sleeping angel in his arms. When Lina was sick his heart had actually burned inside his chest with worry. He'd never experienced anything like that before. Even the dog had captured his heart somehow.

She looked at him again. "What was it like, being in the army?"

He shrugged his shoulders, wondering how to answer. "Some men like it. I didn't. Saw too many men let the power go to their heads. The farther west you go, the easier it is for officers to behave badly. Men like Colonel Dotson are rare. I saw one officer put a man in the stockade because he drank too much one night, and that same man had saved the officer's life in an Indian skirmish the day before. That man would have died for his superior officer, but because his shirt wasn't buttoned all the way the next morning and his shoes weren't shined to the right sheen, he got drug off and punished for it. I can appreciate order and discipline as much as the next man, but some of the eastern rules don't make a lot of sense out here."

"But there are some men like the colonel. Some good ones?"

"Oh, sure. There are some great men in the army." Was she wondering about her husband?

They rode in silence for a bit. Then Hoke, suddenly making up his mind, dismounted and stepped toward the filly. He reached in his shirt pocket, then reached for her hand. "I've been looking for a good time to give this back to you." He laid the blue crocheted bag on her open palm, holding her hand between his own longer than he really had to, enjoying the feel of her skin next to his, and enjoying the sweep of her eyes rolling over each of his fingers. That was the second time she'd examined his hands. He wondered why.

He reluctantly stepped back and remounted as she pulled open the string.

"I don't understand," said Abigail.

"You overpaid me."

She shook her head. "I did not. I underpaid you, if anything."

"You overpaid me a hundred dollars."

"Is this because my money was stolen? I don't want you feeling sorry for us, Mr. Hoke."

"Just Hoke. Look, I don't feel right about keeping it knowing you may have need for it. I told you I was fine with six. I'm trying to do this in private, so don't get up in airs about it, just take it." Realizing he was on the verge of irritable again, he added, "Please."

Abigail put the bag in her pocket and didn't say anything for a while. Just when it started to worry him, she said, "What will you do in Oregon?"

He took his time answering. "I'm not sure I'm going all the way to Oregon."

"Where are you going?"

"Haven't decided yet. What about you?" He turned to look at her.

She looked away. "My husband is supposed to be at Fort Hall."

"Supposed to be?"

"It's a long story."

They'd been climbing and had come to a plateau, far ahead of the train now. Hoke stopped and looked back behind them. The train was like a miniature moving village—like tiny children's play toys.

"Looks like we've got time."

Abigail hesitated. "He never came home," she finally said. "So for a long time I believed he had been killed. But when I tried to claim his death benefits, a gentleman in the War Department said he was alive and serving at Fort Hall. In February I got a letter from him. It was short, but I remember it verbatim. *Abigail, it looks like you tracked me down.*" She turned in the saddle to face him. "How would you take that, Mr. Hoke?"

He opened his mouth to correct her—*just Hoke*—but thought better of it.

If Baldwyn hadn't wanted to be tracked down, maybe Baldwyn didn't want to be married anymore. If Baldwyn didn't want to be married anymore, how was he going to feel when she showed up on his doorstep . . . with four kids and a dog in tow?

But what man in his right mind wouldn't want such a woman? She was the most fascinating creature Hoke had ever met.

He started to answer, then stopped himself and glanced over at her. She was looking down, so he studied her, from her blond wisps of hair that had blown about in the wind, her flushed cheeks washed by the falling tears, the white blouse she wore under a black vest, the green skirt, the tall leather boots. Curse the man who would ever walk out on her . . . who would make her cry.

"I don't know how I'd take it," he said.

Abigail looked up at him with an expression he couldn't read. "I feel like our lives have been hanging in the crook of a question mark for years. I'm tired of feeling helpless and not knowing what the future holds." She nodded once, decisively. "I've come on this trip in search of answers."

Hoke's heart went out to her. Baldwyn had put her in a bad spot. Somehow his behavior didn't match up with the feelings Hoke had gotten about him, though, by watching her and the children. It didn't sound like it matched with her own feelings about Baldwyn, either.

War could do strange things to a man.

Something deep in Hoke's gut was drawing him to Abigail Baldwyn. She was a good-looking woman, but it was more than that. There was something so fine about her—something that drew him like a spell. He didn't understand it and couldn't articulate it, but he was a patient man. He'd wait and see what happened when they got to Fort Hall.

A sudden rumble caused them to look up. To the west, still several miles in front of them, a storm was brewing.

CHAPTER 13

The thunder of the water

May 4, 1866

We experienced our first storm, Mimi—a fearsome thing with lightning popping all around and winds rocking the wagons. My plants were badly beaten. Some of our livestock bolted in the night and we spent half a day getting them back. Our mules were shaken and were as unruly as they have ever been while getting harnessed. The softness of the ground made the wheels sink and it was rough, slow going.

Michael Chessor had been on scout. He came riding past the Baldwyn wagon looking for Colonel Dotson.

Abigail was sitting on the wagon seat darning socks next to Jacob when she heard Chessor tell Dotson, "Creek's pretty swollen up ahead."

Colonel Dotson, the company leaders, and several other men rode out to see. Abigail watched them go with a twisted brow and laid her sewing aside.

❦

Sure enough, the creek had reached the top of its bank. Hoke didn't like the look of it.

"That was a shallow stream when I rode scout yesterday," said Gerald Jenkins. "We might ought to lay by for a day."

"Lay by?" Rudy Schroeder spat. "That's not too deep to cross. I say we go on. We already lay by every Sunday. And we've only covered a few miles today."

John Sutler looked from Rudy to the colonel. "We're already wet from the storm. If we wait and dry out, we'll get wet again when we do cross."

"I say we cross now before it gets any worse," old Tim Peters said, looking up. They all inspected the sky. "Could be more rain on the way."

"Peters, you're the only one that's been over this route," said Colonel Dotson. "You have any trouble at this creek before?"

"No. But I wasn't in a wagon and it wasn't up. I'm sure it'll be fine, though."

Dotson turned to Hoke. "You don't think that's too deep to cross?"

Hoke watched the creek a minute, its water curling and spilling over the jagged edges of the bank. "One way to check." He dismounted, pulled off his boots and socks, and waded into the water. At midpoint, it hit his upper chest. He nudged around the banks, measuring the depths with his feet.

When he sloshed back to the others he said, "Current's pretty strong, but it won't cover the tops of the wagon wheels." He pointed at the bank. "That's probably the best spot. Not too much drop-off, and the bank's low on the other side."

They voted to cross.

When the men got back to camp, Hoke went straight to Abigail's wagon. She was with Jacob, who was driving the team in front. Hoke insisted she let him and James drive the Baldwyn wagons through the swollen waters.

She looked down to his dry boots and back up his wet clothes. "Did you swim the creek?"

He didn't answer, just reached up to help her down. Jacob had already hopped off the seat.

"No, we'll be fine. You go on." Abigail took up the reins Jacob had let drop.

Hoke scowled. "Don't argue with me."

"I'm sure you'll have your hands full helping others. We're fine."

He bit his temper and walked away. Dotson and Jenkins were crossing now. They didn't seem to be having any problems.

Hoke drove his and James's wagon through the restless current, then stayed on the opposite bank to help as others crossed.

❦

The thunder of the water mixed with the bleating of the livestock was so loud no one heard the axle break or Nelda Peters's initial yell. But from the south side of the creek, as they waited their turn to cross, the Baldwyns saw it all—how the wagon dipped down and Nelda fell off the seat. How her husband Timmy jumped in to save her. How they flailed the first few seconds, fighting the current, their heads bobbing up near the oxen. How Timmy pushed Nelda out of the water and back up on the wagon seat just as Orin Peters, Timmy's younger brother, who was driving the rig in front of them, pulled his team up the bank.

Then, as Abigail was letting her breath out, believing Timmy and Nelda were going to be fine, Timmy was sucked back under the water.

Charlie, who had been driving the mule team behind her and Jacob, charged past them on foot and into the creek behind Harry

Sims before Abigail could call out and try to stop him. Hoke was there, too, and Bart Peters, coming from the other side, all racing to get to Timmy Peters in the water.

Harry pulled Timmy's body to the surface first. It took all four men to get him to the opposite bank. Abigail and several others, including the McConnelly sisters, had climbed from their wagons and now stood frozen on the south bank watching.

"Doc!" called Colonel Dotson from the far side of the creek. Doc Isaacs came running with his bag, jumped into the current, and swam to get to Timmy, now stretched out on the opposite bank.

Time slowed as the men got Nelda, who was screaming and flailing, off the stalled wagon, the wheel investigated, and the broken axle repaired. It took a long time as some of the men, including Charlie, used wood planks to help lift the wagon, while others dove under the current to find and solve the problem.

Abigail stood on the bank feeling helpless, her eyes glued on Charlie, willing him to be okay, hating that he was so close to tragedy.

If there was any boy left in Charlie prior to this trip, he was quickly disappearing. Abigail was proud of the man Charlie was becoming, but her heart pined for the innocent youth she'd left in Marston.

She didn't need anyone to wade back over the creek and tell her what was happening. It was clear enough from Nelda's wailing that Timmy hadn't made it.

Irene McConnelly looked at her darkly, as if Abigail were somehow to blame. "What did I ever do to her?" Abigail whispered to Melinda Austelle.

Melinda shook her head. "Her face is just set like that."

When Hoke finally sloshed back through the creek to the south side of the bank, the Baldwyns, minus Charlie, were a somber group, sitting huddled on the sodden grass.

"You going to let me take you over now?" he asked, his voice husky.

Abigail nodded.

Charlie came back over to lead the Baldwyns' first wagon over, Corrine holding things steady in the back. Hoke led the second team. When he yawed their mules up the mud-slick bank, Abigail sat in the back holding on to Lina with one hand and her lockstitch sewing machine with the other. Jacob held Rascal.

Abigail could see Nelda still sitting with her head buried in Christine Dotson's lap. Old Tim Peters stood with glassy eyes, his arms folded tight as he watched the men get the rest of the wagons across.

As the Baldwyns climbed out, Harry Sims approached Colonel Dotson, who stood nearby. "There were a lot of rocks where he was standing. One he was on must've rolled. The wagon wheel hit against one of the bigger rocks. That's what caused the axle to break."

Colonel Dotson swore. "Damn the luck! Sorry, Preacher. But . . . damn the luck! That poor girl."

Nelda clung to Doc Isaacs, who looked up at Abigail with helpless eyes.

Tam Woodford brought Harry a blanket. "Wrap up now, before you catch a cold. You're soaked through."

When Abigail turned back to her children, they were standing together staring at Timmy Peters's limp body on the bank. She picked Lina up. "Come on," she whispered. "Don't stand here and stare. Let's look around and see if there's anything we can do to help. But don't stand here and stare."

"Let's build a fire and get Nelda some dry clothes," said Melinda.

Sue Vandergelden stood near them with her hands on her hips looking toward Nelda and Doc Isaacs. "Can't he do something about her squallin'?"

Abigail and Melinda looked at one another. "She's grieving, Mrs. Vandergelden."

Mrs. Vandergelden looked at Abigail like she'd slapped her. "Well, I don't know why she's got to throw it off on the rest of us!" She turned and stormed back to her wagon.

Rudy Schroeder walked up to Colonel Dotson and said in a low voice, "We ought not to have crossed. That was a bad decision."

Every man within earshot turned on Rudy Schroeder.

"You voted on it, Rudy," snapped the normally jovial Gerald Jenkins, "as did Tim Peters himself. Nobody wanted this to happen, but it did. It doesn't help anything for you to go pointing fingers."

It was as forceful as Abigail had ever heard mild Gerald Jenkins speak, but then . . . all their nerves had been set on edge from the sudden turn of misfortune.

That night there was no singing in the camp. Abigail got through supper and cleanup. But later, long after dark, she slipped out of the wagon to check on her sleeping boys.

She saw Hoke lying under his wagon only a short distance away, his eyes open and watching her. Her body longed to crawl into his bedroll and be held. She wanted someone to promise her that she and her children would finish this journey alive.

♫

One of our men was drowned, Mimi. Some of the women were badly affected.

Abigail laid down the quill and pushed back the letter. She didn't want the ink to spatter or Mimi would guess how badly she herself had been affected.

Days before, they had crossed the Kansas River on a ferry. Men had built ferries and bridges at the major river crossings on the trail and charged a toll for the use of them. Mrs. Vandergelden said it was robbery to charge settlers to cross a bridge or use a ferry. Abigail now felt the charges were justified. There had been no ferry or bridge here, and she would have gladly paid every coin in the blue crocheted bag to use one.

Harry Sims conducted a memorial service just after breakfast. Timmy was buried in a lovely spot under an oak tree as the early-morning sunlight winked through new green leaves.

"I fear Nelda will have a hard time of it," said Melinda as they went back to their wagons.

They had passed several graves on the journey and now left one of their own.

After this, Abigail began to read all the markers more closely and wondered at the lives behind the words. Skeletal remains of many animals also lined the trails, picked clean by wolves and vultures, the bones bleached white by the merciless sun.

In the ramshackle cabin a dozen miles from Fort Hall, Bonnie reached over and stroked his red beard as they lay once again under the horsehair blanket.

"How do you keep this trimmed so neat?"

"I have my methods." He swatted her hand away, not liking to have his face touched.

"I can trim it if you need me to. Since your fingers are missing."

"Somehow I've managed." He threw back the blanket and stood, reaching for his clothes. "I won't be back for a while. I need to go to Laramie."

He had been mulling over the best solution after Abigail's first letter arrived. He wouldn't tell Bonnie. If the Piute woman knew Abigail was headed this way, she would do worse than pout. He didn't need two upset women on his hands.

No . . . there was no need for Bonnie to ever know the difference. Soon enough, Abigail would be nothing more than a bittersweet memory, tucked safely away with the letters in the box.

When the second letter came—the one telling him about Cecil Ryman—the sweetness of her effort to warn him almost made him change his mind. But then she mentioned she was bringing the children. That wasn't what he'd told her to do . . . bringing the children just complicated everything.

Bonnie pouted. "How long will you be gone?"

"Long as it takes."

"To do what?"

"None of your business."

Bonnie crossed her arms and huffed. "What am I supposed to do while you're gone to Laramie?"

"Girl like you? You'll be fine."

CHAPTER 14
Life's pilgrim journey

They arrived at Alcove Springs midday on a warm Saturday. Several members of the wagon party spent the afternoon at a nearby settlement conducting trade negotiations. This proved to be a popular event whenever they came to settlements.

Jacob came running back to camp proudly holding a pair of moccasins. "Charlie got your molasses."

"The people in these towns must be making a fortune," Melinda said, as she, Abigail, and Caroline Atwood all worked on supper.

Abigail smiled as Charlie walked up carrying the molasses and a dozen eggs packed in salt. She wasn't doing badly herself. Charlie had traded two of her needlework hand towels for the items.

The Baldwyns might not starve after all.

"How come you never eat with us, Tam?" called James over to Tam's wagon. Most of Company C had started eating together in the evenings. But Tam never joined them. She ate with two men in Company D.

"Because Harry Sims is a bad cook," she called back. "And Michael Chessor ain't no better. They'd starve if I didn't feed 'em."

"That sounds like me and Hoke." James winked at Corrine. "'Cept that I'm a great cook."

"What are you cooking for us tonight, Mr. Parker?" asked Corrine, holding baby Will on her hip.

"You ladies appear to have it covered. Say, how old are you again?"

"She and Charlie have birthdays in another week," announced Jacob.

"Will that make her old enough to get married?"

"Some girls do get married at sixteen," said Emma, looking at Charlie. "I'll be sixteen in August."

James grinned at Charlie, but Charlie acted like he hadn't heard.

Cold water bubbled into several deep pools at Alcove Springs, a stop on the trail that was a short walk from camp. Abigail rushed through supper so she and the other ladies from Company C could slip back down to the water and bathe before sunset. Since the mud that had been caused by the heavy rains had dried, the dust seemed thicker than ever. A month of travel and they hadn't bathed once! Water was shared with livestock that needed it for drinking, and there had been little privacy with them passing so many settlements and Indian villages. She had tried to wash as best she could with a cloth and the water basin each night but longed to submerge her body in a clean pool of water.

Abigail wasn't alone; soon there was a large group of women at the springs.

Tam Woodford ran off boys who tried to spy. When Tam felt the risk was over, she too ran down to the springs, stripped to her underclothes, and jumped in the water. Lina and Deena Sutler had a grand time splashing on the banks with her. When Prissy Schroeder challenged her to a swimming race, Tam beat her without mercy.

"I believe every female from the wagon train is here." Melinda twisted water out of her hair as she and Abigail sat on the water's edge, their feet dangling in the clear, cold pool.

"I don't see Sue Vandergelden. Or the McConnelly sisters," said Abigail.

"And let us be thankful for it."

Josephine Jenkins approached Audrey Beckett, who was expecting and had waddled down to the springs to sit nearby, resting her legs in the water. "Let me and Chris do that washing for you." Abigail smiled to see Josephine and Christine giggling like schoolgirls as they helped Audrey with her basket of clothes.

"My feet feel like they're going to crack right open," said Audrey.

"Marc has a plaster you should try," said Caroline, who was watching Will splash in the water with Corrine and Emma. "I used it when I was expecting Will and it helped. I can't imagine doing all this walking in that condition."

"Poor Nelda," said Melinda. Nelda had not joined them at the springs, either. No one had known Nelda was expecting until after Timmy died.

Katrina Schroeder walked up to them. "Have any of you had items go missing from your wagons? We're missing a silver spoon and dish I use to feed the twins."

"That's funny," said Tam, who had just finished swimming and had come to sit on the bank. "I'm missing a brass telescope. It was right next to an ivory box that's worth a lot more. It didn't make sense to me that someone would take the telescope and not the box. So I thought I might have misplaced it, but I've been through the wagon half a dozen times and it never has turned up."

Abigail told about her gold coins that were taken in Independence. "Since no one else reported stolen money, I thought it must have been taken by someone from the town."

"I'll talk to George about it," said Christine.

As the evening sun began to sink full and orange on the tree-lined horizon, the women walked slowly back to camp.

Abigail linked her arm through Melinda's. "I feel more like myself. It's been impossible to keep those wagons or any piece of clothing clean."

"Isn't that the truth? Now if I could only get Mr. Austelle and my boys to scrub."

Just then a herd of boys ran past them on their way to the springs. Mr. Austelle and several of the men, including James Parker and Hoke, were right behind them.

Melinda looked at Abigail and giggled. "That'll make the wagon smell nicer."

By the time the men returned the whole camp buzzed with renewed energy, the result of everyone feeling rested and festive.

"You know what we need?" said Tam. "A dance!" She turned to Harry Sims with a mischievous grin. "If you don't ask me to dance, I'll be hoppin' mad."

"Then I'll be sure to ask you." He grinned shyly. Harry had a long handlebar mustache and his hair was thinning on top. He was of only average height but was strong and stocky.

Josephine clapped her hands. "Let's do have a dance! Or is it too soon after Timmy's death?" She asked Orin and Bart Peters how they felt about it and whether they thought it would hurt poor Nelda. Mrs. Josephine had held off singing with the children ever since the accident out of respect for her.

"Timmy wouldn't want people to stop having fun on his account," said Bart.

"Have the dance. Refusin' to live isn't going to bring him back," said old Tim Peters.

Josephine begged the Vandergeldens to let Ned come, and they relented. The smile that appeared on his face was the first one any of the party had seen the boy wear.

James got his guitar, Alec Douglas his fiddle, Harry his harmonica, and Nichodemus Jasper his dulcimer. They practiced while everyone else went to their wagons to spruce up.

Corrine and Lina donned the best dresses they'd brought. "Mama, you should wear your pretty blue dress," said Lina.

"No, she shouldn't," corrected Corrine. "It will be fancier than any of the other ladies' dresses."

"You're wearing your prettiest dress, Corrine. Why can't Mama?"

"Because I'm not married, and she is."

Lina cupped her hand and whispered in Abigail's ear so Corrine couldn't hear. "I think you're the prettiest mother, and I think you should wear the prettiest dress."

"Thank you, sweetheart, but Corrine's probably right." Just yesterday as Abigail passed the McConnelly wagon she'd overhead Irene say to her sister, Diana, "She'll have those hemlines up over her waist next."

They had to have been talking about her. She was the one who had taken up her hemlines after catching her skirt on fire. And she knew her green riding habit was shorter than was customary, but she didn't think there was any harm in it. After all, she'd had knee-length boots on.

Maybe Irene had never seen a split riding skirt in Boston, where she was from. Maybe Irene also thought it was wrong for a married woman to ride horses with an unmarried man. Abigail didn't want to cater to the judgment of a woman like Irene McConnelly, but perhaps she should be more guarded in the future.

May 12, 1866

Mr. McConnelly and his two grown daughters are in Company D. The oldest, Irene, is unpleasant. She said some disparaging things about the South, and Southern soldiers in particular, so I keep my distance and do not remind her that I had a brother who gave his life for the Confederacy. I suspect she has been told this by the Dotsons. Everyone else in this group seems willing to move on from the recent conflict.

The blue of the dress perfectly matched her eyes. But as much as she would have loved to wear it, she tucked it back in a burlap sack and scooted it under the feather bed.

Abigail had washed her other clothes that afternoon and they were still wet, hanging on a rope tied between their two wagons, leaving only the dress she was wearing. It was a soft pink, in a high-waisted style, lighter weight for summer, freshly pressed by rotating irons in the fire and fine enough for a dance out on the trail. She dressed it up with a lace shawl and sprinkled lavender powder on her neck. Then she found a pink ribbon and used it to tie her mother's brooch around her neck. Instead of her usual midcalf boots, she donned daintier ivory boots that buckled around her ankles.

As they were leaving the wagon, Abigail caught a glimpse of gold outside. "Go on, girls, I'm coming," she said, walking back to investigate.

There, in one corner of her box garden, was a new patch of jon-quils—about a dozen of them.

Couples were already dancing when Abigail arrived at the campfire. Word had spread and some folks from the nearby village had joined them.

James Parker whistled long and low as Corrine walked up, but she acted like she didn't hear him. Abigail loved the blue Regency dress on her daughter. The high crossover bodice offset her tiny waist, and the short sleeves, tied with long ivory ribbons, revealed arms as strong as Corrine's will. Another ivory ribbon tied her long hair back.

"You better save me a dance," James told Corrine under his breath.

John and Marnie Sutler were dancing, to the joy of their six chil-dren. Their son Paul watched Corrine, but Cooper Austelle got to her first on Jacob's dare. "Would you like to dance, Corrine?"

She glanced over at Paul, taking Cooper's arm without enthusiasm. "Sure."

Lina, wearing a bib dress of pink-and-white calico with yellow rosettes along the collar, skipped off to sit by Caroline Atwood and baby Will.

"Don't you look like a princess!" Caroline twirled Lina around.

Rascal ran up to Abigail. She turned, looking for Hoke. There he was across the opening talking to the McConnelly sisters, who looked extra pretty in satin frocks. For once, they were animated—especially Irene, who wore a green bonnet with a wide ribbon. It made her face hard to see, even though the men had lit several lanterns around the circle and two fires on either side. Hoke's face was clear enough. He was smiling broadly—he, who hardly ever smiled.

Abigail felt a pang of jealousy followed by guilt. Just because he watered her box gardens and let her ride his white horse didn't mean he cared for her. But of all people for him to be smiling at—*Irene!*

Doc Isaacs approached, looking dapper in a gray vest. He invited Abigail to dance.

~⑨

Hoke was conscious of Abigail's every movement. She and Doc Isaacs made a striking couple, he noted with a scowl. The two talked frequently in the evenings. Both were cultured and educated.

Irene smiled up at Hoke. "I see Mrs. Baldwyn hasn't raised all her skirts above her ankles."

Tipping his hat to her, Hoke excused himself. "Enjoy the rest of your evenin', ma'am."

He heard Irene mumble to Diana, "I thought he was going to ask me to dance."

"Maybe he doesn't dance."

~⑨

Doc Isaacs expertly wove Abigail between the other couples.

"It must be hard to be a physician," said Abigail. "We all want you to work miracles for us, and in the end . . ."

Doc's face fell from mirthful to somber. "I'm just a man."

Abigail was sorry to have caused his mood to change. She squeezed his shoulder with the hand that rested there. "Thank you for your patience when I was unreasonable."

He looked in her eyes. Doc's eyes were blue, like hers. "I don't recall you being unreasonable."

"You have a kindly forgetful memory, then."

He grinned at her mischievously. "So this husband you're rumored to have . . . is he real?"

Abigail laughed. "I hope so. I'm going to a lot of trouble on his account. What about you, Dr. Isaacs?"

"What about me?"

He reminded her so much of her brother Seth. Maybe that was why Abigail had felt drawn to him so quickly.

"Why is there not a Mrs. Isaacs?"

He shook his head, his eyes filled with laughter. "Best ones go quick."

"Well . . . you're young. There's no need to hurry the matter."

Orin Peters cut in. Orin wasn't nearly as polished a dancer as Doc Isaacs, and he concentrated intensely on his feet. When the song ended, Abigail thanked him, but Orin lingered. "It's a nice evenin'," he said after a bit.

"It certainly is." She watched the colonel and Christine Dotson dance past.

"Someone said you lost your mother."

Abigail turned to look at Orin. He'd barely ever spoken to her before. She'd been surprised when he'd cut in on Doc Isaacs. He must have wanted to talk to someone. "I did, about a year ago. When did you lose yours?"

Orin peered down at the ground. "I was a baby. I don't even remember her."

"I know she would have loved to know you—to see you all grown up and dancing." Abigail put a hand on his arm. "I'm truly sorry about your brother, Orin."

He excused himself.

After that Colonel Dotson asked Abigail to dance. Then she danced with Baird Douglas. Baird's brother Paddy stood to the side, smiling and nodding to the music.

"Do you dance, Paddy?" Abigail asked when she and Baird stopped. Paddy shook his head. She looked at the raccoon in his arms. "Does Carson dance?" Paddy grinned and shook his head harder.

"He could dance. If I taught him." He held the raccoon out for her to pet, then pulled him back to sit inside his vest, where Carson liked to ride.

Abigail danced with Charlie next, then swooped over and grabbed Jacob. Hoke tottered on the sidelines with Lina on his feet.

Finally, James Parker, taking a break from his guitar, asked Abigail to dance while Alec played on with his fiddle.

"Mrs. Baldwyn, you are a vision."

She laughed. "I'll take that with a grain of salt, considering the source."

"I do like women," he admitted. "Is Corrine too young for me, you think?"

"Yes, I think."

"Darn. Then Lina's out, too? I was thinking I could get her young and train her like I wanted."

Abigail laughed. It would take a confident woman to snag James Parker.

He whirled her around. Her skirts fanned out and brushed over the holster he wore low on his right hip. Few of the men in this wagon train wore guns all the time, but Hoke and James did.

She nodded her head toward it. "Do you sleep with that gun, Mr. Parker?"

"Yes, ma'am. In my hand."

"You do not!"

James Parker, who kept a verbal jab going with nearly everyone around him, turned serious eyes on her. "It doesn't protect me if I can't get to it. Considering some of the trails Hoke and I have ridden, I've needed it close at hand."

It made Abigail wonder what kind of trails they had ridden. "How long have you and Hoke known each other?"

"Six years. We met as cavalry scouts. He's one of the best men I've ever known."

"How so?"

"You can count on him. If he gives his word on something, he'll do it or die. And he can outwork anybody. You probably haven't noticed." He laughed. "He's like having three men around instead of one. I don't know why he puts up with me—probably because I'm so charming."

Abigail smiled. James Parker *was* charming.

"Hoke also has an uncanny sixth sense that has saved our scalps more than once. He just knows things lots of times without knowing why he knows 'em."

"Why aren't you both married?" It wasn't really any of her business, but Doc's earlier questions had set her mind to wondering.

"Personally, I find it difficult to settle on just one woman. I have several I'm keepin' my eye on in cities all up and down the trail."

Abigail laughed. She didn't doubt it. "You seem to have a good relationship with Tam Woodford."

"Tam?" James furrowed his brow down at Abigail. "Why, she's crazy about Harry Sims, can't you see that?"

"No! Really?" Abigail swung her head around to look at Tam and Harry dancing nearby. Had they been dancing together all night? How had she missed it?

"I thought women had instincts about these things. You're slippin', Mrs. Baldwyn."

"What about Hoke, then? Does he have women all up and down the trail?"

"Oh, no . . . I never a saw a man more pa'ticular about women than Hoke. He's not fussy about what he eats, but he's most pa'ticular about guns, horses, and women."

"He doesn't seem interested in any of our ladies."

"Oh, he's interested."

Abigail's foot faltered. "Really? Who?"

She was embarrassed the moment the words left her lips. James was going to see right through her. But . . . Hoke had been talking to Irene earlier and Irene was attractive.

He raised his eyebrows and looked away. "I can't say."

Abigail stole a peep over James's broad shoulder at Hoke, who was now talking with Christine Dotson. His back was turned but she could see Christine's eyes. Abigail hoped when she got to be Christine's age that her eyes crinkled at the corners.

Hoke turned suddenly and caught her gaze. Excusing himself from Mrs. Dotson, he walked toward her and James.

Abigail's pulse quickened. Once again, she hoped James didn't notice.

৩

Before the dance, when James had seen Hoke planting the flowers in Abigail's box garden, he'd said, "Hoke, you might want to be careful."

"You might want to mind your own business."

"I've never known you to look twice at a woman. You *would* wait and fall for the most out-of-reach female you've ever crossed paths with."

Maybe she was, thought Hoke, but by God, he wanted her to have those flowers that reminded her of the home she'd lost, and him of his mother. When he'd spied those flowers coming back from the springs that afternoon, he couldn't resist digging up a few to add to her collection.

"James," he said now, "let me show Mrs. Baldwyn how to dance."

James tightened his grip on her. "I just showed her."

Hoke glowered.

"All right, then." James looked down at Abigail. "Don't let him step on your feet."

Hoke laid his hand low on her back, pulling her toward him, a reckless thrill shooting the length of him. He'd itched to take this woman in his arms for weeks now—had come close to sweeping her off the white filly that day he returned the blue crocheted bag to her.

Harry Sims whirled past and Tam leaned over to Hoke. "You're holdin' her awful close."

Hoke scowled and spun Abigail away from them, refusing to relax his grip.

His eyes followed Abigail's as they traveled around the circle. "Those two have been talking for a while, your young she-cat and Master Sutler," he said when her gaze landed on Corrine. "It happened while you were consoling Peters."

∽

Abigail looked back at Hoke. Did anything get past this man?

She had been taught to lay her right hand on a man's left when he held it out for her. This created a safe pocket of distance between the dancers' bodies. But Hoke curled his hand over hers and laid it on his heart. It brought her so near to him she could feel the brush of his breath on her forehead.

How long had it been since she'd been held close by a man?

She drove the thought from her head. "Is that Paul Sutler Corrine is talking to?" She looked but couldn't see the young man's face.

"Yes. What'd Peters want?"

Hoke could be so abrupt. Abigail avoided his probing eyes. "I don't know that he wanted anything. Just someone to talk to."

"There's plenty of people here for him to talk to. He's sweet on you."

Abigail scowled up at him. "Don't be ridiculous. I'm at least ten years older than him."

"What's that got to do with anything?"

Hoke was clean shaven and smelled like leather and . . . *what was it?* Trees. He was always chewing on some stick from a certain kind of tree. Abigail had seen him select the stems and whittle them down; a couple of them were in his shirt pocket now. He wore a white shirt and black pants. A gun belt hung low on his left thigh.

"You favor your left hand," she said, looking down at the pearl-handled gun.

"That's right."

"Jacob favors his left hand."

"I noticed that. Been meaning to give him some pointers. I favor my left foot, too, so it's a wonder I can dance."

He smiled suddenly. When he smiled it changed the whole look of his face.

"And you've had a haircut." She bit the inside of her lip as soon as she said it. What lack of control! He was going to know she'd been paying attention.

"Ingrid Schroeder gave haircuts to several of the men this afternoon while you women were at the springs."

Abigail looked away again, avoiding those eyes that tunneled deep, past the surface.

Ingrid Schroeder was about twenty—a pretty girl with a mass of auburn hair and strong German features. Abigail wondered if Ingrid was the object of Hoke's eye. She had seen them talking. It was an intimate thing: cutting a man's hair.

The song ended and Hoke released her. When no one else asked Abigail to dance, he extended his hand again. "One more?"

"Love to. Oh, Mr. Hoke!"

"Just Hoke."

Same low hand on her back . . . same pull of her other hand to his chest. She tried to keep from looking inappropriately pleased.

"Did you put those jonquils in my box?"

"Depends on whether you like 'em."

"I like 'em." She allowed herself a grin.

"Thought you might want some for where you're going."

Abigail was so touched by his words and actions that she didn't trust herself to speak for a minute. "Thank you. That was very thoughtful of you."

This song was a foot-stomper from east Tennessee, played by Nichodemus Jasper. He shocked the whole party with how fast his fingers flew across the small wooden box on his lap. James, who was back at his guitar, couldn't keep pace with him.

Hoke twirled Abigail around, always bringing her close again with his hand low on her back. She was drunk with how good his hand felt on her and didn't trust herself to dance with him much longer. What would Irene say about her next?

When Nichodemus finished, the group cheered. He appeared to grow three inches taller. "I want to play one last song before we end, and I want Nora to sing it with me."

"No, I can't." Nora was a timid bird with nervous mannerisms.

"Come on, Nora, sing this last one with me."

"I'd rather not, Nichodemus."

He insisted he had to have her voice to do the last song or it wouldn't be right. With everyone encouraging her, Nora finally relented.

"This is her favorite song," said Nichodemus behind his hand.

Nora swatted him.

Shy at first, she worked up her courage and began to sing . . . like Gabriel. It wasn't an east Tennessee hill song like Abigail had expected. Instead it was a slave spiritual, one Mimi used to hum when she worked in the kitchen. Nora's words brought Mimi back—Mimi, whose presence had been such a comfort!

> *I want Jesus to walk with me.*
> *I want Jesus to walk with me.*
> *All along life's pilgrim journey,*
> *Oh, I want Jesus to walk with me.*

Hoke didn't ask Abigail if she'd dance with him again—she would have told him no if he had. He simply pulled her close and moved her back and forth to the haunting strums of the dulcimer and Nora's angelic voice.

> *In my trials, he'll walk with me.*
> *In my trials, he'll walk with me.*
> *All along life's pilgrim journey,*
> *Oh, I want Jesus to walk with me.*

As her mind filled with thoughts of Mimi and Marston, Abigail squeezed her eyes closed, Nora's voice wrapping around her like a blanket. Tears stung the corners of her eyes, dropping heavy onto the grass. Soon her cheek lay next to Hoke's shoulder.

> *In my sorrows, he'll walk with me.*
> *In my sorrows, he'll walk with me.*
> *All along life's pilgrim journey,*
> *Oh, I want Jesus to walk with me.*

When the song ended, Abigail became aware of Hoke's broad chest and narrow hips, his body so close, like a chiseled rock but . . . warm . . . alive. And safe. Hoke made everyone feel safe, because he had everything under control.

He held her out away from his body and searched her face.

Josephine was speaking. "Nora, sweetheart, that was the most beautiful thing I ever heard. I can't believe you've been hiding over there while we've been singing. You must share that with us more often!"

Yes, everyone agreed. *Lovely! Simply gorgeous! Please sing more often,* they begged.

Their praise so embarrassed Nora, she bolted from the ring.

Everyone started saying good night and making their way back to their wagons. Abigail turned her head away from Hoke's probing eyes. Before he could speak she raised a hand to silence him and turned to leave.

This was the second time she'd cried in front of him.

❦

As Orin Peters was walking back to the campfire he noticed Abigail's stricken look. "Are you all right, Mrs. Abigail?"

She shook her head and walked away.

He turned to Charlie and Corrine, who stood nearby. "What's wrong? Did someone hurt her feelings?" Then he looked at Hoke.

"No," Corrine answered.

"That song reminds her of Mimi," offered Jacob.

"Who's Mimi?" asked Hoke.

"Our help. Practically our second mama."

"Mimi used to live with us," Charlie explained. "She was supposed to come out here with us, but her sister got sick and Mimi stayed with her instead."

"She used to sing that song," said Corrine, whose own blue eyes had watered to see her mother so affected.

"When Mimi was born," said Charlie, "her father brought her up to the big house to show Grandpa and Grandma Walstone. It was Christmas Day. Evidently, Ma had prayed for a baby sister the night before and nobody knew it. So when Mimi's father showed up with a baby girl the next morning, Ma squealed and said, 'Is she for me? Me?' That's how Mimi got her name."

"I didn't know that's how Mimi got her name," said Lina.

"You never heard Ma tell that? She thought Mimi was the little sister she'd prayed for."

"How old was Ma?"

"About five, like you."

"You're five! I thought you were younger than that," said Prissy Schroeder, who had scuttled up to see what they were talking about.

"She's still four," said Jacob.

"But I'll be five on my next birthday," Lina corrected him, smiling.

"You just had your birthday, Lina," said Jacob. "It won't come again for a while."

Then all the children started asking each other, *How old are you? When is your birthday? How old did you think I was?*

As they chattered, Hoke made his way back to his wagon, mulling over the sacrifice Abigail Baldwyn had made in leaving the safety of what she knew in Tennessee to travel two thousand miles across rough terrain for a man who hadn't even acted like he wanted her to know he was alive.

CHAPTER 15

While the game's on the move

He saddled his horse just before sunset.

"Where are you going, Captain Baldwyn?" asked the sentry on duty as he rode up to the gate. He noticed that it was one of the new recruits.

"To hunt."

"This late?"

"Best time, while the game's on the move."

"You're not supposed to go alone this late in the day, Captain."

"Open the gate. I'll be fine."

The sentry hesitated.

"Open the gate, son," he said again. "I happen to enjoy hunting and I go out for the cook all the time. You can ask him. The cook wants elk and I know where to find some. If I'm not back in three days with an elk slung over this horse, you can feel bad about it then."

The sentry opened the gate and watched him ride out, then closed it behind him.

Once the sentry was no longer in sight, he circled back to the far north side of the fort to pick up the supplies he had lowered over the wall. Then he pointed his horse southeast.

He knew that if he camped in a certain spot, the trapper would find him. Sure enough, when he opened his eyes the next morning, the trapper was sitting on a fallen log, trimming his fingernails with a large knife, watching him.

He threw off his blanket and pulled on his boots. "I thought I was a light sleeper."

The trapper nodded toward the bundle next to him on the ground. "Those guns?"

"Yeah. Henrys."

"Why you bringin' 'em? And where's Bonnie?"

"Bonnie's fine. She's at the cabin. I'm bringing guns—and whiskey—because I have a problem. I need your help."

"What kind o' problem?"

"Wife problem."

"I came to ask you 'bout that. I was down south o' Kearney last month. Met a man who said he aimed to kill you because you killed his brother, Dan."

"Oh, yeah?"

"Said this Dan thought y'all was friends."

"We weren't friends. We served together once. He had a big mouth and I knew he couldn't keep it shut." He swore. "Who saw it? Who told the brother?"

"Man didn't say."

"I'm not too worried about it. Dan Ryman wasn't hard to kill."

"Neither was his brother."

He smiled and cocked his head at the trapper. "That was good of you."

The trapper pointed the knife at him. "Tell me why this Ryman fella thinks he spoke to your wife. Because if I'm remembering right . . . and I always do . . . you said you wasn't married no more."

He took a deep breath and leveled his eyes at the trapper. "I'm not. But there's a woman heading this way who thinks I'm her husband."

"Why does she think it if it ain't so?"

"I borrowed his name."

"Where's she been till now?"

"Tennessee."

"What's makin' her travel out here?"

"Money problems."

"You want to keep her from gettin' here?"

The man known as Robert Baldwyn nodded. "She's with a large group. What's in those wagons has to be a rich bounty. They'll come through Laramie in five or six weeks. I was just there. These were all the guns and whiskey I could get, but I'll get you more in time. Meanwhile, there's a spot about a week out from the fort where the land starts to rise. Scattered evergreens. Make a great place for an ambush."

The trapper pointed the knife at the bundle. "Show me what you got."

The man untied the rope and opened the blanket. "I know this isn't much. I had some trouble at Laramie. But I'm telling you, this train's bound to be a rich load. I know this woman. She's used to having things and she'll be traveling with a well-set group. You can keep it all, and I'll see to it that the army doesn't come after you."

He put his hand in his pocket and pulled out Abigail's picture. "Here's what she looks like."

The trapper reached for it and raised an eyebrow. "You want her dead, or can we have her?"

"Take all the other women in the group you want to, but I prefer you kill her. And anyone with her—she's got four kids. They'll all have yellow hair, like her. And there might be a Negro woman with her. She wasn't real clear about that in her letter."

The trapper put the picture in his pocket. "She won't reach Fort Hall." He retied the bundle and shouldered it.

"I appreciate it."

"I'm not doin' it for you."

As the trapper walked off the man known as Robert asked, "You seen any elk?"

The trapper pointed east. "Four miles that way."

∾

May 20, 1866

Sometimes Mr. Hoke asks Jacob to drive his team—or Cooper Austelle or Lijah Sutler. The boys nearly come to blows over the privilege.

True to their vow, Charlie and Jacob have slept each night on the ground since we left Independence—all but when it stormed. Rascal sleeps between them. (They'll be teeming in fleas, won't they? What was your remedy for those, Mimi?)

Many of the children run barefoot during the day and Jacob has begged me to let him do so, but I insist he wear his boots until we make camp for the evening. No one has been snakebit . . . yet. The snakes probably hear us coming from miles ahead.

∾

Just before they reached Fort Kearney, Audrey Beckett went into labor. She started in the night and Doc said at sunup it might be noon before the baby came.

Colonel Dotson delayed the train's departure.

When Rudy Schroeder suggested to the men that some of them could go on to the fort and some stay behind, Dotson was firm. "We're not splitting."

James had ridden scout days earlier and circled back at the time to see how near the next wagon train was getting. It was a subject the men often discussed: how close was the next group getting? Dotson's goal had been to stay in the lead. But theirs was a large group and the larger the group, the more delays. James had found that the next, smaller train with a dozen wagons was quickly gaining ground.

Doc Isaacs approached the men. He looked tired.

Gerald Jenkins laid a hand on his shoulder. "What's the word on Mrs. Beckett?"

"A few more hours, at least. She's had a hard time of it. I hate to move her too quickly."

"We won't move her today," said Dotson. "The train will stay put."

"But—" Rudy Schroeder started to protest.

Hoke spoke low but they all heard him. "Rudy, the colonel's mind is made and his word is law."

"Fine," said Rudy. "Austelle, how 'bout you come take a look at one of the wheels on my wagon. If we're going to sit here all day, we might as well get something done."

Gerald Jenkins watched Mr. Austelle leave with Rudy and then turned to Dotson and Hoke. "Those Schroeders can be testy."

"Yes, but they're a hardworking lot," said Colonel Dotson.

"You know he imbibes regularly," said Tim Peters.

"Yeah, I know. So does Mrs. Vandergelden. But Schroeder doesn't do it when he's on guard duty."

"Mrs. Vandergelden? How'd you know that?" asked Jenkins.

"You ever look at her eyes? They stay bloodshot. Let's take stock of things today, let the livestock rest, and send out a couple of hunting parties, and more scouts to see how close that next train is getting."

James Parker and Michael Chessor volunteered for the scouting job. Hoke was put in charge of one hunting party and Harry Sims the other.

When Tam Woodford heard Harry was taking a group, she begged to go along. "I can't stand being around all these women fussing over this baby coming. I've got me a rifle. It's an old muzzle-loader, but it shoots fine and I know how to use it."

"Come on, then," said Harry, grinning under his handlebar mustache.

Charlie ran to the Beckett wagon, where Abigail was helping attend to Audrey Beckett, and asked permission to go with Hoke. Hoke could hear them talking as he went to his own wagon for supplies.

When she took her time answering Charlie, Hoke knew her brow must be twisted in that way she had.

"I'd rather you stay close, Charlie, to help with Jacob and Lina while I'm helping Mrs. Beckett."

"Corrine can watch them. Clyde and Cooper are both going. You ought to let Jacob go with us."

It obviously meant a lot to Charlie to go. Hoke had never heard him question one of his mother's decisions.

"No. Jacob stays here and I prefer you stay here, too."

Cooper Austelle ran up to announce, "Hoke says there might be a herd of bison on the other side of the ridge, Charlie!"

"Ma, I know better than to argue, but . . . it's Mr. Hoke!" Hoke was touched to know Charlie wanted to spend time with him. "You know Jake'll have a conniption."

Sure enough, Jacob ran up just then. "Ma! Ma! Mr. Hoke thinks there might be buffalo!"

When Hoke stepped around the corner Abigail's brow was sure enough twisted.

"Why are you telling these boys there might be buffalo nearby?"

"Because there might." He'd seen the herd yesterday and doubted they'd moved far overnight. Jacob had talked nonstop on this trip about wanting to see buffalo. It made Hoke smile to think the boy was about to get his wish.

Abigail cocked her head and gave him a look that preached plenty.

Hoke laid a hand over his heart, wishing he could reach out and smooth the lines in her forehead. "I'll take personal responsibility for their well-bein' if you'll let 'em go."

"Both of them?"

"Why not?"

"You don't think Jacob's too young?"

"Not at all!"

She stepped down from the wagon and pulled him to the side. "Are they dangerous?"

The feel of her hand on his arm made his blood race. "Not unless they stampede."

Her eyes grew wide.

"But it's rare."

"Mr. Hoke!"

"Just Hoke."

Just then Melinda Austelle walked by, on her way back with fresh water. Abigail turned to her. "Melinda? Are you letting your boys go? Is Mr. Austelle going?"

Hoke fumed. She trusted Charles Austelle but didn't trust him? Charles was a good man, but he wasn't any more capable than Hoke was!

Yes, Melinda was letting her boys go, and yes, Mr. Austelle was going. Abigail turned back to Hoke. "I'd die if anything happened to my boys. Promise me you'll watch out for them."

He swept his hat off and bowed low. "I promise to return them in one piece."

"Alive," she demanded.

"I'll do my damnedest."

Her brow did more than twist—it furrowed. "And don't curse in front of them!"

"You boys have a fine gun," Hoke said to Charlie when Charlie handed it to him for inspection. They had stopped near the bison herd.

Hoke ran a hand over the wood stock. It shone. "That's walnut. Nice . . . forty-four rimfire."

Hoke handed the gun to Jacob, who pulled it up toward his shoulder, taking aim on a lone buffalo standing to the side of the herd.

"If you hold it there it's going to break your collarbone," Hoke told him. "Move it over. That's it. And your dominant eye is your left one since you use your left hand, so close your right eye. Pick a spot and close each eye to get a feel for it. See how your barrel moves, depending on which eye is closed? I always keep both eyes open, but you want to take aim with your eye on the same side as your hand on the trigger."

"So I'll always follow my left eye?"

"If that's the hand you got on the trigger. And by the way, don't ever let anybody try to make you do things with your right hand if the left one is what feels natural. Some tools are tricky—like scissors. I got me a pair of left-handed scissors in my wagon if you ever want to use 'em."

Jacob grinned. "I noticed you wore your pistol on your left leg."

Hoke winked at him. "Now look at your target and imagine it's the face of a clock. You want to put the front sight in the rear notch and lay it on six o'clock at the bottom of your clock face. Most people shoot too high. They sight in on the middle of the target. But you'll do better to aim at the base of it. It's natural to raise the barrel as you squeeze the trigger."

"Should I get off my horse?" Jacob was on the dun.

The kid didn't act nervous at all, thought Hoke. Charlie was more cautious. Jacob was fearless—which could be both good and bad.

"It's always served me well to know how to shoot sittin' on mine. If you can hit the target from your horse, you can usually hit it standing on the ground. Doesn't always work the other way. But try to keep the reins in your hand 'cause if your horse isn't used to it, he'll pitch."

Charlie, Cooper, Clyde, Alec Douglas, even Mr. Austelle were all paying close attention to Hoke's words. Cooper and Clyde both gripped their horses' reins a little tighter as he spoke.

"Where's the best place to hit it?" Jacob was concentrating hard.

"Heart or head. Head's better if you can get past the bone structure. A buffalo has a hard head. If you can lay it in one of his eyes or ears it'll go straight to the brain."

Hoke expected Jacob to take a while getting a feel for the gun, but as soon as the boy lined up that bull's massive head on six o'clock in his sight, he pulled the trigger and flipped feet first over the butt of the gray dun, his father's rifle falling to the ground beside him.

Hoke had been kicked plenty himself by both guns and animals and knew every boy had to learn it. He was trying not to laugh at Jacob lying on the ground, scrambling out from under the hooves of his horse—which was also too big for him—when he heard the angry buffalo snort.

Hoke's head whipped around to the buffalo. The kid had nicked him after all, and it made the hairy beast mad.

The dun landed a kick to Jacob's shoulder just as the buffalo charged. Hoke went cold in an instant. The charging bull spooked the rest of the herd and they started to run, too, but by the grace of God, in the opposite direction.

Hoke clamped his legs tight around the stallion, the Winchester out of his holster, in his hands and thrown to his shoulder—*shoot, work the lever, shoot, work the lever, shoot*—but the buffalo was already down. He looked over at Charlie, who stood with the smoking Henry in his hands. Charlie had jumped down from the gelding, scooped up the fallen rifle, and fired the killing shot.

Mr. Austelle had only just gotten his rifle lifted, it all happened so fast.

Hoke looked at Charlie. "Nice work."

Charlie reached for Jacob. "You all right, Jake?"

Jacob looked like he wanted to cry. He eyed the Austelle boys and felt his shoulder. "I think it's broke."

"Here, let's see." Hoke dismounted and felt Jacob's shoulder. "It's popped out. Look yonder at that buffalo and tell me if his eyes are open or not."

As soon as Jacob squinted toward the buffalo, Hoke gave his shoulder a crack and it popped neatly into place.

Jacob yelled.

"How's that feel?" asked Hoke.

Jacob rolled it gingerly. "Sore, but not broke, I guess."

"Blimey! You're good as Doc Isaacs," said Alec Douglas.

"And fast with a gun," said Mr. Austelle.

"Helps if you want to stay alive. And I've popped a few shoulders back in place, includin' my own." He'd popped more than one man's out, too.

Hoke squeezed Jacob's arm at the elbow. "You'll have a nice-size bruise, and it tore the skin a little there." He nodded. "Good job. Shot you a buffalo and took a solid horse kick. Quite a day."

The boy was quiet while they inspected the downed buffalo and field-dressed it, pulling the choice meats out to take back to the wagon train. Then he spoke up suddenly. "Can we keep the hide?"

"Sure," said Hoke. Buffalo hides were heavy, but Jacob was light. They could throw it on his horse. "I'll show you how to tan it when we get it back to camp. We'll make you some more moccasins since those you have are wearing through."

The buffalo was so massive they had to cut it into smaller sections to turn it over. Hoke had the group pile up what was left of the carcass and burn it.

The Austelle boys thought that was silly. "Why take the time to burn it?" asked Cooper.

"It's more respectful. Too many men kill these animals for their hides only, skinning them and leaving them to rot into the landscape.

Indians, on the other hand, use every part of the animal. Think of it as a sweet gift of incense back to God, if you want to. Always clean up after yourself. Leave a spot as good as or better than you found it."

⁓

Abigail and Melinda were by Audrey Beckett's side when Doc Isaacs delivered a skinny red baby. All three women were crying.

"You did good, Doc." Melinda dabbed at her eyes. "How many babies have you helped with?"

"This is my eighth."

"You must think we're silly, crying," said Abigail.

Doc smiled at her. "I don't think you're silly. Crying does a body good sometimes."

Audrey said weakly, "Sam asked could we name the baby 'Nebraska' no matter if it was a boy or a girl." They had arrived in Nebraska Territory a week ago. "He predicted the baby would come here. Evelyn Nebraska Beckett. My mother's name was Evelyn."

They had just gotten little Evelyn washed up and put back in her mother's arms when Alec Douglas ran up to the wagon. "Where's Mrs. Abigail? One o' her boys has been hurt."

His words tore through the canvas and Abigail nearly tripped scrambling out.

"Your youngest is a'right, but he's had a scare. He shot at a buffalo and the rifle knocked him off his horse. Horse kicked him, then it looked like the buffalo was going to charge. Hoke and Charlie took it down, tho'."

Alec had run ahead with the news.

Abigail could see the party coming back, great slabs of bloody meat hanging on the sides of some of the horses behind the riders. Jacob wasn't on his horse. He was riding behind Charlie, his arms wrapped tightly about his brother, his face buried in his back.

Hoke intercepted Abigail before she could get to her sons. "Easy now. He's already embarrassed," he whispered.

Her temper flared. "Why do you keep bringing my children back to me sick or wounded? I shouldn't have let him go. He's just a boy."

"But you're raisin' a man!" he snapped. "And there were more lessons to be had in going."

How dare he tell her how to parent? He didn't have children!

But Abigail held her tongue, knowing there was truth in what he said. With Hoke's words ringing in her ears, she looked at her son. "Are you hurt, Jacob?"

"I'm fine," he muttered, sliding off the horse then jumping back to avoid getting kicked. He was holding his right arm.

"Is it bleeding?"

"A little."

"Better come back to the wagon and let me clean it then," she said matter-of-factly. "Doc Isaacs may need to stitch it."

❧

After he'd gotten the meat prepared for cooking and things cleaned up, Hoke peeped through the canvas cover in the back of her wagon. Jacob was curled up in her lap. She hummed softly as she rocked him and stroked his hair.

How Hoke had longed for a mother's comfort at Jacob's age . . . how he longed for it still.

Corrine came up behind him. "How 'bout you and me get supper started?" he suggested, his voice thick.

"Why?"

"Because your mother's helped deliver a baby and your brothers have been killing buffalo, that's why."

"Fine."

In a little bit, Prissy Schroeder came bounding around the corner. "I heard your little brother got himself kicked by a horse."

"You say one word to him about it, Prissy, and I'll lay you out," said Corrine.

Defeated, Prissy slunk off.

Hoke looked at Corrine admiringly.

"What?" she asked.

"Nothin'."

A few minutes later, after Hoke had got the meat cooking and was ready to go draw some water, he said through the back wagon flap, "Jacob, you need to come help clean these guns and knives we used today."

Jacob looked up at his mother. "It's all right, Ma. I'm all right." Just before he climbed down from her lap, he added, "Thanks," and gave her a kiss.

Her hand went to the spot and lingered.

As he and Jacob walked away, Hoke said low to Corrine, "Let me know if you want any pointers on how to lay Prissy out."

He saw the corners of Corrine's lips curl up as he walked away.

CHAPTER 16

Just before sunrise

The skies wouldn't rain. The sun beat mercilessly as Colonel Dotson's wagon train crossed the plains of Nebraska and water began to run in short supply. When they finally rolled into Fort Kearney, they were a tired, haggard group, buoyed only by the eternal optimism of Gerald and Josephine Jenkins.

May 29, 1866

Fort Kearney was built solely as protection for those trav-
eling the Oregon Trail and yet it is a disappointment.
The farther we get from civilization, the less civilized
are the people in the settlements. Several of the soldiers at
Fort Kearney are Confederates who were taken prisoner
and forced to come west. It makes for a sour mood that
permeates the camp.

Colonel Dotson gathered the company leaders. "Tell your folks to go ahead and do any trading they need to do tonight. Let's get an early start in the morning. This place doesn't bode well with me."

They were camped just outside the fort walls, where they should have felt safer than usual. But deep in the night Abigail woke to the muffled sounds of angry talk. The colonel's voice ripped clearly through the night. "You will not whip these men!"

"What's going on?" whispered Corrine.

"I can't tell, but I'll find out. Stay here." Abigail threw a shawl over her shoulders and crawled out of the back of the wagon, thankful Lina was still asleep.

Charlie and Jacob were in their bedrolls propped on elbows listening and straining to see something in the distance. Rascal's head popped up between them.

"Colonel's over there at the fort with Mr. Jenkins and several others," Charlie said low to Abigail.

She peered at the empty wagon nearby. "Where are Mr. Hoke and Mr. Parker?"

"With the livestock. They're on guard duty."

Sam Beckett walked by in the night.

"What's happened, Mr. Beckett?"

He stepped over to the Baldwyn wagons. "The officers have Michael Chessor and Harry Sims. They want to punish them."

"What for?"

"Couple of drunk soldiers crawled into the McConnelly wagon. Beat up the old man and attacked the ladies."

"What do you mean, attacked them?"

"I mean they had evil intentions." Mr. Beckett looked down at Jacob and Charlie. "But Sims and Chessor intervened before it was too late. Now the officers are mad because their men got soundly whipped."

"Do they need someone to see to their needs?"

"Mr. Austelle might know." Abigail could see Charles Austelle emerging from the darkness.

"Do the McConnelly girls have someone with them, Mr. Austelle?"

"Mrs. Chris and Mrs. Jo are with them, and a couple of the Schroeder women. They're fine. Shook up and mad, but fine."

"Is Mr. McConnelly hurt?"

"He's got a hard knock on the head. Doc Isaacs is with him."

They heard running feet. Hoke burst around the corner of Abigail's wagon, his eyes blazing. Rascal stood up and wagged his tail. When Hoke's eyes found Abigail in the moonlight, his face relaxed.

"James and I were with the stock and just heard. Is everybody else safe?" he asked Mr. Austelle. Before Mr. Austelle could answer, he turned to Abigail. "You're safe?"

Abigail nodded. "It was just the McConnelly wagon, as far as I know."

"That's right," confirmed Mr. Austelle. "I don't think we'll have any more trouble out of anyone—not after the way Chessor and Sims beat those soldiers."

"So they have the men who did it?"

"Yes. Both of them."

"Has the colonel put extra men on watch for the rest of the night?"

"He has. I'll be watching Company C since you and Parker are with the stock."

"Good. Thank you. What are they doing to the soldiers who caused the trouble?"

"They're in the infirmary."

"Good. They need to be court-martialed."

Abigail wondered: Did Hoke feel that way because it was the McConnelly women? Did he really have a fondness for Irene? He was so hard to read. Irene certainly lit up if Hoke ever spoke to her. Would he go there next and check on them?

Should she go check on them? It was upsetting to think one of the wagons had been set upon. What if Charlie and Jacob had been knocked on the head while she and the girls were attacked? A shiver ran between her shoulder blades in spite of the shawl she'd wrapped around herself.

Hoke looked to Charles Austelle. "I'll go back to the stock, but you'll let me know if there's any more trouble, won't you?"

Mr. Austelle nodded.

"You, too, gentlemen?" Hoke peered under the wagon at Charlie and Jacob, who were still on their elbows listening.

"Yes, sir," they answered.

"Maybe you boys should come inside the wagon the rest of the night," said Abigail.

"Mother, we'll be fine out here," insisted Charlie.

"Yeah, Ma. Mr. Hoke just called us gentlemen."

"You stay with 'em, Rascal," commanded Hoke. He nodded at Abigail. "Evenin'."

As Abigail reached up to climb back in the wagon she heard Jacob ask Charlie, "You hear about that body Harry Sims found yesterday?"

"Yeah, said it looked like his throat was cut."

Abigail stopped. "What are you boys talking about?"

"Harry and Tam's group found a man's body when they were out hunting."

"Yeah. Harry said he would have brought the man's boots back to Nichodemus Jasper—you know how poor they are—but both of 'em had big holes in the toes."

"What is it, Ma?" asked Charlie. "Jacob, why'd you mention that where she could hear? Now she's going to make us sleep up in the wagon for sure."

"No." Abigail slowly shook her head, trying to absorb this news. Could it have been Cecil Ryman that Harry's group found? How many men wore boots with holes in both toes? "You can stay as long as Rascal is with you."

Abigail lay awake the rest of the night. Then in the morning, just after the Schroeders' roosters crowed—as they were preparing to leave and Colonel Dotson was letting the captain in charge know he'd be reporting the previous night's incident at the next post—Sue Vandergelden's scream rent the air.

Feet from all over camp went running in her direction. They found her standing over her son's limp body, his bedroll thrown open revealing a small snake curled in the bottom.

It came out that Sue had allowed Ned to sleep under the Vandergeldens' wagon with the youngest Sutler boy, Reuben. When Reuben couldn't wake Ned the next morning, he'd called for Sue.

John Sutler dragged the snake away from Ned's body with a hoe and chopped its head off with a whack. Abigail turned away, nauseated by the morning's turn of events. Doc Isaacs arrived, laying a hand on her shoulder. He bent over Ned's body to check for a pulse, but everyone could see the boy no longer had one.

"Snakes won't usually crawl into a bedroll if someone's in it," said Rudy Schroeder.

"We left our bedrolls." Reuben's voice was laced with fear. "To see what was happening last night."

"It must have crawled in there while he was gone. Bit him when he laid back down." This was from Ty, Ned's father. Hardly anyone had ever heard Ty speak before. Sue did most of the talking for the Vandergeldens.

John Sutler put his hand on Ty's shoulder. "A baby rattler's bite don't feel like much more than a bee sting, but its poison is strong."

Doc Isaacs raised Ned's pants leg and inspected the bite mark on his ankle.

Sue pointed at the dead snake. "That's a rattlesnake?"

"It can't be," Rudy Schroeder said. "It don't have rattles."

Doc Isaacs stood back up. "It's a young one. The rattles haven't come in yet. A young rattlesnake can't control how much venom he injects."

Sue glared at Doc.

A Fort Kearney officer came over to investigate. "Snakes have been an ongoing problem here," he said, shaking his head.

Dotson grabbed him by the neck of his uniform. "Why didn't you say something about that when we arrived?" No one in the group had ever seen the colonel so mad.

The officer tried to back out of the colonel's hold, looking sheepishly around at the crowd of onlookers.

"First the incident with the McConnellys and now this!" The colonel released the man, then threw down an empty tin coffee cup he had been holding. "This is the sorriest group of military men I have ever encountered, and I hold you personally responsible for this boy's death! If we had known there were snakes, we would have had our children in the wagons last night."

Distrusting the sudden weakness of her legs, Abigail looked for a place to sit down. It had been one of the strangest nights she'd ever known. What if one of her boys had been bitten? And what kind of men would they find at Fort Hall?

Every bedroll was checked, but no other snakes were found.

When Colonel Dotson asked Sue what she wanted to do about burying Ned, she became hysterical. "Bury him? What do you mean, bury him? We aren't going to bury him!" Then when John Sutler went to lift the body she screamed, "Don't touch him! Don't you touch my baby!"

It took two hours to get Sue Vandergelden calmed down enough to get Ned's body moved.

Abigail tried to close her ears to Sue's distraught cries. All she could think about was how meanly she had thought of Sue Vandergelden . . . and Ned was her only child.

She located each of her children with her eyes. Charlie and Corrine were talking with Emma and Clyde Austelle by the Baldwyns' front wagon. Everyone not helping with the Vandergeldens was waiting for Colonel Dotson's rollout call. She, Jacob, and Lina were waiting by the back wagon. She looked down at the top of Jacob's unruly hair.

"Jacob, promise me you'll never pick up a baby snake again."

"I wouldn't if it was poisonous."

"Promise me! Not any."

"Yes, ma'am."

Ty said he didn't want to bury Ned at the fort that had been the cause of so much unhappiness. They decided to travel on for a day and then bury Ned. Ty didn't know if he and Sue would continue with the train after that or turn back.

They traveled fourteen miles along the banks of the South Platte River, never stopping for lunch. There had only been two good things about reaching Fort Kearney—replenishing their food stores and reaching the Platte that ran north of it.

Harry gave a moving funeral service.

"Lord, we come to You with hearts broken over this tragedy. We cannot presume to understand, so help us hold fast to each other and to You as we press on in our journey. Receive the soul of Ned Vandergelden, tender and beloved to his parents, into Your paradise and reunite us again someday."

Supper was eaten with heavy hearts.

"Those McConnelly girls may not talk to any of us the rest of the trip," said Melinda as she and Abigail worked on supper. "I tried to go over there and say I was sorry about what happened to 'em, but they went in their wagon when they saw me coming."

"I had a similar experience," Abigail said. Irene had been quite blatant about it—she'd looked Abigail in the eye and just when Abigail had smiled and opened her mouth to speak, Irene had turned her back and walked the other way.

The men dug a small grave on the river's edge and buried Ned there. Children from all the companies laid flowers on the grave. Josephine gathered the children afterward to sing Ned's favorite song. None of the children ran and played that evening; they went to bed early instead. Most people, men included, slept that night in the wagons. A few braved the ground, rolling out and double-checking their beds several times before climbing in. Some laid ropes around because they'd heard a snake wouldn't cross one, but then they jumped at the sight of the ropes, forgetting they had laid them there.

Abigail didn't even have to ask her boys to stay in the wagons that night; they did it without being asked, bringing Rascal up to sleep between them. Many of the children had dogs that slept nearby, but there had been no pets near Reuben and Ned the previous night.

Marnie Sutler, bad as she felt about Ned, got on her knees that night and thanked God it wasn't Reuben they'd buried by the river that evening. Several mothers cried into their pillows thinking how quickly and unexpectedly one of their own could be taken. Audrey Beckett cried the hardest, holding newborn Evelyn and begging God to let her live to adulthood.

∽

Early the next morning, just before sunrise, everyone was awakened by the sound of gunshots—two shots from close by—within the camp.

Some thought soldiers had snuck back to cause trouble, but the shots came from the Vandergelden wagon.

The first rays of daylight revealed a gruesome scene—Sue Vandergelden had first shot her husband in the head, then herself with Ty's .36 caliber Colt Navy pistol. A blood-spattered note was on the pillow beside Ty, where he never woke from a fitful night of sleep.

Bury us by our boy. Give our things to the Jaspers.

Sue lay stretched across the lower half of Ty's body, a rare smile on her face, the gun on the ground near where she'd fallen, a near-empty bottle of Arkansas mash whiskey on the floor.

CHAPTER 17

Dying in these buckskins

The train arrived at Ash Hollow at midday.

Ash Hollow was the steepest elevation drop on the route. It was slow, backbreaking work to get down it. As he worked with James and several of the other men to ease another wagon down the incline, using ropes and pulleys, Hoke wondered if he'd made the right decision coming on this trip. He was anxious to get past the sameness of the plains and see the upper half of the Rockies. They should reach Fort Laramie in another month. South Pass—the entrance to the Rockies—was two weeks the other side of Laramie.

It was mid-June and growing hotter by the day. Sweat poured down his aching back as he dug his heels into the earth and eased on the rope that was threatening to cut through the leather piece wrapped around his hands. James had a sharp welt on his forearm where his rope had slipped and cut it.

As Hoke held his own rope, he let his mind wander. It wandered mostly toward Abigail Baldwyn. They were two months into this trip and his feelings for her had only increased. Worse, now he was attached to her kids. And the dog—that pup was growing paws the size of his horse's hooves!

Charlie especially had captured Hoke's heart. What a hardworking kid, so like his mother in his mannerisms, never complaining about anything, just quietly taking it all in. Charlie stood at the foot of the hill now with Colonel Dotson and Jenkins, helping ease the wagons down and unhitch the ropes. Rascal was trotting back and forth between Hoke at the top of the hill and Charlie at the bottom, supervising the process and nipping at the heels of the mules and oxen when they needed encouragement. Charlie was good to the younger children and respectful to the older women like Mrs. Inez Schroeder. He had jumped right in to help when Timmy Peters drowned.

And that Jacob . . . Jacob was fun to watch. He was all boy, darker haired than his siblings and mischievous by nature. Jacob tried hard to keep up with Charlie, obviously doting on his big brother, as any boy would—but even more so due to the absence of his father. But Jacob didn't have Charlie's calm spirit or levelheadedness. Hoke had gotten so tickled when Jacob took a bead on that buffalo, only to be knocked backward by the kick of a rifle too big for him to handle.

He and Jacob had almost finished tanning the large hide. When they'd ridden back to camp after skinning the buffalo, with Jacob all quiet and humble, Abigail had looked like she'd wanted to tan Hoke's hide—like he'd let her down. He'd felt her disappointment keenly. Then there had been the ugly business at Kearney.

When the Dotsons and Jenkinses cleaned the Vandergelden wagon before giving it to the Jaspers, they found several items hidden near the boy's clothes—Abigail's missing gold coins, a silver bowl and spoon belonging to the Schroeders, Tam's telescope, and several other things. Evidently the boy had slipped around taking whatever appealed to him. He was the last one on the wagon train anyone would have suspected.

Five days ago, Hoke had finally approached Abigail . . .

⁓

She was sewing in her rocker in her usual place near the fire, seated across and well back from the singing and the chatter happening on the other side.

"Can you see well enough for that?"

Abigail didn't seem to realize he was talking to her until he sat down on the ground beside her chair. They hadn't had a good conversation in days. He would build the fire in the mornings, and she'd get her crate of supplies. As she was cleaning up after breakfast, he'd have water waiting for her. If she turned her back, he'd scoop the crate up and put it back in her wagon. In the afternoons he'd have another bucket waiting for her—for her feet. He still watered her plants. They were growing. He'd even nailed another piece of wood to the bottom of each box, as they were starting to get soft in spots. But he and Abigail weren't talking other than her occasional "thanks" and his "don't mind at all."

She looked at him briefly, then continued to sew. "Yes, I can see."

He loved watching her hands by the light of the flickering fire as she deftly worked the needle in and out of the fabric. The needle moved so fast! He didn't see how she kept from sending it through her own fingers.

"What's that you're working on?"

"One of Orin Peters's shirts. It needed mending."

"What are you, Orin's mother?" It annoyed Hoke that Peters hovered around her. It was obvious the kid was sweet on her and that stuck in Hoke's craw.

Abigail shot him an irritated look. "I'm happy to mend shirts for anyone who needs it and doesn't have another woman to ask. I even mended some socks for Mr. Parker a couple of days ago. Do you need anything mended, Mr. Hoke, or does Ingrid Schroeder do your mending along with your haircuts?"

"My hair *is* getting a little long again." He ran a hand through the dark tangled mop on his head, relishing the thought that she might be jealous.

"She's right over there." Abigail nodded toward the Schroeders' wagons, tied a knot, cut the thread, laid Orin's shirt to the side, and picked up her next project—what looked like the yoke of a dress for Lina.

He scowled. "Why are you always goadin' me?"

"I'm not goading you."

"Yes, you are. Look, I'm sorry about Jacob. If you're still mad at me for that, just say so."

"I'm not mad at you for that. You didn't cause it. It scared me is all. My children mean everything to me. We've lost Timmy Peters and the whole Vandergelden family. The McConnelly girls were assaulted and poor Mr. McConnelly hurt. It's very sobering. I sometimes feel heavy with the decisions I'm making, Mr. Hoke. I lost my home and brought my children out here, and for what? The first military post we encounter is . . ."

He watched her fold the material she was working on, back and forth like she was making a fan. She lost her place and started refolding. But then she lost her place again.

She turned to him. "I don't have anyone to ask whether I'm making a mistake or not. I don't have a shoulder to cry on. At least I had Mimi for the past several years. Now, I've left her back in Tennessee. A woman needs some reassurance and someone to halve the burden with. I don't know if you can appreciate that, but why should you? It's not your concern." She folded the pleats again.

Maybe he wanted it to be his concern.

Hoke leaned back and looked up at the stars, tracing the shapes of familiar constellations with his eyes.

She hadn't told him anything he didn't already know. As pleasant as she was with most everyone and as little as she ever complained, he sensed her heart was often heavy and had been heavier of late. It made sense that the Vandergelden tragedy, particularly, would weigh on her, or that she might have fears for herself and her girls where rough, god-less men were concerned. Those incidents had hit all the women hard. He just hated to think he had added to her load with Jacob and the bison because that would mean he'd been part of the cause of what weighed on her.

Hoke wasn't the reason anxiety was gripping Abigail's heart. Every mile that brought them closer to Robert was a mile that brought them closer to their future, but . . . what kind of future would it be? Would Robert be angry she had brought the children? Would he be as altered as his letters seemed to indicate?

It had taken her over a week to pick her pen back up to write to Mimi.

June 12, 1866

> *Forgive me for not writing for several days. We had quite*
> *a tragedy and lost an entire family. I am ashamed to say*
> *I had judged the woman harshly.*
>> *But . . . as awful as her actions were, I understood*
> *her not wanting to leave her son behind on a river bank.*

Abigail had confided her growing anxieties about reuniting with Robert only to Melinda and Christine Dotson, but even with them she was guarded. And she had never mentioned her conversation with Cecil Ryman to anyone. She didn't like placing her burdens on others' shoulders. Every woman out here had her own set of fears and worries. Every woman out here had a hope-filled, but unclear, future.

Josephine Jenkins had taken the Vandergeldens' death particularly hard. She felt she had contributed by drawing Ned out to come to the dance. Christine blamed herself for not realizing how distraught Sue really had been after his death. The colonel knew Sue had a drinking problem. Should he have kept a better watch on her or taken the liquor out of her wagon when Ned died? It was a question that would haunt the Dotsons for the remainder of the trip. The colonel's tolerance for drinking had dipped to an all-time low, which had already led to words between him and Rudy Schroeder.

"Tell me about Mimi," said Hoke, interrupting her thoughts.

Abigail shook her head. "I'm not sure I can talk about her without getting emotional."

"Is that who you write letters to?"

Abigail nodded.

"She can read?"

"She can. I taught Mimi everything I learned—she can even play the piano. I got in a lot of trouble for it." She smiled, remembering. "But it was worth it."

"You can play the piano?"

Abigail smiled again. "A little. We had a box Chickering when I was growing up, and I tried to teach the children whenever we went home to Franklin, but we never had one in Marston, so I've grown rusty. While we're on the subject of musical talents: I like to hear you sing on Sundays. You have a nice voice."

There was something about his voice . . . something deep like the center of the earth, that felt as calming as solid ground, yet stirring as a quake.

"When me and James are out on the trail it gets lonesome. Singing is a way to pass the evenings."

"No chance of being lonesome in this group." She looked across the camp. This was her favorite time of day. She loved sitting here in her usual spot after supper, set back from the fire, watching everyone . . . keeping all four children in her sights.

Right now, Lina was sitting in Christine's lap listening to Josephine practice songs with the younger children. They all adored her. Katrina Schroeder and Faramond's wife, Molly, held Katrina's twins. Little Hannah and Deena Sutler were there, too.

The Kensington sisters and Mrs. Inez sat in their own group tatting and talking about quilt patterns.

Marnie Sutler had a sleeping Reuben in her arms and was walking him back to the wagon. Baird Douglas lay with his head on a sheep while Alec tuned his fiddle. Paddy was nearby trying to show the McConnelly sisters Carson's latest trick. They looked bored with him.

Ingrid Schroeder was talking to her sister, Jocelyn, but looking over at Hoke from time to time. Ingrid often watched him in the evenings as he moved around the campfire. Abigail was keenly aware of Hoke's movements, too, but hoped she was less obvious about it than young Ingrid Schroeder.

Harry, Tam, and James laughed over some clever thing that one of them had said.

Nichodemus and Nora Jasper were walking around the wagon circle, arms linked.

Charlie, the older Sutler boys, Clyde, Emma, and Corrine had their heads together, talking, and Jacob played near them with Cooper and Lijah.

Abigail felt like she knew each family better from quietly watching them as she sewed each evening. Hoke was the hardest one to keep track of. He was always busy—always moving—twisting a rope, nailing a board, pounding a piece of iron, cleaning a gun, rubbing down a horse, or shooting a bottle of grease down somebody's ox's throat to get its bowels moving again.

It was nice to see him stop and sit down for once. It was nice to have him sitting next to her. It felt lonely to sit here by herself and watch Harry and Tam talking and Nora and Nichodemus walking, and to listen to Mr. Austelle and Melinda visiting with the Becketts.

∽

"No, there is no chance of being lonesome here," said Hoke. But he didn't really mean it.

Truth was, being in a group like this and having no one to call his own was lonelier than being by himself on the trail.

Hoke looked around the camp.

Michael Chessor and Duncan Schroeder were on guard duty, which was good.

Colonel Dotson, Jenkins, Tim Peters, and Mr. McConnelly—the latter still bruised and pistol-whipped—stood in a clump talking about the route and the next good water hole.

Jacob and a couple of other boys had sticks for guns and were sneaking up on targets. The Becketts' wagon wheel must have been a skittish deer, because they were crouched low now, moving forward on their forearms, inching in for the kill.

Beckett's head was out of a book for once as he and his wife talked to the Austelles.

Rudy and Faramond Schroeder had their older boys helping with the chickens. Sometimes at night the Schroeders put up a crude yard and let the hens wander and peck. The men were up fetching the hens out of the wagon, handing them down to the boys. Several dogs, including Rascal, watched nearby, hoping one would get away.

"Rascal!" called Hoke. "Come here." Rascal looked at the chickens one last time, his mouth dripping with saliva, then came as commanded. Hoke rewarded him with a good head scratching.

"Sit down." Rascal sat next to him on the grass and put his head on his paws, his eyes darting back and forth between Hoke and the chickens several yards away.

"I don't know what you did to him to make him your dog," said Abigail.

"He's just smart, aren't you, boy?" Rascal sniffed up at Hoke, and Hoke laughed. "I guess he thinks I'm a dog. I probably smell like one."

Rascal licked his hand and Hoke massaged his ears absentmindedly. He felt better with animals than with people. Animals were simpler: just take care of them and they'll take care of you. Wasn't he forever telling James that?

Abigail smiled, running another stitch through the pleats she'd finally folded to suit her. She nodded toward the camp. "Is this more togetherness than you're used to?"

"Yes, it is. Always something to be done, sunup to sundown. It is a temptation just to ride off and leave it some days."

As soon as he said it he wished he could pull the words back. Wasn't that somewhere in Scripture? Something about things that couldn't be recalled? Spoken words, an arrow that's been shot, an opportunity missed.

Abigail's face darkened. "I guess that's the way Robert felt."

Hoke winced, cursing himself for his thoughtlessness. He hadn't even meant it; he was just trying to make a joke.

He had tried to peer inside her mind ever since he met her. He longed to know everything about her. She was hurt. That was apparent. And it would, of course, be hard for her to trust again. If her husband *was* at Fort Hall, they had some damage to repair.

Why had there been so few letters between Abigail and him on the Baldwyns' way out here? Couriers came past the train about once a week and dropped off and picked up mail. She sent regular letters to this Mimi, but . . . he didn't think she'd gotten many—if any—from her husband. Few things escaped Hoke's observation.

He had been convinced her husband didn't exist. How then to explain that one letter she'd mentioned? And what did Baldwyn's "You tracked me down" comment mean? Hoke had turned that one over and over in his head and couldn't make any sense of it.

"Of course, I gave the colonel my word. I signed on for this trip and I don't aim to let anybody down. I'm sorry if I let you down with Jacob."

She laid a hand on his shoulder, which caused him to look up into her eyes.

Her eyes were so blue . . . her hand so warm. She was a toucher—a hugger. He hated it when she touched anyone else, like Doc Isaacs or Orin Peters, but loved those rare moments when she put a hand on him. He wanted to take her in his arms. Tell her he'd take care of her. He wanted her to always look at him the way that she was looking at him now.

Abigail thought again how nice it was to have Hoke sitting next to her. He was real and alive and sitting right here—in the flesh—his sleeves rolled up, revealing his strong forearms.

Why *was* she always goading him? She didn't mean to.

"You didn't let me down. I shouldn't have snapped at you. I should have thanked you for bringing Jacob back safe and helping him make moccasins. I've also been meaning to thank you for nailing that extra wood on my boxes."

"Glad to do it."

She moved her hand off his shoulder and went back to her sewing.

"Say . . ."

She looked back down at him.

"Could you make me a shirt?"

Hoke's shirts were heavy and it had grown hot. Why hadn't she thought to offer? No wonder his sleeves had stayed rolled up lately. "I'd be happy to! Would you like something lighter weight?"

"Yes. I'm dying in these buckskins. Didn't realize it got so hot up here in the north."

"Stand up. I'll measure you. Wait, I need a pencil and my tape." She set down her needlework and went to her wagon.

Hoke followed.

Rascal, released, went back to the chickens.

CHAPTER 18

Thick behind her wagon

Night hung thick behind her wagon, so Hoke lit an oil lamp and set it on the ground. He helped her climb down, the pencil and tape in her hands.

"Lift your arms out," she instructed.

Her fingers walked down his lifted arms as she measured from his shoulder to his wrist, first on one side, then the other.

She wrote *Hoke* (just *Hoke*, he couldn't help but notice) on the wood at the back of the wagon, then jotted letters and numbers below it.

Her hands wrapped the tape around his bicep, forearm, and then wrist as she stood to one side of him and measured the circumference of each.

It caught Hoke off guard when she reached around his broad chest and pulled the tape taut, measuring it at the widest point just under his armpits. He was still recovering from the brush of her breasts when she slid the tape down to his waist.

Damn!

Why hadn't he asked for a shirt before?

She lowered his arms and stepped behind him to measure his back from the neck to the top of his pants.

"How long do you like them?" she asked.

He took her hand and showed her halfway down his buttock. She pulled her hand away as if she'd been burned, turned to the wagon, and wrote down the measurement.

She turned back toward him, looking down at the ground. "You don't, by the way."

Her eyelashes were so long.

"I don't what?" Hoke could barely think straight with the nearness of her, the feel of her hands, those lashes . . .

"You don't smell like a dog."

She reached up.

Without thinking, he pulled her toward him. It was as if they were back at the dance at Alcove Springs. Only this time after laying her hand over his heart, he cradled the back of her head and pulled her lips toward his, his other hand sliding down to that familiar dip in her back so he could move her hips closer.

He hungered for every inch of her.

A faint memory in the back of his mind whispered that this was wrong, but he pushed the thought away. She was responding . . . her lips, soft as running water in a brook; her mouth startled at first, but now open and hungry as his own; her warm hands running down his chest, around his sides, up his arched back and down again.

The feel of her body pressed against his was more stirring than he had imagined, and he had imagined it plenty.

He heard something drop . . . the tape measure maybe . . . and then someone cleared his throat.

Abigail pulled back. Even in the dim lantern light Hoke could see her flush.

Orin Peters glowered at Hoke, then turned to Abigail. "I wondered if you had finished with my shirt. I didn't realize you were . . . busy."

Abigail touched her lips before answering. "I did finish it, Orin. I laid it down . . . somewhere."

Hoke turned to leave, but Abigail caught his arm.

"I need your neck size."

Oh. Was that why she had reached up to him? Not because she wanted him? But only to measure his neck?

Hoke stood rock still, staring a hole through Orin while Abigail reached up again and measured his neck with hands that faintly shook.

Orin couldn't hold his gaze.

Abigail avoided his eyes, too. "I should have this finished in a couple of days."

"Thanks."

Hoke left, cursing Orin Peters and his own lack of self-control.

❧

"I think I laid your shirt by the rocking chair, Orin." Abigail moved in that direction.

Orin caught her sleeve. "I won't tell if you'll give me one."

Fear, embarrassment, and anger all rose like bile in Abigail's throat. "Give you one *what*?"

"Give me a kiss, like you were giving him."

The memory of another man demanding a kiss from her as a form of blackmail came rushing back to her.

Abigail slapped him, the smack of it reverberating all the way back to her confused and pulsing heart.

"Don't ask me to mend any more shirts for you, Orin Peters."

She picked up the lantern and left him standing there.

❧

That had been three days before they reached Ash Hollow. Hoke was wearing his new shirt now as he eased another wagon down the steep descent. It was gold, like the gold that rimmed his eyes, the color of the grass on the prairie. Best shirt he'd ever had. Hadn't taken her long to make it, either.

Three days had passed since the kiss. They hadn't spoken of it.

He had found the shirt folded on a table by his wagon the night before. A perfect fit. When he buttoned it up this morning he'd remembered the feel of her hands pulling the tape across the broadest part of his chest. When he tucked the shirt in, he thought about her measuring from his neck to the middle of his backside.

The shirt now stuck to his back with sweat as he held the rope to help lower the final wagon. They had been lucky to get everyone down the hill without any runaways, but the effort had come at a physical price. Some other travelers lowered their wagons with the help of logs, but logs could start to roll. Banged-up wagons were littered all over the hill as testimony to the dangers of this method. Manpower was the best approach, if you had manpower to do it, but Lord amighty! He'd feel it tomorrow.

He was feeling it now.

"I'll be right down," said James when they finished with the last wagon. "I see me a hunk of log over there I want." He picked up an ax and set off after it.

"What do you need a hunk of log for?"

"I want to make something out of it."

Hoke walked to the back of their wagon and peeled the gold shirt off, splashing water over his chest and wetting a bandana to tie around his neck. He heard a sharp intake of breath as Abigail came around the corner.

When he turned, she averted her glance and held out a fresh shirt.

"I made you another one. I hope you like green." Her words came out fast. "I had time to sew it on the lockstitch machine while we were waiting at the bottom of the hill. Give me that one and I'll wash it for you."

He exchanged shirts with her, amused that she wouldn't look at him, tempted to take her in his arms again, sweat or no sweat, but it was daylight still.

First there had been the awkwardness over Jacob, and now there was a new awkwardness between them since she'd measured him for the shirt.

It was his fault.

He was embarrassed to have let his instincts get the best of him, but the embarrassment was trumped by his desire for her. Try as he might, he could not get the sight of her, the smell of her, and now the taste and feel of her, out of his head.

"If I had a wife I'd ask her for a back rub." Hoke watched her eyes, feeling only marginal guilt at her obvious discomfort.

She refused to look at him. "There's always Ingrid. Or Irene McConnelly. Harry Sims could perform the ceremony after supper."

Leaning against the back of his wagon, feeling worn out from the day's hard work, he buttoned up the green shirt.

"Ingrid's just a kid." And Irene McConnelly was poison. She'd give a man a back rub, all right, and land him in hot water. Hoke had gotten educated on her kind twenty years ago. In fact, Hoke would have bet money that Irene's flirting was what landed Harry Sims and Michael Chessor in trouble with the soldiers at Kearney. Irene had fluttered around Doc Isaacs until she learned he didn't have any money. Then she'd lost interest . . . fast.

But maybe Hoke wasn't much better himself, because now he had put a married woman in an awkward spot.

"Here." Abigail handed him another shirt. "I made this one for James. I guessed his measurements based on yours—longer in the sleeves and a little smaller in the waist. Tell him to let me know if it doesn't fit and I'll make adjustments. Is that one going to work for you?"

Hoke inspected the sleeves.

She was talking fast again, refusing to let her eyes land on him for long. "I made it a little looser in the shoulders so you could move your arms more freely, and I thought—I thought you might like green."

"It's perfect. Thanks. And James will appreciate his. Can we pay you?"

Why wouldn't she look at him? He had his shirt buttoned now.

"After all the two of you have done for us?" She turned to leave.

"Listen, Abigail."

She stopped, her back to him.

Hoke breathed deep, not used to making apologies. "I'm sorry if I . . . misread things the other night."

She, too, breathed deep, and tilted her head to the side, but didn't turn around. "I'm a married woman, Mr. Mathews. I don't want to give you the wrong impression. It's just been a long time since . . ."

He stepped toward her but she bolted.

"James has a nasty cut on his arm," Hoke called after her. "If you see the doc, will you send him over?"

If Orin Peters wasn't hovering around her, Doc Isaacs was.

June 15, 1866

Corrine has learnt to make butter by hanging a tightly lidded jar under the back of the wagon each morning, half filled with cream from the cow's milk. The jar shakes back and forth all day and by evening, we have butter.

Abigail laid her pen down. She didn't want to talk to Mimi about butter; she wanted to talk to Mimi about her feelings for Hoke.

If Mimi were here she would know what had happened just by looking at her. Abigail could hear her now. *Lord, Miz Abigail, I can't believe you gone and kissed another man while traveling out to Mr. Robert!*

Abigail had known Hoke had strong arms and shoulders, but until she measured him for the shirt, she hadn't realized just what a well-built man he was. Robert had only been a boy when they married.

Hoke was no boy.

The only thing to do was stay busy. If she kept busy she might think about Hoke less. And busyness might keep her from running to Harry Sims and confessing everything, as if telling a preacher could absolve her of her sin.

Her two wagons had been among the first lowered down that day. It was rare for her to have time to use the lockstitch machine in the daylight. The train only stopped on Sundays, and Sundays were supposed to be a day of rest, although she cheated and washed the laundry.

So Abigail had stayed busy by sewing. And look where it had led her . . . right back to Hoke's wagon and Hoke with his shirt off! She had actually started to tell him she'd thought green would look good with the gold of his eyes.

Abigail was cloaked in self-reproach.

Thank God it had only been Orin who'd come around the corner. What if it had been one of her children?

If Orin told anyone, she could expose him for what he'd said to her, but the damage would still be done. She wondered how badly it would hurt Charlie, Corrine, Jacob, and Lina if Orin told them what he saw.

～◎～

The man known as Robert Baldwyn hadn't always been patient. But survival had demanded he develop it.

So he waited a month to send the letter, from the morning he met with the trapper. He remembered riding back up to the gate at Fort Hall later that day with an elk slung over his horse, meeting the same young sentry who'd been on guard duty when he left.

"See?" He had smiled widely with his lips, but knew none of it reached his eyes. "No harm done."

Leaving the elk with the cook, he had washed up. In addition to patience, he had learned to be meticulous. He polished the hilt of his sword and the buttons of his jacket, took a stiff brush and buffed his boots, then cleaned a speck off the name he'd had embroidered on his breast pocket.

Then he waited. Four weeks. It would be best if the letter didn't reach her until she arrived at Laramie.

As he touched the quill to his tongue now and prepared to dip it in the ink jar, he instinctively reached into the pocket of his jacket with his other hand for the picture of Abigail, then remembered he'd left it with the trapper.

It didn't matter. The beauty of her face would be forever seared in his mind. Shame, really, that she had to die.

Sweeping the remorse from his head, he wrote: *Welcome to the West, darling.*

When people found his letter to her after she was dead, he wanted it to look like he had been a dedicated husband.

CHAPTER 19
Wide fork of the Platte

Early on a Friday, the wagon train came to the wide fork of the Platte at a spot within sight of Chimney Rock. The colonel decided to take a couple of days to catch up on wagon repairs and wait to cross the river Monday.

"We'll need to take the wheels off for this one and float the wagons over. The Platte's got a swamp-like bottom."

He wanted two rafts built in case any of the wagons took on water, explaining, "Sometimes the workmen just slap the pitch on the wagon bottoms and they leak." If one started to sink, they'd tie the rafts to either side of it to get it safely over.

Reaching the fork of the river was cause for celebration. Friday afternoon some of the older children put together a picnic to eat on the riverbank. Abigail watched Charlie bring more wood to the fire.

"You're happy because Paul Sutler is going," said Charlie to Corrine as she worked on a meat pie, humming a tune. He didn't often tease his sisters, especially not sharp-tongued Corrine.

Corrine raised her brows. "And is Emma Austelle going?"

Charlie grinned. "Maybe."

Once Corrine had finished crimping the crust and slid her pie in the sheet-iron stove, she left with Lina to look for wildflowers.

Charlie turned to Abigail. "Ma, if a girl sits close to you on the wagon seat and seems like she's holding her hand out, would it be all right to hold it or should I ask first?" His face turned pink. "I feel funny asking you, but you *are* a girl. Or you were. I thought about asking Mr. Hoke. I knew he wouldn't tease me for it like Mr. Parker might, but . . . I don't know. It's hard to ask him about it somehow."

Abigail looked at Charlie, wondering what he would think of her if he knew she had kissed Hoke Mathews. She had tried to shake the memory of it—of Hoke's flaming eyes and the feel of his hand possessively moving her against him, then brushing over the curve of her body, of the hunger of his mouth and how he had tasted like the hickory sticks he always chewed. Hoke wouldn't hesitate to take a girl's hand if he wanted it.

"You need a haircut," whispered Abigail, pushing Charlie's bangs away from his eyes. She wanted a good look at him as he was right now, standing on the threshold of adulthood. "If she's holding her hand out there, don't be afraid to take it."

He grinned. "Weren't you my age when you married Pa? How did you know you loved him?"

Abigail shook her head. Had she loved him? Yes . . . she had. Did she still?

She wished she could remember the taste of Robert's kisses.

"I don't know, Charlie. He got in my head and my heart and I wanted to be around him every minute."

"Listen, you won't tell anyone I asked you about this, will you?"

"Of course not!" She leaned in and whispered, "But let me know how it goes."

Just then Lina and Corrine returned with the wildflowers. Almost as soon as Abigail had gotten them arranged, Prissy Schroeder ran up and asked if she could have some to make a necklace.

Abigail pulled out some Queen Anne's lace and violets and handed them to her.

After Prissy left, Corrine hissed, "Why are you always so nice to everybody? Lina just brought those to you. She didn't pick them for Prissy!"

"Corrine, it doesn't cost a thing to be kind. Don't you think people are more inclined to be nice to you if you're nice to them?"

Corrine frowned. "Not her."

Abigail longed to have heart-to-heart conversations with Corrine, but Corrine was Miss Independent about everything. She had started walking and talking earlier than any of the other children. Before she was a year old, she had teetered into the bedroom one morning with a big grin on her face, going to Robert's side of the bed.

"I did it!" It was her first full sentence.

"What did you do, pumpkin?" Robert reached down to scoop her into the bed.

She pointed to her and Charlie's room across the hall. "I did it!" she said again.

"You climbed down? Is that it? And Charlie didn't help you?"

She nodded.

Robert belly-laughed. "I'm going to have to rename you Monkey."

Robert had adored Corrine. And of all the children, she was the most like him.

"What else do you want for your picnic?" Abigail asked her now.

The scowl left Corrine's face and she smiled, thinking.

"You're beautiful when you smile, Corrine." Abigail started to add that she should do it more often when she realized Corrine *had* been smiling more. "Are you glad we came on this trip?"

"I'm not sorry we came." That was a pretty strong affirmation coming from Corrine, who reached for the flour and cleared a space on their worktable. "Do we still have those blackberries the boys found?"

They did. Abigail had let the boys go hunting again once Hoke assured her there were no bison herds nearby. They hadn't come back with any game, but they had with their shirts loaded—and stained—with blackberries.

Corrine grinned. "I'm going to make blackberry biscuits."

"Want my help?"

"No."

"Fine."

Corrine started cutting butter into the bowl of flour.

"I'll at least get you the milk." Abigail grabbed the pail and set off to find the milk cow.

Just before they'd hit the open plains, a bear had killed one of the Douglases' sheep in the night. Wolves and coyotes sometimes stalked the train, too, so the colonel now kept the livestock a good distance away, posting additional guards to watch both them and the wagon train.

Abigail was bent under the Jersey, squeezing the milk out in long, forceful spurts, when she looked up to see Orin Peters watching her.

She nearly kicked over the bucket.

"Orin!" He hadn't come near her since the night she'd slapped him.

"Some folks are getting a party together to ride out and get a closer look at Chimney Rock tomorrow, Mrs. Abigail. Do you want to go?"

It was as if his blackmail proposal and her rebuttal had never happened. Still, she didn't trust him. Her eyes narrowed. "I don't think so."

"It's about eight miles. We'd have to get an early start. Not everyone can go; some need to stay here and watch the stock and wagons."

Abigail gave the teat a final squeeze and said, "I'll stay here."

Orin's face went red. "Well, let me know if you change your mind."

Abigail watched him go with a twist in her brow. Orin Peters was beginning to make her skin crawl.

She picked up the milk bucket and walked back toward the wagons with it, stopping to watch Hoke and the other men as they worked on the rafts. The colonel had collected logs in the last supply wagon before they hit the open plains, just for this purpose.

"Think that'll work?" the colonel asked the men as James tied the last log on one of the rafts with a horsehair rope.

"We can see how they do floatin' this supply wagon over," said John Sutler. "Let's get the wheels off."

Some of the men worked to take the wheels off the supply wagon while the rest lifted up the raft so the younger boys who were helping could pitch the back of it. Hoke's arm muscles bulged as he held the raft. He raked the sweat off his brow with his shoulder, then looked back over it at her, as if he could feel her watching him.

It made her self-conscious, so Abigail lowered her chin and walked on.

$\sim$

Harry, James, and Tam were put in charge of the trip to Chimney Rock.

As Abigail stood by her wagon and grudgingly returned Orin Peters's wave good-bye the next morning, Hoke chuckled behind her ear. "Maybe Orin'll take an interest in Ingrid Schroeder after spending the day with her." Hoke's breath on the back of her neck sent involuntary shivers down Abigail's spine.

"Maybe he will, but then who would cut your hair?" She shot him the kind of sideways smirk he was always giving others.

"I've seen you with scissors. You're not bad." He pointed to his gold shirt as testimony.

Was he saying he wanted her to cut his hair? Abigail shook scandalous thoughts from her head and went to get more water from the Platte.

The water needed to sit several hours before being used so the silt would settle to the bottom.

"Look, Ma," whispered Lina when Abigail got back. Her hands were cupped in her lap. "Mr. Hoke brought me a butterfly." She raised a thumb to show her mother a small white butterfly—the kind that flew by the hundreds over the goldenrod.

"That was nice of him," said Abigail.

"Yeah. I like him."

Abigail wasn't sure if Lina was talking about Hoke or the butterfly.

June 23, 1866

> *I should not like to live on the plains, Mimi, and cannot believe Nebraska will ever be much settled. I miss the rolling hills of Tennessee. There are several pretty wild-flowers, though. The children are helping me collect seeds in case Idaho Territory doesn't have an ample supply of black-eyed Susans, goldenrod, Jacob's Ladder, and prairie lilac. Goldenrod is especially plentiful on the open plains.*

Abigail shaded her eyes, looking from Chimney Rock to the sun. "How soon do you think they'll be back?" she asked Melinda.

"I don't know, before sunset anyway. Don't worry. They're with James. And Hoke is out scoutin'." Hoke and Michael Chessor had crossed the river and ridden out to scout shortly after the others left.

Abigail set down her letter to Mimi and checked on her plants again. She needed to stay busy to keep from worrying. Each time Charlie served on guard duty her heart grew antsy. It felt even worse for Corrine to be so far from the wagon train. Jacob hadn't been allowed to go, and Prissy Schroeder had. But true to his sunny nature, Jacob hadn't pouted about it long.

When Hoke rode back into camp midafternoon, Jacob, Cooper Austelle, and Lijah Sutler ran up to him.

"Let's have games, Mr. Hoke!" cried Jacob.

"We're asking all the men," said Lijah.

"Colonel Dotson's agreed to play," added Cooper.

Doc Isaacs was standing nearby. "You're only asking the men? I bet some of the women would play if you asked them." He winked over at Abigail.

Jacob's head whipped around. "Would you, Ma?"

She shrugged her shoulders. "I *could* outrun most of the boys in school." Truth was, Abigail loved games.

Irene McConnelly, who was walking by just then, let out a cackle.

Abigail turned to the younger woman. "Will you join us, Miss McConnelly?" She suddenly burned with a desire to best Irene at something . . . anything.

"Don't be ridiculous."

These were the first words Irene had spoken to her since the Fort Kearney incident, and they felt like a slap. Abigail was about to ask Irene outright why she disliked her so much when Jacob tugged her skirt.

"Come on, Ma! We're getting started."

Empty feed sacks were collected and lines were drawn on either side of the circle.

The sight of Colonel Dotson hopping in a feed sack sent the smaller children into a frenzy. Abigail soon let go of her anger toward Irene. By the time she and Jacob had tied a bandana around one set of their ankles and raced through the grass, she was laughing as loud as anyone.

When they crossed the line they turned to look at Hoke and Lina behind them. Hoke had told Lina to plant both her feet on his boot and was swinging her along at an awkward gait. Lina had never giggled harder.

When Paddy Douglas outran Colonel Dotson in a footrace later, he beamed and said, "You are not the colonel now, I am!"

Alec told Colonel Dotson, "Now you've gone an' done it. We'll not be able to live with him."

Baird, who was holding Carson, set the coon running after baby Will and the Schroeder twins, who *had* started walking after all. They squealed and clapped their hands.

Heads were bobbing for apples in water-filled tubs when the group returned from Chimney Rock. Mr. Austelle pulled his head from the water. "Melinda! Come and kiss me!"

"Mr. Austelle! Shame on you." Melinda feigned shock and put a hand over her face to hide her laughter.

Prissy ran up to the apple tubs, but Jacob and Lijah barred her from them, saying, "Only the ones who didn't get to go to Chimney Rock can play."

Everyone who hadn't gone to Chimney Rock wanted to know what it was like.

"Corrine drew pictures of it," Clyde Austelle announced.

"Oh, can I see 'em?" asked Melinda.

Corrine reluctantly showed her pictures.

"Well, aren't you smart!" admired Melinda.

"Guess what Harry etched in the rock?" piped Prissy Schroeder. "He wrote 'Harry Sims was here with Tam Woodford.' What do you think that means?"

*Hmmm*s and grins went floating around the camp.

"I think it means Harry Sims was there with Tam Woodford," said Tam, squinting at her. "What were you doin' spyin' on us anyway?"

"I wasn't spyin'." Prissy grinned.

"Of course you were. I know how your little mind works. You remind me of me and for your sake, I hope you outgrow it." Tam eyed Prissy a minute, and then Prissy took off, Tam hot on her heels.

"We'll all get to see Scott's Bluff close up," announced Jacob. "Mr. Peters says it's better than Chimney Rock anyway."

As others started to leave, James stepped over to Corrine to get a look at her pictures. "These are good. I like a talented woman." He craned his long neck down to look her in the eye. "When you tire of Paul Sutler, let me know."

Corrine started to say something, then apparently thought better of it. She hugged her pictures to her chest and stared at James.

"He don't have a lot of sparkle," said James. "You noticed?"

Charlie would tell his mother later that when the group reached the base of Chimney Rock, Corrine had stuck the charcoal pencil she'd brought into the knot of her hair. But it was still hard for her to climb holding the sketch pad.

Before Charlie could help her James said, "Here," and took it from her. He untied his neckerchief, wrapped it around the sketch pad, and slipped it inside his shirt. "I'll try not to sweat on it." He winked at her, then put a hand to her back while she climbed up. "Careful now."

"I'll help her," offered Paul Sutler.

Corrine turned and smiled at them. "I don't need help."

While Jocelyn Schroeder scratched each of the Vandergeldens' names on Chimney Rock and Orin Peters wrote Timmy's and the date of his death, Corrine found a spot away from the others and sketched with her pencil.

"Stop and come eat lunch with us, Corrine," called Paul Sutler.

"I'm not hungry," she mumbled, never taking her eyes from her drawing.

The others climbed all over the rock reading names that had been written by travelers before them and wondering how many miles into the distance they were able to see, but Corrine never moved. When Tam said late in the day, "We gotta go now, Corrine," she reluctantly gave her paper a final stroke and then wrapped her sketch pad back in James's neckerchief.

"No peeking," she said.

He acted hurt. "What do you take me for, Miss Baldwyn?"

As Corrine turned to look behind her at the changing light, she stepped too close to the edge. Paul, who was right beside her, didn't notice. But James did. Just as she realized her mistake and started fighting to regain her balance, James snaked an arm past Paul and grabbed her around the waist.

"Watch where you're steppin' there, darlin'."

Corrine clung to James and peered over the edge at the twenty-foot drop.

"Thank you," she said gratefully.

He winked at her. "Your maw would skin me alive if I let you fall off a cliff." Then James glowered at Paul. "Why don't you go on? I'll help her down."

Charlie concluded his story by saying that Paul had been sullen the whole trip back.

∽

"Mr. Parker," said Corrine, hugging her sketch pad tight, "what makes you think I'd give you the satisfaction of knowing what I think about Paul Sutler or any other boy?"

James grinned. "You gonna keep calling me Mr. Parker when we're married, like Mrs. Austelle does with Charles?"

Corrine rolled her eyes and put her drawings in the wagon, her cheeks burning red while she did it.

∽

Someone proposed a game of hide-and-seek. With the sun sliding below the horizon, it would be harder to find people. Hoke heard the children making all sorts of elaborate rules about where you could and could not hide.

In the end, it was difficult to say who won. The children played the game over and over, first assigning Schroeders to be the "lookers," then Sutlers, Baldwyns, Austelles.

Hoke saw Charlie take Emma Austelle's hand and kiss her when they hid together behind the Jaspers' wagon wheel.

He smiled, remembering what it had been like to kiss the boy's mother. Then he wondered what Charlie would think to know he'd done it. He doubted the lad would take kindly to the news.

When Hoke came back to his and James's wagon, he found James working hard on his block of wood. He'd cut the rough shape of an oval out of it.

"What are you makin' with that?" asked Hoke.

"You'll see."

Thunder rumbled in the distance.

The rain started slow, while they were still crossing the river. It rained hard that night and all the next day.

Colonel Dotson looked out at the gray skies as he stood under a tarp Hoke and James had strung out behind their wagon, then turned back to Hoke. "You were right about this rain comin'. I don't know how you knew, but I sure am glad we crossed the river yesterday, even if it was Sunday."

He and Gerald had been around to every wagon to say, "Just hold tight till this lets up." Those who made the meals did so as best they could.

Mr. Austelle strung a covering off the end of the Austelles' wagon and Abigail and Melinda huddled under it, frying apples and bacon.

Charlie and Clyde carried plates over to Hoke and James when the food was ready and stayed and visited until the men had finished.

Hoke watched the boys run back with the empty plates, then watched Abigail from under his black hat, droplets of rain sliding off the rim past his eyes. Two wet curls were stuck to the back of her neck.

He went and brought the stallion and filly to stand at the back of his and James's wagon, under their tarp, where he rubbed them down with a rag, then a brush.

"You coddle those horses," said James.

"You take care of your animals . . ."

"Yeah, I know. And they'll take care of you." James was working on his block of wood with a flat iron scraper, the shavings piling up at his feet in the back of the wagon.

"Who's watchin' the stock?" asked James.

"Chessor and Sims. Why don't you run 'em out a hot cup of coffee?"

"I'm working on my bowl. Why don't you run it out there?"

"So it's a bowl. Who's it for?"

"I ain't sayin'. None of your damn business, anyway," James muttered.

Hoke finished rubbing down the filly and tossed the brush lightly at James. Then he reached for a couple of tin mugs and sloshed over to where Abigail and Melinda had finished cleaning up from breakfast and were now working on a pot of beans for lunch.

"You ladies got enough coffee for me to take some out to the boys on watch?"

Abigail brightened and reached for the pot. "I'll make some fresh. Have a seat."

Hoke flipped over a wooden box and set it close beside her, under the guise of getting in from the rain. She poured beans in the grinder. He reached for it and said, "I'll do that," taking it from her hand.

He caught Melinda's eyes watching them, but she said nothing. He wondered if Abigail had told Mrs. Austelle what happened when she measured him for the shirt.

Throughout the soggy day, men congregated in clusters to clean guns and to smoke. Rudy Schroeder got sauced and started cursing about the rain, how much time they were losing, and how nobody could tell him when he could or could not drink his own liquor. One of the Schroeders' chickens drowned in the downpour. Katrina and Bridgette plucked and pulled at the wet feathers to get it ready to boil.

Kids ran to neighboring wagons and climbed up with muddy feet, mothers yelling for them to wipe off on rags before they got the whole inside muddy. Jacob, Cooper, and Lijah rolled their pants legs up and stretched out on the back lip of the Baldwyn wagon, which Charlie had let down, giggling as the rain licked their feet.

Lina was trying to keep pace with Jacob and his friends. She rolled her pantaloons up and kept inching closer and closer to the edge. "Careful, Lina," cautioned Charlie. "You don't want to fall out." He picked her up and set her on his own legs, then scooted her out a bit so she could get wet enough to satisfy her.

The Jaspers dozed. Sam Beckett read to Audrey and baby Evelyn. The Kensington sisters quilted and wondered aloud if it rained much in Oregon. Doc Isaacs checked over his pharmaceutical supply while Caroline visited with Corrine and Emma, who'd come to play with baby Will.

The Schroeder kids got out of their wagon and had a fierce mud fight, then lay on the ground and let the rain lick the dirt clumps off. The Baldwyn and Austelle children, who had turned around and propped themselves up on their elbows, watched them enviously, knowing better than to ask their own mothers if they could join in.

The McConnelly sisters sulked and talked bad about everybody else in the train.

Orin Peters slunk around to the McConnelly wagon that afternoon and told Irene and Diana how he'd caught Hoke and Abigail kissing behind the wagon.

Irene raised her eyebrows. "Do tell."

CHAPTER 20

Brooding in the distance

Colonel Dotson and Gerald Jenkins were on scout a mile ahead of the train when a dozen soldiers from Laramie met them.

Seeing their leaders come riding back with the cavalry sent a twitter of excitement rippling down the line of wagons. Word spread that the soldiers had come to escort them to the fort under their protection, and a cheer went up. The train had encountered dozens of people in settlements during the first month of their journey, as the roads through Kansas and Nebraska had been filled with trading posts and Indian villages, but in the past several weeks they'd met only a couple of mail carriers.

The last mail carrier had reported that the smaller train behind them had had a bad run of luck with cholera. Four people had died. They stopped and set up camp at a creek to let the illness finish running its course. It was either that or leave the dying by the side of the trail, which, according to the carrier, was not an altogether uncommon practice.

After supper was eaten, Colonel Dotson, the company leaders, and several other adults gathered around the soldiers. "You're the first train to come through this season," said the lieutenant in charge. Coatman was his name. "And you're a large group, but I'm shocked the Indians haven't tried to steal your horses. The Sioux, especially, have been on a rampage the last year and have burned out nearly every rancher in the area. There's a displaced band of Piutes, too, that have caused a lot of trouble. The Bozeman is closed. Incidents from Laramie on up north along that trail are the worst." He eyed the women in the crowd. "I don't like to tell of the atrocities in mixed company."

Later, Coatman told the group's leaders about an incident that had happened earlier that spring. Laramie officers had invited Sioux leaders to a peace council. While promises were being made to the Indians, a large regiment arrived ready to build up fortifications to the north. When the Sioux realized the US Army had already decided to fortify the north and were meeting with their leaders under false pretenses, they were so angry they started attacking all along the Bozeman Trail. Besides scalping, they'd been known to castrate their victims and pull out their entrails.

"Even down here on the Oregon, trains are supposed to have at least forty people in them, for safety. The government put out that mandate last year. The Indians won't usually attack the larger trains, especially if they're well fortified and guarded. But a lot of settlers are ignoring the mandate and coming in smaller groups. One even came during the winter, which is astounding after the Donner party. A lot of them pay for it, too. You'll see a number of overturned, looted wagons and cabins between here and Fort Hall, including two stage stations. This is the worst two hundred miles on your route. Once you get to Soda Springs you should be fine, although an entire family was killed there a few years ago. People that found them took the wheels off their wagon and buried the whole family inside it."

"We've seen some smoke to the northwest," said Colonel Dotson. "Thin line."

"We have?" Christine looked at him. "That's news to me."

"We didn't want to worry you women. I sent Chessor out to investigate right after all that rain, but any sign of a trail got washed out. We've not seen any smoke since. More than likely it was just a lone rider."

Still . . . the mood of the entire train turned sober. Josephine didn't sing. The children didn't play hide-and-seek. Couples didn't stroll down to the water and back. And Hoke hardly slept. He watched the stallion during the day to see if he pricked his ears, and he watched Rascal at night, believing the dog would wake him if he heard anything out of the ordinary.

June 28, 1866

> *A few days ago we passed a station formerly used by the Pony Express, now abandoned, new telegraph poles strung overhead. It's so vast and lonely out here it is hard to imagine there are settlements at the end of those poles.*
>
> *I continue to waver between confidence and trepidation as we draw nearer our answers, Mimi. It feels like the skies are brooding in the distance.*

They rode into Fort Laramie on June 29, weary and grateful to be near fortified walls.

By the time most settlers arrived at Laramie, the romance of the adventure had long worn off. They'd experienced storms, rivers, sleeplessness, sameness of diet, monotony of landscape, and death.

Sometimes settlers got to Laramie and decided to turn around and go home. Several families on the Dotson train thought about it: Sam and Audrey Beckett with their new baby; the Kensington sisters, who had both been ill with mountain fever; Nichodemus and Nora Jasper, who had inherited several hundred dollars found in the Vandergelden wagon along with a stockpile of whiskey; and Abigail Baldwyn, who was getting colder and colder feet with every step that took her closer to Fort Hall.

All of these people and more considered turning back. But in the end, every family decided to keep moving forward.

❧

Within moments of their arrival at Fort Laramie, a tall soldier walked up to the Baldwyn wagons.

"Mrs. Robert Baldwyn?" he asked.

Abigail held her breath.

"Letter for you, ma'am." He handed her a thick letter addressed in Mimi's handwriting.

"Charlie! Corrine! Jacob! Lina!" The children came running.

"Is it from Pa?" asked Charlie.

"No. Mimi."

Charlie looked disappointed but Corrine said, "Quick, open it!"

Abigail's hands were shaking so violently she couldn't untie the string. Corrine took it. "Here, let me."

May 21, 1866

Dear Mrs. Abigail,

How I hope this letter finds you and the children well. So much has happened since you left. First, Annie B recovered. We all thought she was going to die from whatever it was ailed her, but just when it seemed all was lost, she recovered.

There is a small community of Negroes here and we have formed a church. I surely did enjoy going to that Presbyterian church with you in Marston, but it was nothing like the joy I get worshipping here. The men pitched in and built a simple building. It is only one room with an open back door and side windows to let the breeze flow. The walls cannot contain the singing.

And the cooking! We bring food every Sunday and have a feast like you can't imagine. I am going to feel bad writing this if you and my babies have been suffering for food. I pray that is not so.

Corrine stopped and looked at the others.

"What I wouldn't give for Mimi's cooking right now," said Jacob.

"The letter, Corrine!" Abigail urged her.

If you'll just pour your love into the food like I do, you'll be fine. Same way you pour your love into the fabric when you're working it into a pretty garment. It will put health on my babies' bones, so promise me you'll try.

Corrine raised her eyebrows at Abigail just like Mimi used to do. They all laughed.

"I'm trying, aren't I?" said Abigail. "Now keep reading."

Your father is growing meaner, I do believe. He never was a mean man before the war but some men need a woman to make them tame.

Corrine raised her eyebrows again.

I know you probably think what do I know about it, but surprise, surprise. I have done married, Mrs. Abigail!

Corrine's jaw dropped. Lina put her hand over her mouth.

"It does not say that." Abigail snatched the letter. "Oh my word, it *does* say that."

"My heart got swelled," said Lina. Charlie picked her up as Abigail finished reading out loud.

> *And guess who? The preacher of our new congregation. He never was a slave, but is a free man from upstate New York who came to Tennessee to especially encourage his brothers and sisters as they are figuring out what they want for their lives.*
>
> *Just think, if Annie B hadn't fallen ill, I would have gone to Independence with you and missed meeting my Thomas. He is a good man, Mrs. Abigail.*

Abigail stopped reading for a minute, her throat growing tight.

> *I know you would approve of him. Even though our courtship was short, the Lord, He whispered in my ear that it was the right thing to do.*

Abigail stopped reading again, her throat threatening now to close.

> *You know I listen when the Lord talks, and now He has gone and taken care of me. He is going to . . .*

This time when Abigail stopped reading, Corrine smiled and took the letter from her hands to finish.

> *He is going to take care of you, too. (I know, because He whispered it in my ear.) And I understand why you sent me my freedom papers. Don't think I don't appreciate it. But my love to you was always free. You need to know that.*

Abigail pinched the bridge of her nose as Corrine continued reading.

Thad and Mrs. Sue Anne had their new baby, right on the heels of the other one. They named him Seth Robert and wanted you to know. Your father has not rejected him. We all take this as a good sign.

My love and hugs to the children. I have enclosed a letter for each of them. I wrote Lina's in big letters because I know she is still learning.

Corrine handed out the letters and gave the first one back to Abigail.

Signed, Mrs. Thomas Hargrove (but you can still call me Mimi).

∽

Abigail was so happy to have heard from Mimi that when the soldiers threw a dance in their train's honor later that evening, she wore her blue dress. Corrine didn't say a word about it.

The waist piece was fashioned like a corset worn over a white blouse. A dyed blue string laced up the front and the bottom of the Swiss waist dipped to a low V, pointing down to a wide flounced skirt. It wasn't on a hoop but still swung slow and wide, thanks to the stiffness of an underskirt of crinoline.

The dress sent quite a buzz through the soldier ranks.

Hoke was standing beside Lieutenant Coatman and several other men when she came into the fort's dining hall. The lieutenant turned to him. "Did someone tell me she was married?"

"I don't know, did they?" Hoke didn't like for so many men to be following her with their eyes. "You know any of the men at Fort Hall?"

Coatman's eyes lingered on her. "A few. What's his name?"

Hoke didn't like where Coatman's eyes were concentrating.

"Baldwyn," he said flatly.

Coatman nodded, his eyes never leaving Abigail. "Yeah. He's been here."

Hoke's eyes bored through him. "Robert Baldwyn?"

"Yeah." Coatman frowned up at Hoke, then looked back at Abigail. "Lucky man."

A hard blow to Hoke's stomach couldn't have hurt more. In spite of all evidence that seemed to prove the man's existence, he had not wanted to believe him real.

"When was he here last?" Hoke asked.

"Month and a half ago, maybe?" Coatman crossed his arms. "Never said a word about his wife coming."

When another soldier came over to ask the lieutenant a question, Hoke stepped to the wall opposite Abigail Baldwyn.

He was just breathing normally again when Irene approached him. "You've never asked me to dance, Hoke Mathews, and I'm starting to get my feelings hurt."

"We can't have that." He bowed. "Miss McConnelly, shall we?"

She smiled. "It's actually Mrs. Stinson, but I was married such a short time everybody still thinks of me as Irene McConnelly."

"Begging your pardon then, Mrs. Stinson." He led her onto the dance floor.

"You know, you're hard to read," she said.

"How's that?"

"You don't talk much. Mr. Parker, now, he is very sociable."

"Would you like me to get him for you?"

"No!" She held tight to Hoke's arm.

Hoke did not place his hand low on her back nor lay her hand on his chest like he had with Abigail Baldwyn. He refused to look over Irene's head at Abigail but knew when she passed on the dance floor. He seemed always to be aware of her movements, as if she held him by a string.

Colonel Dotson soon cut in to dance with Irene. She watched Hoke move away with a sharp crease in her forehead.

Hoke asked Christine Dotson to dance next, then Josephine, Melinda, Caroline Atwood, who looked extra pretty in a yellow gingham frock, and finally Ingrid Schroeder. He moved with little feeling. His heart belonged to the woman in blue . . . and she could never be his.

He watched her dance with several of the soldiers . . . like a rich sapphire floating in a sea of tarnished brass. What could he ever have offered her? He was an orphan who came from nothing and had amounted to little more than nothing.

⁓

The soldiers had their own musicians, which freed up James, Alec, and Nichodemus to enjoy the dance. As soon as Corrine had entered the room, James had waltzed over, taken her arm, and led her to the dance floor. Corrine wore a floor-length dress for the first time and had put up her hair, aging five years in an hour.

Her cheeks flushed and she said, "Are you asking me to dance, Mr. Parker?"

"Nope." He put his arm around her waist.

"Isn't this dancing?"

"It is. But I didn't ask."

She stopped and stood still. "A gentleman ought to ask."

"Miss Baldwyn? May I have the pleasure?" When she started to dance again he said, "I didn't ask because I didn't want to give you a chance to say no. Now, if you're holdin' a dance card, I imagine it's goin' to fill up once I let you go. You just make sure you leave the last spot open for me." He winked. "I want to be the first and last man you dance with tonight."

Corrine didn't say she would or she wouldn't, but a soft blush stole into her cheeks.

The evening was nearing its end when Alec Douglas asked if he could play one more.

"I feel so inspired by that blue dress Mrs. Abigail is wearin' that I wanted to play one o' the Douglas clan's favorite Scottish ballads, 'Blue Bell of Scotland.' It was our mother's favorite. It's Paddy's favorite, too. Right, Paddy?"

Paddy nodded shyly and looked down at Carson, the raccoon riding as usual in the sling inside Paddy's vest.

"Baird, ye have to sing it with me," said Alec. "Big an' loud now."

Ah! where and ah! where is your highland laddie gone?
Ah! where and ah! where is your highland laddie gone?
He's gone across the ocean in search of wealth to roam
and 'tis oh! in my heart I wish him safe at home.
He's gone across the ocean in search of wealth to roam
and 'tis oh! in my heart I wish him safe at home.

Abigail had never heard the song before. She was struck by how parts of it were a reflection of her own story. How many times had her heart wished for Robert to be safely home?

Oh! where and oh! where does your highland laddie dwell?
Oh! where and oh! where does your highland laddie dwell?

Why had Robert chosen to dwell in Idaho Territory when his family waited for him in Tennessee?

His bonnet's of the faxon green, his waistcoat's of the plad,

Robert had always looked good in green. Was that why she'd made Hoke a green shirt? Had she wondered if he'd look as good as Robert in it?

Suppose and suppose your highland lad should die?
Suppose and suppose your highland lad should die?
The bagpipe should play over him I'd sit me down and cry
And 'tis oh! in my heart I hope he may not die.
The bagpipe should play over him I'd sit me down and cry
And 'tis oh! in my heart I hope he may not die.

Abigail had been convinced that Robert had died. She'd grieved. Then the news had come that he was alive. She should have been happy. Was she happy? How could she be when she didn't know if he loved her . . . or wanted her . . . anymore?

⁓

By the song's end nearly everyone was staring at Abigail. She looked so self-conscious and miserable that Hoke's heart went out to her. He decided he would ask her to dance, after all, just to get her moving out of the eye of the room. But as he started across the floor a soldier cut him off. "I heard that pretty lady in the blue dress was Cap'n Baldwyn's wife. Is that true?"

Hoke stopped. "Why? Do you know him?"

"Yeah. I've had dealings with him."

"What kind of dealings?"

"Not overly pleasant ones. He came here to restock on guns not long ago, but we were low ourselves. He wasn't none too happy about it. I can't believe he's got an upscale wife like that."

"Why not?"

"Don't get me wrong, he's kind of a dandy, but men don't hold him in very high regard."

"Why? What sort of man is he?"

"Struts like a banty rooster. Carries a fancy hilt sword. Acts like he's better than anybody else."

"Does he have reason to be arrogant?"

The soldier raked back over Abigail with his eyes. "I didn't think he did, but . . . maybe I'd be arrogant, too, if I had that to come home to."

But the man didn't go home to her, thought Hoke.

Seeing the way this man looked at Abigail and thinking of the bad spot Baldwyn had put her in lit Hoke's ire so bad it was all he could do not to grab the lusty-eyed soldier by the neck and pin him to the wall.

He inwardly swore, then turned and left the room.

As he left he heard someone propose they all sing "My Country, 'Tis of Thee," as the Fourth of July was only days away.

Rascal, who was lying near the porch steps, jumped up as Hoke came out the door. Nick and Nora were outside, selling whiskey to the soldiers. When Hoke stormed by, they tried to hide what they were doing, knowing the colonel wouldn't approve and thinking Hoke wouldn't, either. But in his current mood he was glad to happen on them.

He took a bottle from Nick's hand as he passed, then walked out of hearing distance, away from the lights, and stared off into the darkness. Rascal sat at his feet, watching him expectantly.

When Rascal's head swung back toward the mess hall, Hoke whipped around, the Colt in his hand. He saw Abigail walking away carrying a sleeping Lina, the child's head on her shoulder.

Had Abigail been coming out to see him? Why had she stopped? Should he go after her? Why would he? What did he have to say? *I hear your husband is alive and that he's a disrespected blaggard.*

Hoke holstered the gun and took another swig.

CHAPTER 21

Bugs crawling in the sugar sack

When Abigail got back to her wagon, she laid Lina down and peeled off the blue dress. She had worn it because she'd wanted *him* to see her in it.

Last time he had danced only with her; this time he'd danced with everyone *but* her.

Abigail hadn't seen when Hoke left the dance, but she had felt it. A cold breeze had swept in and swirled around her . . . the fool in the blue dress.

The Douglas boys hadn't meant to wound her by drawing attention to her—they didn't know the state of her heart. Mimi's letter had caused it to swell. Then the sight of Hoke dancing with Irene, and later, an awkward conversation with Lieutenant Coatman, had jerked her heart first one way then another. Now it was sore and raw.

What did she care if Hoke danced with Irene? And what did she care if he drank whiskey in the moonlight? What was any of that to her?

And so what if Lieutenant Coatman had given her a strange look when he said as she was leaving the dance with Lina, "I've met your husband."

She had stopped, surprised. "You have? How is he?"

"Opinionated. And stubborn."

While those were qualities she remembered, Abigail had expected Coatman to say something nice. She waited for him to laugh and follow up with a compliment—perhaps about Robert's attention to detail, his sense of fairness, his strong intelligence and competence. But that was all Coatman had to say before he smiled wanly and left the dining hall, renewing Abigail's fears that Robert had changed.

Still . . . Robert was her husband. Mimi had said that if ever there was a woman who could help a man find himself again, it was Abigail. So if an opinionated, stubborn husband was her cross to bear, she would bear it. And she would face the task with all the grace she could muster. After all, she owed it to her children to put their family back together.

Hoke could dance with Irene, kiss *her* behind the wagons, and drink whiskey by the barrel. None of that was anything to her.

Or was it?

⁓

Dotson had announced the night before that they would leave after breakfast. The camp flurried that morning as folks made final trades with the soldiers, packed their gear, and got the teams ready. A sergeant walked another letter over to the Baldwyn wagons. Its postmark read *Franklin*.

Abigail had been certain they would hear from Robert while they were at Laramie. "There's nothing from Fort Hall?" she asked the sergeant.

"No, ma'am."

She mustered a smile. "Thank you." It wasn't the soldier's fault Robert hadn't written.

Charlie, who was walking by, stopped, seeing the letter in her hand. "Is that from Pa?"

"No. I think it's from Thad. It's his handwriting." She opened the letter.

> *May 29, 1866*
>
> *Dear Sis,*
> *I send this letter on behalf of Father and all the family.*
> *We miss you and the children and pray you are well.*
> *With Arlon's help, we cleared a hundred acres and plant-*
> *ed tobacco. It's coming in nicely. Sue Anne and I had our*
> *new baby. We named him Seth Robert.*

Abigail and Charlie exchanged a smile.

> *Nathan married Nora Clark. That will not be a surprise*
> *as they courted so long.*
> *You may be interested to know that the girl who*
> *disappeared from Marston a few years ago was found.*
> *Everyone thought she was killed, like her mother and sis-*
> *ters were, while her father and brothers were off fighting.*
> *But she's alive and has been reunited with what's left of*
> *her family. She can't be much older than Corrine.*

"Louella Dale," said Charlie.

"She was seventeen when she disappeared, wasn't she?"

"That would make her nineteen now. She had a twin brother."

"How wonderful that she's alive and has been reunited with her family!" Maybe it was a sign . . . maybe this was how God whispered in Mimi's ear.

> *I don't know any other tales. Franklin continues to recon-*
> *struct. We looked at horses the army was selling back,*
> *but they were all worn out and shell-shocked. Arlon's*

mules are the best working stock we've got. Mimi said
you bought mules for your wagons.

Father is declining in health and mind. I'm sorry he
was difficult last time you were here. He'd be sorry, too, if
he could think straight. I hate to know you're so far away,
but we pray for you. Send us word when you get where
you're going.

Thad Walstone

Charlie put his arm around her. "Not much farther now, Ma."

Abigail hugged him. "How are things with Emma Austelle?"

"Good." He grinned.

"You going to be all right to stay in Idaho Territory while she travels on to Oregon?"

Charlie nodded, but the look on his face let her know he had wrestled with it. "I think so."

He left to hitch the teams.

Abigail had just swung a leg over the dun's saddle when the sergeant came running back to her and handed her another letter.

"I just found this one, Mrs. Baldwyn. It was so small I overlooked it at first."

Her heart missed a beat. It was from Robert. "Thank you."

He tipped his hat. "I hope you have a safe, pleasant journey to Fort Hall."

Abigail wondered if she should call Charlie back, and all the children, before opening it. Company C was second in formation today. She looked over and saw that Charlie was lifting Lina into their first wagon. Corrine and Jacob were already on the seat of their second one, waiting to move into line.

Nervous about what it might say, she tore open the letter.

Welcome to the West, darling. It thrills me to know you are coming. We
can have a happy life here, you and me.

It was brief, but reassuring. Abigail smiled and put the letter in her skirt pocket. Yes . . . this had to be what it felt like to have God whisper in your ear. But it bothered her that he still didn't mention the children or offer an explanation about Cecil Ryman's claims.

꙳

The trapper had made a quiet camp within sight of Laramie. A large but lean man, he moved as light as the Indians he'd lived with for the majority of his life. He had no trouble spotting Abigail Baldwyn or her children.

Her blue dress had been especially nice.

He had watched the wagon train arrive at Laramie, watched them circle up, watched them have their dance. He had crept through the untended wagons, feeding raw meat to the dogs to keep them quiet—had seen the gold and supplies, the whiskey stores, and the numerous rifles stored in the wagons throughout the camp.

He took nothing and left no prints with the soles of his moccasins. But he had identified which wagons he wanted, and he knew what all the Baldwyns looked like—the cute kid she carried sleeping in her arms, the pretty girl with the long ponytail, the boys who slept beneath the wagon.

It was sweet when they gathered around to read the letter from home.

To kill them there would have been easy, but he would wait until they were away from the fort, in the spot Robert Baldwyn had mentioned. He wanted the gold. And he knew a band of Piutes that would love that whiskey and appreciate those rifles.

꙳

July 2, 1866

I can hardly believe you are married, Mimi. May God bless your future and your marriage as richly as you deserve.

Thad wrote. He says Louella Dale from Treetop Ridge was reunited with her family. What a happy ending! It gives me hope. Robert wrote, too, and appears pleased to know we are coming.

In spite of these good omens, it makes me melancholy to count the grave markers left along this trail. Since Ash Hollow the numbers have increased.

Yesterday we heard about a man who stood on his wagon to look for Indians and lost his balance, shooting himself in the head as he fell. It seems it's accidents and illness that take the better part of the lives lost out here, not Indians and nature.

∽

Abigail wondered why she felt so jumpy.

Hoke also seemed on edge. He said little to her and little to anyone else. She thought back to his comment about feeling tempted to ride off from the group and wondered if there had, after all, been some truth to it.

Irene McConnelly had ridden with him the day they left Laramie—not on the white filly, but her own horse. And Abigail spied them that evening talking by the campfire. Ingrid had given him another haircut, too—and after Hoke had made that comment to Abigail about how *she* was good with scissors!

Abigail fumed at herself for keeping track of all his movements. Hadn't she vowed to stop thinking about him? Wasn't she traveling toward a husband who was thrilled she was coming?

Her temper grew short.

The second day after leaving Laramie, when she found dirt clumps scattered across the floor in the second wagon, she pulled everything out, swept and scrubbed, then packed it all back in. Later, when she found bugs crawling in the sugar sack she threw it against the wagon wheel.

"Mother!" Corrine picked up the bag and tried to keep any more from spilling out of a hole now torn in the side. "We need this sugar. It's our last bag!"

"I'm sick of finding bugs in it!"

Melinda walked over. "Bring it over here, Corrine, and we'll sift through it good and get 'em out. I've saved an old bag we can refill it in."

Abigail put her hand to her forehead. "I'm sorry."

She walked to a nearby creek and sat down on the bank. Melinda joined her there as the sun bent down and kissed the horizon.

"I'm sick of that dirty floor," mumbled Abigail.

"And I'm sick of livin' so close to livestock."

"And I'm sick of my lumpy mattress."

"And I'm sick of the sun scorchin' my skin through this muslin. And havin' to ask other women to hold their skirts out and hide me when I need to tinkle. And wakin' up ever' mornin' to the Schroeders' roosters callin'. I'm not havin' me any roosters when we build our place."

"I'm sick of not having any privacy." A smile curled the corners of Abigail's lips. "A woman can't even have a fit in private around here."

Melinda put an arm around her shoulders. "But you know what I'm not sick of? Look yonder at that sunset. I ain't got sick of that yet, have you?"

Abigail leaned her head over on Melinda's shoulder. "I'm scared, Melinda."

"Scared of what, sweetheart?"

"I don't know." But as soon as Abigail said the words, she did know.

Back in Independence, she had thought to travel with this group of people only for the sake of safety and convenience. She'd seen this train as a vehicle meant to take her back to her husband, to the man she belonged to, so she could try to repair damage she had caused by not supporting him.

It had not occurred to her then that she would grow to love the people on this train. But she had. In fact, she now felt a stronger sense of community with this small group of people than she had felt with the whole town of Marston, where she had spent her married years.

This was the first time Abigail had ever picked up the reins of her own life. She'd had nothing to do with the place where she was born, nothing to do with where Robert had lived. But the bonds she had formed on this journey were hers, a result of choices *she* had made. And they felt good. She wasn't ready to give them up, especially not for a man who had abandoned his family.

"This is all we've got, Melinda," whispered Abigail. "That lumpy mattress, one bag of buggy sugar, those dirt-clumped floors. We left everything else behind, and this is all we've got."

Melinda squeezed her. "It's all any of us got, sweetheart. And each other."

Abigail raised her head up and looked at her. "That's just it. That's what I was going to say. It's enough—better than enough. We've got each other. But when we get to Fort Hall, I'll lose you." Her voice cracked. "At first I was scared Robert didn't love me anymore, or that I wouldn't love him when I found him. Now I'm scared of losing you . . . the Dotsons . . . this sense of belonging. I don't want to have to start all over again on Robert's terms."

"Is there not any chance he'll come with us?"

"I don't know." Abigail looked into the deepening shadows of the creek bank. Crickets and frogs had begun to serenade them. "Lieutenant Coatman says he's opinionated and stubborn."

Melinda cocked her head. "You'll have to be persuasive, then."

The corners of Abigail's mouth curled. "You can always make me smile, Melinda Austelle." Mimi had that quality, too.

Abigail rubbed her forehead. "Maybe I'm worrying over nothing. Yesterday, when I was driving the wagon and Lina was on the seat beside me, she asked, 'Ma, aren't you happy?' And I said, 'Of course I am, sweetheart. What makes you ask?'

"And she said, 'Your eyes look sad.'"

"That child," said Melinda. "An angel if there ever was one."

"I told her I felt nervous in my heart and that I was sorry I wasn't doing a good job of hiding it. She said, 'Why would you try to hide your heart?'

"'Because I don't want my worry to make anyone else worry,' I said. 'Especially not you.'

"'You don't think I'm old enough to help?' she asked. I told her she did help—that she was the best help I had, and that when I looked at her I knew somehow that everything would turn out like it should.

"But I lied to her, Melinda. When I look at my children I wonder if I'm doing right by them. First I worried that I shouldn't have brought them out here. But it turned out to be the best thing I've ever done for any of us. Now I don't know whether I'm meant to join Robert or whether we ought to keep going."

Melinda shook her head, thinking. After a while she said, "I can't tell you what to do or how it will all turn out, but you've got them no matter what. You'll always be where you're supposed to be as long as you're with those children."

"You're right. I better go get them ready for bed."

As she and Melinda walked back to the wagons, Abigail remembered the feeling of Lina's sticky little hands reaching up to her face yesterday, and the words she had whispered up to her:

"Look at me more."

CHAPTER 22

From the rocks and ground
around the train

July 9, 1866

*Today we crossed the Platte for the final time. It is a unique
river, shallow and muddy, nearly two miles wide. It felt
like we were Israelites crossing the Red Sea. Several times
I looked behind me to see if the Egyptians were coming.*

Abigail was walking with Marnie Sutler. The train had reached
Mitchell Pass and the foot of the Black Hills. Aspens and evergreens
dotted the landscape, a welcome sight after the flat monotony of the
prairie. The women had just begun feeling the ascent in their legs—legs
that had grown strong from three months of travel—and the oxen and
mules leaned into their yokes and harnesses.

A large shepherd mix belonging to the Schroeders barked and
darted toward a stand of cedars as a faint *zzziipp* whispered past Abigail's

ear. Lijah Sutler, who was driving the nearest wagon, cried out in pain. Abigail looked over to see a black-tailed arrow extending from his arm. She watched in horror as a second arrow from the thicket caught the dog in the throat, cutting his snarls short.

Hoke, who was riding near the front of the train, slapped the white filly's rump and wheeled around sharply.

Marnie ran toward Lijah as Hoke yelled, "Circle up!" Then he grabbed the reins of the first wagon—driven by Phillip, the oldest Sutler boy. Lijah's wagon had been second in line. Hoke turned the team and swung them around to start to form the outer circle. Rascal, always near the heels of Hoke's horse, had a hard time keeping up.

They had talked about what to do if they were ever attacked but had hoped they would never need to act on the plan. The lead company was to swing away from the attack to form the first half of the outer circle; the second company was to swing in the same direction for the first half of the inner circle; the third company would fall in behind the first company to close the outer loop, leaving space for the fourth company to pull in and close the inner one. The last wagon would close in the gap. Women and children were to take cover inside the inner-circle wagons, and the men were to go to the center of the ring—Dotson's command post—to receive instructions.

Thankfully, the train wasn't as spread out as usual. Dotson had been keeping them tighter since they left Laramie, knowing this was Indian country.

Abigail helped Marnie pull Lijah into the back of the wagon, then grabbed the reins and led his team into formation behind Phillip's. They were the first two wagons in Company D, which had been leading the train today. Hoke nodded to her.

"Sutler!" shouted Hoke to Phillip, who had secured his own team. "Get back here and tie this team. Go on down the line as they come up." He pointed at Abigail. "Get back to your family!"

❧

Hoke's chest swelled with pride at Abigail's quick actions, but he wanted her inside the loop so he wouldn't have to worry about her.

Company A was in the rear, which meant that the Kensington sisters were in the last wagon and would need help. Hoke rode back through the line shouting instructions to the drivers.

He saw Abigail jump down and run toward her own wagons. Company C was second in formation.

More Indians had leapt from the trees. Arrows zipped like sideways rain. It was hard to tell how many there were; everything was happening so fast. The Indians were on foot. They had emerged from the rocks and ground around the train.

❧

Charlie got in line behind James, their two wagons forming the first part of the inner circle. Abigail saw him hand the reins to Corrine and climb into the back to get the rifle. James hobbled the lead team, then ran back to help Corrine tie her horses to the back of his wagon.

"I've got 'em!" she yelled. "See if Jacob needs help."

"All right," said James, "but get inside as soon as they're tied."

Abigail jumped in the back of the wagon just as Charlie's feet cleared the buckboard on his way out. "Charlie!" she called. But he was gone.

"Oh, God, watch out for him," she prayed, knowing Charlie had never heard her.

Her hands trembling, she clawed for the box that held the pistol—a .36 caliber Navy Colt exactly like the one Sue Vandergelden had used. Robert had wanted her to have something small that she could handle but still powerful enough to get the job done. *It got Sue's job done*, she thought with a shiver.

She broke the gun open and checked. Five shots. Robert had said to leave it resting on an empty chamber with the children around. She closed the cylinder and clicked it over so the gun was ready to fire. She grabbed another box of cartridges and percussion caps and stuffed them in her skirt pocket. She looked around. Was that everything she needed?

Outside the wagon there were shouts and cries, then an eerie high-pitched whooping. That had to be Indians. Of course it was Indians! They were under attack. Hadn't she seen the arrow in Lijah's arm? She'd begun to react before the truth of the situation had really sunk in. A reckless thrill shot through her chest followed by a sinking fear. It could just as easily have been one of her boys who'd been shot.

Would they lose anyone? Everyone? Where were her children? *Lina!* Cold fear flooded her chest again. Lina had been at the back of the train with Josephine Jenkins in Company A.

Corrine was still working to tie the reins to the wagon in front of her, the mules pitching their heads wildly. The wagon jerked and Abigail was flung to the side, but she held on to the pistol. Corrine snapped the leather in frustration. "Settle down!"

"When you get them tied, come in here," yelled Abigail, scrambling to get her balance. "I'll bring Jacob and Lina to you. Stay in here with them—no matter what happens." She climbed over the back and dropped to the ground.

Jacob was just pulling their second wagon into formation. Abigail reached for him as James took the reins to tie. The mules were wild with fear and hard to handle, but Jacob had done it. His face was white from the effort.

"You did so well!" Abigail gave him a squeeze. "Get inside with Corrine. I'm going to get Lina."

Abigail spun around, taking stock and counting. Company A would be about fifteen wagons back. The attack was coming from the northwest, at the front. Her children were on the southeast side. *Thank*

God! She could see Colonel Dotson stationed at the center of the circle, directing the men.

"Beckett, get over here," he yelled. "Put your gun away; get your notepad and pencil. Charlie here is a marksman with a .44 Henry. I'm sending him to the far right front by Sutler. Write that down. Listen for his shots and when he gets to six, let me know."

He turned to Paddy Douglas. Paddy had stuck pretty close to the colonel since the children had played games at the river's split. Paddy had followed Colonel Dotson to the center when the attack started. "You know where we put that ammunition in my wagon? It's the one Baird's driving today. Run and get as much as you can carry in your shirtfront. Hold your shirt up like this and cradle it—your pockets won't be big enough. Don't worry about your coon, he'll hold on. Bring that ammunition right back here to us—powder, balls, grease, and some paper cartridges. Secure 'em good. Don't drop 'em. You're a fast runner—don't think I forgot."

"Son!" said Dotson, as one of the Sutler boys ran up, "go find Harry Sims and relieve him of his wagon. He'll be at the back of Company D, over there. Tell him I need him on the front."

Everyone appeared relatively calm, but Abigail's heart was pounding so hard it felt like it would rip from her chest. She saw Jacob climbing in the back of their first wagon with Corrine like she'd told him to do. *Good.* She didn't need him trying to be a man right now. It was enough to have Charlie to worry about. Where had Charlie gone? She looked around and found him: there he was with John Sutler, in a firing position behind one of the Sutlers' wagons.

Emma Austelle ran past her with one of the Schroeder twins on her hip. "Get in the wagon with Corrine and Jacob," instructed Abigail, pointing to it. She tried to count the moving wagons again to locate the front of Company A.

Where was Lina?

Shots rang out and the whoops grew closer. Her heart was gripped with fear for her youngest daughter.

Hoke had needed only a moment to take it all in. He'd counted fifteen Indians but didn't trust his number; they darted in and out of the brush so fast. It was smart of them to attack just as the train hit a steep part of the ascent. The Indians were on foot, so they probably just wanted horses. But it didn't make sense for them to attack in the daytime like this—they'd have had a better chance at the horses after dark. Who had been on scout duty? Why hadn't he noticed any sign of the imminent attack? Hoke blamed himself for not having been more vigilant.

Everyone had been quick to respond to the crisis, he noted with pride, and was staying pretty calm—at least for now.

Rudy Schroeder yawed his team to the left and swung around in formation. His wagon was on the outside, the first of Company B to get in place. As soon as the team halted, Rudy grabbed his shotgun and jumped from the seat, handing the reins to his wife. Then he began making his way down the line, instructing and lending a hand to each of the Schroeder wagons as they pulled up, helping the men restrain the livestock and getting the women to inner-circle wagons, telling them to hunker down.

Few of them did. They were rummaging for guns and extra ammunition and poking children's heads down when they bobbed up, the children's eyes filled with wonder.

"Faramond!" barked the colonel. "You got that repeating rifle ready? Send your nephew there and run it over to James Parker. Bring back his Winchester and reload it for him. Duncan, you keep track of Michael Chessor."

Hoke smiled at the colonel. He'd been paying attention and was putting each man on a task he was well suited for. The Schroeders weren't marksmen, but they were cool under pressure, so he'd put Schroeders on reloading and restocking from the middle. Where was Gerald Jenkins? he wondered, and then realized he'd be back with

Company A, still getting them into formation. Hoke knew the colonel would want Jenkins in the middle.

"I count fifteen! All on that northwest slope!" yelled Hoke to Dotson as he charged past on his way to get Jenkins.

Someone yelled, "Women and children to the inside!"

Men continued running toward Colonel Dotson as soon as they got their teams tied, then running off to wherever he'd directed them. The men with guns threw their shoulders against the wagon wheels and fired at the elusive attackers who kept leaping out, then disappearing again into the brush.

Hoke spotted Nichodemus Jasper. "Come help these sisters in the back. They're last in line and need to close the gap." Then he swung back up the line, continuing to shout instructions and oversee the train. He really needed to get off the filly.

Doc Isaacs ran to the colonel. "What can I do?"

"Get over to the Sutler wagon. One of their boys was hit. Stay there so we'll know where to find you if anyone else goes down."

Hoke saw Abigail standing between the outer and inner circle with a Navy Colt in her hand. She was turning from side to side, counting wagons. He'd seen Emma Austelle climbing into the back of the Baldwyn wagon, one of the Schroeder babies in her arms. Corrine and Jacob had been pulling her in. But where was Lina?

Hoke swung wide, drawing some fire away from the train. When a brown shoulder poked up from behind a rock, he lifted his Winchester and squeezed off a shot, then pulled on his horse, zigzagged wildly, and galloped to the back of the train as he worked the lever to fill the chamber, his eyes scanning for the snowy-white hair of Lina Baldwyn.

And then he found her, running with Josephine Jenkins, her eyes wide and frightened.

Company A was just pulling into formation. Everything was chaos—the attack was coming from the other end of the train, and the folks down here were still trying to process what was happening. The men were still tying the teams and grabbing their guns. Nichodemus Jasper was seeing to the Kensington sisters' wagon now. Tam Woodford had come back to help, too. She was herding the sisters to a wagon on the inside of the circle.

Nelda Peters, who was on Doc's orders for bed rest, poked her head out of the canvas while Orin jumped from the wagon seat to restrain his team. Josephine had Lina by the hand and appeared to be looking for Abigail.

"Hand her to me," yelled Hoke.

Josephine lifted Lina up.

"Jump on, angel," he instructed, scooping her up with his arm that held the rifle, reins in his other hand. Lina linked her arms and legs around him and buried her face in his chest, frightened by the noise and the shooting. He couldn't have lost her in an avalanche.

"Tam!" called Hoke. "Take Gerald's job so he can get to the middle!"

When Hoke rode up with Lina, Abigail's whole body sagged with relief. Stretching out her arms, she pried her daughter off and looked up at him with large, grateful eyes.

"Get in your wagon," he said gruffly.

Abigail ran to the wagon and lifted Lina up to Corrine. Katrina Schroeder ran by with one of the twins. "Your other one's in here!" shouted Abigail, waving her over.

Hoke cursed when he saw Abigail run away from her wagon again. He wheeled to the back to check on Jasper, then rode back up to Dotson. "We're closing the gap now!"

"Good man," returned Dotson as he charged by. "You! Austelle! Run these over to your pa yonder, and keep your head down."

Baird and Alec Douglas were fast, so when they ran up, Dotson kept them working the line with fresh guns. "Gerald, go plug that hole in the middle there, by Austelle. You're the next best shooter I got. Good to see you. Rudy. You be Gerald's loader. He's got a .44 rimfire."

"Where's he going?" said Rudy, watching Hoke ride off.

"Everywhere, that's where," said Dotson smiling. "God's providence he's mounted today, but damn the luck of it being the white horse."

$\curvearrowright$

"Get in here, Abigail Baldwyn!" yelled Bridgette Schroeder as Abigail ran past.

Ignoring her, Abigail ran for the northwest line, then stopped suddenly. A few of the Indians were starting to circle around. It was hard to tell how many, they were so quick to dart from tree to rock to bush.

Abigail had never seen men so naked before. Feathers stuck out of their hair and paint covered their faces and chests. These were nothing like the docile Indians they had encountered during their first month on the journey. These men were fierce and terrifying.

Once during the war, she and the children had traveled to see her sick mother in Franklin. The fighting had come within a few miles of her father's land. Early that morning they heard scattered shots. At midday Abigail had climbed a hill on the edge of the land with Mimi and Arlon. She would never forget the scene she'd spied two miles in the distance: neat lines of blue soldiers stood on one side, and neat lines of gray stood on the other. Later, after Abigail and the others had left, the real fighting had begun, but at that moment, from the hill's vantage point, it had reminded her of a patchwork quilt.

This was nothing like a patchwork quilt. This was brutal and steady. The Indians came in waves, patient as the sea slapping at a man-made vessel.

Abigail raised her pistol and aimed at one of the Indians as he stepped from behind a cedar and came into full view.

She couldn't shoot. It felt wrong.

But when the Indian raised his bow and pointed an arrow at Jocelyn Schroeder, who was turning around in a daze, Abigail didn't even think about it. She pulled the trigger.

In horror she watched his body jerk backward.

"Get to the inside, Jocelyn!" Abigail's voice came out like a stranger's—hoarse and raw.

Jocelyn looked at her in horror and did as she was told.

Abigail's hand shook so badly she could hardly hold the gun. She had only wanted to see Charlie—to know that he was safe. But now she was caught in a dilemma: the men didn't seem to notice that some of the Indians were circling around. Should she run to tell Dotson, she wondered?

Abigail heard someone yell in pain to her left. She didn't turn to look; she kept her eyes on those three—no four!—Indians she saw circling and moving closer.

Hoke was suddenly beside her, off his horse now that all the wagons were set. "Dammit, Abigail, get to the inside!"

Just then an Indian slipped past the outer ring of wagons. Hoke shot him, then swatted at Abigail with the butt end of his rifle, trying to move her back toward the inner ring. Bullets were flying everywhere— Abigail saw one rip through the canvas of a wagon close by, one that she hoped was unoccupied. Nearby a dog yelped, having been stepped on by a nervous mule.

"Abby!" Hoke was shouting at her. She turned to look at him, then craned her neck as she looked past him at an Indian raising his rifle.

Taking the pistol in both hands to steady it, Abigail stepped to the right and shot.

Hoke wheeled around as the Indian fell, part of his head blown off, the bullet having caught it at an upward angle.

After that there was a sudden whoop followed by the sound of horses stampeding on the other side of the ring. Then abruptly the shots and shouting stopped, and there was only the lingering pound of the horses' hooves as they topped the rise and flew over the hill.

Abigail shook all over, her eyes fixated on the part of the Indian's head that lay glistening on the ground. She still held the pistol in both hands, though they were shaking violently. Her legs were shaking, too, and her arms . . . her heart was even shaking, as if her whole body were freezing.

Hoke took the Colt from her hands, shoved it in the back of his waistband, set his rifle on the ground beside Rascal, who was still barking, and lowered her arms to her sides.

"Hush now," he scolded the dog, touching him briefly on the head. Rascal quieted but paced around nervously.

"I—can't—stop—shaking," she whispered, the words ragged and jerky. It surprised her she could speak at all. Her whole body felt jumpy and her gaze was frozen to the Indian's head—a pool of pink-and-white liquid mixing with red blood on the grass. It was much more awful than the sight of bloody slabs of meat. She was responsible for it. She had caused it.

Hoke took her by the shoulders and turned her around so her back was to the Indian and to him. Then he slid his hands down her arms and held her tight. "It's all right," he crooned, the same way he talked to his horses. "It's over. They're gone. You did good. Everybody's all right. You're all right."

Abigail breathed deep, in and out, her body pulsating, her ear on fire from the closeness of his mouth. She relaxed and laid her head back, loving how good it felt to be held by this strong, capable man she had grown to trust. He had brought Lina to her. He was always watching out for her and her children. She was so grateful for his strength. She didn't want to have to be strong. She didn't want to have to be both father and mother to her children.

Her eyes rolled back.

$\sim\!\!\!\circ$

Abigail went limp. Hoke nearly dropped her. He scooped an arm under her legs to lift her up.

That was when he saw the blood on her blouse and skirt.

CHAPTER 23

Purple flowers and the smell of lavender

Hoke set her down and tore the clothes at her side to get a better look. Rascal was barking again. A bullet had passed through the fleshy part of Abigail's right side, below the rib cage and above the hip bone.

It was a lucky spot and he didn't think anything vital had been hit, but blood was pouring out. Had that caused her to faint? Or was it just nerves catching up with her?

He pulled off a long, wide section of her skirt, ripped two pieces from it, plugged a wad of fabric in each hole in her side, then wrapped another piece around her body to tie them in place. He lifted her up and carried her to her wagon.

"Go get the doc!" he told Emma Austelle, who was the first to poke her head out as he approached. "He's at the Sutler wagon."

Women who had been hiding inside the Baldwyns' wagon spilled out to make room. Corrine's eyes were wide. Jacob put his arm around Lina, who looked like she was going to cry.

"Is Mama dead?" Lina asked Hoke in a high-pitched voice, fear on her golden face.

It broke his heart.

"No, baby doll, your mama's going to be just fine. She lost some blood and had a fright is all. Bullet came clean out the back, so it can't hurt her anymore. Doc'll tell us if anything vital was hit, but I don't think it was. She had a scare . . . we've all had a scare . . . but your mother's tough. You know that, right?" He smiled to reassure her—and to reassure himself—petting Lina's golden ringlets with his blood-free hand.

Lina nodded as tears pooled in her eyes.

"You know if Mr. Hoke says it, it's true, Lina." Jacob squeezed his sister's shoulders. "He's not the kind to go soft on you just 'cause you're young."

Hoke put his hand on Jacob's head. God, he loved these kids.

Charlie appeared at the back of the wagon. "I heard Mama was hurt!"

Hoke took Corrine's hand and put it on Abigail's side. "Put pressure on it until Doc Isaacs gets here. Mrs. Schroeder, will you get some water? Jacob, start a fire out here in case Doc needs the water boiled. There'll be others wounded. It might take him a while to get here. Charlie, help me out here."

When he climbed down from the wagon, he took Charlie aside. "Your mother's goin' to be all right." He nodded toward one of the fallen Indians. "We need to get these bodies cleared out of the way." The dogs were already starting to sniff and lick at the blood. "The women and children are going to be upset enough without seeing all this."

∽

Charlie swallowed hard. He was pleased Mr. Hoke treated him like a man and not one of the children, and he didn't want to show how rattled and upset he felt. But if anything should happen to his mama, he would never forgive himself for suggesting they come west.

He had shot at several Indians—just like Mr. Hoke had told him to, putting the sight in the notch and squeezing off at six o'clock on the target—but hadn't hit any. He also watched John Sutler kill one of the attackers. Mr. Sutler was very cool about it.

It all happened so fast—arrows whizzing, bullets flying. Charlie started to shoot at one Indian even before getting into position, over-eager to impress because the colonel had showed faith in him. But Mr. Sutler put a hand on his rifle barrel. "Careful," was all he said. Charlie looked past the end of his rifle then and saw Jocelyn Schroeder run by. He might have hit her! What a fool he would have been. He was grateful Mr. Sutler had been there and hoped the man didn't think him an idiot.

To Charlie, everything had seemed like chaos. On his right, Harry Sims fought hand-to-hand with an Indian. Charlie watched him stab the Indian in the neck and twist the handle.

Mr. Sims carried a bowie knife—thicker than Mr. Hoke's and ten inches long. He kept it sharp, too. Charlie had seen him sharpen it lots of times when they sat around the campfire. It was great for tanning a hide. An animal's flesh peeled off like butter under the influence of that knife, just like the buffalo's flesh had when they used Mr. Hoke's to tan the hide on the one they killed. But Charlie had never thought about what that blade could do to a man's neck before he saw it firsthand.

He felt sick now remembering it.

Clyde Austelle, who had been standing behind him after bringing Mr. Sutler a gun, had doubled over and retched at the sight. And Mr. Sims was a preacher! Toughest preacher Charlie had ever known.

Charlie's respect for men like Hoke and Harry Sims and John Sutler had shot way up. And for Michael Chessor—only twenty, not much older than him—who had raced past him toward the front, snarling like a bobcat.

Hoke had been everywhere Charlie looked—racing down the line with the command to circle up the wagons . . . firing his rifle from his hip into the cedars at the north end of the train . . . racing up and down the line of men behind the wheels yelling, "Hold 'em off! Watch that one on the bank!"

He'd steered women and children to the inside and encouraged the men. He seemed to know where everyone was and exactly what was happening. Mr. Hoke was normally reserved and collected, but he sure could command attention when conditions called for it.

Charlie appreciated Dotson's foresight and tactical planning, too. The way he'd told them to circle those wagons, and the way he stationed himself in the center so he could see what was happening, was smart. And each man only had to do one thing. That was smart thinking, too.

Dotson's cool planning and solid decision making, coupled with Hoke's quick action and ability to get up and down the line, was what had saved them, according to Charlie's way of thinking.

When Hoke reached his wagon he pulled out two shovels and handed one to Charlie.

Colonel Dotson hurried over. "Hoke! Charlie! Looks like they've moved on, but James and Gerald are riding out to scout around and make sure they don't double back. How's Mrs. Baldwyn?"

"I think she'll be fine. Doc's with her now," Hoke said.

Charlie looked toward the wagon. He hadn't seen Doc Isaacs arrive.

"He got there when I was handing you the shovel," Hoke told him. "Mrs. Austelle's with her, too."

The colonel gave Charlie's shoulder a squeeze and pointed to the blood on Hoke's shirt. "You weren't hit, were you?"

Hoke shook his head and glanced at Charlie. "Must be hers."

Pointing to the dead Indian on the ground, Hoke said, "He'd have killed me if your mother hadn't shot him. Looked like you were holding your own, too."

Charlie felt pride rush to his face.

Hoke started shoveling over the blood on the ground. Charlie got to work, too, doing exactly what Hoke was doing.

"How many of ours are hurt?" Hoke asked.

"Five that I know of," said Dotson. "I've nearly finished making the rounds. Duncan Schroeder is the worst. He was shot twice—I don't know how, he wasn't even on the front line. Doc says one didn't miss his heart an inch. Shot in the leg, too. Harry Sims had a tussle and got stabbed a couple of times, but the cuts aren't too deep. Tam and the Jaspers are tending him. Baird Douglas was speared in the shoulder. Lijah Sutler took an arrow at the start. McConnelly turned his ankle pretty bad gettin' out of his wagon. Guess that makes six with Mrs. Baldwyn. And six Indians on the ground. They carted off some of their wounded, too. That's pretty good odds. I don't think those Indians had a lot of guns. You notice what they did have?"

"Yeah, I noticed." Hoke stepped over, picked up the rifle the Indian had dropped, and handed it to Charlie. "Army commissioned. Same kind they had at Laramie. Either they've picked 'em off dead soldiers or someone out here's supplying to 'em. Wouldn't be the first time."

"I'm surprised they attacked us like they did," said the colonel. Charlie handed him the rifle and got back to work. "They must have wanted those horses pretty bad, and for some reason weren't as patient as normal. Lucky break for us."

"You think they were put up to it?" asked Hoke.

"I don't know. I don't want to jump to conclusions and upset anybody without cause. Let's get these bodies cleaned up and move on to a better spot. We've got some livestock to round up, too. You think we need to go after the horses they took?"

"How bad do you want 'em back?"

"I can live just fine without all of 'em, but you know Rudy Schroeder'll throw a fit if I don't offer. Two of 'em were his. At any rate, we don't have to decide this minute."

As Dotson left, Jenkins joined Hoke and Charlie. Together they dug a deep grave in a low spot a hundred yards from the wagon train. Then they went back to get the bodies. The most horrific site was the one where Abigail had saved Hoke's life. As Hoke picked up a piece of the Indian's head he bent down for a closer look at the body. A small leather bag was looped over one shoulder. Hoke cut it off.

"Jenkins," he said in a low voice, not looking at Charlie. "Come here."

The men opened the bag and looked at something they found inside it. Jenkins muttered, "Good God." They looked closer at the dead man on the ground.

Jenkins turned the body with his foot. "That's not an Indian. That's a white man with a shaved head, dressed like an Indian."

Charlie stepped over for a closer look. "What was in the pouch?"

Jenkins and Hoke exchanged a look.

"Picture of a white woman," said Hoke. "See if you recognize her." He held out the worn picture. Charlie's heart dropped. It was of his mother.

"Who is he?" demanded Charlie. "How did he have that?" His veins had turned to ice. It didn't make any sense why a white man would be dressed like an Indian and have his mother's picture in his pouch.

"Let's not say anything about this to anyone yet." Jenkins put the picture in his pocket. "I'll talk to the colonel. But Charlie, let's not say anything to your mother or your brother and sisters about this. It may just be a strange coincidence."

It wasn't a strange coincidence. Charlie could feel it in his gut. "No, sir. I won't say anything about it. But I want to know what y'all are thinking, and I want to be included in any efforts to find an explanation."

Hoke nodded at Charlie. "Fair enough."

Colonel Dotson moved the train to a camp four miles from the attack spot.

Once he'd gotten the rest of Company C settled, Hoke stopped by to check on Abigail. As he peered into the back of the wagon he caught a glimpse of her with her dress off, lying in her underclothes, Doc Isaacs dressing her wound. She had regained consciousness and looked out at Hoke over the back of the wagon with those big blue eyes. Her expression . . . was it pain? Longing? Gratitude? Or embarrassment?

Corrine blocked his view and said, "Mother's not decent. You can come back later." She closed the flap before he could protest. But Doc Isaacs was still in there. Doc got to see her not decent.

Hoke had intended to stop back by but ended up talking with Colonel Dotson and the other men until long after dark, going over the events of the day. What had worked well? What hadn't? Who among them had proved his merit? Who hadn't? Did anyone think they should go after the horses? "If so, say it now," said Dotson, looking hard at Rudy Schroeder. But Rudy didn't ask him to. The Schroeders were all worried about Duncan, and with good reason. Duncan Schroeder was the only one Doc Isaacs couldn't promise would make it.

On his way back to the wagon to bed down for the night, Hoke stood beside Abigail's box garden for several minutes, twisting his hat in his hands. It was easy to spot her wagons with those box gardens on the side. He needed to tie up that cherry tree again, before it started to lean. And this purple flower had really grown. What had she called it? A dahlia.

He lightly touched one of the blooms, thinking of how purple flowers would always remind him of her now—purple flowers and the smell of lavender.

She'd scared him. She'd really scared him.

He'd quit asking himself weeks ago why this woman made him crazy and had just resigned himself to the fact that she did.

Why the hell had she not stayed in the wagon with her children like he'd told her to? When he'd seen the group of Indians break off from the others and swing around during the attack, few of the other men had noticed. Even Dotson hadn't noticed yet. But she had. She had looked like she was trying to decide whether to shout to the men nearest her or to just run and tackle those Indians on her own.

He grinned and shook his head. She probably would have tackled those Indians on her own if he hadn't run over and tried to push her to the inner circle.

She might have saved his life, but she had put it in danger, too. She was a distraction to him. He never would have turned his back to that Indian if she hadn't been there. He'd been worried about the visibility of the white horse, while the bigger danger had been his feelings for Abigail. Still . . . she did save his life. She would have done the same for anybody, but it was *him*. She was a woman a man could count on . . . except to stay put in the wagon.

Hoke's mind traveled back to what had gnawed at him the rest of that day. How had that man come to have her picture in his pouch? It gave Hoke a bad feeling.

That night he slept in fits. He finally gave up and took over the watch. Charlie was up at daybreak asking to scout around with him and James.

"Go ask your mother if she's awake, but don't wake her if she's resting," Hoke said. "She might rather keep you close today."

Charlie was back shortly. "She says as long as it's with you and Mr. Parker, I can go."

"How's she feelin' this morning?" asked James.

"She looked good."

"She always looks good."

Charlie and Hoke both gave James a dark look.

"What? Y'all don't think so?"

❧

Charlie rode with new respect for Hoke and James—they had the most tracking experience of anyone in the group.

"Here's where horses were tied. Indian ponies are unshod," Hoke told Charlie. "You know the difference in their tracks?"

Charlie nodded.

"There's a whiskey bottle over here," said James.

Charlie turned to Hoke. "You and Colonel Dotson said yesterday they had army-commissioned rifles. You think someone at Fort Laramie sold them guns and whiskey?"

"Laramie or Fort Hall. Sold 'em or gave 'em to 'em."

"Why would they give Indians guns? Aren't they supposed to protect settlers from the Indians?"

"If white men—soldiers or not—can get Indians to attack a train, then they don't have to."

"But why would they want to?" asked Charlie.

"Different reasons. Money. More guns. Horses. Supplies." Hoke looked Charlie in the eye. "Women."

Charlie scowled.

"Then the army goes after the Indians who attack the trains when it was really white men putting them up to it—white men waiting in the background to collect on the spoils," added James. "We've also known soldiers to sell guns and whiskey to the very Indians they're fighting. To line their own pockets or serve some personal scheme."

Charlie shook his head. "I can't believe white men would do such low things."

"Bein' white don't make a man good; we've known several who adopted low behavior."

"James is right," Hoke said. "Happens more than you might think, Charlie, especially in parts of the country where laws are scarce, and that's where you're livin' now. If these Indians were really after horses, they would've attacked when we were circled up at night. Instead, they hit us on the ascent, when we were spread out. Makes me think they had their eye on certain targets."

They found where the Indians had camped for the night—about six miles from the train—with spatters of blood on the ground.

"Two or three wounded," said James. "This one here lost quite a bit of blood, but I don't see a body."

From all indications the Indians had moved on.

"Maybe these Indians only wanted horses," surmised James. "Or maybe they just wanted us to know they don't appreciate their land being invaded. Ever since the Grattan Massacre of '54 the Sioux have been mad." James turned to Charlie. "The Grattan Massacre started over a misunderstanding about a cow."

"I don't think they'll be back," said Hoke.

"How can you be sure?" asked Charlie.

"I'm not. It's just a gut feeling."

"Hoke's gut feelings are usually right," said James.

"I still don't understand why that white man was with them and how he came to have my mother's picture."

Hoke looked Charlie in the eye. "I can't answer that." One last time he surveyed the scene where the Indians had camped. "They were after something, but whatever it was, I think they got more resistance than they bargained for."

CHAPTER 24
Neither silly nor vain

July 10, 1866

My dahlia has flowered, Mimi. It has large, purple blooms—exquisite blooms to match the beauty of the land. We're coming out of the plains and into hills that appear to have been caressed by the hand of God.

And the hand of God is holding us as we begin to travel through them.

～☯～

Hoke stood outside the Baldwyn wagon twisting his hat in his hands, the laughter that floated out choking his heart with jealousy. He had just turned to leave when Corrine lifted the back flap and said, "Hey! Mama's been asking for you."

"I better go check on some of the other patients before we roll out." Doc Isaacs climbed out with his bag and grinned at Hoke. "You were great yesterday."

Hoke nodded to him coolly. "I'm just glad more folks didn't get hurt. Glad *you* didn't get hurt."

"Glad you didn't, either. I have a feeling you wouldn't make a willing patient."

Hoke tried not to seethe as he watched the man walk away. The doc was too smiley to suit Hoke's taste.

Following on the doctor's heels, Corrine called over her shoulder, "Ma, I'm going to see Emma but I'll be back before we leave." When she climbed down, Hoke offered a hand and she took it.

"Thank you."

It was a more docile Corrine than he'd ever witnessed. He turned with raised eyebrows toward Abigail. "Is that your same wildcat of a daughter?"

"It probably won't last any longer than I'm lying here. Are you going to come in, or do I have to shout at you through the flap?"

Hoke stepped up and swung a leg over, using for only the second time the steps he'd made for her, feeling like an intruder into the private world of Abigail Baldwyn. He'd carried her in here yesterday but had hardly noticed the surroundings at the time. As he might have expected, it was nothing like the inside of his wagon, or most wagons. It looked more like a bedroom in a fine home than it did the back bed of a wagon.

He sat gingerly in the rocking chair, feeling like he might break it, and touched the side of the bed. "Is this a real bed?" Most people who slept in their wagons slept on piles of blankets. Some had straw or feather mattresses or sacks filled with old papers and feed bags.

Abigail tried to sit up and winced. "No."

He reached for her. "Don't—"

"I'm fine. Just sore, is all. I made cloth trunks for our clothes and quilts. And we brought quite a bit of extra cloth, as you know. Aren't you glad? I like that shirt, by the way. Where'd you get it?"

He grinned. "Lady friend made it for me." It was the second shirt she'd made—the one the same color as her riding skirt. His gold shirt still had her blood on it, but Mrs. Austelle was working to get that out for him.

He was pleased to see the return of her sass and humor.

"We've put the feather mattresses on our cloth trunks," she continued, "and while it's not as comfortable as my bed back home, it's much more comfortable than the ground where the boys sleep every night."

A lot of folks slept on the ground, including him. In fact, he slept only a few feet from this wagon of hers, sometimes watching her body's outline on the canvas in the light of an oil lamp as she wrote letters and read books to her girls. She read the Bible or poems to them every night. He liked to hear her read Scripture, but there was something about the poems he found mesmerizing, maybe because they were new to him.

On cooler nights, when sound carried best, he could hear their conversations. One night not long ago, Lina had begged, "Mama, sing that song you made up for me."

"What song did I make up for you?"

"You know, what's a mama gonna do?"

She laughed. "I made that song up for Corrine, sweetheart, before you were born."

"You did?" Corrine asked.

"You don't remember me singing it to you before Lina was born?"

"No. Maybe. I never really thought about it."

"All right then," said Lina. "Sing us *Corrine's* song."

What's a mama gonna do,
With a girl like you?
What's a mama gonna say,
When you play all day?
What's a mama gonna try,
When all you wanna do is cry?
What's a mama gonna do,
With a girl like you?

"Keep me." Lina giggled. "I love that song."

Hoke felt like he knew the exact look Lina had given her mother right then, and the thought made his throat tighten.

"Should I keep Corrine, too?" Abigail had asked Lina, "Even when she turns her back and refuses to join in?"

"Yes. You should keep us both because you love us both."

"Yes, ma'am. That I do."

Hoke smiled, remembering that night.

Abigail lay crossways so she could better visit with folks. There was just enough room at the end of her bed for the rocking chair and a beautifully carved box that served as a low table that held a washbasin. The rocking chair was usually kept in the second wagon, but someone had brought it in here for visitors. He ran his hand down the side of the carved box, admiring the craftsmanship.

"My father built that, from a cherry tree off our land. It's the only piece I saved when we sold all our things in Marston—that and the rug." A large blue braided rug with flecks of yellow and green covered the floor. Some cloth bags made from matching colors hung on both sides of the wagon. That was a smart idea—it kept things from rolling around inside. He looked down at the seat of the rocking chair and noticed that the same colors in the bags had been woven into it.

"I did that on purpose," Abigail said when he commented on it. "The children laugh at me for wanting things to look nice, but I can't seem to help it. I took fabric strips left over from the bags and wrapped them around some of the twine to get that color effect. Well . . . you saw me do it, I guess."

Yes . . . they had quarreled after.

A mirror was positioned smartly on one side over the carved box. This was where she combed her hair each night and morning and washed her face in the basin.

"It's a sight neater and prettier than my wagon," Hoke said.

"Men don't think about making things pretty."

"True." But he still admired beauty, and he admired functionality.

A quilt covered the bed beneath her. She was dressed and her hair loose around her shoulders. He'd only ever seen strands that escaped the loose knot of it when she rode the white filly, and hadn't realized she had so much. It hung long, past the swell of her breasts. He noticed again how soft and white her bare feet looked.

He wanted to wrap his hands around her feet, or run them through her loose hair. Instead, he touched the quilt. It was yellow, blue, and white . . . ginghams, checks, and solids.

"Did you make this?"

"My mother did."

"What's this pattern?" He'd heard the women talking about quilt patterns. This one was full of triangles in circles.

"My mother called it a pickle dish. See how the diamonds shape an oval, like a pickle dish? She used material from some of my girlhood dresses for these pieces."

"There's such a thing as a dish just for pickles?" Was she teasing him? He had not sat at a lot of fine tables in his lifetime and couldn't believe there was such a thing.

"Yes."

She smiled and took his hand to trace the outline of the dish, sending a warm current through his veins. "These form ovals like four different dishes to make the entire circle. A pickle dish of fine crystal has ridges around the edges, like these diamonds."

"Why?"

"I don't know. It just does." There was no teasing in her eyes. She didn't fault him for not knowing.

Careful not to move his hand away, loving the feel of her touch, Hoke looked around the wagon, breathing in the scent of lavender that had stirred in the air when she reached for his hand. "What? You didn't bring a pickle dish on this trip? You don't have a real one to show me?"

She laughed and let go of his hand. "No. I don't even like pickles. I don't like the sour taste or smell of vinegar."

Sour smells made him think of blood. "That reminds me, I tore up that outfit you were wearing yesterday. I'm sorry about that, but I needed something quick to plug the holes in your side."

She winced. "Don't worry about it. I'm sure it was already ruined. Corrine has probably salvaged the trimming and got rid of the rest, not wanting to upset me."

Today she wore a calico blouse, lilac with small buttons up the front and little pleats lining either side. It reminded him of the pleats she'd kept refolding the night they had their last good conversation, before he kissed her and made things awkward between them.

Her deep-purple skirts fanned out over the bed.

Abigail smoothed the wide black sash tied loosely around her waist. As Hoke drank in her surroundings with his ever-thirsty eyes, she grew more self-conscious.

Did it meet his approval?

Why should she care what he thought of her or her surroundings? But she did care. She wanted his approval. She wanted him to think well of her, and not regard her as silly for wanting to match the chair and fabric bags to the rug, or vain for covering her seeping bandages with a black sash or having a mirror nailed to the side of the wagon.

❩

Hoke thought her neither silly nor vain. He thought her fine.

They both started talking at once.

"Thank you for—" began Abigail.

"I wanted to say—" He stopped.

She laughed. "You first."

Hoke wasn't used to feeling shy or tongue-tied. "No, you," he insisted.

Her eyes held his. "Thank you for yesterday. When you brought Lina to me—I don't know how to tell you how much that meant to me. And I'm so embarrassed that I fainted! I've never done that before."

"Embarrassed?" He was incredulous. "You saved my life!"

She brushed the claim away. "I don't know about that."

But his eyes and voice were insistent. "Yes, you did. You saved my life. And before that, you were rounding up women and children and throwing 'em in your wagons. You knew those Indians were circling back around to attack from the other side, and true to your nature, you didn't squeal and you didn't run. You started shooting at 'em—runnin' right toward danger. You wouldn't listen to me when I told you plainly to stay put in your wagon." He shook his head. "I should have known you wouldn't listen to me . . . damn hardheaded woman."

He wanted to kiss her something fierce. He wanted to crawl up on that clothes-trunk bed and wrap her in his arms and bury his face in her hair, and he might have, but was afraid of hurting her—that, and she had a husband. He couldn't believe he'd let himself feel this way about a woman with a husband. His instincts usually served him better.

Abigail grinned, and then her expression grew more somber and she swallowed hard. "I've never killed anything."

"I know too well that's a god-awful feelin'. And I don't mean to make it worse, but I believe you killed two."

Her brows pinched tightly, but he kept going. "Altogether, the twenty-four able-bodied men of this wagon train killed four Indians in that skirmish yesterday, and you killed two. If I were putting together a small group to defend this train, I'd want you on my side, Mrs. Baldwyn."

"A lot of bullets fly in skirmishes like we had yesterday. I've been part of more than I care to count. But not many find their mark so well. In fact, a lot that do find their mark are pure accidents, like the bullet you took might have been."

Hoke scowled and shook his head. "The more I think about it, the more I think old man McConnelly might have shot you by accident. The Indians had rifles. A rifle shot would have—"

"Oh, no! He might have hurt someone."

Hoke scowled harder. "What do you call this?" He pointed to her side.

"I mean, what if someone else had been hurt?"

He leaned in. "What, *you* don't matter?"

"No, I mean . . . I'm just glad it was me if it had to be someone. And it's not bad. Well, it's sore, to be sure, but I'm not in danger of dying, according to Marc."

Hoke pulled back. "Marc, is it?"

Abigail had said the word innocently enough but was pleased at Hoke's reaction. He was jealous. She felt wicked for loving the fact that he was jealous and the way his forehead crinkled when he was irritated.

He *had* to still care for her then, even if he had snubbed her at the Fort Laramie dance.

A thousand times she had relived the kiss they'd shared when she'd measured him for the shirt. She could still feel his strong arms around her from yesterday, too, when he'd held her and told her that everything was all right, just before she lost consciousness.

Her face flushed at the memory.

~

Hoke noticed the flush in Abigail's cheeks and wondered if he'd hit a nerve by mentioning the doc. Trying to restrain his irritation, he said, "At any rate, I'm glad you're a dead shot. Oh, and here's your gun back."

He reached to the back of his waistband and pulled out her Colt, running his hand over the barrel. "I cleaned it and reloaded it for you. You don't have to keep it on an empty chamber. It's got a safety peg right here it'll sit on between rotations."

Her eyes looked surprised. "How did you know I kept it on an empty chamber?"

Hoke bet Marc Isaacs wouldn't have known that fact. "You only fired twice, and there were three bullets in the chamber."

"I feel better if it's sitting on an empty one."

"Well, I'm just tellin' you because you might need that sixth bullet sometime. That safety peg'll keep the hammer from hittin' the percussion cap even if it falls."

"That's just what . . . I thought it would be safer with children around."

Hoke slid his hand over the barrel again. He loved the smooth, solid feel of it. "It was better on some of the older guns, but on this Navy revolver you're fine to load every chamber. You've got six in there now. Normally a .36 wouldn't take such a big chunk out of a man, but it sure took a plug out of that fella who was behind me."

She winced. "Please don't describe it that way. You say it like it's a good thing, but it's awful. I killed a person. I was having a hard enough time without you saying I might have killed two."

No one but Hoke, Colonel Dotson, Jenkins, and Charlie knew that one of the men she'd killed had her picture in his leather pouch. Hoke wondered how that news would have made her feel. He didn't like the feel of it at all himself.

He nodded. "I know. Believe me, I know. And I'm not tryin' to make light of it, but if it had to be me or him, I'm glad he's dead and I'm not. Where do you keep this?"

She pointed to the cherry box.

He moved the wash tin and opened the lid. After laying the gun back in its case he noticed a stack of books inside. "Mind if I look at these?"

"No, go ahead."

They were good books—Charles Dickens and William Wordsworth. He would have expected no less.

"You're welcome to borrow any of those."

"I'd like that. I haven't read this one." He pulled out Wordsworth's *Poems, in Two Volumes.*

"You've read Dickens?"

Why did she say that like she was surprised? Bet she wouldn't be surprised if *Marc* had read them.

"I have. Just because I didn't go to school very long doesn't mean I don't read. '*It was the best of times, it was the worst of times,*'" he quoted, "'*it was the age of wisdom, it was the age of foolishness . . . it was the spring of hope, it was the winter of despair*'—I think that's the beginning of this one, anyway. I like Dickens."

Hoke had carried *A Tale of Two Cities* in his saddlebag a long time before trading it for his fold-up pocketknife. He lost count of how many times he'd read it, especially that passage at the beginning. Just like his old Bible. The Bible was the only thing he had that had once been his father's, so it was still in his saddlebag. He read it cover to cover as a kid, then cover to cover again, several times over, trying to figure out why his father had put such stock in it—and trying to figure out why God would allow any boy to end up alone in the world.

Reading that Bible made him less angry when he saw that God suffered, too.

"Dickens wrote that about England," Hoke said. "But it sounds like things out here, don't it?"

Abigail smiled and shook her head. "You never cease to amaze me. Why don't you take the poetry book since you've not read it? It's mine to lend. The two Dickens books belonged to Robert."

He noticed she'd said *belonged*. Sometimes she referred to Robert in the past tense, and sometimes in the present. Should he tell her what the soldier at Laramie had said about her husband? No, he decided. It would seem mean-spirited if he did.

"Thank you." He kept the book out and closed the top of the cherry box. "I'll take good care of it and get it back to you."

"Be sure to read the one about the daffodils . . . 'I Wandered Lonely as a Cloud.' That one and 'Resolution and Independence' are my favorite two."

He nodded, holding the book in his hand and staring at her so hard she began to squirm.

She lowered her lashes. "Were you going to say something before?"

"What?"

"Before. You and I started talking at the same time. Were you going to say something else?"

Just that I wish your husband weren't alive and that I'm in love with you. You're driving me crazy and distracting me with your yellow patchwork quilt and your cherry box and your bare feet and your golden hair and your blue eyes and the way you smell like lavender.

"No," Hoke said. "Just, thank you for shooting that Indian. Oh . . . and I wanted to tell you that Charlie did good yesterday and this morning. He's a good one. They're all good . . . good children." He wished they were his.

Hoke put his hands on his knees; he'd stayed too long.

"Thank you again, Hoke."

Just Hoke. It was sweet music to his ears. She put her hand on his as he stood up.

He brought it to his lips and kissed it softly. "You have lovely hands, Abby." Then he took his hat and the book and left.

Abigail lay still for a long time and thought about him, her hand hot from the kiss, her heart beating so hard it made the bullet wound in her side throb.

CHAPTER 25

Blood-orange sunsets

July 13, 1866

I remembered your remedy for fleas, Mimi. Lavender! How could I have forgotten? Now if only I knew a remedy for weevils in the sugar sack.

A steady stream of visitors helped Abigail keep her mind off Hoke. Paddy Douglas brought Carson to visit. One of the coon's legs was wrapped on a splint.

"He got dropped and stepped on during the attack," explained Paddy. "But Doc Isaacs reset it and it's healing nicely. Since you're both laid up, I thought you might enjoy each other's company."

Abigail laid a hand on Alec Douglas's arm, grateful he had come with Paddy to see her. When Paddy talked, his round eyes darted and pitched, like the tempo of his words, and hardly ever rested on the person he was talking to. He talked more than he used to, ever since he beat the colonel when they raced at the fork of the Platte River.

"I was one of the colonel's best runners when we had the attack," he reminded Abigail. "I brought bullets just like the colonel said. I didn't drop a one."

"He's taught Carson a new trick," Alec told Abigail. "Show her, Paddy."

Paddy grinned and held out a bag. "Give Mrs. Baldwyn her present, Carson." Carson reached in and pulled out a small bundle of flowers, tied with a string.

"Oh!" Abigail clapped. "How sweet! Thank you, Carson. And thank you, Paddy." She reached to hug them and winced, wondering if her side would ever stop feeling like it was on fire. "How is Baird doing today?"

"Some better," said Alec. Baird had taken a spear in his shoulder during the Indian attack. He'd been fine at first but then started a fever. "Doc thinks he'll pull through. He's still runnin' fever, tho'."

"Doc says fever is not all bad," said Paddy.

"That's right, Paddy. Doc says it's a lad's way o' fightin' infection."

"But it don't feel good," continued Paddy.

"No, he don't feel his proper self yet. We're happy to know you're feelin' better, Mrs. Abigail."

"Can I mend anything for him, for any of you?"

"Oh, no, ma'am. We've had so many offers from the lady folk, we don't want for nothin'. In fact, Paddy and I are gonna get fat if folks don't stop bein' so good to us."

"We've had two cobblers already." Paddy held up two fingers. "And Carson has had three ears of corn." He added another finger.

Alec grinned at Abigail. "He can count to ten, can't you, Paddy? We never got past ten 'cause that's all the fingers he's got."

Alec and Paddy Douglas weren't her only visitors. So many people brought Abigail flowers while she recovered that she started weaving them together and made a covering as wide as her bed. She kept adding to it, like she was weaving a quilt, letting the flowers dry and working the tapestry on a light cloth that she rolled it up in each night.

Some of the Schroeders even visited. Mrs. Inez brought two loaves of bread and Rudy and his wife, Olga, sent a cured ham and a dozen eggs.

"I take it they've forgiven you at long last for Rascal eating their chicken," said Melinda when she stopped by. "Now we know what it takes to get back in their good graces. Gettin' shot savin' one of their young'uns. You should've got shot sooner!"

"Melinda," scolded Abigail, holding her hand to her bandages. "You're making my side hurt!"

Melinda smiled mischievously. "Mr. Austelle told the colonel he figured out why the Schroeders don't shoot well. The only meat they ever eat is pork, and it's not hard to take aim on a domesticated pig."

After spending five days in the wagon, Abigail got Charlie to help her down to join the others for supper. Doc Isaacs rushed over and told her she shouldn't be getting out this soon, but she insisted, so he got her rocker and set it close to the fire.

Abigail smiled proudly at Corrine. She had taken over the cooking without complaint. Lina brought her mother a plate. Caroline Atwood came to sit with her until Will grew fussy and had to be put to bed. Doc Isaacs walked back over to her and said, "Feel like stretching your legs a little?"

"I'd love to."

She took the arm he offered and they strolled slowly around the outer circle of wagons. Alec got out his fiddle and Nichodemus and Nora were soon singing. The older children danced and played in groups while the mothers started getting younger children to bed. Abigail could see Jacob with Cooper and Lijah under the Austelles' wagon, making plans to reenact the Indian attack. Lijah had bounced back the quickest—children were always the ones who did.

"You're to be commended for saving his arm," said Abigail.

"The arrow missed the bone, so I can't claim to have worked any miracle."

"I get to be Hoke," they heard Jacob say. "You be Colonel Dotson, Cooper. Lijah, after you get shot with the arrow, you can be Harry Sims. We need more people. Go see if your sister Hannah wants to play."

Abigail looked around for her other children. Lina was with Mrs. Josephine listening to the Jaspers sing. And Corrine and Charlie were talking with Clyde and Emma Austelle.

Doc pointed to the three boys under the wagon. "Earlier they were plotting a prank on the McConnelly sisters."

"I hope it wasn't too bad."

"No worse than what they deserve."

Abigail lightly slapped his arm. "I still feel bad for what they went through." Of course, neither Irene nor Diana had been by to express their concern about her getting shot. But that had not surprised her.

"It didn't make them any nicer," said Doc Isaacs.

As they passed the next wagon Abigail caught a glimpse of Hoke on the other side of camp, leaning against a wagon wheel and talking with James, who was sanding a block of wood. Hoke was chewing on a stick, watching her and Doc Isaacs.

Abigail's hand turned hot on Doc's arm as she thought about the kiss Hoke had planted there a few days ago. He hadn't been back to see her since.

Sleep had begun to elude her. She didn't know if it was the fear of getting closer to Fort Hall that was the cause, or just that she'd been in her bed too long. Twice she'd awakened and noticed light coming through the canvas of Hoke's wagon. When she eased her linseed-oiled cover up, she could see his outline in the light of an oil lamp, reading what she suspected was her book of poetry.

"Marc, what do you know about Hoke?"

Doc gripped the hand she had laid in the crook of his arm a little tighter. "Not much really. I did hear a rumor about him in

Independence, that he'd killed a man when he was young. Something to do with a woman of ill repute. A jury found him innocent, but he left town after the trial and stayed gone twenty years. I don't tell you that to smear his name, I tell you that because I think it explains why he's so guarded all the time. He seems like a good man. He's certainly a capable man. I feel safer with him around."

Abigail was curious to know more details but knew she'd never ask for them. Once again she imagined what it would be like for Charlie or Jacob to be left alone, to have to grow up fast . . . to face hard things. "You think that's why he's blunt?"

"He's definitely authoritative." Doc grinned. "But Hoke can be gentle with the children. They sure respect him."

Abigail was surprised Hoke had never married and had children of his own. It made her wonder about Marc Isaacs's past. He was certainly going to make a good father.

"Were you close to Caroline's husband?"

"He was my dearest friend."

"I didn't realize that."

"We were roommates in medical school."

"How did he die?"

"Dysentery. It was a real lesson in humility for a couple of young physicians. My loyalty to Caroline is doublefold. She's my sister—my only sibling—our parents are both gone. And her child is the son of my closest friend. I promised William I'd help raise him."

Just then Jacob came running past them, calling to Hannah Sutler, "Dammit, Abigail! I told you to git to your wagon!" Abigail reached out and grabbed him, wincing from the sharp pain in her side.

"Watch your language, young man!"

Jacob stomped his foot. "Aw, Ma. We're having the Indian attack."

"Well you can have it without using salty language, Jacob."

"But—"

"No *but*s.'"

"Yes, ma'am."

"Do I need to put some more lavender in your hair?" she asked, running her hand through his mousy locks. "Are the fleas bothering you?"

Jacob rolled his eyes. "No, I'm fine. Can I play now?" He went back to Hannah. "Git to the wagon." He rolled his eyes at his mother.

Abigail looked at Doc Isaacs in apology.

He laughed. "That reminds me, I meant to tell you about Jacob. Yesterday, he and the youngest Austelle boy were crawling, pulling themselves on their arms, making big waves in the grass without knowing it. Hoke and James saw them and decided to have a little fun. James said, just loud enough for them to hear, 'Hoke, go get your gun, I see Indians crawlin' up to the train.' Before he said that, you could see the grass moving. But then it stopped." Doc laughed. "In fact, it might have shaken a little in fear."

Abigail had no trouble picturing the scene.

"Hoke said, 'James, I don't believe that's Indians. That's a crouching mountain lion is what that is. Why look, it's not just one, but two of 'em! Don't worry, I've got 'em in my gunsights.' Then Hoke pointed his revolver in the air and clicked the hammer back.

"Jacob and Cooper stood up and yelled, 'Don't shoot, Mr. Hoke! It's not really mountain lions! It's us!' I thought I was going to split my side it was so funny. We sat around at supper last night and retold that several times."

"Jacob's never been short on imagination." She decided to change the subject. "How is Nelda Peters?"

Doc's face turned sad. "Better. Right after the baby came . . . you heard it was stillborn?"

Abigail nodded.

"She shouldn't have delivered for several more weeks, but the baby had already died. I thought we were going to lose Nelda, too, she bled so much. Sorry." He looked down. "That was more than you needed to know. The night after an Indian attack is not an easy time to give birth. She was scared to make a sound—scared she'd put us all in danger, I think. Her heart raced the whole time. And then she was worried the baby would cry and make noise, only he didn't."

Doc shook his head. "She was going to name him Timmy, she said."

Abigail gripped his arm more tightly. "How is she handling it?"

"She's pretty heartbroken. I've got bags of laudanum, turpentine, castor oil, quinine, blue moss, calomel, Epsom salts, McLean's pills . . . you name it . . . but I don't have a thing for a broken heart. They didn't teach us how to cure that."

"What's the blue moss for?"

"Works good on mountain fever, especially if you combine it with calomel and laudanum. Worked a charm on the Schroeders, but it hasn't helped Baird Douglas's fever."

Abigail searched back through her mind. "I don't remember you using that on Lina."

"Well, I did." He patted her hand. "You weren't quite yourself when Lina was sick, so I'm not surprised you don't remember."

Abigail smiled at him apologetically. "I need to visit Nelda."

"Wait and make sure you don't get a fever."

"I'm not going to get a fever. And you're wrong."

He stopped walking. "About what?"

"You do have something it takes to mend a broken heart."

He looked at her quizzically.

"Time and the sweet attentions of a good man can do a woman a world of good."

Abigail liked Doc and there was something about Nelda. She seemed right for him, and Caroline and Nelda were close.

Doc's mouth fell open. "I can't believe you're playing matchmaker after our conversation at Alcove Springs about me not needing to be in any rush to look for a wife."

Abigail lifted her shoulders, innocently. "I'm not suggesting you rush. I'm only suggesting that you would be good for Nelda. Whether Nelda would be good for *you* is for you to decide. Now give me a hug."

He held his arms out and she wrapped hers around him. "You've done so much for me, and I'm grateful. I can't help wanting to see you happy."

 ∽

Hoke swore under his breath when Abigail and Doc Isaacs's laughter floated over to him.

Doc's attentions had picked up more than he felt necessary. Sure, Abigail had been shot, but so had Duncan Schroeder. Doc spent a lot more time with Abigail than he did with Duncan, and Duncan wasn't out of the woods yet.

He stalked over to her rocking chair and picked it up, setting it in the boys' wagon, then watched as *Marc* hugged Abigail and helped her climb the steps Hoke had built for her.

 ∽

The man known as Robert Baldwyn made camp in the usual place. He waited three days, but the trapper never showed. Before going back to the fort he rode out to the cabin to check on Bonnie.

"You seen your father?" he asked.

"Not for a while. Why?"

"No reason."

When he got back to the fort, Robert sharpened his sword.

 ∽

The Rocky Mountains are lovely, Mimi. The highest peaks are capped with white, and the bottoms are purple in the evenings against blood-orange sunsets. It must be the purity of the air that makes the tones so deep.

Someone rapped hard on the side of her wagon. The train had stopped for the noonday meal and Abigail was resting. She pulled back the cloth. There stood Tam Woodford smiling broadly. "You can come to my weddin' if you promise not to wear that blue dress!"

Abigail scrambled to get down and hug her neck. "Congratulations, Tam! Why can't I wear my blue dress?"

Tam crinkled her nose. "'Cause I want Harry to look at *me*, that's why."

"Is the dress sinful?"

"No, it's just gorgeous and has the prettiest detailing I ever saw."

"When's the wedding?"

"This Sunday."

"Do you want to wear it?"

Tam looked at Abigail's middle, then her own. "It ain't gonna fit this waist."

"I could let it out. Or do you want me to make you a dress?"

"Mrs. Abigail, you're trying to recover!"

"Sewing's not hard." Abigail's mind starting working out the options. "I can add detailing to something you've already got, or I can start from scratch. Oh, please let me! It will give me something to do while I have to ride in the wagon. Which will it be?"

They talked about what color would look best—Tam wanted to wear white, with a veil and lots of lace, real girly, which surprised Abigail. Tam had a tan dress and Abigail said they could add some white lace to it and put some thickness in the skirt so it would billow a bit more.

For the next few days she and Tam measured and planned and basted.

On Sunday, after Harry Sims had preached a short sermon, Colonel Dotson married Harry and Tam on a creek bank just west of the Continental Divide.

Just before the wedding, Tam had stood behind the Baldwyns' second wagon, looking radiant. "I hardly know myself and I sure don't recognize this dress."

She turned as Abigail, Corrine, and Melinda all held up mirrors so she could see herself. Abigail thought she felt Hoke's eyes watching her in the glass, but when she peered past the wagon she instead saw James Parker, who was looking at Corrine.

༕

When they reached Soda Springs, Colonel Dotson decided that the train would stay several days to let those who were recovering enjoy the pools that were said to have healing effects. Abigail lay in a warm pool each day in a lightweight dress, the water bubbling and fizzing as she lowered herself in. Lina climbed in with her one day. "It tickles!"

"It feels like God is stitching me back up," said Abigail. Her heart might soon be mended, too. In a matter of days she should know how things stood between her and Robert.

Some of the pools had alkali in them. The men worked hard to keep the stock out of the poisoned pools, but it was harder to keep the small animals out. Rascal got sick after drinking some of the water.

"Alkali is a nuisance!" declared Hoke.

Charlie and Jacob held Rascal while Hoke shot fresh water down his throat with a bottle, to flush out the poison.

Hoke rubbed his ears a long time afterward, watching Abigail from a distance. When she climbed out of the pool her wet clothes stuck to her skin, accentuating the shape of the woman who had now seeped into his bloodstream like a poison.

"Hurts, don't it?" he muttered to the dog. "I hope you've learned your lesson."

Back on the plains, when they'd walked across a stretch of dry alkali, the men had cut leather pieces and covered all the stock's feet to keep them from burning. Rascal had chewed his off twice and got sores on the pads of his feet, but it never made him sick like this.

The Baldwyn children all fussed over him and worried he would die, but the fresh water did him good. He was up and running by the next day.

Baird Douglas, whose fever had finally broken, especially benefited from soaking in the pools. Duncan Schroeder was still too weak to be lifted down to the pools, so several of the Schroeder women—including his wife, Katrina, and his mother, Mrs. Inez—gathered water by the bucketsful to pour over him as they prayed for his healing.

It wasn't enough. Duncan Schroeder died the last night they camped by the springs. The Schroeders were as somber as they'd ever been as Duncan was buried before the train moved out the following morning.

CHAPTER 26

Balls are loaded, caps are on

He sat on his big red roan and waited with the men in his unit, watching Sergeant Smith approach with a tall, dark stranger on a fine-looking stallion. A black dog was at the horse's heels, as if the man, horse, and dog all came as a set.

"Cap'n Baldwyn!" called Sergeant Smith as he came within earshot. "Wagon train's coming." Smith nodded his head toward the man beside him. "This scout from the train says your wife and children are part of the company."

He steeled his jaw. So . . . the trapper had indeed failed. He'd really thought the old serpent could pull it off. Now what would he do? He wondered what had happened, and whether the trapper was dead.

Checking his thoughts, he looked around at his men, then let his eyes roll over the scout, horse, and dog. They were all staring at him. The scout's eyes, especially, bore into him hard.

"Were you expecting your family?" asked Sergeant Smith.

"I was not."

The scout's fierce eyes narrowed. "You didn't get word she was coming?"

"I was not . . . expecting her this soon." He smiled at the scout. The man didn't smile back. "You're sure it's her?" Who was this hard, handsome scout scrutinizing him so closely? And what was it to *him*?

"I'm sure it's Abigail Baldwyn from Marston, Tennessee, lookin' for her husband, Captain Robert Baldwyn of the 113th regiment servin' at Fort Hall." The dark stranger's eyes continued to burrow into him. "That you?"

He smiled widely this time . . . victoriously . . . and pointed to the name embroidered on his chest. "That's me. Men, I need a moment. How far away is the train?"

"About an hour out," one of the soldiers answered.

๑๑

Hoke felt a sharp, instant dislike for Robert Baldwyn. Why? Was it simple jealousy? Because his heart was racing wild with the bitter sensation.

He had wanted to believe this man did not exist. Even after Laramie, and after hearing Abigail talk about Robert, Hoke's gut had refused to accept what logic had shouted. But here Robert was: alive and, from what Hoke's gut was telling him, not the type of man to whom he could begrudgingly concede her.

Was he being influenced by the comments made by the soldier at Laramie? Hoke prided himself on his ability to read other men accurately. He couldn't afford to lose that skill—not out here in this land where a man's wits and guts were his two most critical weapons.

But, no. There was something amiss about this man. Whatever kind of man he had been before, the Robert Baldwyn who sat on this big red roan in front of him now was more than just arrogant.

Hoke let his eyes run over Baldwyn again, from his overly shiny boots up to his neatly trimmed beard. His uniform was crisp . . . impeccable.

The other men looked hot and dusty. Did he launder his clothes every day, as if expecting an audience with the president? A fancy sword hung at his side. Some men still used bayonets out here, but this was a big gold-handled rapier. It was something old Spanish fighters would have used—an impractical weapon in these parts and times.

He searched the man's face for any resemblance to Charlie, Corrine, Jacob, and Lina but couldn't find it. Maybe he just couldn't be objective.

Of course he couldn't be objective.

"She'll probably head this way when she hears you're this close," he said. "There were a couple of others with me when we crossed paths with your sergeant. They rode back to the train." As much as Hoke had wanted to see Abigail's reaction when she heard her husband was close, he had wanted to see this man even more. He'd wanted to size him up before Abigail got to him.

Baldwyn turned to Sergeant Smith. "Ride back to the train. Send Mrs. Baldwyn on ahead—just her. I'd like a little time with her." He looked hard at Hoke. "Surely you can understand a man wanting to spend time . . . privately . . . with his wife?"

Hoke shot daggers at him with his eyes.

Baldwyn looked down at the ground with an air of drama. "I'm afraid I'm going to be emotional, men. I'd like just a moment to compose myself and get ready to receive my wife." He looked back up at Hoke. "Is she still good-looking?"

Hoke answered with another glare.

"Of course she is," Baldwyn answered himself. "Are you married— I'm sorry, I don't know your name."

"Mathews." *And you better call me Mister.*

"Are you married, Mr. Mathews?"

"No." Hoke wheeled his horse around. He had to get out of here. He'd seen enough. He'd never be married. *To hell with it!* And to hell and double hell with Captain Robert C. Baldwyn.

"I'll let her know you're waitin' for her," he spat as he kicked his heels to the stallion.

Rascal shot after him, working hard to keep pace with the horse that carried the man who held his allegiance.

◦◦◦

The man known as Robert Baldwyn turned to Sergeant Smith. "Did that scout seem unhappy to you?"

Smith didn't answer. He knew Smith didn't like him, but he didn't care.

"Go with him," he ordered. "All of you. Go meet the train and send Mrs. Baldwyn on to me. Just her, Smith. Okay? I'd like a chance to talk to her alone before I see anyone else. Don't let that scout come back with her. Tell him you'll accompany Mrs. Baldwyn instead, but send her on and keep a fair distance. I fear it will be an emotional reunion and would rather not have an audience."

"Yes, sir," said Smith. "I understand, sir."

◦◦◦

August 7, 1866

We have arrived in Idaho Territory, Mimi.

Abigail set down her quill and crawled from the wagon. She pulled off her hat, wiped the day's dust and a thin sheen of sweat from her brow, then took off her vest and fanned her face, wondering where Hoke was. She missed the regular bucket of water he always had waiting for her . . . and she missed him.

Lina danced over with a pail full of berries. "Can we have cobbler, Mama? Mrs. Chris and Mrs. Jo found blackberries and sent us some!"

Abigail looked in the pail at the ripe berries—dark as the night. She ate one. It was so sweet they'd need little sugar. That was good considering they were so low.

"Sure, precious."

She smiled as Lina raced to tell Corrine. It felt so good to be back to normal that Abigail didn't even mind the cooking chores. Her side had finally quit hurting, but she still had the scabs, one where the bullet had gone in and one where it went out. She'd always have the scars.

Charlie came sprinting toward her. "Ma! Ma!"

Her heart missed a beat, thinking something had happened to Jacob.

"You're not going to believe this," said Charlie breathlessly. "Pa's here."

His words hung in the air.

She looked sharply around. Where was Hoke? Tears sprang to her eyes and she blushed with shame. "Where?" she whispered.

"A few miles west of here. Bart and Orin Peters were with Mr. Hoke scouting ahead and they met some soldiers from the 113th who said Pa was with them. Well, he wasn't right there with them, he was back a ways. Mr. Hoke rode out to meet him while Bart and Orin rode back this way to tell us. Jacob's getting the horses hitched. Come on!"

"Wait a minute, Charlie! Slow down. I need a minute to think." She trembled all over and longed to see Hoke. Why had he gone ahead instead of coming back to tell her this news himself?

No . . . she could guess why. It was just like him to scout out the danger.

What would Robert look like after five years? she wondered. What if things were awkward between them? How would things *not* be awkward between them? What had she planned to say? Why had she come on this trip? Oh, she couldn't remember!

She grabbed Charlie's arm to keep him from running back to Jacob. "I'd rather see him by myself first. Before you children see him."

The excitement fled from Charlie's face, but she knew it was the right decision.

What if war and time had changed him? *Of course they would have changed him!* Lieutenant Coatman's words came back to her . . . *opinionated and stubborn* . . . as did Cecil Ryman's claim that Robert had killed his brother without cause.

It was going to be a shock to the children to see him, having built him up in their minds. She needed to get past seeing him herself before she could focus on the children.

Maybe it had been a mistake to come. Maybe they should have left well enough alone. But here they were . . . too late now.

Charlie's eyes pleaded with her. "Mother, no. We're going with you."

Abigail planted her feet. "Charlie, you have to trust me on this. I need to see him first. I need a chance to talk to him and . . . compose myself." A hard tremor in her voice made it sound strange to her own ears.

Charlie put his hands on his hips and shook his head. Three months ago he would have argued with her and they both knew it. But the events of the past three months had matured Charlie Baldwyn into a man.

He didn't like it. He didn't agree. But he looked her in the eye and said, "Yes, ma'am."

Abigail pulled him close and kissed his cheek.

The worry on his face was sharp. "Are you sure you don't want me to ride out with you, Ma?" he whispered. "I could hold back, but be close by."

"No, son. I need you to be here for your brother and sisters. Get them ready, will you? And maybe tidy things up in the wagons?"

Charlie shook his head again, but the tension drained from his shoulders. "Of course."

"Corrine can get supper. Tell her there are some new potatoes ready next to the dahlia. They'd be good with onions. And Lina wants a cobbler."

The normalcy of giving Charlie chores made her feel better. But her legs were shaky as she found Jacob with James, who was saddling the gray dun for her.

Suddenly people were everywhere, asking questions. Was it true? What providence! Was she going out to meet him? Did she want some of the men to go with her? What about the children? What about supper? How could they help?

Abigail thanked them and said she'd be fine riding out on her own. She preferred to ride out alone. It would give her time to think.

With trembling hands, she grasped the saddle horn and swung up onto the dun, wondering if she should smooth her hair or wash her face.

She decided against it. Instead, she set her face to the west and rode out to meet her husband.

⁓

Three miles out Abigail spotted a rider. Even if Rascal hadn't been running at his side she would have known it was Hoke. Few men rode with such ease on a horse, and few men had a mount so beautiful as the stallion.

His face looked ominous as he approached. At first she thought he was going to ride right past her without speaking, but he stopped suddenly, wheeled around, and turned to trot beside her. Seeing him was a relief, but also troubling.

She loved him.

She allowed herself to think it at last: she loved Hoke Mathews. He might once have loved her, too, but love wasn't presently reflected in his eyes.

Abigail had stopped wanting to find Robert weeks ago, in the moment she'd laid the blue crocheted bag into Hoke's perfect, strong hand at the corral in Independence—before he'd ever held her dancing or kissed her behind the wagon. This was the man she wanted the freedom to love: This brooding man beside her. This man who would now never be hers.

Hoke wouldn't want her if he knew how fickle she was. She had driven Robert away by not supporting him, and now, after coming all this way to patch things up, she'd given her heart to someone else.

Robert was alive. It didn't feel real. She was outside her own body watching a scene play out, her heart turned as lifeless as a stone.

In moments Abigail would be her husband's again, and Hoke would be left with nothing but the taste of hope gone sour. Hope deferred made a heart sick . . . he'd read that in Scripture. And while he'd felt abandonment and shame before, and experienced fear and all the ferociousness of nature, he'd never felt a knife cut as sharp as did the deferment of his hope for her.

When she had been shot he'd had something to do: check to see if the bullet was out, try to stop the bleeding, get her to the wagon and fetch the doc.

The memory of it washed over him and he longed to have her back at the Indian fight, trembling and needing him to calm her.

He wanted her to want him—*him!* Not that arrogant man he'd just met. *Damn Robert Baldwyn for being alive!*

He kicked the stallion forward and blocked her path, unable for the first time to look her in the eye. "Don't go."

She didn't answer. When he looked back up he saw her eyes were filled.

It ripped his heart out.

Could she really have once loved that man he'd just met? If so, then she wasn't the woman he'd believed her to be. Or had Hoke's keen judgment become all twisted?

God amighty, he was miserable! He wished he'd never met this woman and never come on this train. Now what would he do? He couldn't stay within a thousand miles of her if she was living with that man.

"I have to, Hoke." He'd never heard her voice so strained.

He gritted his teeth. A group of riders appeared ahead—the 113th. Hoke had ridden hard; they had loped along. This was it, then . . . the last moment he'd ever have in private with her.

"Did you bring your gun?" he asked, thickly.

She looked surprised. "No. Why would I need it?"

Hoke unwound his pommel holster, dismounted, and reached for her saddle, fastening the holster to it. "Take this with you. It's a little bigger than the one you're used to, but you can handle it." It was a .44 Army Colt. "Balls are loaded, caps are on. All six cylinders . . . ready to fire."

Her brow was twisted. He wished to God she wouldn't look at him that way!

"Hoke, I'm sure I don't need it. I hate to take your—"

"Take it!" His voice was raw. "It'll make me feel better."

The soldiers drew up as he remounted the stallion.

"Mrs. Baldwyn?" said Sergeant Smith, who approached them with obvious trepidation. "The captain is waiting just ahead for you, ma'am. Not much more than a mile there by a creek. He was hoping he could see you alone before coming back to the rest of your family."

Smith warily watched Hoke.

"Yes, of course," said Abigail, also looking at Hoke, then back to the sergeant. "That's best."

Hoke sat still on his horse. It took every bit of effort he had not to move, not to kill every one of these men, take her in his arms, and ride off with her. That was what it felt like he should do. If he did that, he would be protecting her. But from what? Her own husband?

He willed himself not to move while Abigail urged the dun forward.

CHAPTER 27

Like a low-hanging storm cloud

The man stood by a stream in a small grove of aspens with his back to her, his boot propped on a fallen log. He heard her approach and dismount but didn't turn around.

She'd come this far. Let her come a little farther.

༄

Abigail noted how tall he looked. His shoulders had never been so wide. Robert had been a slender man—now he was robust. She tied her horse to a tree and walked toward him, her legs like jelly beneath her skirts.

"Is it really you, Robert? You seem taller. Stronger." She was nearly to him.

He turned and took his hat off.

She stopped cold, her eyes frozen to his red beard and hair.

It wasn't Robert.

"Hadley! What are *you* doing here? I was told Robert was waiting alone. Where is he?" She looked around but there was only one horse tied nearby.

Hadley laughed. "Abigail Walstone, I believe you've gotten prettier. How is that possible? What? No hug for good old Hadley Wiles?"

He opened his arms but she stayed rooted to the spot.

"I thought you'd be glad to see me again." His eyes were icy. "To have a chance to make up for that last time when we parted on awkward terms."

"Where's Robert?" she whispered. It was as loud as she could make her voice work.

"Come on, Abigail. Aren't you even going to hug me? Aren't you just a little bit glad to see me?"

The strange edge to his voice frightened her. She was trying not to panic, but . . . why was Hadley here? And where was Robert?

"You know, you've thrown me like a wild mustang coming out here. I mean . . . I got your letters, of course." The turn of his mouth grew hard. "You haven't given me a lot of choice here, Abigail. Things could have gone a little easier for you if you'd acted glad to see me this time."

Hadley was poison. She had hoped to never see him again.

Abigail willed herself to move, to take a step back toward her horse. Her horse . . . there was a gun on the pommel! James had once told her Hoke had a sixth sense. She should have taken that to heart. She should have put Hoke's gun in her pocket.

Hadley stepped left, putting himself between her and her horse. "Where you goin' so fast? We got a lot to talk about."

Abigail's eyes shot to his chest. His shirt said *Baldwyn* on the pocket. His stripes were captain's stripes.

Hadley cocked his head. "I realize it may take you a while to get used to the idea, but I . . . this wasn't how I had planned to break the news to you."

Abigail inched backward. "I don't know what you're talking about, Hadley. I'm looking for Robert. What have you done with him?"

"I am Robert." He stepped closer. "The new edition. *That* Robert died some time ago. Only weeks after he left Marston, best I can calculate."

He took another step toward her. Then another.

Abigail shook her head. "Liar! He's been sending me letters."

Hadley threw his head back and laughed, stepping closer. "That wasn't him, love. That was *me*. Haven't you figured this out yet? I thought you were smarter than that."

She looked at the name on his chest again. "You're impersonating Robert?" She was going to be sick.

"Yes, love. It was me sending you those sweet letters. I've been Robert Baldwyn for a while now. Since just after the last time I saw you, matter of fact. Maybe now I'll get that kiss . . . and more."

He stepped closer.

Abigail swallowed to keep the bile down as the truth swept over her. She looked at Hadley's right hand. Two fingers were missing.

He held out the hand and flicked his remaining fingers. "That part was true. Which is why I had to keep my gloves on last time I saw you."

What a fool she'd been!

The content of the letters had reflected an altered Robert, but to think that Hadley had stepped into his shoes and clothing . . . who had ever heard of such a thing? She suddenly thought of the children: the children would be crushed.

She and Hadley had grown up together. He had asked her to marry him when they were young. Even then he'd sent chills down her spine. Then, not long after Robert had left, Hadley showed up on her doorstep.

Corrine had seen the whole thing, she'd discovered later—how Hadley had swaggered up the sidewalk to where Abigail was pruning her plants.

"Hadley! We heard you had been killed."

"Army makes mistakes sometimes." He grinned, then started to chuckle.

The hair at the base of her scalp had prickled then, like it prickled now. "What's funny?" she had asked him.

"I was just thinking how I know something about your husband I bet you'd like to know."

"What?"

"I'll tell you for a kiss."

When Abigail told him to leave, he grabbed her wrist and said, "If you knew what it was, you'd do more than kiss me. You'd let me in your bed."

She jerked her hand free and slapped him for such an insult, then ordered him off her property. He got halfway down the walk before he turned. "I'll give you one more chance, Abigail Walstone." His eyes were narrow, his tone menacing. "Would you marry me if you had it to do over? Me, instead of Robert Baldwyn?"

"Never."

Anger flashed in his eyes. "You sure about that? You sure you don't want to give it a try?"

An equal anger flashed in her own. "Don't come back here, Hadley."

The memory of the encounter washed over Abigail as she took another step back.

"Why?" she asked.

She needed to get out of here. No one else was coming. But—hope rose in her chest—there was a gun on her pommel! Hoke's words came back to her: *Balls are loaded, caps are on. All six cylinders . . . ready to fire.*

"Robert Baldwyn had some things going for him," Hadley was saying. "A title, the respect of men . . . you. But he had the misfortune of getting killed in a battle where the troops were widely scattered."

"You fought for the Confederacy." She searched her mind for the details. "In a regiment from Nashville. Same regiment as Robert's cousin. We heard you'd been killed. Somewhere in Virginia." Abigail took another step back.

"It didn't take me long to see the writing on the wall," he said, stepping closer. "The Union was better dressed, better fed, better supplied.

And they had Henry rifles. There was no way we were going to win. I admire Robert Baldwyn for figuring that out so early. He was an intelligent man, Abigail. You did all right."

Hadley's nonchalance made her blood boil. "How did you get his jacket?"

Hadley took another step forward. "As fate would have it, I was coming through Virginia when I happened on a field of dead soldiers that hadn't been ransacked yet. I was looking for better boots in my size when I turned over your dearly departed, shot in the—" He cocked his head. "Do you care to know where he was shot?"

Tears slid down her cheeks. What a monster. How could he be so cavalier?

"I'm sorry, love, but it was significant because he was shot in the head. That meant no holes in the uniform, which was important for me. And the luck of coming across someone I knew . . . that was gold, Abigail. I couldn't have pulled it off without that. I didn't know Robert so well as some, but I knew he only had one brother, who conveniently died himself before the war was over—thanks for letting me know about that. And I knew you, having grown up with you. I knew you *well*, having been in love with you once already."

Hadley inched closer—too close.

When Abigail turned to run he caught her arm and yanked her off balance. Then he twisted her arm behind her back.

She cried out as pain shot up her shoulder. Another inch and the bone would snap.

"You can't leave. It's rude! I'm in the middle of a story here."

His breath rolled into her nose. For all his spit and polish, it was foul . . . perhaps because it bubbled up from a foul, cold soul. The bullet holes in her side that hadn't hurt in days began to throb and pulse again.

"I hatched a quick plan and swapped coats and boots." Hadley pointed her toward his horse. She had no choice but to go where he guided her, but she dragged her feet as slowly as she dared.

"His jacket was a little snug but it had lieutenant's stripes. That was sure better than what I had. I slipped on over to Ohio, putting enough distance between me and the next regiment to the south that nobody would know what Robert Baldwyn was supposed to look like. Luckily they reassigned me fast and didn't send me back—but the men in his original unit had all been wiped out anyway."

Hadley eased up on her arm a little. But when Abigail tried to straighten it out, he jerked it back up, sending a shooting pain through her elbow.

"I suddenly had power, Abigail. Men listened to me and respected what I had to say, all because of that jacket and those stripes." He laughed, putting his mouth close to her ear. "And there was a letter from you in the pocket. Your picture, too. I'd show it to you, but I gave it to a man who was supposed to stop you. Let that be a lesson—if you want a job done right, you need to do it yourself."

He continued to push her forward. They were close to his horse, now. "Every man I showed that picture to was pea-green jealous. Bonnie, too.

"I started writing you letters. And even better, you started writing *me* letters. You were finally talking sweet to me, Miss Stuck-Up Little Walstone." He dug his elbow in her back.

Abigail cringed.

"I *had* you! You didn't know it was me, but I had you, Abigail."

The look on his face was like that of a happy spider, ready to wrap its prey.

Abigail fought to draw breath into her lungs. The pain in her arm and side was shooting and sharp but now overshadowed by the efforts of her chest to rise and fall.

What did it feel like to die?

Hoke thought she was with her husband. He wouldn't interfere. He wouldn't come for her. She'd made Charlie stay back at the wagon train to wait for her, too. Now she understood why the letters had never talked about the children.

Would Hadley kill her?

She would not die, so help her God! She would not leave her children as orphans. Hoke had been an orphan.

Hadley's breath blew hot on her neck. "Do you have any idea how much I loved your letters? You have written me the sweetest things. That you loved me . . . that you missed me and wanted me to come home to you. Which I did once, but"—he clucked his tongue—"you didn't know it.

"I offered to tell you, for a kiss. It's going to take more than a kiss this time, sweetheart."

⁓

It wasn't easy dragging Abigail toward his horse.

"When it looked like the war was nearly over," he grunted, kicking at the feet she'd planted on the ground, "I asked for the transfer out here. I was a better Union soldier once I switched sides and became Robert Baldwyn. I was promoted to captain—remember when I wrote you about that?"

He stopped to catch his breath and studied a spot at the top of her collarbone.

"I haven't been celibate," he admitted. "Bonnie's the bastard child of a supplier I traded with, but I'm thinking we've made our last deal. She's not too bright. I've never had bright. So this will be a nice change for me."

Abigail tried to free her arm to slap him. "If you have defamed Robert's name, so help me, I'll kill you."

He tightened his grip and jerked her next to his horse, where he had some rope in the saddlebags. Abigail groaned in pain, which he found thrilling.

Leaning close to her ear again he said, "I'd like to see you try, wife."

"I am not your wife." She pulled and jerked.

He held her tight. "That's right. You turned me down. How old were we? Thirteen? But now, I'm Robert Baldwyn. And you said yes to Robert Baldwyn. It's time I enjoyed my privileges. If the game's about over, then by God I *will* enjoy my privileges."

"I'm not going anywhere with you."

"Yes, you are. I got a nice little cabin. Bonnie's not going to like it, but I can deal with her. I figure we got one good night before your new beau comes looking for you."

"I don't know what beau you're referring to."

"Yes, you do." He had a hard time holding her, but managed to keep her arms pinned and get the rope he needed. "That dark-headed scout—he was sick to see me. Wanted to hit me so bad he couldn't hardly sit on his fancy horse. I figure he's got it bad for you, and look at you . . . who wouldn't? Now be a good wife and remember you're married to me. I'd hate to mess up your pretty face, but don't think I won't. Just ask Bonnie."

Before he turned her around to tie her arms, he kissed her forcefully on the mouth.

She wrenched her head away and spat on him. So he slapped her— hard across the face. Then he wrestled her to the ground, tied her hands behind her back, and threw her over the front of his horse.

"By God, you're a handful." He wiped his face and brushed the grass and dust off his clothes. He didn't like to get his captain's uniform dirty.

Hadley grabbed the reins of her dun, swung up on his big roan behind her, and headed down the middle of the creek for several hundred yards before cutting up a gravel bed that led to the south.

❧

Hoke rode into camp with the soldiers, his thoughts brewing.

How long would Abigail and Baldwyn be? Should he ride out and check on things? No . . . that could be humiliating. But he was antsy . . . restless as a caged panther.

Charlie and Jacob sought him out.

"Did you see him, Mr. Hoke? How did he look?"

"Strong." And arrogant . . . just like the soldier at Laramie had said.

Hoke couldn't bear to talk to anyone right now. Where was his ax? He needed something to do. Swinging the heavy head of an ax into a tough, hard log might help.

Hoke looked around for a hardwood tree. Hickories had grown scarce.

Jacob slapped the fair-haired older brother he adored on the back. "Looks just like Charlie, don't he?" Hoke turned to leave.

"Aw, you don't even remember him," said Charlie. "You've only seen pictures."

"He has a fine red beard, I can tell you that much." This came from one of the soldiers who'd ridden in with Hoke.

"Red?" asked Charlie. "Pa's hair's not red; why would he have a red beard?"

Hoke stopped.

"Why, of course his hair's red." The soldier laughed. "You just haven't seen him in a long time, son, you probably don't remember it right."

Hoke whipped his head around to Charlie. "You got a likeness of your father?"

"Yes, sir, in the wagon."

"Go get it." He needed to see that picture.

Hoke filled his canteen and watered his horse. He asked James to pack a food sack. He took his knife—an Arkansas toothpick with a coffin-shaped handle and eleven-inch blade—and tied its sheath to his left leg below the holster. His sidearm—another Army Colt with pearl handles—rode low on his hip, a thin strap tied around his thigh at its base. He cracked it open to look in the cylinder, then snapped it back in place and cradled it in the leather. He checked the extra ammunition he always kept in his saddlebags—.44 cartridges for the rifle, .44 balls, powder, and grease for the Colt, along with two extra prepacked cylinders. He stuffed one in each pocket. He pulled out the rifle and checked the chamber, then sheathed it back in the stallion's saddle.

His quick movements stirred the air like a low-hanging storm cloud.

Charlie came back carrying their family pictures in a small brown packet. Corrine and Lina were with him.

"What's going on, Mr. Hoke?" Corrine's brow was twisted like her mother's. "And how come you're wearing your knife like that?"

He stepped toward Charlie. "I want to check these tintypes."

A couple of the soldiers, including the one who'd said Captain Baldwyn had red hair, came over to look, too.

The first picture Charlie showed them was of Captain Baldwyn in his uniform.

Jacob was right. This man looked just like Charlie would in another few years—different eyes, but the same nose and chin.

"That was taken right after he joined up. He mailed it back to Mama. He was just a lieutenant then," said Jacob. "And this is Ma and Pa the day they married. Those are our uncles in the back there. That one is Seth. He was killed."

"That's not him." Hoke looked at the soldiers for an explanation. "That's not the man I just met."

One of the soldiers was still looking at the pictures. "There's Captain Baldwyn." He pointed to a man standing in the background in Abigail and Robert's wedding picture.

Corrine's breath caught. "No, that's Hadley Wiles. He asked Mother to marry him once when they were younger, and he made some unwanted advances on her again a few years ago. I saw it."

Hoke's heart lifted briefly . . . then sank like a stone.

He dropped the pictures and ran to his horse. Charlie was right behind him. "I'm going with you!" he yelled.

"No! Stay here." Hoke stopped long enough to turn and look Charlie in the eye. "Charlie, I don't know what I'm going to find. If he's taken her, I can track 'em better alone. And hold the dog here. I can't worry about anything or anybody else makin' noise."

"If he's taken her?" repeated Charlie.

Hoke could see the boy was trying to work it out in his mind, but he was out of time. "Hold the dog," he repeated.

Charlie and Jacob grabbed Rascal and held him tight.

James poked a food sack and a flask of whiskey in Hoke's saddlebag.

"You think I'm going to need that?" Hoke said in a low voice about the whiskey. They looked at each other for a second.

"I pray God will give thy horse strength, Hoke. And that He'll clothe his neck with thunder. That's from Job 39, by the way. And this whiskey'll give you strength and clothe your neck with thunder. It settles a man's nerves, whether he's having his worst day, or his best."

Pray it's my best. Hoke couldn't say it out loud. His throat squeezed at James's words like somebody had him in a choke hold.

James laid a hand on his shoulder. "You want me to come?"

Hoke shook his head. This was something he needed to do alone.

"I'll see to things here, then." James clapped him on the back. "Keep your head clear."

James scooped Lina up in one arm and put the other around Corrine.

Hoke put his foot in the stirrup and felt a tug on his sleeve.

Lina's big eyes met his. "I want my mama."

"I'll get her for you, baby."

He kissed her on the forehead, then kicked the stallion and rode. Hard.

❧

Word quickly spread through the camp and folks hurried over to ask questions. Colonel Dotson and Christine ran up just as Hoke rode off.

"George, shouldn't you go with him?" asked Christine.

Colonel Dotson shook his head and considered the falling blanket of evening. "No, I believe he can handle it. If they're not back by first light, we'll strike out after 'em."

CHAPTER 28
The smell of the roan

Abigail lay facedown over Hadley's horse, her hands tied tightly behind her back. When he had first thrown her over, the jolt slammed the air out of her lungs. When he mounted the horse beside her, he pushed her hard against the pommel. She fought for breath. The hard leather of the saddle and the roll caused by the top of the roan's shoulders when it started to move dug hard into her stomach.

Finally, her chest heaved and her lungs filled again, causing every nerve in her side to surge with pain.

When she tried to lift her head, Hadley smacked it back down, the smell of the roan filling her nostrils.

"I was crazy about you, you know," Hadley said. "From the time we were young. Why did you never care for me?"

It took every effort to breathe. How did he expect her to talk? "I thought of you as a friend," she managed to get out.

"No, you didn't. You were nice enough until I asked you to marry me that time. Then you wouldn't have anything to do with me. But you sure lit up when Robert Baldwyn came to town."

"Our families have always known each other, Hadley. I was sad when I heard you'd been killed."

"I bet you were. Did you cry, Abigail? Did you shed tears for me? You sure didn't act relieved when you saw me on your sidewalk. Back there by the creek, either. Wouldn't even hug me."

"I wasn't expecting to see you. Either time."

All Abigail could see now was the ground moving below the roan's hooves. It was getting dark. How far had they gone? Would anyone come looking for her tonight? It was unlikely, she thought with sinking hope. *God help me*, she prayed.

"If you'd given me the least bit of encouragement, Abigail, I would have told you Robert had been killed and not me. But you scorned me. So you brought it on yourself. At least I had the letters. You acted like you wanted me in your letters. 'Cept that last one from Marston. You seemed angry in that last one."

She *had* been angry but had tried not to show it.

～⁓

Hadley looked down at her on the horse in front of him.

"You still got a nice shape, sweetheart, even after having four kids." He ran his hand over her backside, then began unfastening her shirt buttons in the back.

"Hadley, don't." She squirmed and tried to swat his hands away.

He liked making her squirm. "Do you remember dancing with me at the Tidwells' party before you ran off with Baldwyn?"

"I didn't run off with him. Hadley, stop!"

"We were fifteen then, you and me. You were the first girl I ever loved . . . prettiest girl at the Marston schoolhouse. Remember playing down on the banks of the Piney River when we were younger? Those were good days, weren't they? After you ran off and got married I left

Franklin for a while. Went down to Atlanta. It set me on a different path. I scraped low in the barrel until the war started."

He rubbed her back, disappointed that her underclothes still covered most of it, even with her buttons undone to the waist. He had thought to try for the cabin tonight, but it was still miles away. Night was falling, and besides, Bonnie was at the cabin. She wouldn't like him showing up with Abigail. A thought occurred to him.

"Say, your group have any trouble along the way?"

Abigail didn't answer. He smacked the back of her head. "Hey, I'm talking to you. You have any problem with Indians or attacks or anything?"

"Once."

"When?"

"After we left Laramie."

"And?" He waited but she didn't answer. He reached down and grabbed a wad of her hair, lifting her head up. "What happened?"

Abigail cried out in pain. "Our leader is smart. We fought them off."

"Anybody hurt? Killed?"

"We had some injuries."

"You kill any of *them*? A bald man?"

Hadley smacked the back of her head again when she didn't answer. "I'll take this pistol and blow your pretty little brains out if you don't tell me."

"Yes!" she cried. "One of the Indians was bald."

Now he knew for sure he wasn't taking her to the cabin. When Bonnie learned her father had been killed, she'd be mad. And if Bonnie learned he was the one who had sent her pa on his death mission, the Piute was apt to stab him.

Looked like it was time for him to cut and run. Abigail would have to go soon. He couldn't afford for her to slow him down.

Hadley wondered if someone from the wagon train would come looking for her tonight, or if they'd think the reunited couple wanted time alone before returning. That was what he was banking on.

"I thought we had a good thing going in those letters, Abigail."
He ran his hand over her backside again. "But I can't pretend I'm not
excited to finally get to play married with you."

∽

When Hadley wasn't smacking her or pulling her head up by the hair,
Abigail's face rubbed against the side of the roan, the sweat of its coat
slick against her face. She remembered standing next to the corral in
Independence and Hoke saying, *Horses sweat.*

He was right. Mules didn't. She hadn't known that before taking
this trip.

The saddle pommel hit her right at the site of her bullet wound,
knocking it with every roll of the horse's shoulders, ripping at the scabs.

She would have begged him to rein in the horse and let her off, to
untie her hands, if she wasn't scared of what he'd do to her once they
stopped.

As if reading her mind, he stopped, slid off the roan, then reached
up and jerked her down to him, his eyes cold in the moonlight.

"You be nice next time I kiss you or you won't last long." He told
her to sit down while he made camp.

Abigail's arms throbbed with pain. "Will you please untie me?"

"Let's see how you act, first."

It was difficult to sit with her hands behind her back, but Abigail
did as she was told.

Hadley pulled supplies out of his pack and started a small fire. He
didn't seem worried that anyone might be following them. When he
wasn't looking, Abigail dug her heels into the earth and moved them
around to widen the holes. She wanted to leave clear signs that someone
had been here.

How long had it been since she left Hoke? Two hours? Three? It
was dark now, save for the faint light of the moon. How would she get

through this night? The rope around her wrists burned and cut her skin. She wanted to feel her side but couldn't with her hands tied.

"Hadley, my wrists are bleeding; will you please cut these ropes?"

He had coffee going and bacon frying. "You going to behave yourself?"

"Yes."

He moved a large rock over and sat on it across from her, raking over her with his eyes.

It made her skin crawl. "Tell me about your life before the war," she said, hoping to change his mood.

"I told you, I went to Atlanta."

"Anywhere else?"

"All through east Tennessee, then in Kentucky, working where I could. Helped lay some track, mined . . . a few other things. I never had a respectable job. I wasn't the same person you knew back in Franklin. I even had a wife for a while. Bet you didn't know that. Not even my family knows that. She was a good-for-nothing woman . . . rough-as-they-come mountain family. She ran off and I didn't much care. When talk of the war started, I decided to work my way home."

By the firelight Abigail could see that Hadley's full beard was neatly trimmed. He had matured into a strong, handsome man. But his eyes were cold and distant. She sensed deep hurt behind them and remembered that Hadley's father had been particularly harsh. And Hadley, even as a child, had always seemed restless, wanting . . . forever longing for what he didn't have.

Hadley stood up then, poured himself some coffee and ate some bacon, watching her with wolf's eyes.

She needed to keep him talking or moving, keep him from looking at her that way. "Can I have some coffee?" she asked.

He only had one cup, so he drank what he'd poured, refilled it, and brought it to her. Rather than holding it to her lips as she'd expected, he untied the ropes. Grateful, she took a couple of hot, bitter swallows and set the cup down.

If she threw the coffee on him, would it burn him? Could she get to her horse fast enough to get away? Her blouse was still unbuttoned in the back, and the evening air was cool. She shivered while trying to work out a plan of escape, gathering her courage.

Hadley walked to his horse, took down his bedroll, and unrolled it. Pulling out a blanket, he put it around her shoulders. Then he took his finger and ran it down her throat and down the center of her chest. Abigail closed her eyes and focused on keeping her body from jerking away, trying hard not to do the wrong thing and make him angry.

She didn't move when he kissed her neck, but when he pulled down her blouse and the chemise beneath it, and sought the top of her shoulder with his lips, she shoved him away and scrambled to get up and run.

She had to get to her horse! Get the gun on the pommel!

As Hadley hit the ground he reached up and grabbed her foot, knocking her off balance. He pulled her back to him.

Abigail screamed as she fell.

❧

Hoke flew on the stallion until he got within sight of where he'd last seen Wiles. This was why a man needed a horse like the stallion. He eased in, gripping the rifle in his left hand. This was why a man needed a side-loading sixteen-shooter. He stopped the stallion, sheathed the rifle, and dismounted, slipping the knife out of its sheath and into his right hand and the Colt out of its holster and into his left as he scouted around for signs of Wiles and Abigail. This was why a man needed a six-cylinder Colt and a bowie knife like the toothpick. He stopped every few steps to listen.

Nothing.

How long had it been since she'd reached Wiles? A half hour? Hour? Longer? Why hadn't he insisted on coming with her? All of Hoke's instincts had told him something was wrong. This could be the biggest mistake he'd ever made, and now her life and his heart—not to mention the hearts of those children—were in danger.

Darkness was setting in. If he lit a match to see better, he'd give his position away. Was Wiles lying in wait for him? What if he'd killed Abigail and was hiding nearby?

Hoke couldn't bear the thought.

More likely, Wiles had taken her, thinking he couldn't be tracked until morning. Pretty smart of him to act like he wanted time alone with her . . . and Abigail had played right into it.

So had he.

Hoke swore repeatedly at himself for sending her into a trap. Between curses, he prayed she hadn't been harmed. Those kids needed her. He blamed himself, but what reason had there been for him not to believe what he was told? He'd thought Wiles was really Baldwyn. All the soldiers had acted like he was Baldwyn. How long had the man been playing this game?

Once he was convinced that Wiles had gone, Hoke lit a match and built a small fire. Wiles would move along the creek but in which direction? Hoke needed light to see where he had come out of the water.

It took some time, but he finally found the spot and followed it several yards. Initially Wiles had gone south. Hoke recognized Abigail's horse's tracks, which were lighter than they should have been.

The red roan's tracks were deep, so it held both riders. Hoke had already determined that Abigail hadn't gone willingly, having found the spot on the grass where they'd tussled. It looked like Wiles had pinned her down, probably to tie her hands—*please, God, let that be all it was*—then dragged her a couple of yards to his horse. The grass was pretty beat down there.

He liked to think Abigail had done that on purpose, to make it easier for someone to read the signs. There was no blood. Thank God for that.

Would she know he would come for her?

Of course he would come for her.

How could she doubt it? But she couldn't know that he would have made the discovery and come after her so soon. That was the one great break for Hoke.

He kicked dirt over the fire and moved off to the south, his instincts guiding him better than what little he had seen of a trail.

Wiles would stay near the creek, Hoke was sure. He might try to make it look like he was moving away from it, but he would eventually swing back around. He was a fussy man, overdressed and particular. He'd want a place to wash his hands.

The stallion, responding to his touch, stepped quietly as Hoke picked his way along the brush near the creek. How long would Wiles ride before he stopped? That was one advantage Wiles had. He knew this area and Hoke didn't.

Hoke rode steady for several miles, following his gut and the bend of the creek. It was pitch-black out now, save for the mottled moon overhead in the early August sky.

Surely Wiles had stopped to make camp by now. Hoke decided he must have changed direction. He was just swinging back around to search a wider circle when he heard a scream. It came from his left.

He kicked the stallion in that direction.

CHAPTER 29

Coffin-shaped knife handle

When Hoke came crashing through the brush, Wiles was trying to pin Abigail's flailing arms to the ground with his knees. In an instant, Hoke took in the scene unfolding in the firelight: Abigail fighting like a cougar, Wiles slapping her with the back of his hand, blood dripping from her head.

Hoke was off his horse and running toward them before he knew he had dismounted.

∽

Hadley, furious at the interruption, rolled off Abigail and came up with his fists ready. He'd lived pretty hard and knew a thing or two about fighting.

"You're back, Mathews. I was hoping I'd seen the last of you."

The scout's eyes were as fierce as ever. "*Mister* Mathews to you."

Hadley sized Mathews up, from the hard line of his mouth down to his ivory pistol, coffin-handled bowie, and dusty black boots. He appeared a worthy opponent, but Hadley still felt a sense of superiority. "I believe I've got a few pounds on you."

"It's not going to help you."

Hadley nodded at Abigail, who was still lying on the ground. "You'll have to kill me if you want to take her out of here."

The firelight danced in Mathews's eyes. "Glad to."

"What a bother," groaned Hadley. None of this was going as he had hoped.

Hadley punched with his right and Mathews deflected the blow. Next, he swung a left and caught a piece of Mathews's right shoulder as the man came around with his left. When it hit Hadley's jaw he felt the crack all the way down his spine.

He had known the scout looked strong, but *damn!* The man could hit.

⟲

Like bulls they squared off. Then they punched.

Relief at Hoke's arrival flowed through Abigail, but so did fear. What if Hoke got hurt? Or worse?

First it looked like Hoke had the upper hand, then Hadley, then Hoke again. They separated, stepped back, and circled each other. Hadley pulled out his sword and twisted it so it would gleam in the firelight.

"I bet you've never seen one of these before." The blade was long and thin, attached to a fancy handle. "It's two hundred years old. See the hilt? Protects the hand. Which is good for me, 'cause I already lost two of my fingers." He swished it in the air to demonstrate its effect. "But don't worry. I can still thrust. It's made for thrusting."

Hoke looked unimpressed. "What'd that set you back? Or did you steal it, like you been stealin' other things?"

Hadley laughed, wiping his mouth with the back of his free hand. "Pretty clever, wasn't it? I knew somebody might find me out one of these days, but it surely was fun while it lasted. I'm going to keep right on enjoying myself, too, once I run my rapier through your heart and take her."

"Right here." Hoke pointed to his chest with two stiff fingers. "All the way up to your fancy little hilt if you can get it in there, 'cause I got a hard heart."

Hadley's eyes briefly cut over to Abigail, who was crawling away from them. "I suspected you'd taken a shine to my wife."

"She ain't your wife."

"All our marriage needed was consummation. We were just about to see to that when you so rudely interrupted. Too bad you didn't bring your fencing sword." Hadley thrust at him and Hoke stepped backward, the blade slicing through the side of his shirt, whispering past his skin.

Abigail gasped. Her breath came in ragged spurts and her ears still rang from Hadley's slaps. It was hard to think straight. Only weeks ago she'd been shot. She felt like she might faint again.

No! She had to stay alert. She had to help Hoke.

Hoke was here. He didn't have a sword, or a knife or anything. No wait, *he did*. His pistol was strapped to his side. She could see it. Why hadn't he pulled it from the holster? And there was something else on his leg. A knife. She'd seen him use that knife before but had never seen it strapped to his leg. He always kept a smaller knife in his left pocket, too, the one he used to poke holes in the tops of lightning bug jars for Jacob and Lina.

Why didn't Hoke get out one of his knives? Or just shoot Hadley? Hadley didn't have a gun on him. Where was Hadley's gun? *On his horse!* She should get it. Or get the one Hoke had tied to her horse's pommel. *Yes!* It was loaded and ready to go.

She groped her way on hands and knees toward the horses, past the light of the fire, trying to keep her eyes on the men as they fought.

When she stood up, the blood drained from her head and she fell to her knees.

Hadley thrust again, and Hoke feinted left. Hadley thrust left. Hoke stepped to the right and punched him in the jaw. Enraged, Hadley slashed wildly with the sword.

Hoke caught his arm and smashed it over his knee. Abigail heard it crack. Hadley cried out in pain and dropped the sword. Enraged, he reached into his boot with his other hand and pulled out a derringer, pointing it at Hoke with a shaking hand.

"At this range, I won't miss."

Abigail threw herself to her feet and reached for the gray dun in the darkness.

Hoke lunged and knocked Hadley down before he could get off the shot. They rolled over the ground, punching and hitting each other. Abigail found the pommel and pulled on the Army Colt. To her horror, it was tied down. She fought with the string, unlooping it as fast as her fingers would go.

Hoke was down and Hadley was on top of him when a shot ripped and echoed through the still night air, just as Abigail got Hoke's gun free. She thought she was too late—that Hoke had been killed—and held the pistol in two shaking hands ready to shoot Hadley when he came for her.

Then Hadley's body rolled off Hoke's, a bloody coffin-shaped knife handle sticking out of his stomach.

A low, involuntary sob shook out of her throat as a cascade of emotions swept over her like a waterfall. Horror. Relief. And disbelief that Hoke was alive.

She dropped to the ground and laid down the gun, the dun side-stepping nervously beside her, upset by the events of the evening.

Hoke threw off Hadley's leg, got up, and slowly came to her. He knelt down and cradled her head in his hands, looking deep in her eyes, then pulling her forehead to his.

She loved the feel of his skin touching hers, the brush of his hair over her eyes.

∽

Hoke's breath grew steady. She was safe. *God, thank you. Thank you, God.* She was safe.

"You came," she whispered.

"I came," he answered.

∽

Abigail raised her head to look at him. He was here. She was safe. Everyone was safe when Hoke was around.

The fire was dying out. Hoke went to stoke it.

Her nose dripped and her head and side were pounding. It was pitch-dark now. She wiped at her nose—what came off on her hand was hot and smelled like blood. It *was* blood. And it was coming from her head, not her nose. She touched it gingerly. Now she knew why her head was throbbing.

"Come here so we can get a look at that head wound," Hoke said. He followed her eyes to the front of his yellow shirt. "Let me change that." He went to the stallion and pulled an old buckskin shirt out of the saddlebag, along with his canteen. Splashing the blood off his chest, he pulled on the buckskin, then pulled out the bottle of whiskey.

Lacking the strength to stand, Abigail crawled toward what remained of the fire. Her blouse hung loose on one shoulder. Hoke reached around her and buttoned it. She'd heard him splashing water but could still smell his sweat, and the sweat of the stallion, on him. Or maybe it was the smell of the buckskin shirt.

Whatever it was, the smell was nice . . . masculine. She wanted to see, smell, taste, touch everything that had to do with Hoke—the waft of pine that always encircled him, the sound of his movements, the flame that constantly flickered in his eyes.

"I guess this is ruined," he said of the gold shirt, which was now wadded on the ground. "Mrs. Austelle had just got the bloodstains out. It was my favorite shirt, too."

"I can repair it. There's still some cloth on the bolt."

"We can think about that later." Hoke inspected her head wound. Then he rolled up his shirtsleeves, uncorked the whiskey, saturated the bandana, and prepared to bathe her head and wrists.

"This is going to sting," he said softly.

"All right."

She winced when he held the cloth to her head. He pulled her close and blew on the wound, then dabbed at her wrists and blew on them, too. She followed his every move with dull eyes, feeling passive and heart-spent.

"I knew somethin' didn't feel right about him, and I fault myself for not trustin' my instincts," Hoke said as he worked. "All of this could have been avoided if I had."

"Don't you dare blame yourself for any of this! I might not have made it until morning if you hadn't come." Her voice cracked.

She watched his hands—oh, how she loved his hands! They were the most beautiful hands she'd ever seen, with a faint layer of black hair curling on the backs of them . . . strong, yet incredibly gentle.

Abigail stared at the fire, finally feeling warm and safe, exhaustion wrapped around her. She felt her side.

"Do we need to look at that?" Hoke asked.

"I'm pretty sure the scabs pulled off, with all that twisting and getting thrown up over the side of a horse." She laughed weakly and pulled at her clothes. The blouse was easy to pull from the skirt, but the chemise she wore underneath was longer. "I don't know why we wear so many layers."

"Want me to cut through 'em?"

She nodded.

Hoke took out his pocketknife and cut a fist-sized gap in the side of her clothes. Then he lit a stick in the fire and held it up so they could see better. The scabs were off Abigail's wounds, as she'd suspected.

"It's worse on the front hole than the back," he told her. He dabbed whiskey on the bandana again. The sharp sting when he applied it to her wound stole her breath.

"Doc's got a good ointment when we get back to the train. It helped when James got that cut on his arm." Hoke threw the stick back on the fire.

She covered back up, feeling self-conscious about her bareness and his nearness . . . and about her new status of freedom. "How did you know to come?"

"One of the soldiers mentioned his red beard. The kids said your husband didn't have red hair. So I asked if they had a picture. One of them was a picture of your weddin' day. Wiles happened to be standing in the background and one of the soldiers spotted him."

"I never noticed Hadley in that picture before. He's dead, Hoke. Hadley said he found Robert dead in a field." She bit her lip. She felt like she'd always known it, from the moment she realized she was pregnant with Lina.

Robert had wanted a fourth child. And he had hoped for another girl. He had been elated during Abigail's fourth pregnancy. But shortly after they learned she was pregnant, Robert became ill with scarlet fever. The doctor told them Robert wouldn't father any more. That was why Robert had been so upset with her when she rode horses with Seth and lost the fourth baby. And that was why, when they learned that Abigail was expecting a fifth child, shortly after Robert left, Mimi called Lina the miracle baby.

"You know what's so awful?" Abigail asked Hoke now, gripping his sleeve. "I told Mimi it would have been better if Robert had died in the war. I said that standing in my kitchen in February. What a terrible thing for me to say." She hung her head.

~

Hoke put his hand under her chin and raised it back up.

"Words you said in February didn't reach back and cause a thing to happen years ago." He started to add that he was sorry, but he wasn't. Robert's choices had led her here, to him.

He found the coffee cup, emptied it, and refilled it with whiskey. First he took a swig to calm his own nerves. *A man's best day*, he thought wryly.

"Here." He handed her the cup. "Drink this, and don't get all female about it."

She did as she was told, jerking her head at the bitterness of the whiskey. Then she laughed.

"What?" he asked.

"First the Indian fight . . . now this." Her laughter changed to tears. "I'll be fine . . . eventually. I think. I've just never had events to quite compare." Her eyelids drooped. "My head keeps swimming."

Hoke looked at Hadley's body. "Let me bury him, then I'll get you to a better camp a little ways off. We'll go back to the train at first light."

He felt her eyes watching him as he looked in his pack for something to dig with and then pulled out a tomahawk he kept for a broad range of purposes. It would have to do for a shovel. He turned to her and said in a voice filled with regret, "I'm sorry you had to see this."

He raked out a shallow grave, pulled Hadley's body into it, and started to cover it with dirt and rocks.

"Wait!" Abigail said suddenly. "He's wearing Robert's ring. Can I have it?"

Hoke slid the ring off Wiles's finger, then cut off the top part of the pocket that had *Baldwyn* sewn across it, and handed them both to Abigail. She twisted Robert's ring onto her thumb. Then she reached for Hoke's knife and shredded the false name into pieces and let them fall to the ground.

"He wasn't at all like Hadley." Her blue eyes brimmed with fresh tears. "Robert was like Corrine—and Charlie and Jacob, and you a little. You would have liked him, I think." She shook her head. "It all makes sense now and I feel so foolish. I don't even know where Robert's buried. Or if he ever got buried."

Hoke didn't know what to say, so he didn't say anything. Words weren't going to mend what was broken in her heart; only time could.

He would wait.

By the time he got a new camp made and had rolled out his bedding, she was asleep on the ground, the fire down to its embers. He picked her up and carried her to the new campsite and settled her into his bedroll. He'd sleep on the ground. He'd slept straight on the ground lots of times.

She stirred. "Will you hold me?"

Feeling a surge in his chest like he'd never felt before, he moved into the bedroll behind her, wrapping his arms around her beneath the blanket. She took one of his hands and kissed the open palm, then tucked it next to her cheek.

"Now I know why Lina goes to sleep when she rides with you."

"Why?" he whispered.

"Feels so safe." Her breathing grew even again.

Hoke lay with Abigail in his arms and closed his eyes, two tears seeping out of the sides and running down his grizzled face. She was alive . . . and not bound to another man. He buried his nose in her hair the way he'd longed to for weeks.

⌒

An old memory showed up in Abigail's dreams. Robert stood tall in the hallway of the house in Marston with Corrine on his back, where she always loved to ride, her small hands running playfully through his golden locks of hair.

"Charlie, come here!" called Robert. "Let's measure you before I go in the morning. That way, when I get back we can see how tall you've gotten." He pulled Corrine over his head. "You, too, pumpkin. Abigail, bring Jacob."

Each of the children stood in the doorway while Robert measured them, etching the mark at the top of their heads with his knife, then adding their names and the date at the top. "I shouldn't be gone long, but the way you kids grow—like your mama's garden plants—I won't be surprised if you're taller when I get home."

He laid a hand on Jacob's head. "Son, I'm going to miss that wild hair of yours every morning." Next he shook Charlie's hand, smiling at his firstborn proudly. Then he kissed Corrine on the forehead. "My little pumpkin. My little princess."

Later, after the children were in bed, Robert told Abigail, "I can't very well defend the laws of our land if I ignore the Constitution we were founded on. Hopefully, you'll see fit to forgive me by the time I get back."

"I'm not against the Constitution, Robert. I just don't want you taking aim at my brothers and them at you."

He shook his head and reached for her hand. "Let's not get into this again. We'll work it out when I get back."

But he never got back.

CHAPTER 30

A glory to her

When Abigail woke, she saw that the sun had long preceded her. Bacon crackled on the fire and a creek gurgled nearby, water running over rocks in the shallows. Hoke was on the bank, shaving. She sat up. Her head spun.

Had yesterday really happened? It must have, because she was sitting on a bedroll in a small camp near a stream. The wagon train was nowhere in sight.

The children! She had to get back to them. Like Melinda had said, her place was with them.

Abigail stood and her head reeled. She might have fallen if Hoke hadn't suddenly been there to steady her.

"Whoa, there. I didn't want to rush you. Sit tight and eat somethin' before we head out. Your strength is gone. How's that head doing?"

He insisted on dabbing whiskey on her head and wrists again to keep the cuts from getting infected, and handed her the rag so she could treat her side.

"You want another drink?"

"You trying to get me drunk?"

He grinned. "Always a good sign when your sass comes back."

At the first bite of bacon she realized how hungry she was. Health to the bones—that was what Mimi used to say to encourage the children to eat their breakfast.

What would Mimi think when she learned about all this?

The sun continued to rise, its warmth seeping through her body. Abigail felt clammy from having slept in her clothes.

"Mind if I wash before we leave?"

"No, go ahead. I'll get us packed to go."

Hoke handed her a bar of soap he kept wrapped in an oilskin in his saddlebag, along with a comb and the bandana. "Only rag I've got. And here's a little piece of a mirror I use for shavin'."

She reached out to feel the smoothness of his face. He caught her hand, his eyes simmering. "You do that and we'll never get out of here."

Her cheeks warm, Abigail took the items and went down to the stream, her strength returning with every step.

⌒9

Hoke didn't even pretend not to stare as he packed up the camp. He was a man and she was a woman . . . a beautiful woman who was no longer forbidden.

He smiled every time he thought about it. Life was more hope-filled than he'd ever known it.

Abigail stood behind a tree but Hoke could see her. She slipped off her boots, wiggled out of her skirt and stockings, then pulled the blouse up over her head. Still in her chemise and bloomers, she waded out to the deepest part of the stream and submerged herself. Then she scrubbed, as if working hard to get the Wiles off.

She lay still for a few minutes like she had at Soda Springs, ducking her head back into the water several times, baptizing herself, apparently enjoying the feel of the sun kissing her face each time she poked it back up through the surface.

Water was healing.

Finally she crawled out, redressed over her wet underclothes, and came back to where he was waiting. As she wrung out her hair she looked at peace.

"Sorry. I used most of your soap bar." She handed what was left to him. "And I'll break this comb if I keep trying to run it though my hair. I've lost almost all my hairpins. And I'm wet underneath these clothes," she laughed, "but I'll dry out eventually."

His eyes combed over her hair. "'If a woman has long hair, it is a glory to her.'"

She raised her eyebrows. "First Corinthians."

He raised his back at her. "Chapter eleven."

$\sim$

Abigail thought for a moment that he was going to kiss her—she wanted him to—but then she dropped her head. She didn't want him to think she was forward. Hadn't she only just learned that her husband was dead? And last night she had asked Hoke to hold her. This morning she had reached out to stroke his cheek.

Hoke put his hands around her waist. "Jump." He lifted her up and she winced. "Oh. I forgot about your side."

"It's fine." She would have been disappointed if he'd cupped his hands for her foot.

They rode out.

Four miles later they met the search party. Colonel Dotson led it, Charlie by his side. James was there, and Doc Isaacs and Mr. Austelle, along with three soldiers from the 113th.

Charlie's relief was apparent. Doc Isaacs gave her a big hug and said, "Caroline sure will be glad to see you. It was all I could do to keep her from chasing after you herself last night."

"Melinda, too," chimed Mr. Austelle.

"Let me look at that head." Doc peered close at her. "I can stitch that back at the train if you want—like I did Jacob's. It might leave you with a smaller scar."

Abigail watched Hoke's forehead crease as Doc fussed over her. She was embarrassed that everyone had gone to such trouble on her account.

Hoke took the colonel, James, and the soldiers to the side to explain to them what had happened. Abigail heard the soldiers question him hard, as if they didn't believe him at first. But Colonel Dotson said, "This man has no reason to lie about what happened, Sergeant. Question Mrs. Baldwyn about it, when she's ready. You'll surely trust that she's telling you the truth. As you saw in those pictures, the man who claimed to be your captain wasn't Robert Baldwyn. This is his family. They should know."

Charlie looked at Abigail, his eyes sad. "So it's true? Hadley Wiles was pretending to be Pa?"

"Yes, Charlie." She took his hand and led him away from the others. "I don't know if you remember the letter from Grandma telling me that Hadley had been killed in Virginia early in the war. The only reason you might remember it is because she mentioned how Hadley used to be sweet on me. The Wileses were our neighbors. But it was your father who was really killed. Hadley switched their uniforms and passed himself off as your father."

The disappointment on Charlie's face made Abigail's heart ache. "Why would he do such a thing?"

"I guess because it was a chance to make himself over—to get a promotion in rank and finally be respected by other men."

Charlie's eyes flashed. "But he wrote you letters! He led us to believe our father was still alive." Charlie looked off in the distance. "That is the most underhanded, dirty thing I ever heard of."

Abigail wished there were something she could say to smooth the hurt lines of her son's forehead. "It was a low thing to do, Charlie, but harboring anger will only end up hurting you. He won't feel it. He's gone now."

He whipped his eyes back to hers. "What happened to him?"

Abigail glanced over at Hoke, who was watching them. Charlie saw it.

"Mr. Hoke kill him?" He darkly pointed at the cut on her head. "Did Wiles do that to you?"

Abigail nodded. "Yes."

Hatred danced in his eyes. "Then it's a good thing Mr. Hoke killed him. Because if he hadn't, I would have."

"Charlie!" She didn't want her son to be filled with hate. Hadley had been filled with hate, and look what it led him to do.

But Charlie walked away, shaking his head.

James Parker strolled over and put his hand on Abigail's shoulder. "He'll be fine, Mrs. Baldwyn. He's hurt to know his pa's gone, and he's hurt to know you've been hurt." He smiled. "You've got a fine young man there. I hope you know that. You've done good raisin' him."

How she had grown to love this giant of a man! She hugged James's waist, which hit her nearly chest high.

"Don't go gettin' sweet on me, now. I wouldn't want to have to wrangle with Hoke."

She twisted her brow up at him.

James chuckled. "Oh, don't act like you don't know what I'm talkin' about."

The soldiers from the 113th asked to see the campsite where Wiles was buried. They wanted to verify the details of what happened for the report they would have to write. Hoke and Colonel Dotson rode with them. The others rode back to the wagon train.

The instant she saw them, Abigail slid off the dun and scooped Lina, Jacob, and Corrine into her arms. When James Parker held out his arms to Corrine and said, "Hug me, too," Corrine rolled her eyes at him.

⁂

Mr. Parker hadn't teased Corrine last night. He'd treated her like an adult.

Everyone else in camp had tiptoed around the kids and talked about everything but what was really going on.

But when the others left to go to their own wagons, Mr. Parker stayed with the Baldwyns.

"I ever tell y'all about the time Hoke could feel the mountain lion?" he said nonchalantly, moving his bedroll near the boys' under the second Baldwyn wagon.

No, they said, but they wanted him to. They wanted to know that Mr. Hoke had the power to save their mother.

Mr. Parker told them the story and ended by saying, "Man's got an uncanny sixth sense. And he could track a ghost over solid rock."

After Lina went to sleep, Corrine crawled back out of the first wagon to look out in the darkness in the direction Hoke had gone. Mr. Parker came and stood with her.

They stood without a word for several minutes, then he said softly, "He's got her by now. I'm sure of it. But late as it is, it makes more sense to sit tight than to pick back through the brush in the dark."

Mr. Parker, for all his lighthearted talk, could say just the right thing at a heavy moment.

Corrine turned to him with wet eyes. "I don't ever mean to be difficult."

She didn't know why she was so often short with others. It had become a habit more than anything—a type of defense against being hurt. But if anything should happen to her mother, after Corrine had been so sassy to her . . .

She would never forgive herself.

"Aw, sweetheart, you're not difficult." James put his hand under her chin and lifted it to its normal position, winking at her. "You're fiery! Fiery is a good thing."

"Mama doesn't think it's a good thing."

"I 'spect your mother just wants to do right by you, Corrine. A little reassurance from you time-to-time that she *is* would probably ease her mind."

James was right.

As Corrine rolled her eyes at James now, she thought back to her conviction to be sweeter and kissed her mother on the cheek.

Abigail, looking surprised and pleased, laid her hand over the spot. Corrine hadn't kissed her mother since before her father left.

Lina tugged at Abigail's skirt. "We saved you some cobbler, Mama."

❧

The mystery of Robert's behavior has been solved, Mimi. Hadley Wiles is the one who wrote the letters. He won't be writing any more.

CHAPTER 31

About the split

From Soda Springs, most groups traveled north to Fort Hall, where they came to the Snake River. They followed the Snake south again to the split where the California Trail turned west. Since there was no longer any reason for them to stop at Fort Hall, and since there was the awkward business of one of the train's men having killed one of the fort's men, Colonel Dotson decided to take a shorter route, directly west from Soda Springs, that had become popular in recent years.

The mountains continued to rise around them. Abigail wondered if the land had grown more beautiful, or if her eyes were now just seeing it in a new, more brilliant light. The peace that had settled on her the morning after Hadley's death flowed through the channels of her veins. There were still questions—like how she would provide for the children—but they were less frightening to her now.

All the talk since Soda Springs—besides that concerning the incident with Wiles—had been about which families were splitting off where. What was everyone's final destination?

Dotson was planning to travel to the bend of the Snake just inside Oregon Territory. It was more popular for settlers to travel farther on, up the Snake and over the mountains, then follow the Columbia River to Oregon City. That was what the Becketts and McConnellys were going to do.

"We've come this far," Sam Beckett said to the men. "Don't you want to push on and see the Pacific?"

"I've seen it," said Tim Peters. "Looks just like the water on the eastern side."

The Schroeders, and now the Jaspers, would head down to California. Which route would Hoke take? He hadn't told anyone.

Irene walked over to Hoke's and James's side of camp one evening. "Mr. Parker, Mr. Mathews, you fellows haven't said where you're going yet."

Hoke and James always took supper with the Baldwyns. The Austelles, Marc Isaacs, Caroline Atwood, and Nelda Peters often brought their plates over, too. Nelda said her reason was to be near little Will, as it was helping her over the loss of her own baby. But Abigail and Melinda thought it was so she could be close to Doc Isaacs.

♲

Hoke looked over his plate and scowled at Irene.

She had laid it on thick since Laramie—even thicker after he'd got back with Abigail. But Hoke's mind was made. He was only biding his time until Abigail was over the loss of her husband.

Knowing she was free of Captain Baldwyn and having ascertained that Doc was showing more interest in Nelda Peters had relieved his mind considerably. But out of respect for her husband's memory and out of respect for the children, he didn't want to approach her too soon. That was why he couldn't say what his plans were. They all depended on whether she'd have him, and he hadn't asked her yet.

"Hoke and I been talkin' about that, Irene, haven't we, Hoke? We're leanin' toward California."

Hoke looked at James sideways.

"Yeah . . ." said James, "California just might be the place. We've never tried our hands at prospecting, but I think we'd be good at it. And if that doesn't work we can probably sing for a livin' in a show somewhere. I'm gettin' good on that guitar with all the practice I've had on this trip. Don't you think so, Hoke?"

"You're a regular maestro, James."

"We probably won't be able to keep the women off us."

Doc laughed.

"Um-hum," James continued. "The more I study on it, the more I think that's what we need to do. And we got to stick together, me and Hoke, because you know he wouldn't last a week without me, hard a worker as I am and lazy as he is." James winked at Corrine. "Ain't that right, Corrine?"

Corrine shook her head and turned away, but Hoke still saw her grin.

Irene frowned. "You can't be serious. Why would anybody want to go to California when Oregon City is the place to go? Don't you want to see the ocean?"

"We saw it in Texas," said James. "It *is* somethin' to see, but almighty sandy."

Irene turned to Hoke. "Oregon City is already a nice established town."

"Hoke and I don't like established towns," said James. "We prefer the open land."

"California's not going to be open land, it's going to be full of miners and prospectors and people like the Schroeders. Besides, I'm sure there's all kinds of open land near Oregon City and all kinds of places for a ranch. Isn't that what you said you were thinking about, Hoke? A horse and cattle ranch?"

"Um-hum." Hoke was careful not to look at Abigail. He'd worked hard to keep his feelings for her in check and didn't want to give himself away, but he was dying to know what she thought about the idea of a horse and cattle ranch.

Would she like to be a rancher's wife?

She and the children had lived in town back in Tennessee. She might rather set up a dress shop on the main street and live on the floor above. That was what Tim Peters and his clan were going to do—live upstairs from their general store. Hoke didn't much relish the thought of living over a dress shop.

Of course, if she married him, she wouldn't need a dress shop. If she married him, he'd take care of her . . . *if* she married him.

She ought to be an important man's wife, Hoke told himself. The governor's wife or somebody else's. But hadn't she responded to *his* kisses behind the wagon? Hadn't she wanted to be in *his* arms?

When they got back to the wagon train after he'd killed Wiles, Hoke felt like everyone sized him up differently than they had before. He recognized the old familiar shame cloud that hovered every time he'd ever taken a life. This incident hadn't been like defending the train against Indians. This had been a soldier—the man who had claimed to be Abigail's husband. If Hoke took right up courting her, wouldn't that make him look guilty of something? At the very least, wouldn't that make him look like a brute?

He cared about the opinions of some of these folks, especially George and Christine Dotson. He didn't want them to think he didn't deserve Abigail. Hoke wanted their approval.

"I can see you ranching," said Doc Isaacs to Hoke. "You'll be good at that."

"What would it take to talk you fellows into Oregon City?" asked Irene.

"Oh, I feel certain we could be talked into it," said James lightly. "What are you offerin', Irene?"

She rolled her eyes. "Mr. Parker, you are awful."

Abigail was gathering supper dishes, acting like she wasn't listening.

James asked, "What are you doin', Mrs. Baldwyn?"

"Collecting the supper dishes."

"No, I mean about the split."

Abigail kept her eyes on the stack of plates in her hands. "I'm not sure. The children want to stay with the main group, but we haven't . . . said for sure. Are you finished with that plate?"

Hoke was sitting next to James. He handed his plate over to her without looking up. She took it, not looking at him.

Irene's eyes followed Abigail as she finished collecting plates and took them to wash. Then Irene sat down on the other side of Hoke, craning her head, searching out his gaze until he looked at her. "What would it take to talk you into going to Oregon City?"

Hoke chanced a quick glance at Abigail. He only tolerated Irene because he wasn't ready for everyone to know his thoughts. His pride was at stake. When he did make his play for Abigail Baldwyn—which had to be soon, with both splits inching closer—if she refused him it would hurt like hell. He'd need a convenient fork in the road to travel down to lick his wounds.

No one had wept for Hoke Mathews for twenty-five years. He had told himself that was what he preferred—that freedom was the better choice. But the freedom he really treasured was freedom from vulnerability. Long ago he'd learned that if he kept moving and working, it dulled the pain of loneliness. Never again, he'd vowed as a ten-year-old boy left alone in the world, would he love someone and take a chance on losing them. Never again would he allow himself to be laid open by love's sharp-edged sword. But here he had gone and risked it.

Hoke shook his head at Irene. "I don't know. Maybe I will."

Irene smiled up at him as Hoke stood. "I've got guard duty." He took off his hat. "Beggin' your leave, Mrs. Stinson. Everyone. I enjoyed my supper, ladies. Thank you."

Abigail felt him leave but didn't turn around.

She was growing confused. Hadn't she and Hoke shared something intimate? Hadn't he come for her? Why, then, would he share his dreams of ranching with Irene and not her? Had he decided that taking on a wife and four children was more *togetherness* than he could tolerate?

Only yesterday when she and Hoke had passed each other between the wagons like they'd done a hundred times, Hoke had stepped back to give her space . . . like he was afraid of brushing up against her.

Maybe I will, he'd told Irene. *Maybe I will.*

Abigail had trouble getting the words out of her head.

ᘒ

My heart is changing, Mimi. I can feel the difference in my chest. I'm tender and new, like a seedling pushing up through the lingering leaves of winter. I cry easier and laugh louder.

I'm trying to let go of the doubts, the fears, the worries, and the hurt, and to see the world through a different set of eyes—eyes that see with hope and peace and promise.

Food supplies had grown low as a result of bypassing Fort Hall, but everyone still managed to contribute something to a final picnic before the split.

"Mrs. Abigail, I meant to get you to show me how to crochet one of them hairnets," said Bridgette Schroeder mournfully. "I just loved that one you wore at the dance in Laramie."

"Oh, I'm glad you said something. I have gifts for you." Abigail hopped up and ran to her wagon. It had taken a few late nights, but she had crocheted hairnets for all the women splitting off and sewn pink bonnets for the Schroeder twins.

When she crawled back down from the wagon, Hoke was walking by. He stepped over to help her down since her arms were full, putting his hands around her waist as she backed out of the wagon.

"How's that side feelin'?"

The unexpected warmth of his hands sent hot shivers up her spine. "Better. Thank you."

He reached for her hand that lay on top of the items she held and turned it to look at her wrist. "Those cuts are healing, too."

She nodded, afraid to meet his eyes as his thumb ran over the outline of her scars. She held her breath, waiting for him to take her in his arms.

He let go of her hand.

She looked down and turned to leave, then stopped. "Hoke?"

"Yes?"

"Did you decide to stay with Dotson's group?"

"For now. You?"

Why was he acting so distant? "Yes."

He smiled. "Good."

Abigail walked back to the picnic wondering why she couldn't muster the courage to tell him how she felt. She had trouble offering her heart when he didn't act hungry for it, that was why. Her heart was too bruised from five years of twisting.

She handed hairnets and bonnets to the Schroeders and Nora Jasper. "I hope you like them."

"Oh, you shouldn't have!" said Olga Schroeder.

"These are beautiful," added Katrina, looking at her twins. She was facing life without Duncan now.

"Show me how to wear it," begged Bridgette.

This started a profusion of gift giving, hug swapping, tears, and promises to write among the women. The children went off to play a final round of hide-and-seek and the men stood by and watched the women, asking each other things like:

"What do you think Peters's final mile count is going to be?"

"How much did you pay for that team of mules at Laramie?"

"Do you think Beckett's wheels are going to hold out all the way to Oregon City? He's got the sorriest wheels on that wagon I ever saw."

⟡

Hoke reached into the pocket of his shirt as he and James sat on their horses in the waning afternoon light. They were on guard duty. "My last two hickory sticks." He offered one to James. "Looks like I'm going to have to find me a new kind of stem to chew . . . or take up smokin' after all. I haven't seen a hickory tree in weeks, have you?"

James shook his head and pointed to a fir tree standing tall, stretching toward a bright moon overhead. "Tried those? That's a strong wood. Be a good framing wood for a house, don't you think?"

Hoke nodded. "Yes, I do."

"You could lay out a big place with wood like that. Speaking of . . . when you planning to lay your feelings on Mrs. Baldwyn?"

"What's your hurry where that's concerned?"

"Well, I got to figure out what I'm doing, Hoke, and something tells me you'll be framing a farmhouse soon."

"Not a farmhouse—a ranch house."

"Excuse me, then, a ranch house. God forbid you take up farming. Although if you settle down with Abigail Baldwyn, it looks like you'll be plantin' a garden, complete with flowers and cherry trees."

"Maybe I will. But that's not farming."

"When you goin' to ask her?"

"When I'm ready." Hoke scowled at him. "When I think she's ready."

"She's ready. Can't you see that? You're confusing the hell out of that woman."

"What makes you think? She tell you her feelings about me, is that it?"

James huffed. "I got eyes, don't I? I can see she's crazy about you. I don't know why, stubborn and set in your ways as you are, but you finally lucked out. It's not like you to shirk a task."

Hoke scowled again. "I'm giving her time, James—time to grieve—she never had that. And time to decide what she wants."

"What about what *you* want?"

"I want what she wants."

"What if she wants you to be a farmer?"

They swapped grins.

"We'd have to negotiate on that one," said Hoke. "Why don't you go on up to Oregon City with Irene, get her off my back? I don't know why she's taken a sudden shine to me when you're the one all smooth with the ladies."

"Irene's a looker. But she's not Mrs. James Parker."

"Who is?"

"Who knows?" James stroked his beard with his hand. "It's a mystery yet to be revealed. Michael Chessor and I talked about going back down to Kansas for that herd you and I saw. I thought we could run 'em up here and sell 'em to a local rancher if I knew any. Ranchers in the area, that is."

"I'll buy 'em from you. I'll even put up part of the money on the front end. If I stay here. If I don't stay in Oregon, I'll go with you and we'll find us another rancher to sell 'em to. I thought Chessor was going on to Oregon City chasing that youngest McConnelly."

"They had a fuss. The oldest Sutler boy may go with us, too, and Bart Peters is thinking about it if his dad's willing to part with both of 'em."

"Both of 'em? Orin's working the store, isn't he?"

James turned in his saddle to look at Hoke. "Orin's going to California in the morning."

"Really? How'd I miss that?"

"I don't know. It's been all the talk since Scott's Bluff."

"He take up with Ingrid?"

"No, Jocelyn. I swear, Hoke, where you been? Have you not heard about him and Jocelyn? How their hands touched when they were carving names at Chimney Rock? Have you not noticed he quit buzzing around Abigail and took up with the Schroeders?"

James turned back to watching the stock and shook his head. "Orin's one of those that flits from girl to girl."

Hoke threw him a sideways smirk. "You're one to talk."

"I handle my charm responsibly."

"You sure about that? Don't make a young girl like you if you're just going to ride off and leave her."

James scowled a full minute, then sighed. "I aim to be back before she hits her prime, if you must know."

"You better not stay gone long, then. Is that who the bowl's for?"

James shook his head. "I hate it when you turn out smarter than I give you credit for."

"Don't pout about it."

"I ain't poutin'. And stop tryin' to change the subject. We were talking about you, not me. You need to tell Mrs. Baldwyn how you feel about her so you can free both your minds."

"I don't know what makes you think you're an expert on women."

"Oh, I *know* women, Hoke! I've made quite a study of 'em. A man should never leave a woman wondering how he feels about her—that's a sin in my book. Women are beautiful, complex creatures that need a lot of strokin'. And they're worth it. You take care of her and she'll take care of you. Now where have I heard that?"

Hoke reached for his canteen, unscrewed the lid, and took a swig. Then he handed it out to James. "Coffee. You want some?"

James took it and drank deep. Then he wiped a hand across his mouth and continued. "That's why Mrs. Baldwyn's so crazy about you. You water her plants."

He handed the canteen back to Hoke. "That was brilliant. You surprised me on that one. But you can't just water the plants, Hoke. You got to talk to her, too. You got to tell her how you feel. I know that don't come natural to you, that's why I'm tellin' you to do it. I figure I haven't ridden with you all these years for nothin'. Loving women is the only thing I'm better at than you are, so I owe it to you to give you this advice. I won't keep harpin' about it, but I wanted to get it off my chest."

Hoke took another swig of coffee. "You feel better?"

"Yes, I do."

"Just as long as you feel better, James."

They exchanged sideways smirks.

Hoke knew James was right. He'd talk to her soon.

CHAPTER 32
The sudden flow of emotion

As she rounded the corner with a hot pot of water, Abigail only caught the tail end of what Irene McConnelly was saying to a group of women. Audrey Beckett was there, along with Marnie Sutler, Nelda Peters, and Irene's sister, Diana.

". . . can't be a decent woman to have stayed out all night with Mr. Mathews like that, and to force him to kill that man who claimed to be her husband. I would hate to have that on *my* conscience."

Abigail looked down at the cookpot in her hands, wanting desperately to douse Irene with its greasy contents. That little loose-mouthed tart!

The very idea! Abigail liked those other women sitting there. Were they *all* talking about her? How dare Irene smear her reputation by implying she had contrived to cause problems and put Hoke in an awkward position.

"Makes me wonder if she planned with that man all along to run off together and somehow Mr. Mathews foiled it. Her husband was supposedly gone for years, and that youngest one is what—only three or four? She's a lot more white-headed than the others, too. What if she's not really the same man's as those other—"

Irene jumped up when she realized Abigail was standing just inches away from her with a steaming pot.

The group was stunned into silence, the other women looking ashamed to have been caught listening to Irene's gossip by the object of her slander.

"You can say whatever you want to about me, Irene McConnelly . . . Stinson . . . whoever you are. I don't know why you would. I don't know how I ever offended you. But there is not one drop of truth in any low remark I've heard you say. So stop. And don't *ever* talk about my children again—especially not a child who is nothing but a gift straight from God—a child whose heart and conception are as pure as the driven snow. Understand?"

Irene just looked at her.

Abigail set the pot down. "I asked you a question, Irene. I asked if you understood me." She was near to shouting.

Others in the camp crept over to investigate.

"What's all this?" asked old man McConnelly.

"Your daughter has said mean-spirited things about an innocent child." Abigail took a deep breath, trying to calm down.

"I just think some of the facts in your stories don't add up," said Irene.

"My *stories?*" The needle on Abigail's ire shot up again. "You think I'm making up stories, Irene?"

"I know about you and Hoke Mathews kissing behind the wagons, Mrs. Uppity!"

Irene's announcement didn't embarrass Abigail, it only served to make her madder.

"And I find it a little hard to believe your husband's been dead so long and no one knew about it. I got informed right away when my husband was killed." Irene looked around at the growing circle of onlookers. "Well, hasn't anyone else wondered about it? How an entirely different man could be writing her letters and her not know it? And meanwhile she's carrying on with other men?"

Zzzzzzip went the arrow, straight to Abigail's heart. Her cheeks burned hot with shame.

Irene had flung the dagger directly on the nerve. How tender was the spot where Abigail asked herself those same questions . . . accusing, blaming, cursing her own blindness and stupidity.

Yes, how could she not have known? She was surely the world's biggest living fool. To have someone else ask the same questions—and Irene, of all people—brought her pride to a new low and her defenses to a new high.

Abigail lunged, meaning to shut Irene's mean mouth before her words ripped out what was left of Abigail's heart. But Hoke was suddenly there, hooking his arm around her waist, pulling her away.

She clawed at his hands, those hands she had so recently loved. "Leave me alone! Get back! Out of my way!"

But he held her fast and refused to let her go.

She wheeled on him. "Just who do you think you are?"

"Abby," he chided. "Cool down."

"Don't patronize me! And don't tell me what to do. What gives you the right?" She jerked an arm loose and punched him in the stomach. It was like hitting a boulder. But she'd had to hit something, and he was the obstacle in her way.

Suddenly all four of the Baldwyn children were there and while Abigail was vaguely aware of it, she couldn't seem to stop herself. The torrents of her feelings had gotten beyond her ability to hold.

Hoke easily deflected her blows.

They had become a spectacle. Caroline Atwood's mouth was open and Josephine Jenkins tried to cover Lina's eyes.

Hoke feinted left as she swung an arm, and then he scooped her up below the knees and threw her over his shoulder.

"Put me down!" Abigail beat on his back, pulling and tearing at the golden shirt she had just pieced back together. That shirt—like her heart—kept getting ripped and bloodstained.

"Put! Me! Down!"

"Show's over," Hoke told the onlookers. "Go on about your business."

"Where are you taking me?" she demanded as he walked away from the wagons.

"To cool off."

"I never said you could call me Abby." She punched his back. "My father calls me Abby and we are *not* on good terms."

"I didn't ask your permission!" The sudden passion in his voice startled her. This was the old Hoke—the pre-Hadley Hoke.

❦

Hoke walked toward the creek, Abigail wriggling on his shoulder like a mewling calf, before he unceremoniously dumped her in a waist-high pool of water.

Her body landed with a slap, the cold water engulfing her in a sudden freeze that, by all appearances, only made her hotter. Hoke turned to leave but, indignant, Abigail shot up and came after him, knocking him off balance and sending him sprawling on the bank.

He got up, despite her flailing and slapping at him, and held her at arm's length.

❦

James Parker, Colonel Dotson, Gerald Jenkins, Mr. Austelle, and Doc Isaacs watched from a rise on a small hill several yards away.

"My money's on Mrs. Baldwyn," said James.

Colonel Dotson shook his head. "She's no match for Hoke."

"I don't know . . ." James chewed on a maple stick. He and Hoke had decided sugar maple was the best-tasting option out here. "She's givin' him as good a run for his money as anyone I've ever seen."

"That's 'cause he won't hit her back," said Mr. Austelle.

Doc Isaacs looked concerned. "He better not hit her back."

"Or we'd have to step in," said Mr. Austelle.

Jenkins shook his head. "I don't relish the thought. What set her off like that, anyway?"

"Irene ruffled her feathers." James chuckled. "She's always so composed, you know? I knew Corrine had spirit, but . . . I figured she got it from her pa."

Abigail had gotten past Hoke's defenses and socked him in the ear. Irritated, he threatened to hold her head under the water.

"You don't think he'd hurt her, do you?" asked Doc Isaacs.

"Naw, he's in love with her," said the colonel.

The other four men turned in unison and looked at Colonel Dotson in surprise. James had known it, of course, but he'd thought Hoke had done a fair job of concealing it from the others.

"I could tell it that day he met her, before we left Independence. That's why I put her wagon in his company."

"But she was supposed to be married!" said Jenkins.

Dotson grinned. "Wicked of me, wasn't it."

⁓

With Hoke's arms locked around her, her skin soaked and her hair fallen out of its knot, Abigail finally ran out of steam. She ducked her head out of Hoke's hold, backed up to a shallow sand bed, and sat down hard on the uneven rocks that lined it.

The water was muddy brown from their fighting. She heard it trickling downstream for the first time. Her boots felt strange filled with water, and her clothes stuck to her body, the skirt dragging heavily and swirling in the current. It wasn't like the last time she'd gone into a creek, seeking to purge herself of Hadley.

Her knees splayed out with her elbows resting on them . . . a most unladylike position. Abigail tried so hard to conduct herself with grace and dignity. But Irene had gotten the better of her.

She hated to have so publicly displayed that she was human after all. But . . . there was also a certain measure of relief in it.

Hoke took his gun from its holster and laid it on the sand bank before sitting down beside her. "You sure pack a wallop." He smoothed his black mane and felt his jaw, which needed a shave again. "And you tore my favorite shirt." He cast her a dark, sideways glance. "Every time I get this shirt fixed, somethin' else happens to it."

"I'll fix it," she offered, her energy spent. "I thought you were going to shoot me, for a minute, taking that gun out."

"I don't like to get it wet."

They sat for several minutes, each collecting their breath and their thoughts.

Finally, Hoke ran his hand around her hip and said, "Come here." He pulled her close, raking her butt across the sand and gravel.

She leaned her head on his shoulder. "Why is it always you? Every time I need something, it's always you that shows up and takes care of it."

"That is odd, isn't it?" Hoke looked up the hill at James. "Now I've gone and got attached to you."

"I'm sorry."

"I'm not."

Abigail pulled back and looked him in the eyes—those piercing, gold-rimmed eyes. "You have? You're not? You don't think I've manipulated you? Because . . ." Hurt sprang up in her voice. "That's what Irene said. Did you tell her that on one of your rides together?"

"Oh, stop it." He pushed a wet leaf off her forehead. "You know how I feel about you."

"I do?"

"You ought to. James says I'm not good at showing it. He's felt the need to give me pointers of late." Hoke plucked a stick out of her hair and grinned. "I like you so well I've decided to sell you my white horse."

Abigail raised her eyebrows. "That much?" Then they fell again. "Did you forget I'm low on money? Because I haven't forgotten. I'm going to have to sell an awful lot of needlework to buy a house."

"I'll build you one."

"*You'll* build me one?" She knew hurt and doubt were both written on her face, but her ability to hide her feelings was depleted. "When? You told Irene McConnelly you might go to Oregon City!"

"Woman"—Hoke looked her deep in the eyes—"why would I be sittin' here pickin' creek trash out of your hair if I planned to go to Oregon City with Irene McConnelly?"

A warm rush—better than whiskey—started from the base of her neck and flowed toward her damaged heart. "Are you sure you don't just feel sorry for me?"

Hoke's eyes blazed. "*Sorry for you?* I don't feel *sorry* for you. I *want* you. I want everything you've got."

Abigail raised her eyebrows.

"I was just giving you a little time before I ask you to marry me, that's all."

She felt a slow, silly grin spread across her face. Then she scowled again. "Why?"

"Why was I going to ask you to marry me?"

"No, why were you *waiting*? If you knew how sick and tired I was of the very word *waiting*—"

Hoke pulled her into the crook of his arm so fast she didn't have time to finish her sentence. His kiss sent her head sinking back toward the water. He pulled her body over his and together they began to float downstream, spinning in the current: first the back of her head bobbing up, then his, causing the men on the hillside to walk back to the wagon train out of common decency.

❦

"Well . . . it's nice to see they got that worked out," said the colonel.

❦

Hoke and Abigail finally hit a shallow spot in the creek and came up for air. He pushed the wet hair off her face.

She pulled back and let her arms float in the water. "I tried not to need you, Hoke. I wanted to pull my own weight."

"You have pulled your own weight, but what's wrong with lettin' somebody else make your life a little easier?"

Abigail looked down. "It's bad if you leave me one day."

God amighty, she had long lashes! Those blue eyes were going to be his. "Hey, look at me."

Hoke lifted her chin and forced her eyes to meet his. "I will never leave you—at least not of my own accord. That's my promise to you, and I don't break my promises." Then he added low, "Robert didn't leave you of his own accord, either."

Her face threatened to crumple, but he wasn't having any more of it.

Standing up, he pulled her from the water. "Marry me now. Not because you need me, just because you want me."

"Now? With my hair looking like this?"

"I like it that way. Come on." He stepped out on the bank taking it in strides, water sloshing in his boots, pulling her behind him, back to where his gun lay.

He picked it up and stuffed it in its holster, then turned up the bank back toward camp, never letting go of her hand.

"Hoke, wait a minute!"

He stopped and turned. "You're not backing out?"

"Don't you think we should give it a day or two?"

He took her in his arms again, kissing her slower this time, exploring not only her lips but also the curve of her neck and the space behind her left ear. "No," he breathed huskily. "You said you were tired of waitin'."

She pushed on his chest. "It seems so impulsive. I hate for people to think I'm being rash."

He cradled her head in his hands. "If you knew how much willpower I've had to call on while you chased your fake husband all the way out here, you wouldn't think this was impulsive." He pulled her along several more steps, then stopped and turned again. "Do you have any idea how crazy you've made me?"

He kissed her again. Good Lord, it felt good!

"Charlie!" yelled Hoke when they got back to the wagons. "Come here, and bring Jacob." He pulled Abigail over to where Corrine was getting supper.

"Where'd you go?" asked Corrine. "And why are y'all all wet?"

"We're having a family meeting," said Hoke. "Go get Lina."

⁓

Corrine looked at her mother, then at Hoke, then back to her mother. They were all wet, holding hands, with silly grins on their faces. And her mother looked . . . sheepish.

She went to find Lina.

In a minute all four children were there, along with several others: Colonel Dotson and Mrs. Chris, Melinda, James, Doc Isaacs, and Tam.

"Charlie, Corrine, Jacob, Lina . . . I aim to marry your mother," announced Hoke, holding Abigail's hand tightly to his chest. "Any objections?"

Lina put both hands over her mouth. The children looked at each other, then back to Hoke and Abigail. They shook their heads. No objections.

"All right, then. Tam, where's Harry?"

"Do you mean to marry her this instant?" Tam looked at James, who was watching Corrine's reaction. Corrine stole one quick look at James before looking away.

"Yes, I do." Hoke clutched Abigail's hand to his chest as if he'd never let it go. "I mean to marry her this instant."

The sound of a metal pot hitting the iron of a wagon wheel made them all turn and look. Irene McConnelly eyed them darkly from across camp, the pot rolling to a stop at her feet.

The group ignored her and turned back to Hoke and Abigail.

Tam nudged Abigail. "Well, say something!"

Abigail had fallen silent under the vehemence of Hoke's feelings. His whole body stirred and his eyes swirled like lava. Abigail, by contrast, was the picture of peace . . . perfect peace.

"I love him," she said simply.

Hoke was quick to shut his eyes, but everyone could see the sudden flow of emotion that rushed to them, so powerful was the effect of Abigail's words on him.

When he could talk again, he growled, "Where's Harry?"

CHAPTER 33

A most vehement flame

Harry was located and Abigail, insisting that she'd at least like to be dry and wearing her best, held Hoke off long enough to don the blue dress. She also hinted that he might like to shave. Since the gold shirt was wet, he wore his green one.

As they stood before Harry—with Charlie and Jacob standing up for Hoke and Corrine and Lina standing up for Abigail, a profusion of wildflowers in their hands—Abigail whispered in Hoke's ear, "Are you still charging me for the white horse?"

He gave her a sideways smirk. "We'll work somethin' out."

"*Set me as a seal upon thine heart,*" read Harry, "*as a seal upon thine arm: for love is strong as death . . . the coals thereof are coals of fire, which hath a most vehement flame.*"

⁓

Hoke's announcement that he wanted to marry their mother hadn't completely taken Charlie by surprise, but it had Jacob. Later, when they were lying on their bedrolls looking up at the stars, Jacob sat up and turned to his older brother. "Hoke's our new father, Charlie!"

Charlie laughed. "Yeah, I guess so." He looked up at the wagon where his mother and Hoke would stay together in a day or two. It was their first night as a married couple, though, and Hoke had made a little camp off-site for just the two of them. He said he didn't want to be under the ears and noses of the wagon train—not yet.

Charlie thought about Emma and wondered what it felt like to be married. He hadn't kissed her again since that time playing hide-and-seek, but he thought about it all the time.

"It's weird," said Jacob looking out in the direction of Hoke's camp.

Charlie glanced that way, too, then back up at the stars. "I don't know. It doesn't feel that weird to me."

"It changes Mama's name, don't it? What about us, does it change our name?"

"No. I'm keeping Pa's name." Charlie respected Hoke, but his father's name was all he had of Robert Baldwyn—that and his memories.

"Yeah, me too."

Charlie knew he still hung the moon for his little brother, and he didn't take it lightly.

"But Mr. Hoke is pretty spectacular, as men go," continued Jacob. "He's so . . . tough. You think he's tougher than Mr. Sutler?"

"Oh, yeah."

"Tougher than Mr. Sims?"

Charlie grinned over at him. "Yes, Jake. I think he's tougher than all of 'em, except maybe Colonel Dotson, but the colonel's getting old. Did you see Hoke that day the Indians attacked? And he killed a man to save our mother. I reckon he's earned the right to marry her."

"You don't think he'll whip us, do you?"

"Naw. You kidding? I don't think he'll act a lot different than he's been actin'."

"Yeah. He already acted like our pa, didn't he? He took us huntin'."

"Yes, he did." Charlie grinned over at Jacob again. "I'd think twice before making him mad, though."

Jacob nodded. "Yeah, I 'spect we better."

◦৩

Corrine and Lina had a different conversation in the wagon.

"Corrine," whispered Lina in her ear. "Mr. Hoke is our father."

Corrine rolled onto her side so Lina could scoot in closer. Lina had grown used to sleeping in the crook of her mother's arm on this trip. Corrine wondered how that was going to work now that Hoke was part of the family.

"Stepfather," she corrected. "Strange, isn't it?"

Lina laid her small hand on Corrine's arm. "No. I asked Jesus to make Mr. Hoke my father."

"You did? When?"

"Remember when the Indians came? And Mama got a bullet in her side? Right after that."

Corrine studied the top of her younger sister's head in the moonlight that streamed in through the opening of the canvas. "How did you know our real father wasn't coming back?"

"Jesus told me. Pa's with Him."

It took Corrine off guard. "In heaven? Did you dream that, Lina?"

Lina looked up at her and blinked. "I guess it was a dream." She inched her head under Corrine's chin. "I love Mr. Hoke. He took me to Mama. I knew she liked him."

Corrine stroked Lina's hair absently. "I guess I did, too. She's always been different around him, like she was trying to act like she didn't like him." It was the same way Corrine acted around Mr. Parker. She didn't want anybody to know she liked Mr. Parker—especially not Mr. Parker.

"You don't mind, do you, Corrine? You're not mad at Mama, are you?"

"I haven't decided yet. She could have waited longer than five seconds after finding out Pa was dead."

Lina reached up and patted her cheek. "Don't be mad. I hate it when y'all argue."

"It's just weird, that's all."

"You'll be married one day, Corrine."

"No, I don't think I will." Paul Sutler was boring and James Parker was probably only teasing with her. She wasn't having any of it.

⁓

Hoke made them a crude shelter in the side of a hill walled by a thick stand of cedars. The fire had burned low. They lay on a bed of pine needles covered by blankets. Hoke was propped on one elbow playing with the end of a lock of Abigail's straw-colored tresses. "There are things I want you to know . . . but I'm not used to tellin' 'em."

She traced his jawline with the back of her hand. "We've got time. You can tell me when you're ready."

He caught her hand. "I hope you're going to listen to me from now on. 'Cause twice you've scared me senseless."

"I'm sorry." She reached up with her other hand and ran her fingers through his black mane the way he always did. "I'll be cutting your hair from now on."

He took both her hands in his so she'd look him in the eye. "I'm bein' serious. I didn't think I could feel this way. I didn't expect to ever love anyone or have them love me."

"Hoke, you're bound to have broken hearts all the way to Texas and back. You're too sure of yourself for me to believe you've had no experience with women."

He shook his head. He wasn't explaining this right.

"I remember sittin' on a hill one time in the snow. I was fifteen, and spied this family having dinner. It was night, but all lit up outside because of the moonlight bouncin' off the white. The light from their window glowed for miles. Some of their neighbors had come over in a farm wagon to eat with 'em. They all looked so happy. I sat on that hill and cried—a fifteen-year-old boy. Cried so hard it made ice on my cheeks. I'd already been on my own five years. I'd even killed a man." Hoke closed his eyes against the memory. "I've seen some awful things, Abigail. I've done some awful things. I don't deserve you."

He released her hands and lay on his back beside her. It hurt to think how much he loved her . . . how much loving her made him afraid of ever losing her . . . or of ever doing wrong by her.

Abigail sat up and leaned over him. She kissed his hands . . . his head . . . his eyes . . . his lips.

"You deserve good things, Hoke Mathews. I'm sorry you've had to wait so long for them."

"That man I killed back in Independence . . . I thought I was doing the right thing. A woman had screamed for me to help her. Then later she threw herself on me and I realized what had happened. She wanted him dead and used me for it. I was ashamed to have been so gullible."

Understanding registered in her eyes. "That's why I lost my temper with Irene. I was ashamed I'd been gullible with Hadley Wiles."

Hoke took her face in his hands. "When Wiles had you, I was so scared."

"Well you've got me now," she whispered.

Hoke flipped her over on her back and finally pulled her hips in as close as he damn well pleased.

⌒

Some husbands, after marriage, turned less attentive in getting down dish crates or helping a woman step up on a wagon bed. But not Hoke. Hoke kept watering the flowers.

∽

Corrine was at the sawhorse table sprinkling flour on a board and getting ready to knead the dough when James spoke from behind her.

"You ever make beaten biscuits?"

"No. What are beaten biscuits?" She turned. He was leaning against the edge of the wagon and she could tell he was hiding something behind his back. After giving him a quizzical look, she turned back to her work.

He strolled over to the table, his hands still behind him.

"You beat the dough out real flat, then stack it up like a fan to bake it. Here, I'll show you." He set a big wooden bowl on the table.

"Where'd you get the bowl?"

"I made it."

She ran her hand over it admiringly. It was long and narrow and smooth as glass. "It's nice. What wood is it?"

"Oak. I picked it up back at Ash Hollow. It's twenty-six inches by sixteen."

"So that's what you've been working on." She'd seen him shaving out a block of wood . . . whittling, chipping, sanding.

"I made it for you."

She looked up at his face to see if he was teasing. But there was no smirk on his lips like there was normally—no jesting in his eyes.

"You make good biscuits. My grandmaw had a bowl like this. I wanted you to have one."

Corrine didn't know what to say. No man had ever made her a gift before. She caressed the bowl again and looked at him, short of words.

He seemed pleased.

"Thank you," she said, finally. "You want to show me how to make those biscuits with it?"

He grinned and took the dough in his hands.

"You got to beat it real flat, like this. It's an old slave technique." He took a section of the dough and laid it in the bowl, beating the mixture with the strong, flat part of his palm until the whole inside was lined with a thin layer of it. He then took a tin scraper and cut the dough into strips.

"If you use a sharp blade it'll cut the wood," he explained. "I used oak 'cause it's hard, but it'll get nicks eventually. I can sand it out again every year or so for you."

Every year or so? Was James Parker planning on sticking around, then?

He took a strip of dough and folded it first one way, then the other, until he had a fat, square block. He handed it to her, to put in the pan. Then he layered another strip.

When he handed her the last square, he said, "I'm twenty-six. Is that too old for you?"

She tried to think of something clever to say but couldn't. "Mr. Parker, you're always teasing, and I don't quite know how to take you sometimes."

Flustered, she reached for the empty bowl to clean it.

He took her hands and turned her toward him. She met his eyes, trying to keep the color from rising in her cheeks.

"I know," he said. "I like cuttin' up. But I'm not cuttin' up now. When we get where we're goin', I plan to stay the winter. Come spring, I aim to ride back down this trail to Kansas for a herd of horses. It may take me another year to break 'em and get 'em back up here. But that'll give me the money I need to build my own place.

"In that year I'm gone, I expect word's going to get out about the prettiest girl that ever came to Oregon. Young fools like Paul Sutler are goin' to muster their courage and start swarmin' like mayflies. 'Fore that happens, I wanted you to know how I felt."

"And how do you feel, Mr. Parker?" she asked, with a lift of her chin.

He grinned. "I like the way you lift your chin. And I like the thought of eatin' your biscuits when I'm old. So I aim to court you when I get back."

Corrine didn't know what to say. Her heart was pounding at the thought of being courted by this tall, bearded man whose outlook was so naturally lighter than her own. But for some reason she was afraid for him to know it. "I may not cotton to the idea of being courted by a hairy-faced cutup who wears a gun on his hip."

James narrowed his eyes and nodded. "When I shave my beard, you'll know it. And you'll know why."

"What's that supposed to mean?"

"It means, little missy," he said, putting his bearded face close to hers, "that I may just turn you over my shoulder and haul *you* off to the creek."

He winked and left her standing with her ears and cheeks burning.

❧

At Fort Boise, there was another letter from Mimi.

August 1, 1866

Dear Abigail,
You will have got to Fort Hall and your answers by now.
I know it is so because the Lord, He whispered it to me. I
expect—and you tell me if I heard Him right—that you'll
be moving on to Oregon with the colonel and all the rest of
them. And I expect you won't be homesteading alone. I am
so certain of this that I have sent my letter to Fort Boise.
They can send it on back to Fort Hall if I got it wrong.

I have some bad news. Your father passed away on
Sunday, July 29. He wasn't sick long—pneumonia down

in his lungs. He went down fast and sent for me so he could ask about you. Said he'd had a dream. Robert was standing on the left side of Jesus and your mother was standing on the right. When he woke he sent for the local preacher and begged forgiveness. Said he felt as if he'd sent Robert to his death by being ornery with him. He was worried he might have sent you to yours, too, by not giving you money and stopping you from going to Independence. He asked about each of the children and the dog and I told him you were all fine—better than fine! I told him you were like yourself again—strong and brave and standing on your own solid feet.

I said, "You know she's got the best children in the world. I can say that because I helped raise them." And he said I was right.

Mr. Thad and Mrs. Sue Anne's baby is growing. He has a head full of black hair—a first in the Walstone family.

The church here is growing. It's the singing that brings them in—that and Thomas's preaching. He's a good husband, Mrs. Abigail. A real good husband. I do hope you get to experience that again.

Give all my babies a hug and a kiss—yourself, too. I miss you all so bad sometimes I ache, but the Lord tells me you're in good hands and all I can do is trust Him. Tell Corrine I want a painting of the family soon, so I can see how everyone has grown. Make sure the dog is in it.

Mrs. Thomas Hargrove (Mimi)

P.S. Lay you an unlit match on top of that sugar. A weevil doesn't like the smell of sulfur.

Abigail wiped tears from her face as she folded Mimi's letter.

"What's the matter?" asked Hoke in alarm. Lina lay asleep on the bed between them, Hoke playing with her hair, which he found a miracle of softness.

When Hoke had brought Abigail the letter after dinner, delivered from a soldier from Fort Boise, he'd found her with Lina curled on her lap. He then carried Lina to their wagon since Emma Austelle was spending the night with Corrine in the second wagon. Abigail had just settled in beside him and Lina to read the letter.

"My father died."

"Oh, darlin', I'm so sorry." He reached over, careful not to squeeze Lina, and kissed his wife's forehead, his thumb raking away her tears. "You want me to get the children?"

"No, I'll tell them tomorrow." She blew out the candle and scooted Lina down so she could lay her head on Hoke's chest.

He held her for several minutes, running his fingers up and down the strong spine of her back. "Will you be all right if I leave?" he said after a while.

"You promised you would never leave me, Hoke."

He grinned. "I only mean for a few hours, to help with guard duty. Colonel's been nice to give me a break, but I need to get back to it. Beckett's out there tonight and I don't feel good about his ability to keep my girls safe. Besides, I'm going to get soft if I sleep in here much longer. I haven't slept this much on a real bed since I was a kid." He put his face in her hair.

God amighty, he loved her hair! And her eyes . . . and her lips . . .

Abigail looked up at him. "You call this a real bed? You're not going to make me sleep on the floor when we have a house, are you?"

"I guess not. But maybe we can make a little pallet out under the stars sometimes? Like on our weddin' night?"

Abigail smiled. "I will never grow tired of the fire that simmers in your eyes."

His eyes grew serious. "I'm sorry about your father."

"Me too. Will you come back before morning?"

"You can count on it. If any other man tries to crawl in here besides me, shoot him."

She reached for one more kiss. "I love you."

It got him in a choke hold every time.

⟎

September 5, 1866

Dearest Mimi,

Thank you for writing to me about Daddy. I knew the finality of our decision and that I would likely never see any of my family again this side of eternity, but it is still a jolt to hear about Daddy's death.

I have happy news to share and have waited to tell it all in one letter.

First, I married Hoke Mathews. Guess what his real name is? David. His father gave him the nickname "Hoke" because they laid him under a chokeberry tree when they cleared their homestead in Kentucky. (Do you remember what a chokeberry bush looks like, Mimi? It has a lovely white bloom. The dark berries are bitter, but can be made into a sweet wine or jam when they've had a chance to ripen.) After his mother died, being called David made him sad. So he went by Hoke instead.

I am struck by similarities to David and Abigail in the Bible. It's as if Mother prophesied when she named me. Robert was not like Nabal, but Hadley certainly was . . . "churlish and evil in his doings." And while I

*would not describe Hoke as ruddy, he is handsome and
fearless like King David.*

*Abigail rode her donkey out into the wilderness to
meet him. We have that in common, too. In reading back
over 1 Samuel 25 I have a new favorite passage, in verse 18:
"Abigail made haste." I told Hoke I was tired of waiting.
That's why I made haste to marry him when he asked me
so soon after learning of Robert's death. I hope you and
my brothers will not think me rash. The children all gave
their blessing and are proud, I believe, to have him in our
family. He, too, is a good man, Mimi. You would like him
very much.*

*The second piece of good news is that we have at last
arrived at our destination. Colonel Dotson has decided to
stay and settle near a young town, just platted last year,
called Baker City. Five years ago a man found gold on
the Powder River in this area. So folks have been coming
here ever since. The surrounding land is most beautiful
and with those who have already come here, supplies are
readily available. It is still young enough of a town to
satisfy Colonel Dotson, and he is convinced it is an ideal
location to attract the railroads. So send future corre-
spondence to Mrs. David "Hoke" Mathews, Baker City,
Oregon. Hoke is at the land office now with several of the
other men to stake the claim for our acreage.*

*Once we are settled, I will write longer letters to both
you and Thad. I also need to let Mrs. Helton know we
won't be coming back to Independence.*

Until then, all my love,
Abigail

CHARACTER LIST

COLONEL DOTSON'S WAGON TRAIN

COMPANY A

* *Gerald and Josephine Jenkins*—Leader of Company A and Colonel Dotson's longtime friend and his wife, sister of Christine Dotson, who leads the children in camp singing
* *Alec, Baird, and Paddy Douglas*—Brothers from Scotland who have sheep and drive wagons for Gerald Jenkins and Colonel Dotson; Alec plays the fiddle; Paddy is simple-minded
* *George and Christine Dotson*—Retired army colonel and leader of the wagon train and his wife, a mother figure to many on the train
* *Tim, Orin, and Bart Peters*—Widower planning to open a general store and his two grown sons
* *Timmy and Nelda Peters*—Tim's oldest son and his wife, who is expecting
* *The Kensington sisters*—Older spinster sisters who plan to open a library

COMPANY B

- ❖ *Rudy and Olga Schroeder*—Leader of Company B and oldest brother of the Schroeder clan and his wife
- ❖ *Prissy Schroeder*—Youngest of Rudy and Olga's three children
- ❖ *Inez Schroeder*—Mother of Rudy, Faramond, Bridgette, and Duncan; matriarch of the Schroeder clan
- ❖ *Bridgette Schroeder*—Unmarried daughter of Inez
- ❖ *Faramond and Molly Schroeder*—Second of Inez's sons and his wife; his name is pronounced "Fairman" by his family
- ❖ *Ingrid and Jocelyn Schroeder*—The oldest two daughters of Faramond and Molly
- ❖ *Duncan and Katrina Schroeder*—Inez's youngest and quietest son and his wife; they have twin infant daughters

COMPANY C

- ❖ *Hoke Mathews*—Leader of Company C and former US Marshal
- ❖ *James Parker*—Hoke's fun-loving riding partner
- ❖ *Abigail Baldwyn*—Mother of four who is searching for information about her husband, army captain Robert Baldwyn
- ❖ *Charlie Baldwyn*—Abigail's older son
- ❖ *Corrine Baldwyn*—Abigail's older daughter
- ❖ *Jacob Baldwyn*—Abigail's younger son
- ❖ *Lina Baldwyn*—Abigail's younger daughter, her "miracle" child

❖ *Charles and Melinda Austelle*—The blacksmith and his wife

❖ *Emma, Clyde, and Cooper*—The Austelle children

❖ *Marc Isaacs*—Young doctor caring for his widowed sister and her son

❖ *Caroline and Will Atwood*—Doc Isaacs's widowed sister and her infant son

❖ *Sam and Audrey Beckett*—Writer and his wife, who is expecting

❖ *Tam Woodford*—Mountain woman

COMPANY D

❖ *John and Marnie Sutler*—Leader of Company D and his wife; they have six children

❖ *Phillip*, *Paul* (who cares for Corrine), *Hannah*, *Lijah* (Jacob's friend), *Reuben*, and *Deena*—The Sutler children

❖ *Mr. McConnelly*—Man from Boston traveling with his two grown daughters

❖ *Irene and Diana McConnelly*—Mr. McConnelly's disagreeable daughters

❖ *Ty and Sue Vandergelden*—A browbeaten husband and his contentious wife

❖ *Ned Vandergelden*—The unhappy child of Ty and Sue

❖ *Nichodemus and Nora Jasper*—Young, poor married couple; Nichodemus plays an Appalachian dulcimer and Nora sings like an angel

❖ *Michael Chessor*—Young adventurer

❖ *Harry Sims*—Preacher who proves himself a capable frontiersman

MARSTON

- *Mimi*—Abigail's former slave and her one, true friend
- *Annie B and Arlon*—Mimi's sister and her husband, who works the land for Leo Walstone
- *Leo Walstone*—Abigail's embittered father
- *Thad Walstone*—Abigail's oldest brother, married to Sue Anne
- *Nathan Walstone*—Abigail's youngest brother, who marries Nora Clark

OTHER

- *Bonnie*—Indian woman
- *Trapper*—Man connected to a band of Piute Indians
- *Cecil Ryman*—Man looking to avenge the murder of his brother, Dan
- *Hadley Wiles*—Childhood acquaintance of Abigail

ACKNOWLEDGMENTS

It's a sunny day in late summer. As I write in my journal I am so over-whelmed with gratitude that my heart expands like a balloon that's been filled with a sudden burst of air.

For thirty years I held the dream of writing a novel close to my chest, revealing it to few, thinking the task too hard and myself too inca-pable. Five years ago I dusted off one of my ideas and began working on it . . . trying one more time. Were it not for Matt Hearn following God's leading to introduce me to Dana Chamblee Carpenter, my friend and writing critique partner, I might have lost heart again. But Dana kept me accountable, kept me working, and pushed me to attend the writer's conference that led to me signing with my agent.

A simple thank-you is insufficient to the depth of gratitude I feel for her, but I offer it all the same.

Others who believed in my ability to produce a book long before I believed in it myself include my mother, my husband, my two daughters, my friends Sue and Doug, and a host of other supporters and encouragers.

My mother, Joan, has been a steady force in my life—she is the woman who planted and watered my love of words by reading us qual-ity books when my brothers and I were young.

My husband, Stan, believes in what he believes in with his whole heart. To hear him tell it, I deserve a Pulitzer.

My youngest, Shelby, was like a breath of the purest air to my writing aspirations and was a staunch supporter from early in the dusting-off stages. And Jordan, who doesn't compliment lightly, said Hoke was hot.

My friend Sue Richardson was one of the first to fan the flames of my writing dreams.

Doug Bates invited me on his radio program one Christmas when I wrote for a small-town newspaper. He passionately loves words, people, universities, and God, and he quotes poetry when I need encouragement.

That host of others I mentioned includes three friends who I am sorry to say didn't live long enough to read my finished product. (Chris, Ellen, and Donna, I can't wait to tell you all about it when I see you again.)

Thank you, Jennifer Fisher, for your editing help as I figured out how to tell a story. Thank you, Jessie Kirkland, for believing in me and serving as my agent. Thank you, Erin Calligan Mooney at Amazon Publishing, for seeing this story's potential. Thank you, Shari MacDonald Strong, for serving as my editor—what a pleasant experience you made it! Thank you, Waterfall Press team, for helping me get Hoke and Abigail into the hands of readers.

To borrow from Donne, no writer is an island; we are all attached to a continent, part of the main. I now can appreciate how many talented individuals it takes to bring a book to fruition, and am deeply grateful for every moment of time and piece of input offered.

Writers are sensitive souls, seeking to let words flow in answer to a burn that can feel like a curse. Nothing soothes me . . . and perhaps you . . . quite like words. I am indebted to every writer who has strung them together well, for they have taught me about myself and about life.

I pray my own words do a little of the same for others.

ABOUT THE AUTHOR

Photo © 2015 Shelby M'lynn Mick

Leaving Independence is Leanne Wood Smith's first historical novel. In addition to writing, she teaches for a university in Nashville, Tennessee, where she lives with her husband, two daughters, and son-in-law. Leanne believes that when something calls to you, you should journey toward it. Visit her website at www.leannewsmith.com for inspiration in pursuing personal and career-related dreams.